Jacqueline Briskin was born i   **P9-AGF-071**
and grew up in Beverly Hills. She is
the author of the highly acclaimed
bestseller *Paloverde*.

Also by Jacqueline Briskin

Paloverde

Jacqueline Briskin

Rich Friends

A MAYFLOWER BOOK

GRANADA
London Toronto Sydney New York

Published by Granada Publishing Limited in 1981

ISBN 0 583 13320 7

First published in Great Britain by
Granada Publishing Limited 1980
Copyright © Jacqueline Briskin 1976
All rights reserved
Published by arrangement with Delacorte Press, New York

Granada Publishing Limited
Frogmore, St Albans, Herts AL2 2NF
and
3 Upper James Street, London W1R 4BP
866 United Nations Plaza, New York, NY 10017, USA
117 York Street, Sydney, NSW 2000, Australia
100 Skyway Avenue, Rexdale, Ontario, M9W 3A6, Canada
PO Box 84165, Greenside, 2034 Johannesburg, South Africa
61 Beach Road, Auckland, New Zealand

Made and printed in Great Britain by
Richard Clay (The Chaucer Press) Ltd
Bungay, Suffolk
Set in Linotype Baskerville

Granada ®
Granada Publishing ®

This, with all our love, is for

Rich
Liz
Donna
Ralph

who have brought us much joy.

ACKNOWLEDGMENTS

Lyrics from 'Kozmic Blues',
© Strong Arm Music/Wingate Music Corp. 1969.
All Rights Reserved, International Copyright Secured,
Reprinted with permission of the Publisher.

Lines from 'Into My Heart an Air That Kills' from
'A Shropshire Lad' – Authorized Edition – from
The Collected Poems of A. E. Housman.

Reprinted by permission of The Society of Authors as
the literary representative of the Estate of A. E.
Housman, and Jonathan Cape Ltd., publishers of
A. E. Housman's *Collected Poems*.

Then

Chapter One

I

On this particular blazing Saturday afternoon in June 1946, the cloudless sky above Glendale appeared a deeper blue than normal. The air held crystal clarity. Sound travelled immense distances, and you could hear a far-away whistle of the Southern Pacific passing through, hear the tinkle of a Good Humour truck with its trail of excited children's voices.

Glendale is one of the numerous suburbs that form Los Angeles. It is barricaded on the north by the tall, gloomy San Gabriel Mountains, which sometimes in a cold winter have a gravel of snow and after a hot summer will turn dry and black. As if to deny this living harshness, the eternal green necropolis of Forest Lawn coils in the heart of Glendale. Westwards sprawls the San Fernando Valley – in those days a cheap whore selling her body without plan to GI housing tracts and factories. Driving east over the tall Arroyo Seco Bridge – nicknamed Suicide Bridge – puts you in wealthy Pasadena. Large homes separated and hidden by acres of pruned shrubbery. In Pasadena lived some of the Van Vliets, the supermarket Van Vliets. (The family was large, intertwining through Los Angeles with other good families rather like royalty.) Pasadenans did not look down on Glendale. They were oblivious of the neighbouring suburb.

In Glendale, houses were small, edged with well-watered grass. Trim Protestant spires rose through billowing summer green of elm, sycamore, birch. If that afternoon you had ventured onto the wide, sunstruck business streets, no crowd would have jostled you, you wouldn't have been annoyed by the hot dog- or chili bowl-shape stands seen in other areas – there was a local ordinance against such extrusions.

When movie studios wanted a middle-class reaction,

9

they held a sneak preview at the Alexander. For Glendale, wedged into a city already known as futuristic, oddball, home of lotus eaters, was a core of insular America. Here, people overlooked the terrible chasm of the recent war, gazing back to our earlier time of naïveté. Glendale was the honest, true place that Kate Smith's hearty voice sang of, the unambiguous good life that Norman Rockwell's *Saturday Evening Post* covers had engraved on our hearts. Teachers here enthused about equality to white faces. And the people did believe they dwelt in the best of all possible melting pots – refusing to admit within the boundaries of their suburb any evidence to the contrary. A few veterans might privately brood on implications of their recent horrors, but for the most part a man adjusted, slipping his ruptured duck in his wide, civvy lapel, returning to clear up his desk. Glendale had no use for the foreign craze of fifty-minute hours.

The young faced the future as the young always have everywhere, as a new chapter to be written, dice yet to be thrown. It was impossible for them to gauge how marked the pages, how weighted the die, in this Truman era, in the dawn of the atomic age.

Beverly Linde, who was eighteen, stood in the hedged drive of a tile-roofed bungalow. She was lighting a cigarette. In the back garden Em and Sheridan Reed's wedding reception had been in full, sweaty swing for almost two hours. Em (née Wynan) was the elder sister of Caroline Wynan, Beverly's best friend. And Beverly knew she had only a few minutes' grace before Caroline came and dragged her back. In the green shade of the ivy hedge, though, Beverly was freed of the crowd, able to forget her self-consciousness, forget that she was so different from the other young people whose voices she could hear. Sometimes she thought she was different because she was Jewish. Since this was a fact she never mentioned unless pressed to the wall, she hadn't been able to discuss it, not even with Caroline. Or maybe, more simply, it was be-

10

cause she enjoyed being alone. Sketching. Painting. Before she had started school, when she was very young, she had been happy. That was before she knew it was contemptible to enjoy solitude.

She was a slender girl with soft brown hair. Her mouth, under the too-dark lipstick of the time, gave an impression of great gentleness. She wasn't pretty, but that didn't matter, not once you noticed the eyes. The eyes were memorable. Amber eyes that darkened when she was upset, eyes that one would swear could see things invisible.

She wasn't a real smoker. She puffed, gazing dreamily through the wisps. Cordell Road was lined with eucalyptus: with their sad, moulting bark, the trees reminded Beverly of a parade of elderly circus camels.

A pod clunked on a well-kept-up pre-war Nash that undoubtedly belonged to one of Dr and Mrs Wynan's family friends. (Dr Wynan's lacklustre dental practice was drawn from these friends.) The battered jalopies were owned by dates of the Omega Deltas, the bride's sorority sisters who were also Beverly and Caroline's sorority sisters. The Lincoln Continentals, the Cadillacs with jump seats, had borne Mrs Wynan's relations, the Van Vliets, from Pasadena and other wealthy sections. The black Daimler with the coloured chauffeur leaning against the bonnet belonged to Mrs Hendryk Van Vliet, the bride's grandmother. The limousine was far too aristocratic for Cordell Road. *The Van Vliets, you know, Van Vliet's supermarkets*, Beverly had heard other guests whisper. *Mrs Wynan is one – her mother is the real big shot.* And they would throw awed glances at Mrs Van Vliet, a tiny, imperious old lady who wore her hazelnut-size diamond and huge emerald as if they sprang from the bones of her wrinkled, elegant fingers.

Beverly took another puff. I shouldn't be out here. Why aren't I at the back, drinking champagne and laughing and enjoying myself like everyone else? Why? Nobody sneaks away from parties. I'm the most abnormal hermit. Why solitude ... These thoughts were too vague to put into words. They were more like a haze of guilt surrounding that mysterious element: her dislocation from other people.

She gazed around, hugging the perfect California summer afternoon to herself. In desert clarity, the purple-creased San Gabriel Mountains seemed touchable. Shadows half-covered the Wynans' house, painted for the occasion, and on this side, rough stucco didn't appear its brutal new salmon but a deep, lovely garnet. Again Beverly examined the eucalyptus. They really are pathetic, she thought, and went over to trace shaggy bark with two fingers, as if she were caressing an animal. Her smile was dreamy, gentle. And agonizingly vulnerable.

2

Behind the house, the reception. In russet shadows of the liquid amber trees, hatted women chatted and laughing men held flanged glasses. Across the lawn two small girls pirouetted, organdie skirts ballooning. A young masculine voice shouted, 'Charge!' and a burst of laughter rose from the patio. Here, despite the blazing slant of afternoon sun, young people crowded. A waiter with growing dark half moons under his white sleeves dispensed tepid California champagne, slowly and ungenerously – he was down to three bottles. Nearby, another damask-covered picnic table, this dedicated to food. Hot sun had hardened circles of bread into shells around pastel spreads that gave off sharp odours of anchovy and devilled ham: green and white mints stuck together and napkins no longer fanned to show silver-imprinted names: MARILYN AND SHERIDAN. Caroline Wynan maintained less hours had been spent negotiating the entire Japanese peace treaty than deciding whether to print her sister's given name or the initial by which she'd always been known. Mrs Wynan and Em finally had opted for MARILYN. Van Vliets would be in attendance, and therefore, they had concluded, utmost formality was in order.

The long, wavery line had kissed the bride, congratulated the groom, exclaimed to Dr and Mrs Wynan how lovely the ceremony at St Mark's Episcopal had been, and now the couple stood by themselves on the path leading from the patio to the barbecue.

Em, a short, small-boned girl, was surprisingly ample of bosom, an endowment she disguised. Her rayon-satin wedding dress was ruched in the matronly style of Princess Elizabeth. Under Max Factor pancake were the ghosts of wrinkles to come, slight parentheses from the corners of her tilted nose to her mouth: her sandy hair had been permed two days earlier – the froth of tulle mercifully hid most of the resulting frizz. Yet Em, in her diminutive way, was appealing, especially when she smiled. And she was smiling up at Sheridan.

Em always had been popular with girls. With boys, not so. The men her age – twenty-two – had spent four years of their lives making democracy live, yet from her infrequent blind dates with servicemen, she knew, just knew, she didn't have the same flirtatious knack as her high-handed younger sister. With men sometimes Em was afflicted by a nervous stammer. She had met Sheridan a few weeks after he had started the University of Southern California on the GI Bill. Newspapers and magazines might be full of statistics, the returned warriors marrying at an unprecedented rate, but Em – how could Em see this wedding as anything short of a miracle? From time to time she reassured herself by gripping Sheridan's hand, the left one with the gold ring, size 9, $12.50. Her size 4 had cost him the same. When she had asked the jeweller why, he had thrown in the engraving: TO S, FOREVER, M and TO M, FOREVER, S. If Em had known how to rephrase the question politely, she would have asked again. She liked rational explanations. She liked fairness. It was irrational and unfair, both, making Sheridan pay the same for half the amount of gold.

Sheridan's double-breasted, hired tuxedo stretched across wide shoulders. Under close-cropped dark hair, his big features might easily have been considered homely if it weren't for a tautness across his cheekbones and around his full, dark lips. It was this brooding tension – actually a kind of anger – that gave Sheridan tremendous SA, or so the Omega Deltas agreed. (That he was attractive to other girls excited Em almost as much as it worried her.) He had two more years until he was a pharmacist. She had just graduated and her teaching credential was going to help support them – so many girls were putting GI husbands through college nowadays, and Em in her serious way had decided this was a tremendous advance over Mother's time: she would be an equal partner in Sheridan's career.

Sheridan glanced around. 'The kissing's over,' he said, lifting his free hand, glancing at his steel watch. 'We can hit the road.'

She gripped his fingers tighter. 'There's still the cake.'

'Let 'em eat cake,' Sheridan said with his short laugh, 'when we're gone.'

'I have to c-cut it.'

'Bring it on, then.'

'I can't. I mean, the bride sh-shouldn't,' little Em stammered. How could she argue with Sheridan?

He bent swiftly, saying in her small, flat ear, 'If we stick around too long, they'll get the idea we're not eager.'

Darts like needles stuck downwards in the pit of Em's stomach. She wasn't. Eager. She was terrified. She had taken the blood tests, Mazzini and Kahn, and afterwards Dr Porter had given her pre-marital counselling. Which meant he'd examined her on a leather table with spread metal stirrups (pure torture) and said he'd fit her for a diaphragm after the honeymoon, when the hymen was broken. Back in his office he had pencilled male and female organs. Em stared at his memo pad, hypnotized. In cramped second-floor bedrooms of the Omega Delta house she and her friends often discussed aberrations like the man and woman not fitting or getting stuck and re-

14

maining that way until separated by the fire service. Dr Porter's voice was cheerful, easy, yet his words were infinitely more disturbing. This was about to happen. Happen to her! 'Orgasm,' he had paused, then gone on to tell her she would know she'd achieved it when she felt an urge similar to the need to urinate. And she wasn't even one for petting!

Sheridan's muscular arm snaked around her and she felt his warm, dampish side pressing affectionately against her. Again she was overwhelmed by the miracle. They were married. She would be a good wife, she vowed earnestly. Would, would, would.

'I'll find Caroline. She'll get Lucidda to wheel it out.'

'Atsmygirl.'

Em rose on her grass-stained white shoes. Nearsighted, she had refused to wear glasses on her day of days. She squinted to find her sister, who was also her maid of honour.

Near the pyracantha hedge stood Caroline, face shadowed by a wide-brimmed horsehair hat, gesturing and chattering with Van Vliets. The Family, the entire group dressed with impeccable simplicity for a garden wedding, adults and children alike endowed with a terrifying (to Em) air of self-possession that said they owned any bit of earth that they chose to stand on. Em grew nervous, awkward with her wealthy Van Vliet relations, all of them, even her grandmother.

Em gathered her bridal train under one arm and, veiled head high, tugged Sheridan's hand. At the same moment Caroline, seeing her, patted her grandmother's arm in farewell and came over with the forthright confidence of a prima ballerina. Em heaved a sigh of relief. She wouldn't have to talk to Them.

Tiny beads of sweat stood out on Caroline's forehead, and her normally pink cheeks were crimson. Almost nineteen, she was a tall girl with a healthy, full-blooded Edwardian handsomeness. And great style. Despite her maid of honour's dress with its dowdy sweetheart neckline (the bride's choice) Caroline managed to look chic.

Or *chick*, as she purposefully mispronounced it. Caroline's black hair was set in a loose pageboy with a few strands permitted to drift casually onto her forehead, drawing attention to her sparkling blue eyes and the colour in her cheeks, to her blue eyes and cheeks so rosy. Her graduated pearls were knotted to the fashionable choker length. In Caroline's attractive presence, Em felt her bridal splendour disappear. Em, shrinking and fading like a rag doll washed in the Bendix. She was used to it. The only time she let it get to her came when she saw Caroline with the Family. This alone she envied her sister: her ease with Them. Sheridan slowed, his hand tightening on hers, an unspoken admission that They unnerved him, too.

'Hot!' Caroline fanned herself vigorously. 'Sweaty the bride, and so on.' She laughed. Caroline's laughter was a rare gift. People melted on its receipt. It emerged from deep in Caroline's chest and had an almost raucous note like a calliope, a joyous, golden invitation to have some fun. Em couldn't help smiling. Tall Caroline embraced her short elder sister with one arm while with the other she drew Sheridan closer, breathing a champagne-scented kiss in the air between them.

'The cake,' Sheridan said.

'Cake?' Caroline fluttered black lashes.

He made a cutting gesture.

'Oh *that* cake. Luv, it's about time. The bubbly's run dry.' Caroline laughed again, and Em, anxious as she was, couldn't keep back an echoing chuckle. 'Mother!' Caroline exclaimed. 'Why on earth she kept *in*sisting we didn't need another case! We children were meant to be blotting up the fruit punch. Remember, Em, I –'

Sheridan interrupted, 'We'll get it cut now.'

'Aye aye, sir.' Caroline's salute tilted her wide-brimmed hat.

And she started for the patio, moving with agonizing slowness, or so it seemed to Em, pausing to smile, laugh, speak, touch an arm, an eternity before a wisp of pink skirt narrowly escaped being trapped by the screen door.

3

Caroline leaned against the Bendix, staring at the three-tiered cake. Stiff it was, and less digestible-looking than the china bride and groom simpering under a quadruple arch of tightly folded fabric flowers. Trust Em and Mother! In their conventional minds a wedding cake *must* look like this. Caroline, tossing her hat to the linoleum, started to unfold cloth flowers.

These impingements of the family (or, as her parents and Em capitalized, the Family – like the Holy One) grated on Caroline's healthy nerves. The house was wildly neat, the arrangements so faw-ncy that something inevitably went wrong. For example, at her eighteenth birthday tea last August 13th, the Wynans' ancient golden retriever lifted a leg to Uncle Richard's white flannels. Of course the family – and Caroline – had thought this hilarious, and – equally of course – any mention of the great pee incident still reduced Mother to quivering middle-aged curds and apologies. Poor Mother. As if any act of a Glendale dog could disturb them.

Caroline glanced through the uncurtained service porch window and saw Van Vliets standing apart from other guests. The family. Handsome. Witty. Descendants of the hard-working little Dutchman who in 1858 had travelled from New York by steamer to Panama, losing three fingers to snakebite as he crossed the Isthmus on his journey to the fly-infested village of Los Angeles. Here, everything profited him. His original stock of tea, bottles of spice, yeast powders, and dishes (along with the flour that the china had been packed in) he parlayed into a thriving grocery business near the Plaza. The village grew into a town, Southern Pacific railroad ties were laid, he opened another shop, and another. His lush, black-haired bride was heiress to the Garcia land grant. The resulting Van Vliets came in two sizes. Dark, tall, rosy ones, like Caroline. Little ones, like Em, who generally were fair. The small blond ones, strangely, all had narrow, pinch-tilted noses as if God had taken thumb and forefinger, tweaking to give His little Van Vliets distinction.

Mrs Wynan alone had the size of a dark one with the light hair and tilted nose of a small one. On her broad, flat face, the Van Vliet nose spread too wide. She resembled a shy Hereford. She was the eldest child, but that didn't prevent her from being terrified of her two worldly brothers and their elegant wives. And of her cousins, so many years younger. Even of her own mother. They in turn were amused. She was so Glendale. No other life would have fitted Mrs Wynan as well as this, with her squirrel-jawed, loving, unsuccessful dentist husband, her two daughters, needlework of some kind eternally in her large, doughy hands.

Poor Mother. Caroline pushed at a shining black strand. Poor Mother. But Caroline knew *she* herself didn't fit in smug, snug Glendale. She never mentioned her mother's patronymic – wild horses couldn't drag the name from her – yet in her rare bad moments she had a rune to cast: I am a Van Vliet of the Van Vliets.

The china bride and groom teetered.

'Omigawd,' Caroline muttered, hastily grabbing to save it. She managed a wire arch of flowers and crushed two rosettes. Glaring at the damage, she leaned forward, searching the garden for Beverly. Seventy guests with insects swarming above them. She scanned the view beyond the screen door. Attended by their crew-cut boyfriends were her dowdy Omega Delta sisters. (She had been bid by good houses, Tri Delt and Theta, but it never had entered Caroline's loyal head to pledge a different house from Em.)

Caroline hurried through the square kitchen, opening the back door. Dustbins overflowed with torn silver wrapping, ribbons, and excelsior. She saw Beverly.

'Ahhah!' Caroline cried. 'Caught you!'

Party noises funnelled down the narrow drive. Beverly

18

didn't hear. Handbag under her arm, head bent on long, slender neck, she lit a Tareyton. She really is unique, Caroline thought. Why *must* she be so anti-social?

Though totally dissimilar, the two had been best friends since a cold, clear afternoon when Miss Marron, the grey-haired witch who ruled third grade, had dispatched them with a note to the principal. *Making a disturbance*, Miss Marron had written. Belching, she meant. Beverly hadn't. Caroline had. As they walked, Beverly murmured her admiration of Caroline, surely the world's champion ventriloquist belcher, and Caroline praised Beverly's heroism, not snitching. When they reached the slotted shade of the pergola, Caroline said, 'Let's be best friends.' 'You mean that?' Beverly's soft voice raised in surprise. 'Sure.' 'Honestly and truly?' 'Forever and ever,' Caroline vowed. Surprisingly, they *had* remained a joint force during the wars of adolescence. And unknown to Beverly, Caroline had got her pledged to Omega Delta in an epic chapter-room session. 'I don't give a damn about the alums and their tacky prejudices! She's witty and talented and better than anyone else we're bidding and she's *my best friend*!' Small Em, always striving to be fair-minded, had risen from her president's desk to agree with Caroline. This past year Caroline hadn't seen quite so much of Beverly. Nothing planned. She still felt as warm, but the best-friend season was past. They were growing up. So, Caroline wondered as she watched Beverly take that first drag, why should she feel this sense of loss? Well, who else knew how unguarded Beverly was?

Beverly realized she was being watched. 'Sneaking one,' she said, holding up the hand with the cigarette. 'You know Mother.'

'I know you.' Caroline deepened her voice. 'I vant to be alone.' She decided her Garbo was definitely lesser Wynan. She remembered something. 'Lloyd's here.'

'He is? But he said about five.'

'A tall V-12 paying his ree-spects to your parents. Anyone else fit the description?' Caroline shook her head. 'A real hardship case you've got there.'

Beverly stubbed out the fresh cigarette, starting for the garden.

'Hold on! I *need* you.'

'But Lloyd – he must be ready for a transfusion.' Beverly's voice trembled.

Lloyd was shy, true, but the depth of Beverly's sensitivity got to Caroline. 'Your fine artistic hand, luv, is unique,' she asserted. 'And the cake's a horror.'

So Beverly, the art major, loosened cloth flowers with slender, deft fingers while listening to Caroline's gossip about the guests, joining in the infectious laughter.

'Interested in the destination?' Caroline asked.

Beverly looked up, her mouth opening a little. Surprised. Em had kept everyone, including her sister and parents, in the dark about the location of her honeymoon.

Caroline smiled tantalizingly, holding a long Fire and Ice fingernail to her matching magenta lips. 'Don't breathe a word. Sequoia. Keep working. Sheridan's bought a double sleeping bag from the Sears catalogue.' Caroline winced. 'Imagine. Sears! Em's going to lose it under the open sky.'

'Like Olie de Havilland and Charlie Boyer in *Hold Back the Dawn*.' Beverly's tone was properly sophisticated, yet a sigh escaped.

'It means no, N-O bathroom. That Sheridan! He didn't even *ask* her.'

After a moment Beverly asked, 'Caroline, don't you, well, need a bathroom for, uhh, junk?'

They looked at one another, bewildered. Neck they did, plenty, Caroline and Beverly. Neither, though, took part in those mungy little chats at the Omega Delta house – Caroline felt considerably more worldwise than anyone *there*. Mrs Wynan and Mrs Linde, thank God, weren't the sort to have comfy talks. When the time came, the two girls agreed, the man would know.

'Em saw Dr Porter,' Caroline said finally. 'She must be fully equipped and informed.'

'Ca-a-aroline,' called a male voice outside the screen

door. 'Where you hiding?'

'Ain't nobody here but us chickens.' Caroline bent to retrieve her maid of honour hat, smiling into the sunlight. From this angle the young man must have quite a view. Black hair spilling over pink cheeks and firm breast tops. She said to Beverly, 'That's good enough. I'll get Lucidda to wheel out the monstrosity. Go rescue Lloyd.'

She ran into the baking heat of the patio.

Beverly went the long way around, moving dreamily through the kitchen. Outside, she saw Lloyd, shifting his weight from one long, bell-bottomed leg to the other as he faced her parents. Beverly hurried, her high heels sinking in grass, around clusters of laughing guests.

Lloyd: a quiet, mathematically inclined Catholic boy who played Bach on his oboe, smelled of peppermint, and came from St Paul, a leftover from Caltech's Navy officer-training programme. He was wearing his whites.

Lloyd saw her first. His smile showed lower teeth. Mr Linde turned. His smile showed dentures that Dr Wynan had fiddled over endlessly.

Mrs Linde said, 'We've been wondering where you were, dear.' Her voice was firm, assured.

'Helping Caroline fix the cake.'

'Daddy and I have to leave before she cuts it.' Mrs Linde glanced at her small gold Bulova. 'You'll stay, won't you? It's the correct thing to do.'

'I want to.' Beverly glanced at Lloyd.

He flushed happily, saying, 'I'll walk you home.'

Mrs Linde said, 'We've already made our apologies to the Wynans and' – she smiled – 'the Reeds. There's fried chicken in the refrigerator for you – and Lloyd, too.'

'Thank you, Mrs Linde,' Lloyd said.

'We're eating at the Los Feliz Brown Derby,' said Mr Linde. Invariably, he told his daughter where he could be reached. 'We're playing bridge after. At the Marcuses'.'

At this possibly Jewish-sounding name Beverly tensed, aching (1) to fly, (2) to murder this desire, and (3) to sneak a look in her compact to make sure her face wasn't be-

21

traying her. Without realizing, she moved closer to Lloyd. She didn't notice the gathering of fine wrinkles around her mother's mouth or the deepening of worry lines above the bridge of her father's spectacles.

The Lindes' concern was unnecessary. They could have asked Beverly how interested she was in Lloyd, and most likely she would have replied that she enjoyed his quiet company, and no more. But the Lindes didn't ask. They prided themselves on being circumspect, non-interfering (and therefore non-Jewish) parents. Assimilated. Yet, at the moment that Beverly took a step towards Lloyd – long, skinny, Catholic Lloyd – Mr and Mrs Linde glanced at one another. Each saw fear reflected.

4

Lucidda, an invited guest and also the Wynans' daily maid (Glendale police made life intolerable for any black servant who stayed overnight) bumped the cloth-draped kitchen trolley across the worn wood doorstep. A boy shouted, 'The cake!' and champagne-lubricated young throats took up his chant. 'The bride cuts the cake, the bride cuts the cake.' Em and Sheridan made their way to the patio, followed by Dr and Mrs Wynan. Sheridan's parents had remained in Wichita, unable to waste money on fares and new clothes. Three mousy bridesmaids appeared, as did the roseate Caroline. The photographer posed the bridal party behind the tiered cake. Everyone crowded up three patio steps, the Family making a phalanx, protecting Mrs Van Vliet, the only surviving grandparent.

'A lovely boy,' Mrs Van Vliet pronounced in a voice as light and clear as ringing crystal. 'He and Em make a fine couple.'

Em slid the first piece of cake onto a plate and, glancing

anxiously up at her husband, tiptoed to fork-feed him. 'No more pictures,' he said, closing his mouth on spongy whiteness.

Old Mrs Van Vliet, next to Caroline, raised her smart flowered hat towards her granddaughter's ear, murmuring, 'The Christian feeds the lion.'

'Well, well,' Caroline whispered back.

'Did you ever see such an expression?'

'*You* said he was a lovely boy.'

'An appropriate remark for Glendale.'

Caroline reached out for borrowed china with its cube of cake. 'Here, ancestress,' she said loudly.

'At my eldest grandchild's wedding,' Mrs Van Vliet said in her normal, clear tone, 'I don't need reminders of the ageing process. And I prefer to eat sitting down. Come inside, Caroline.' She handed Caroline back the plate. Someone opened the French windows to the living-room and Mrs Van Vliet proceeded like one used to having doors opened. Regally.

Caroline shouldered the windows closed, wondering, as did everyone, how old was her grandmother? Mrs Van Vliet kept her age secret, but she must be well into her seventies. Not that she looked younger. Her face was tapestried with amused wrinkles, her beautifully waved hair completely white, yet she gave off an indefinable scent, the odour of youth. She made you think of a young girl dressed in a trim old body. She was vain of her appearance, and under plucked white brows her eyes snapped with wit. Caroline admired her grandmother almost as much as she loved her. She didn't realize how alike they were. Mrs Van Vliet did, which was why Caroline was her favourite grandchild.

'Blessed cool,' Mrs Van Vliet breathed, sitting straight-backed on one of the pair of dun tweed couches that flanked the fireplace. She gazed at puppy-stained hooked rugs, crocheted afghans, purplish needlepoint footstools, crewelled pillows, the results of her daughter's thick, industrious fingers and total lack of taste, smiling when she came to the jarring note of elegance, a gilt-framed, life-size portrait of herself holding a single white camellia, painted during her first pregnancy. For this reason alone she had given it to Mrs Wynan. Mrs Van Vliet did not part easily with possessions.

Still smiling, she drew off one French kid glove. The great diamond flashed light in the dim room. Caroline handed her the cake plate.

'He is attractive.' Mrs Van Vliet nibbled, made a moue, set down her fork. 'Common but attractive.'

'Em is *crazy* about Sheridan, Sheridan is *wild* for her.'

'Don't get on your high horse with me.'

'I'm –'

'You're loyal,' Mrs Van Vliet said. 'You are, Caroline. Just look how you stand by the little Linde girl – stop frowning. Do you want wrinkles? You know I'm no bigot. A snob, certainly, but not a bigot. Frankly, I've always seen Em with someone like herself.'

'From a richer family, you mean?'

'Money isn't what we're talking about. Though I daresay he's impressed.'

'With what? This?' It was Caroline's turn to glance around the comfortable, ugly room. 'Our fort-yoon.' She and Em received an annual income of $712.50 from Van Vliet's preferred stock.

'Coming from good people doesn't mean much to those who do. I hope he won't take it out on Em. But, Caroline, it's you we're thinking about.'

'We are?'

'Yes.'

'Grandmama,' Caroline sighed, accenting – as always – Grandmama in the French manner.

'Listen to me. The most important quality in a husband is that he's good to you.'

'Words of wisdom, I'm sure, old luv. But let's not get ahead of ourselves.'

'You girls are marrying younger and younger.'

'For *love*.'

'That's a bonus.'

'And how is this wondrous *good* quality apparent?'

'There are ways.'

'That only you know? I promise I'll bring over any prospect.'

'Do that little thing,' her grandmother said, the small, ringed hand closing on Caroline's large, well-shaped hand. 'Is there one?'

'Not as far as human eye can see.'

'I want you to be happy.' Veined fingers tightened. 'You must be happy.'

'That sounds like an order.'

'It is. You're my reincarnation. Didn't you know?'

5

Beverly watched Caroline undo the tiny satin-covered buttons at the back of Em's wedding dress.

Caroline said, 'You've got a stain, Mrs Reed.'

'How? Back there?' neat little Em wondered. And at the same minute Beverly said, 'I can't get used to it. Mrs Reed.' And Caroline cried, 'Mrs Reed, *Mrs* Reed!'

Mrs Reed stepped out of ivory satin and stiff, hooped underskirt. 'My room's so bare.' The beds and dresser already had been moved to the apartment. Boxes were stacked along one wall.

'It's jammed with loot,' Caroline pointed out.

'But the room's not mine,' Em said earnestly. 'This isn't my home, not any more.'

'Yes,' Caroline exclaimed. 'No,' Beverly murmured. They meant the same thing. Em shook talc on her shoulders and under her arms, smoothing with a big puff. Beverly picked up the heavy dress.

'A wedding,' Em went on in the same sober tone, 'is an end to something.'

'It sure is, luv!' Caroline laughed.

Beverly laughed, too. Em didn't. And Beverly noticed

her expression as the small, cruelly frizzed blonde head emerged between the straps of a new slip.

'Em,' Beverly said, softly, 'you're a whole new person. Think on it.'

Caroline said, 'I bet Lloyd asks *you*.'

'You kill me.' Beverly.

'He will. But me, *I*'ll be stuck forever. An old maid.'

'That'll be the day,' Beverly said, twisting the top of the quilted hanger, attaching it to the top of the closet door, high, so the train wouldn't touch the floorboards.

Caroline reached out, one well-shaped arm about her sister, the other circling her best friend, and then the three of them were hugging one another in a fierce embrace. Beverly was Caroline's friend, not Em's, yet Beverly felt a welling of tears. This moment, she thought, is an hour-glass, endings sifting to become beginnings, this moment is a deep, endless seal on our three lives. This moment is crucial to our future. Later, Beverly would look back and wonder whether she had been given some precognition, whether she had somehow blundered into future knowledge of the Laocoön twinings of an unborn generation. But at the moment her ideas were soaring and growing until she could no longer decipher them.

The square little room was filled with girl odours, light sweat, Camay, various colognes. Atoms of talc hung in warm air. Party chatter came through crisscrossed-curtained windows and a glass crashed on patio tiles. The three girls kept hugging one another wordlessly. Caroline, Em, Beverly. They were close, close.

Em and Sheridan, rice pelting around them, ran to Dr and Mrs Wynan's wedding gift, a 1941 Ford coupé, the newest-model car anyone could buy in Glendale. Late models had just started off Detroit's reconverted assembly lines but these were being sold in communities more able to pay huge under-the-counter bonuses. Em, blushing and anxiously flicking rice from her tan going-away suit, moved to the middle of the seat. Sheridan slammed into reverse. Down the hedged drive jerked the Ford, crushing empty cans tied to the rear bumper. Guests were over-flowing the front yard onto the street. A few ladies, Mrs Wynan among them, dabbed at tears. Omega Deltas clutched tiny white boxes of cake – they dwelt in an age beyond superstition, yet this sliver of wedding cake was something on which to dream up a husband. Caroline's high colour was intensified by excitement. Beverly stood a little apart. Sheridan inched the Ford through the crowd, moving into blue shadows of eucalyptus, Goodbye, good luck, goodbye, God bless you.

'Live happily always,' Beverly called. 'Be happy forever and ever.'

Chapter Two

I

That night, after eating their cold fried chicken, Beverly and Lloyd sat on the couch, which smelled of upholstery shampoo. On the record player was one of Lloyd's records, a Bach fugue.

'Yesterday,' Lloyd said, 'a man from du Pont was on campus.'

He rarely spoke during Bach. Beverly pulled away. She saw herself twinned in his pupils.

'About when the Navy's through with us.'

'Oh?'

'They're big on research.'

'Du Pont?'

'Uh-huh.'

'Is that in New Jersey?'

'Delaware,' Lloyd said. 'They're interested in me.'

'Lloyd, that's wonderful.'

'I'm not in them.'

'But didn't you want research?'

'Here,' he said. 'In California.'

The light from the floor lamp shone through his hair. He's going thin in front, Beverly thought. The idea rather pleased her. Mr Linde was bald. She smiled.

'It's quite a place to live, Los Angeles,' he said. His sun-chapped lips remained expectantly parted. Woodwinds rose in orderly progression. She felt her smile turn rigid. He swallowed, drawing her head back to his shoulder.

'Good,' Lloyd admired behind her.

She jumped. It was the following Monday afternoon, and she hadn't heard him enter the backyard. She clutched her charcoal, hunching protectively over her pad. She'd been sketching the wisteria, and to have anyone look at her work, unfinished or not, made her squirm. She would have preferred to turn over the big pad, but mightn't that hurt Llyod's feelings?

'Have you resigned from the US Navy?' she asked.

'John's covering for me,' he said. He was peering over her shoulder. With a few black and grey lines she had captured pendant blossoms. He said, 'I never realized you were so good. Aren't you going to finish?'

She shook her head.

'Beverly. Don't!'

But already she was ripping, crushing the sheet in one hand. 'It's rotten, rotten,' she said, dropping the ball of paper.

He sat on the grass, raising long, skinny legs to bridge fallen lavender blooms. 'You weren't thinking of good or rotten before I came.'

'I wasn't thinking, period.'

'Then?'

'I was working. Lloyd, could you do a calculus problem if I were in your room?'

He flushed. 'Now,' he said, 'we get down to the basic differences.'

'Girls feel the same,' she said. 'Or haven't you noticed?'

They both reddened. A robin landed nearby, poking his yellow beak in mud surrounding the leaky sprinkler head.

'It's nice and cool here,' Lloyd said.

'I love summer.'

'Why?'

'Oh, I have time to draw. And I'm not forced into the ominous world of people.'

'About du Pont,' he said. 'You wouldn't want to live anywhere but Los Angeles, would you?'

And reached for her hand, the one clenched around charcoal. Now, Lloyd might have stretched his body along the length of hers, open mouth to open mouth, he might have kissed her small breasts which were astonishingly white and shaped like peaches, but this, taking her hand, was on another plane. At that time a boy and girl didn't hold hands, not if mothers were likely to see from a window, not unless the couple were engaged – or at the very least, pinned. Beverly and Lloyd, both, had been raised to this fine distinction. She jerked back her hand. Lloyd's face glowed with naked hurt. And the world of lavender blossoms and fernlike leaves rushed around Beverly. She never had taken pleasure in conquests. She could not, like Caroline, inflict the teasing ambiguities of flirtation. She could not bear the thought of causing minor humiliation in anyone, much less Lloyd. He gave a muted, nervous cough. Here, Caroline would have laughed and made rapport. Beverly could not trust herself to speak. Charcoal snapped in her fist.

After a while Lloyd spoke. 'See the way the sun comes through the branches?'

'I was trying to get that on paper.'

'When I was little,' he said, 'there was this stained-glass window in church. All colours of pink and red, and sometimes the light would slant like this. I figured it was a ramp to Jesus and his angels.'

Beverly could scarcely breathe.

Next Wednesday morning, early, she drove to USC, filling out her next semester's schedule. Afterwards, she didn't get back in Mrs Linde's Hudson. She walked north, past the statue of Tommy Trojan on his horse. Hot already, waves shimmered off the streets around campus. After a while she came to a large Catholic church. St Mary's. Covering her soft brown hair with a scarf that she didn't tie – it was too hot – she entered. The church was empty, smelled of incense, wax, and peace. Knotting the silk, she sank into the last pew. An old Mexican woman limped in, pausing to genuflect before kneeling at the leather rail in front of the altar. Beads clicked. Sibilant whispers.

Beverly gazed up at the cross.

Lloyd, she thought, Lloyd. I'm here to think about him. In most girls it would be histrionic, coming to an alien church to contemplate a boyfriend, but Beverly had not chosen her ground with drama in mind. For all her self-consciousness about being Jewish, in every other matter she lived on the naked point of innocence. She acted instinctively, without artifice or hypocrisy or malice. She was here for one reason: the place seemed right to sort out emotions about a Catholic.

First, she thought, the necking. It's fine. But . . . She was passionate, and with two of her high school boyfriends she had ached to go the limit. With Lloyd, though, she never had felt any substantial urges. We both enjoy classical music. And Lloyd, thank God, would rather take in a picture show than a beer spree. He never makes derogatory cracks about any group. (This was vitally important to Beverly, who had spent the better part of her childhood playing deaf to such cracks.) When he plays his oboe his brow gets all crinkled.

And as usual when she tried to think to a concise end, her mind wandered. Without realizing, she leaned forward, resting her arms on the next pew. The position was awkward. She inched forward, resting her weight on her knees. The same position as the Mexican woman. How strange, Beverly thought. The old woman's praying.

'I want to pray,' she whispered.

Pray?

The Lindes didn't belong to a temple. Ritually they celebrated Christmas with an Open House, and shared their Thanksgiving turkey with the Harleys, who were English — Thad Harley was Howard Linde's partner in the accounting firm of Harley and Linde. Other holidays, the Jewish ones, were observed by Mr and Mrs Linde and Beverly, alone, gulping a festive dinner with a general air of embarrassment because Willeen, the coloured daily maid, was serving them. Years later, Beverly read of the *marranos*, those Jews forcibly converted by the Inquisition, who lived exactly as their neighbours, yet for generations held on to one particular aspect of the faith of their fathers, sometimes merely changing body linen for Friday night or turning to a wall as death overtook them: Beverly was reminded of the manner her family had practised Judaism, furtively eating a large meal from the good Lenox on the High Holy Days.

A lean priest rustled up the centre aisle. He was looking at her curiously. Or so she imagined. All at once her mouth tasted bad, metallic, as if she'd been sucking a penny.

What am I doing in a church?

I don't belong here.

Pushing to her feet, she fled, racing through hot streets. By the time she reached Mrs Linde's Hudson sweat rolled from her and she was gasping in terrible heaves.

That night she phoned Lloyd. In a breathy, embarrassed murmur, she told him she couldn't, uhh, keep seeing him, at least not every Saturday night.

At the end of August she came down with mumps which worsened to mumps meningitis. Four long white boxes of roses, American Beauties, arrived with cards from Lloyd.

She had fully recuperated on the afternoon that Mrs Linde came into her room with a letter. 'Dear, Aunt Pauline would like you to come to New York.' She handed Beverly the folded sheet. 'How nice of her,' Beverly said. 'Daddy and I think it would be good for you.' There was an unspoken corollary to Mrs Linde's remark: to get away from Catholic boys who send red roses. More than anything, Beverly wished she could talk out her bewilderment with her mother. It was impossible. The Lindes were oblique people. They had bought this brick house in Glendale, which was not then (and is still not) a suburb of liberalism. The particular section they had chosen had no other Jewish families, yet they had proceeded to act with their daughter as if she were no different from their neighbours. (In school, with honest cruelty, the children had made Beverly aware of these differences.) Later, the Lindes did admit one minor peculiarity, like having an extra molar. We marry only those with one too many teeth. Beverly had accepted her parents' paradoxes. Now her eyes blurred. Weepy. She was undone by their concern. She wanted to reassure her mother that she didn't love Lloyd. This, however, was a time and place of reticence, and Mrs Linde – to the end of her days – considered discussion of one's emotional landscape a breach of propriety. So Beverly said, 'Thank you, Mother,' and hugged Mrs Linde. Unyielding all-in-one corset. 'You're such a funny, sensitive child,' Mrs Linde said, extricating herself. 'We decided since you can't be in college this semester, it's a perfect opportunity for you to see New York.'

2

'My father,' Dan said, 'thinks I'm getting too involved.'

New York. Beverly had been taken by Dan Grossblatt for Sunday brunch at Steinberg's and Dan had ordered for both of them. Lox, cream cheese, and bagels. Cream cheese, of course, she knew. Lox she recognized as smoked salmon, but she'd never been exposed to a bagel. When she'd asked what it was, Dan, laughing, had assumed she was putting him on. Now, biting into the tough bun, she stared at him. Cream cheese squished out with a bit of salmon. She bent to let them fall, unobtrusively as possible, onto her plate.

Finishing chewing, she asked, 'Involved?'

He reached for her pickled tomato. 'If you didn't want it, why order?'

'You ordered.'

They smiled at one another. A bald waiter passed, his tray leaking odours of rich, brown butter.

'How'd he know you are? Involved?' Asking, she realized her stupidity. Dan lived at home, someplace in New Rochelle, and since they'd met sixteen days earlier, he'd taken her out every night.

'You had to start the phoning.' Dan grinned. He was the one who called. Two or three times a day, at odd hours. Friday morning, though, at the Museum of Modern Art she'd been transfixed, overwhelmed by Monet's

Waterlilies and knowing she must share with him, had called his father's factory in Brooklyn, S&G Shoes. Dan worked there.

'Did he say anything else?'

'Sure.'

She tilted her head questioningly.

'He's got a girl for me to meet. She's loaded. A *shad-chan* found –'

'A *shad* – a what?'

'A marriage broker.'

Slowly she wiped fishy cream cheese from her fingers, gazing at him. Voices and blue coils of smoke rose from the next table. Dan went to services Saturday mornings, ate no shellfish or any part of a pig, never creamed his coffee after a meat meal: this, without really thinking it through, she had accepted. Dan was religious. Lloyd confessed and got up early for Mass, the Wynans went every Sunday morning to St Mark's. Dan did these things. A marriage broker? She kept staring into almond-shaped blue eyes set above broad Slavic cheekbones. This was Dan Grossblatt. Her Dan. Twenty-six. When he stood he would be the same height as she in Cuban heels. (He was so full of vitality that she never felt too tall.) He was warm. He was generous – but got pretty brutal if she mentioned it. As a kid he had listened to 'The Happiness Boys', Billy Jones and Ernie Hare, had known Ming of Mongo and the Katzenjammers and Tom Swift, had half-backed his high school football team, had graduated from the University of Michigan, had been mustered out a captain in the Army, he was hot for the King Cole Trio, he laughed at Bob Hope and Red Skelton, one after the other, on Sunday nights. Dan was, God knows, more all-American than Lloyd with his slide rule and Bach. Yet here he was, Dan, talking matter-of-factly about something from another world, another age. A marriage broker?

'That's some expression,' he said.

'I didn't know there were those people. Not anymore. Why? What does your father want?'

'A rich girl for me.'

'She's probably hideous,' Beverly said. 'Is she?'

'What? Loaded?'

'Pretty?'

'Like Lana Turner, he heard, and what's so hot about that? I told him to forget it.' Dan traced the threadlike scar under her lip and she kissed his finger with a tiny, popping sound.

'Buzz,' he said quietly. 'You're right. I'm no Jack Armstrong.'

Beverly, although sensitive to people's pain, was fairly dense about their other emotions. But she understood Dan. He understood her. They were deeply in love, but that wasn't why they understood one another. Dan never hid his feelings from her. His warmth, she realized, drew her out. Also he was shrewd about people. Often – like now – he could tell her what she was thinking.

When they left Steinberg's a soft rain fell. 'Come on,' Dan said, taking her hand, starting to run. Sodden leaves mushed under the boots she'd chosen at Saks. In the park were swings that waited for children who didn't play in the rain. Dan gripped a metal chain. 'Here,' he said. 'Dan, I never can get myself started.' 'So I'll push you.' And he did, shouting, 'Pump!' each time. Beverly, laughing, kicking her new boots on the upswing, tucking them under as she went back. 'Enough, Dan,' she called, 'I'm under my own steam.' But he kept shoving his palms on her back until she semi-circled as high as possible. He sat on the next swing. Bare twigs pendulous with water raced at her. Every breath delighted. Already Dan was as high as she. Rain matted his thick brown hair and he looked, as always, packed with energy. He started to laugh. She laughed, too. 'Oh Dan. Dan, Dan, Dan.'

That was the night he told her.

They were outside Aunt Pauline's building in his new Packard convertible, a welcome-home gift from his father, bought, Dan had told her, with an exorbitant bonus.

He had been at the liberation of Buchenwald.

Words came at her. She couldn't duck. Limepit mass graves. Shower rooms with shower heads that held poison

35

gas. Ovens. SS injection experiments. Skeleton corpses by the thousands, cadaverous survivors unable to eat, survivors dying in the hour of their liberation. Before that night he hadn't mentioned it. (She had, of course, read disquieting snips in newspapers.)

'It was raining, and my uniform was soaked. Whenever I smell wet wool I smell ... Oh God! Those other smells.' He shuddered, gripping the wheel. 'And the faces – when people starve, they look alike, know that? The identical face. A skull with huge, caved eyes. And the corpses were yellow and flat, stacked neatly as lumber in a sawmill. Men, women, children – there weren't many children. Know what hell is? A huge, muddy place with living corpses and dead lumber.'

She was shivering. He gazed at the streetlight, as if there were some answer to be found in electricity. And told her about the Frenchman. Somehow the one Frenchman's tale reached deeper in her than all the number-tattooed victims of Buchenwald. Dan had found him on a road south of Paris, walking erratically beneath dripping plane trees. Dan had stopped the jeep to give him a lift. The Frenchman's soaking coat (courtesy of the US Army) was open and so was his striped slave jacket.

'I don't know how he got that far, Buzz. He was so thin I could see his heart beating. Like a fist opening and closing.' Dan clenched and unclenched his hand. 'But he kept telling me he was fine. Very strong. After a while I figured it. They ran a selection. Workers in this line live. All others in that line. To die. Either/or. He'd been in a world where his only right to exist was his being able to work. He spoke pretty good English. He told me he was on his way home. He was from Lyons. His wife and kids, he said, should be there. He'd been separated from them at Drancy – that was the camp depot for France. They'd agreed they would get back to Lyons as soon as possible afterwards. He said it over and over, they would be in Lyons, soon he'd see them. Yvonne, that was his wife. And Jacques, his son, and little Marie. Buzz, I can still hear the way he said the name. P'teet M'ree. Very soft, like that. And all the time I could see his heart. We talked about New York. In 'thirty-eight he was here, a business trip. He was a lawyer.'

High heels clattered on the sidewalk, fading. Lonely.

'We were talking about the Statue of Liberty one minute. Then he was dead. Just like that.' Dan was silent again. Finally he shrugged. 'I got together nine other Jewish guys and we said *kaddish*.'

Said what? Did it matter? Always Beverly had sensed a flaw of horror under everyday surfaces, and now she was inundated with the evidence.

'That's why I keep things,' Dan said. 'If I forget thee, O Jerusalem.' He paused.

'Go on.'

'I'm willing to go through the whole *schmear* because I believe in God. And it's my way of remembering.'

'Ritual is a form of remem –'

Her mouth froze. In dim shadows cast by the streetlight, she saw his face. Violent. Furious. He gripped her shoulder, hurting.

'You don't know what the shit you're talking about!'

'Catholics don't eat meat Fridays because –'

'Catholics! The lawyer told me his wife was a devout Catholic! Of Jewish extraction. Did I say I went to Lyons to find her?'

Beverly shook her head.

'The last anyone knew of her was Buchenwald. Maybe I did find her. She could've been one of those corpses – no! Hell, how could she've lasted that long?' Dan's fingers cut harder into her flesh. 'All those stacked bodies had one common denominator. Whether they call themselves Catholic, Lutheran, atheist, agnostic, they were Jews. Jews. The great assimilated along with the Hasidim. My father's family in Lodz. All Jews.' Dan released her shoulder. She didn't permit herself to move. 'Nothing to do with religion.' Dan's normally ebullient voice was levelly cold. 'That Frenchwoman. You. Me. They wanted to rid the earth of us.'

She felt his words more than heard them.

She became part of the vast, festering wound of their generation of Jews. The survivors who asked: *Why not me? If the others, then why not someday me?* She was, and would forever be, haunted by the skeletal wraiths. Her heart never could make the necessary adjustment. Never. Yet at that second she was mostly terrified by Dan's fury. She reacted in her own way. She withdrew. Shifting on new leather as far as possible from him, she said, 'You don't need anything to make you remember.'

'So?'

'Then it's not the point. Giving up cigars on Saturday and wearing a cap to pray, I can't understand why you won't admit it's ritual.' Her voice came out too thin.

'You're a damn stupid broad,' he said, adding with careful viciousness. 'What's the point of you?'

Tears came. She leaned her head against the icy window, ashamed her weakness could be seen by Dan, who must know her muffled sobs were only in small part for the tortured millions, the French lawyer and his family. She wept for herself. She wept like a prisoner thrust back into solitary confinement. She felt a handkerchief pushed into her hand. She blew her nose into smells of freshly ironed linen and tobacco, fine and happy odours of the living: she reached blindly. Dan's large, warm hand clasped hers. She slid across the seat. He buried his face in her neck.

'Who says you can't smell in your dreams?' His face was wet, too.

She stroked his hair, which was crisp and coarse. Many people are able to deny evil. Beverly couldn't. Evil is. Her mind wasn't neat, analytical, small. What Dan had told her she could never explain away in philosophical or psychological terms. Evil is. She held him, stroking his coarse brown hair.

3

She argued with Dan.

They argued whether to see the James Mason movie at the nearby art house or *The Big Sleep* – Dan considered Lauren Bacall hot stuff. They argued if Beverly would nurse their future babies, Dan said he didn't want her to, he didn't want her breasts sagging, he was crazy about her breasts, they were small but pretty and the nipples were gentle, know that? They argued about the formation of a Zionist state, a subject about which she knew nothing (beyond hearing her parents agree they were against such a country) and one where Dan had put his money where his mouth was, and they argued about *Guernica*, although he was ignorant of Picasso's intent. Dan never caught on they were arguing. His idea of good conversation happened to coincide with Beverly's idea of argument. Their longest, continuing battle: she wanted to go the limit. He wanted to wait.

They were sprawling, discomforted by the steering wheel, safe from police flashlights under the Grossblatts' stone *porte-cochère*. Dan's fingers traced her quivering thigh. She made her suggestion for the fifth – or was it the sixth? – time that night. He removed his hand.

'Not here,' he said.

'Someplace?'

'We should find some flea-bitten dump and sign in as Mr and Mrs Smith?' He kissed her nose. 'What've you done to me?' A pair more kisses. 'I used to spend all my time selling girls they should register with me.'

'I'm sold.'

She had confessed to him that she'd petted above the waist and – on a few occasions – below, and he, amused, had asked how come she hadn't noticed a certain physiological fact about the male sex organ? Had she assumed a man normally kept it strapped down? Oh, in retrospect her ignorance was monumental. 'I want it to be right,' he whispered, curving her fingers around himself. 'Buzz, know how great we're going to be together?'

Three times Beverly ate in the Grossblatts' huge brick pile in New Rochelle. Next to the front door, nailed to the arched oaken jamb, was a blue enamel case with Hebrew lettering. Dan kissed his fingers to it as they went in. The mezuzah, he explained, contained a parchment inscribed with the *Shema* (passages from Deuteronomy) plus the visible name of God. *Shaddai*. The mezuzah blessed this house. Beverly thought the huge stone pile barren rather than blessed. Gloria, the youngest, was away at Ohio State. The middle child, Sgt Victor M. Grossblatt, USMC, had been brought home from Iwo Jima under an American flag, and the Grossblatts in their bitter grief (Dan told Beverly) had blamed one another for letting Vic enlist under-age. Now Mr Grossblatt never spoke to his wife. To Beverly he spoke in his harsh gutturals as little as possible. He had come from Lodz at fourteen, a penniless cobbler's apprentice without family or a word of English. By the time he turned thirty the man was a millionaire, and today nobody knew how many millions he was worth, only himself and *Shaddai*.

'My mother,' Dan said, 'has a diamond in the vault. Three and a bit.' Mrs Grossblatt, short, with a wide, freckled nose, fussed over Beverly's appetite. Beverly liked her anyway.

'Want to look at settings?' Dan asked.

Beverly said nothing.

'Before we get it made up, I should introduce myself to your parents? Ask for your hand?'

Another cold, drizzly Sunday, they were heading for the park.

'Well?' he asked finally.

'Have you told your father?'

'Screw my father.' Dan put his arm round her shoulder. 'Why nervous?'

'Who's nervous?'

'Any girl who doesn't want a three-carat ring.' His fingers squeezed through layers of fabric, wet and dry. 'Buzz, listen, once he sees he can't have his own way, you'll be his idea. It's been very tough on them since Vic. A wedding'll cheer them up. A wedding is for families – hey! Watch it!'

She avoided the puddle, walking apart from Dan.

Families.

Her very problem. Families. Idiot, she told herself, cretin. Wasn't it incredible she never once had considered that marriage is no island? Marriage is a social contract. Marriage is the Grossblatts and the Lindes, marriage is Dan with Caroline and Em and Sheridan and the Omega Deltas. Dan never would accommodate himself to Glendale, and she would feel a nail go in for each shrug, each Yiddish expression, anything that might be construed as loud, including a three-carat ring on a nineteen-year-old girl. A fierce osteomyelitis of shame weakened her bones. Was this the measure of her love? (But how could anyone have her identity mercilessly imprisoned for nineteen years, then expect love, however deep, to throw open every jail door?)

Dan grabbed her elbow, halting her on the brink of a water-filled gutter. He gripped both her shoulders, turning her to face him. Drops caught in his hair. His heavy features were wet. They stared at one another, and she felt that warm, aching need quiver in the pit of her stomach. Her eyes grew moist. 'You need a keeper,' he whispered. A car swished by, splattering their legs. Neither noticed. And in that minute her future seemed simple. She would have a difficult time, sure, but not for long. They would be married. They would be together always.

'Your folks have only one daughter, such as she is,' he said. His arm around her, he started to walk briskly. 'We'll do this right, I'll come out to Los Angeles, right, right, oh, I did right by my wife and my seventeen kids

41

and my peanut stand and my old grey mare ...' He marched faster and faster until they were both laughing breathless into the rain.

4

In Los Angeles Dan spent days with the local S&G rep. Dan had force and humour. He was a natural. Christmas, when wholesalers take off because nobody writes an order, he sold shoes by the gross. Nights he took Beverly out. The Lindes made no comment. But Beverly knew what they thought of him.

Breakfast. Mr Linde had just left for work, Mrs Linde, handsome in a cashmere sweater set and the smell of Yardley's, finished her first cup of coffee and Beverly scrubbed a cocoa stain from her pink robe – since the mumps, Mrs Linde hadn't insisted she dress for breakfast. The previous night Dan had been to dinner, the first time he'd been invited, a jarringly awkward evening.

'Mother.' Beverly clenched her napkin to keep her hands from shaking, 'I'm asking Dan to the Open House.'

'Oh?' Mrs Linde, for once rattled, touched her springy grey-black hair. 'Are you sure that's the correct thing?' *Behave correctly* was the motto blazoned on Mrs Linde's firm beating heart.

Beverly said, lied, she was sure.

'I got the impression that Dan is, well, quite religious.'

'He is.'

'Then don't you think a Christmas party might offend him?'

No doubt about it.

'And he won't know anyone. He hasn't met Caroline or Em or Sheridan or Lloyd or –'

'I haven't asked Lloyd.'

'I see.' Mrs Linde poured her second cup of coffee. 'Well, you've always invited your own guests.'

'You don't want him.'

'Beverly! What on earth has gotten into you? I only asked if you thought it right to ask Dan to this particular party.'

'Mother.' From the kitchen came a deafening roar, the maid using the WasteKing. Beverly, under cover of grinding garbage, asked, 'I was just wondering how you and Daddy would feel if he and I . . .'

The disposal stopped. Beverly's words, *if he and I*, hung in the sunlit breakfast nook. To Beverly it seemed that she and her mother were like the red-jacketed hunters in the paired prints on the wall, forever suspended above an English hedgerow. They were trapped, unable to hurdle *if he and I . . .*

Mrs Linde recovered. 'He's quite a bit older.'

'Seven years.'

'I know this is difficult for you to believe,' Mrs Linde said, smiling, 'but you aren't the most mature nineteen.'

'I am nineteen, though.'

'You enjoy your painting, listening to music. Sensitive, quiet things. Dan, even knowing him as little as I do, is a dominating person. And aggressive.'

Beverly stared at her mother.

Mrs Linde looked down at her coffee. 'He comes from an entirely different background.'

'Orthodox.' Beverly was thrust back into childhood. She despised her sullen tone.

'That's not all. There're differences maybe you can't realize. Attitudes. For example, I wonder if Mr Grossblatt respects his wife the way Daddy respects me.' (Here Mrs Linde was playing a little dirty pool: her sister-in-law had written that the Grossblatts were estranged, something to do with the death of a younger son.) 'We learn from what we see at home. Behaviour patterns.'

'He's nothing like his father.'

'Dear, you haven't known Dan long enough to form judgments.'

43

'He's warm and kind and good and generous.'

'I'm sure he is.' Powder showed in Mrs Linde's paper-fine wrinkles. 'This is the reason your father and I always let you make your own decisions. So that when something important comes along, you'll know how to behave.' With a click, Wedgwood cup met saucer. 'Go ahead and invite Dan. The Open House will be a nice way for him to meet your friends.'

Oh God, Beverly thought, again scrubbing cocoa. God.

The living-room drapes were drawn, the record player blared 'Adeste Fideles', and a Douglas fir with blinking, multicoloured lights cast its spasmodic glow over some twenty guests. Glasses tinkled, men made jovial talk while their spouses covertly glanced at one another's legs to see who had succumbed to Dior's calf-covering New Look.

Beverly leaned against the Knabe spinet, hearing but not listening as Caroline's latest, Gene Matheny, discussed this column he wanted to write for *The Daily Bruin*. To Beverly, people appeared in sharp outline, a caricaturist's sketch, with one predominating feature. Gene Matheny was Tolerance. Tall, slightly built, he had a long face that resembled an intelligent hound dog's. Because of his fair, scrubbed-looking complexion as much as his unfailing sense of decency, Caroline often called him Clean Gene. He went to UCLA, he had a social conscience. When he spoke about his beliefs he would press his thumbnail down on his lower lip. Beverly, watching him, thought, If Mother wants a mismatched couple, she should get a load of Gene Matheny and Caroline Wynan.

Caroline, in her new crimson taffeta, picked one-handed along with 'Adeste Fideles', laughing as she hit a clinker.

Sheridan and Em sat side by side on bridge chairs. Em's solemn, small-chinned face, lifted towards Gene, was drawn. She was nearly seven months pregnant. Caroline privately maintained this condition was caused solely by lack of adequate toilet facilities in Sequoia. Em never commented. Her bodily processes appeared focused on building the large, peaked stomach over which her hands clasped protectively. A few minutes earlier, Caroline had whispered to Beverly, 'Dr Porter suspects we have here twins, but mum's the *word*. You know how she is. Sheridan's in one foul mood, so ply him with bourbon.' Sheridan made no pretence of listening to Gene. His deep-set eyes were shadowed. Tired, Beverly thought. For a month, Sheridan had been delivering nights for Cambro's Drugs over on Colorado Boulevard. Who could live on a GI cheque?

Gene was saying, '... convinced him some people aren't hot for sorority and fraternity news ... maybe do ... column on world politics ...'

Draught sucked smoke. The front door had opened.

'I'm dying!' Caroline cried. 'It must be *him*.'

It was. Beverly raced for the door.

Dan, glancing around the tree-lit scene, his thick brows shooting up, bellicose as the MGM lion about to roar. He said nothing. 'Come have a drink,' Beverly said, tugging him through the living-room past Gene, Caroline, Em, and Sheridan, who gazed with open curiosity. In the dining-room Dan stopped to greet Mr Linde and to present a gold-wrapped chocolate box to Mrs Linde. Mrs Linde introduced him to the Harleys, and Thad Harley (Mr Linde's partner) said in his veddy British accent that it just can't be Christmas, not with such masses of flowers and sunshine, then Beverly and Dan, drinks in hand, moved on to listen to a heated masculine discussion of the upcoming Rose Bowl game, and Dan, from Michigan and therefore loyal to the Big Ten, said Illinois by thirty points, and the men tackled him, saying UCLA would win by two touchdowns at least, and Mrs Linde tapped Beverly's shoulder, saying, 'Dear, you mustn't forget your guests,' so Beverly mumbled to Dan she was going into the living-room, turning quickly, hoping he'd continue to do battle for the Illini.

He followed her.

Grasping his hand with her icy one, she introduced him to Caroline and Gene, to Em and Sheridan. She stumbled over names.

Caroline invariably blanketed awkward situations with talk. Spooning eggnog, dripping on her chin, a triangular blob she remained blissfully unaware of, she chattered about a favourite subject of Gene's: State Senator Tenney's blowing in from Sacramento to huff and puff on liberal professors at UCLA. 'He's about,' she declared, 'to attempt mass conflagration of any he thinks bow in the direction of Moscow.'

'And quite a few others,' Gene interpolated.

'The faculty won't *stand* for it!' Caroline.

'They will,' Em said. Over her smock her freckled hands clenched. Lately Em had become depressingly aware that fair play does not the real world make. 'People with families think twice about losing their jobs.'

'But Em, the way the Tenney Committee works,' Gene said, 'is against the state constitution.'

Dan asked, 'Going into law – it is Gene, isn't it?'

'Yes. Gene. No. Teaching.'

'At the university level,' Caroline added. 'And, of course, write.'

At the word write, Gene's pleasant, hound-dog face turned red.

And Em asked, 'Dan, where did you go to school?'

'The University of Michigan.'

'Oh?' Sheridan's finger drummed on his glass. 'Grossblatt? I should've thought you'd've gone to an Eastern college.'

This was one of those inexplicable lulls in party conversation, otherwise you never would have heard the slight inflection in Sheridan's voice as he said Eastern. His meaning was obvious to Beverly. Admittedly, though, she was a specialist. So was Dan. His smile disappeared.

'Why?'

'Beverly said you live in New York.' Sheridan's tone was morose, chilly.

'And that limits my choice of colleges?'

The tension around Sheridan's lips was heavy, as was his dislike. He said nothing. He did not need to.

'We are,' Dan snapped, 'allowed out of state.'

46

Em pushed back a sandy bang. 'C-Columbia's one of the best sch-schools.'

Caroline held up her empty glass. 'All gone,' she cried. 'Gene, get me another. And Beverly's is empty, too. Poor thing, she's dying of thirst, aren't you, luv?'

Dan took Beverly's glass, putting it on the piano, 'Already she's *shikker*,' he said.

Beverly's face burned. She was pretty stewed, but she could see only too clearly Gene's questioning expression, three other pairs of eyes glazed with bewilderment. None of them knew the word. She herself had learned it from Dan, a Yiddish expression and one she was positive he'd used with malice aforethought.

'You're right,' she said to Dan. 'I need some air.' And pulled him past a group of PTA ladies, through the door, down the short hall to her bedroom.

It was cool and smelled, faintly, of Apple Blossom cologne that she'd sprayed on two hours earlier. She kicked the door shut. Laughter and sounds of Christmas revelry were muffled, receding in waves. Dan didn't put his arms around her. Their being alone, though, was comfort. She was sober enough to know they shouldn't be in here, drunk enough not to care.

She kissed his chin.

'Uhh-uh.'

'Why not?' She kissed his mouth lightly, touching her tongue to his lower lip. His breathing slowed. She could feel *it* pressing against her. Closing her eyes, she traced the twin tendons at the back of his neck. Freshly trimmed hair prickled her fingertips.

Loud party noises. The door had opened.

Mrs Linde stood in the hall, her face a pale egg suspended in gloom. Beverly stepped back, hoping in her wild confusion that her mother wouldn't notice Dan's pants. Dumb, she thought. Stupid. When his chin looks as if someone used it to clear magenta from a paintbrush.

'Beverly,' Mrs Linde said calmly, 'I need help with the ham biscuits.'

The floor changed directions.

Dan gripped her arm. 'Okay?' he asked.

'Beverly.' Mother's voice.

'Frances, she's not feeling well.'

Beverly opened her eyes and for the briefest moment saw aversion ripple through her mother's face. Her mother and Dan were staring at her. Beverly comprehended that she was a duelling ground, but she was too befuddled to understand what the combatants expected of her.

'Come on,' Dan said. 'We'll walk around the block.'

'Beverly, your guests.'

Dan and her mother kept speaking, and in the living-room Bing dreamed of a white Christmas.

'Get your coat.' Dan's voice was angry. Rasping. Was it the Scotch? She heard not him, but his father's gutturals. Maybe Dan was his father. Maybe. What did she really know about Dan except she loved him? Except right now she hated him.

'I'm fine,' she said.

Her mother blocked the hall. 'First go wash your face, dear,' said Mrs Linde. 'And remember. Use a fresh napkin in the biscuit basket.'

Beverly dawdled over the washbasin.

When she emerged, Dan was leaning against the arch between dining- and living-rooms, talking with vigorous gestures to Gene, who listened, his head tilted attentively. Dan, smiling at her, kept talking. Loudly. About the good works of the B'nai B'rith Anti-Defamation League. In Glendale, Jewish people spoke of such matters quietly and always among themselves. Beverly wished she could erase Dan and his voice. At the table, tall Sheridan, holding a canapé, bent over bulgy little Em. As Beverly approached, they fell silent, and Em's cheeks, under the pancake make-up, flooded with colour. Beverly had a quick drink. Caroline, laughing with the Tinkers, didn't ask Beverly to join them. Beverly offered beaten biscuits through the living-room. She could hear Dan's voice. She had another quick one.

Finally, around six, she closed the front door on Caroline and Gene and the Reeds. She headed again for the reproduction sideboard which today served as a bar. She was dizzy, nauseated, and had to make an effort to appear (almost) sober.

'Quit while you're on your feet,' Dan said in her ear.

'It's a party.'

'You're ready to keel over.'

'Why'd you have to talk about that to Gene?' she asked. Never before had she used this low, furious tone. Never. A stranger was talking. *In vino veritas.* That stranger is me.

'The Anti-Defamation League?'

'Yes.'

'He was interested.' Bellicose. 'And why the hell shouldn't I talk about it?'

'And did you have to make that scene with Sheridan? About nothing?' This definitely is not me.

She started to move away. Dan grabbed her arm, examining her. The Christmas tree, a blinking rainbow pyramid, 'O Little Town of Bethlehem', a smell of pine, a fall of laughter, and the two of them facing one another.

The muscles around Dan's eyes contorted. 'So that's what's with you,' he said.

Beverly twisted from his grasp.

A drink later, she heard Mr Harley's polite voice being marched over by Dan, something about the British having no right to be in Palestine, something about a White Paper being reneged on. From time to time she caught Dan examining her with an expression she was far too drunk to interpret. He left as the disembodied tones of Lionel Barrymore started to creak out the story of Scrooge.

5

It rained on 5 January, on the night before Dan was to leave.

He was staying at the Biltmore, and he and Beverly ate in the Grill. Over his porterhouse he told of his day in various shoe stores. She looked into his face. She knew misery when she saw it, but he continued talking in a pleasant tone. He was standing. He must've signed the cheque. A convention of California Men's Clothiers, yellow identification cards on their lapels, crowded the vast lobby. Dan stopped at a gilt easel with a true-colour photograph of Tanya Someone, appearing nightly. He said, 'We'll go hear her.'

'No.'

'It's wet out,' Dan said. 'She's convenient.'

'No,' Beverly repeated.

'Where do you want, then?'

'Your room.'

A threesome of Men's Clothiers eyed Beverly up, down, up again.

'To talk. I won't rape you. Dan, please?'

The men were listening. Dan shrugged, heading for the broad steps that led to the elevator hall. Neither of them spoke on their way to his room. Lighting a cigar, he lounged on the bed made up as a couch. Its perpendicular mate was turned down. She sat on the chair. Gusts of water slashed at windows.

'Lucky it wasn't like this New Year's,' he said. And conversed about the Rose Bowl. He'd been close on those thirty points, Illinois having skunked UCLA 45–14. She twisted her handbag strap.

I must start, she thought, I must.

She was in this impersonal room to put an end to co-cooned silences, to conversations breaking mid-sentence, to ambiguity about future letters. It was dead for him, she

50

assumed, but she wanted it interred as it had lived. With honesty. She wanted to know cause of death. Even if the results of the autopsy killed her. She almost laughed. Wasn't she taking herself a mite seriously? If God didn't believe in her, how could she take herself so seriously?

Dan gestured at the windows. 'This keeps up, they'll close the airport.'

'Dan.' Her heart was pounding furiously. 'Listen, I'm very smart. It's obvious we're through, and it happened when I got drunk at the Open House. The thing is, I'm not sure why.' She swallowed painfully. 'I mean, what happened?'

He was standing. 'That Tanya, can she be all bad if she's booked here?'

'You'll be gone tomorrow. Dan, you're the only person I ever could talk to. Please?'

He sat again, tapping a cigar ash. 'All right. Where shall we begin? Your parents?'

'It's us I need to understand.'

'For openers, then. Don't you think your mother talked a lot about age?'

'No. I guess. Maybe.' Yes. Of course. And hadn't Beverly eaten every meal to conversations about the quiet, unostentatious virtues?

'Dirty old man!' he snorted. 'A first for me.'

'Parents always think their children are children.'

'On the button, in your case.' He spoke loudly. She jumped, and felt better. Being argumentative was more natural to Dan than the past few days' careful politeness. 'And about this Lloyd Rawlings?'

She flushed. 'They couldn't use their Civic Light Opera tickets. They gave them to Lloyd, a Christmas present.'

'And you don't call that running interference? Listen, there's one thing you ought to know. Your parents don't give one damn what's right for you. They worry about their friends. And put that word, "friends", in quotes.'

'We're here to talk about us, not them.'

'I embarrass them. I admit I'm Jewish.'

'A lot of people there were. The Crowns, the Garets –'

Dan interrupted. 'It's a new one on me.' Bewilderment creased his forehead. 'Jewish parents who'd rather have their daughter take on a poor *goy* than –'

'They think we're more alike . . .' Her voice trailed away. 'Besides, Lloyd's not poor. He's bourgeois.' She didn't much care for that bourgeois. Pretentious. 'Middle class. Like us. Middle middle. You try to fit in with everyone else, like it's a *Saturday Evening Post* world. Besides, money's not all that important to them.'

'*Mazeltov!*' he exploded. 'And you don't know what you're talking about. Christmas trees, carols, the whole *schmear*, that's fitting in? There's nothing about their own God or their own past they want, so they horn in on someone else's.'

He's right, she thought, then her blood raced, and glands, loyal-to-her-parents glands that she hadn't realized existed in her, secreted hot acid in her arteries. She was on her feet, sorority white-cotton gloves, bag dropping unnoticed to beige carpet.

'Just because they aren't fanatics –'

'They're the worst kind!'

'They respect all sorts of people.'

'Respect, hell! They want to be them. They'll do anything, including wipe themselves out, to avoid being what they are. In Germany they supported Hitler. They gave him money. At the beginning they gave him money. They hated themselves that much!'

Cheekbones raised, Dan's face distorted as if he'd run the mile. Dan, looking into his not-so-private hell, a nightmare world that shrank Beverly's problems to nothing.

'They're not like that,' she said quietly. 'You don't understand them.'

'The hell I don't!'

Her filial anger returned for a weak second round. 'Just one afternoon couldn't you have behaved decently?'

'Decently? What's that mean?' Dan was talking in a deep, ferocious rumble, as if his voice came from a place beyond his control or volition. 'Okay, okay, you're hot to have it out. I'd never seen this side of you, that's all, and –'

'Dan –'

'– and it hit me you despise being Jewish enough to kill everything else you are.'

She didn't say anything.

'And you were wishing you could kill me off, too.'

She bowed her head.

'Weren't you?'

She bent for her bag and gloves.

'Weren't you?'

'Yes,' she whispered.

And at the admission, with no warning, tears came. She turned, resting her head on the chair back. Her crying made no sound. Rain alone was audible. Beverly was not a girl who could excuse herself. She couldn't simply think, It didn't work out between us, that's all. There was no way she could convince herself that her parents were at fault. She thought herself the worst monster. She tried to stop her tears by thinking of the rain, it had rained so much of the time they'd been together. And eventually the crying stopped.

Dan gave her a minute or two's grace. 'Beverly? Look at me.'

God, no. She must be a holy wreck. She couldn't know it, but grief pared her features to delicate bones: beautiful amber eyes dominated the face. Grief, that was Beverly's colour.

'Buzz?'

This time she looked.

He grimaced unhappily, stubbing out his cigar. 'Buy you a drink,' he said, crossing the room. He pulled her to her feet.

'Who else do you know who can have silent hysterics?'

'Look, I ... Buzz.'

The kiss started out light, but turned all tongues and teeth and a struggle to get every part of their bodies closer. He was tugging at her side zipper. She took over. No words. Unlaced shoes, hosiery like brown snakes on a white garter belt, slip, lace bra, panties, socks, everything falling to the carpet, and in the middle, Beverly and Dan. His hands moved up and down her hips. He led her to the turned-down bed.

Urgency left them. It was as if hotel sheets were hot water, they moved so languorously. He traced the almost invisible scar under her lower lip and she kissed his finger. He slid a hand between them, circling her navel. Waiting. And she almost stopped breathing. Waiting. Now she blessed the rain, it was a noisy curtain shutting them off from time and the world. She never had any physical shame with Dan, and she guided his hand down, reaching for him, her hand curving around the pulsing hardness, the smooth skin like a glove, veins at the back, rubbery ridge. She had avoided looking at *it* and was glad they were under covers so she couldn't see *it*. Why? She didn't know why. She loved every part of him, the hair in his armpits, which wasn't beige like the rest of his body hair but a sort of reddish-brown, the flat mole the colour of a cough sweet on his left shoulder, she loved the smell of him, cigar, underarm sweat and all, she loved the way his body stuck lightly to her body, his moist, warm breath penetrating her ear, his heart beating against her squashed breasts. She loved him more than she ever had.

'Buzz,' he said against her hair, 'it's me, not you.'

'No.'

'I just couldn't take it. You're the gentlest girl, some-place off by yourself, so gentle. Don't let them ruin everything for you.'

She put both arms around him, feeling the crisp hairs on incurve of spine. He moved onto her. His shoulders and chest were strange like this, naked. He smiled dreamily down.

'S'a nice room,' she murmured.

'Shouldn't it be, at these prices?'

'In a good hotel,' she whispered.

'So they tell me.'

'No fleas biting.'

'Not one.'

'You're not Mr Smith.'

'Nope.'

'I'm not Mrs Smith.'

'You aren't registered, even.'

They whispered inanities, touching one another's lips, their breath conveying the depth of their feeling, pain and regret and flowing need. Far away a siren howled, then there was just the rain, softer now.

'Any other girl,' he said, 'would be trying to patch things up. Thank you, Buzz.'

'You're shaking.'

'You, too.'

'Do people always?' she asked.

He shook his head.

'I want,' she whispered.

'Yes.'

'You do?'

'More than anything in my life.'

'Now?'

'Yes, now. I have to get a –' All at once he forced himself off her, saying, 'Oh God. Am I really this big a bastard?'

'Please?' She shifted in the bed. 'Dan, can I, this?'

'Yes, ahh, like that. Buzz ...'

And so, a victim to Dan's loyalty to the ancient code, you don't lay a Jewish virgin unless you intend marriage, Beverly was a virgin, semidemihemiquaver, but a virgin nonetheless when she married Philip Schorer.

Chapter Three

I

It didn't rain again until a Tuesday late in February.

Em, aware of the patter on the roof shingles, snuggled deeper into her blankets. Her small bedside radio was tuned to a station where an organ rose majestically and her thin little face grew eager: 'Stella Dallas' was one of her favourites. Her anticipation shamed her. Still, what else could she do? After Christmas she'd got so huge she could barely totter around the apartment. Dr Porter had ordered her to bed.

The first six months of her pregnancy, Em had felt contemptible, like a child who's done something nasty in her pants: to justify the fast-growing evidence of her misdeed, she had prepared feverishly for her new role, devouring books by Spock, Gesell and Ilg, any expert in the field of child development. Now, though, her body unequivocally invaded and alien, she had sunk into mindless acceptance.

'Ahh, Stella, how can I tell you.'

Em retrieved lipstick and brush from her drawer, carefully painting her dry mouth. She wore a pink bedjacket crocheted by her mother, and her limp blonde hair was neatly curled at the ends. Here, at least, she hadn't let herself go. Later she would turn on the oven. In it was a lamb stew that Caroline had dropped off on her way to class – every day either she or Mrs Wynan would pop in with a casserole so at least Em rested easy knowing Sheridan always ate a hot dinner.

Em's head tilted. The staircase was shuddering under a man's shoes. Sheridan had a heavy step. But it was way too early for him. A key scraped in the front door.

'Sheridan?' Em called, hastily turning the black knob. Stella faded mid-sigh. 'Sheridan?'

He came into the pocket-sized bedroom.

'You're soaked through,' she said.

'Rain'll do that.'

'You're so early.'

His lips grew taut. She had learned to dread this angry white at the corners of his mouth. But why should he be angry? All she'd done was mention his being home.

He stripped off his loafers, dark with rain, and his sopping argyles, knitted from dangling spindles by Mrs Wynan. At last Em ventured, 'It's Tuesday. You have a lab until five.'

'School's out.'

'Because of the rain?'

'You take every word literally.'

Pushing up in bed, wincing, she peered through her glasses at him. 'Sh-Sheridan, I don't understand.'

'I had an appointment with Mr Cambro at twelve, so I came right on home.' Sheridan used their wedding-present Ford to deliver emergency night prescriptions for Mr Cambro.

'What's wrong?'

'Nothing's wrong. Tom Marshall's quitting. We were talking about me taking Tom's job.'

'But Tom works full-time.'

'A six-day week,' Sheridan agreed.

'You can't handle that, not with your schedule.'

'You might as well know the worst.' With a sardonic grin, he deposited water-heavy socks in the clothes hamper. 'I've dropped out.'

'You what?'

'Cashed in my chips.'

'But we never even discussed it!'

'Why should we? My mind's made up.'

His full meaning sank in. 'You won't have a degree,' Em cried. 'You won't be a pharmacist. Ohhh, Sheridan.'

'It's no three-alarm fire,' he snapped, heading for the kitchen, returning with a slice of white bread smeared with peanut butter.

'Fall, I'll get another teaching position,' she said. At notification of her pregnancy, the Los Angeles Unified

School District, naturally, had cancelled her contract.

'Cambro's starting me Monday.'

'I'll send for the papers.'

'Don't you listen?'

'Yes, but –'

'It's settled, so lay off will you, Em?'

She wouldn't. Couldn't. 'I'll apply now.'

'And what'll you do with the twins? Drown 'em?'

'Dr Porter could make out only one heartbeat.'

'He's looked at your belly, though.'

Through Max Factor pancake, patches of red appeared. She pulled blankets higher, over that horrendous mound with the navel popping like a cherry on top of a sundae.

Sheridan had been pacing barefoot. He stopped, wagging bread over her. 'Listen, Em, I know it gripes you, and I understand it. You want the big future. But you picked the wrong guy. I'm too old for this homework crap. I'm not about to brown-nose some 4F prof into an *A*.'

'But you'll have wasted two and a half years, and –'

'And I've got me a wife and kids to support. I need money. Cambro's giving me one fifty-five to start. Don't look like that, Em. Your hubby'll be out there prescribing St Joseph's and Midol with the best of 'em.' His cheerful words didn't track with his expression.

Poor Sheridan, Em thought with a quick rush of sympathy. My poor sweetie. She wanted to cuddle his face against her swollen breasts. She wanted to express her very real sympathy and her equally genuine gratitude for his never once having thrown the pregnancy up to her. But watching his strong teeth clamp on white bread and peanut butter, she found herself wondering. Is he taking the course of least resistance?

The question hurt, turned her traitor, yet doubts already were planted within Em. Sheridan, she knew, tested 130, Binet, yet at finals, lower IQs walked off with the grades. For the longest time she had assumed Sheridan's tight, ridiculing smile turned professors against him. Then she'd realized he did as poorly on anonymously corrected blue books. The past month, in her serious, methodical way, Em had worked out the reason for this low performance level. Sheridan was afraid. His classes filled him with dread, not knowledge. She had taken so long reaching this conclusion because Sheridan was no physical coward – in the bottom drawer of their chest he had stored medals dangling from faded ribbons, medals he'd earned across the Pacific. Em, always endeavouring to see both sides, concluded her husband had reason to fear education. She'd never met his parents – they hadn't been able to afford the trip from Wichita for the wedding. From Sheridan's remarks, however, she knew they were poor, mean-poor, obsequious to, yet belittling of, those above them. His three elder brothers, returning from active duty, had gone back to their assembly jobs at Kelvinator. Sheridan alone had taken up the gauntlet of the GI Bill. And at USC, a private institution where well-off students accepted college as their due. Last semester Sheridan had gone down two grade points (all those chem labs!), which meant this semester he had to earn better than Cs.

Chewing, he sat on the end of her twin bed. He's delighted to drop out, Em thought. It's a relief. And in the Reed family, clerking in a drugstore is a step up. Over my dead body, she thought.

'You haven't told anyone?' she asked anxiously. 'In Admissions, I mean?'

'Not yet.'

'Good. I'll talk to my parents.'

'About what?'

'My Van Vliet stock.'

He gave her a dark look.

'Our st-stock. It's preferred, so we can't s-sell, but –'

'What're you getting at?'

'It can be c-collateral. You won't let me work – you're right. A b-baby's first years are formative. But I'm sure we can borrow enough.'

'For what?'

'You must finish.'

'Listen to me, Em, and listen good. We're getting this

59

straight for once and all. To cut down utilities, us boys bathed once a week in the same water. I didn't take piano lessons, I don't have a cashmere sweater to my name. Face it, I'm ordinary. And there's one thing us ordinary joes do. Support our families. Next Monday I'm starting.'

'Sheridan, Upper Division is hard for everybody. After a while it gets easier. There's nothing to be afraid of.'

'Afraid?'

And swallowing the last of his peanut butter sandwich, he raised his right hand. Slowly. Deliberately. A sharp sound rang inside her skull. The slap wasn't hard. But it jarred into her brain an image: Sheridan's black-and-white snapshot of his father, a fat, brutal-shouldered man who, or so she'd been told, wore a hernia truss from moving overstuffed Kansas upholstery and who had beaten his sons (his wife, too, Sheridan hinted) with his belt buckle, a man who hadn't gone beyond sixth grade. In that brief moment Em realized how much she despised the poor. Tears glittering behind her glasses, she stared at Sheridan.

'Just letting you know,' he muttered, 'who wears the pants in the family. We won't have any more, Em. And that's that.'

Her tears, flowing now, bore no relationship to the slight sting on her cheek. She wept because she was realizing the violence (and unfairness) of her prejudice against the background of the man who had rescued her, miraculously, from spinsterhood, the man whom recently, in the eyes of God, she'd vowed to cherish and obey. Unlike Caroline, Em cared little for luxuries. It wasn't important to her that Sheridan make a lot of money. Rather, it was the idea that without a college degree, without a profession, he would be only a cut, a very small cut, above his father's class. She wept because until now she hadn't realized how ruthless her snobbish proclivities were. It must be the Van Vliet in me, she thought. And argued no more.

Sheridan moved on the bed, stroking thin, pale hair,

breathing peanut butter on her, calling her his little puffy.

2

Exactly nine months to the day of their wedding, Sheridan drove Em to the hospital. Her labour was hard and protracted, lasting over thirty hours. She did not, however, beg for additional painkillers. There was no talk – as there might have been – of a Caesarean section. In due time she was given a spinal. Around noon on 28 March, she gave birth, normally, to twin sons. The first weighed in at eight pounds two ounces, the second, who was longer, at seven-thirteen. A huge burden, Dr Porter told the bleary-eyed father, for so tiny a woman.

'Boys,' Sheridan beamed, proud. 'Twins.'
'Fraternal, not identical.'

3

When Sheridan came to the hospital that evening, he kissed her freshly rouged cheek, presenting her with gladioli. 'Should've bought two bunches,' he grinned, sitting next to the bed.

'What do you think of Van Vliet?' she asked.
'For a supermarket?'
'For one of the names.'
'Roger, after my father. We already decided.'
'We have two babies.' (Em, until she'd been wakened by the delivery-room nurse with the news, had refused to speak of this eventuality.)

'And you aren't calling either of 'em after a market, Em.'

'A Family name.'

He shifted uneasily on the chair. 'Yours.'

She lay back on the hospital pillow. This was not a gesture of weakness – she'd been strengthened immeasurably by her two-day battle – but because she had a splitting headache.

'Vliet for short,' she said.

'No.'

She stared him down. I'll win, she thought. This was the first time she had considered their marriage in terms of victor and vanquished. I'll win.

She did. In less than a minute he surrendered.

'Which one?' he asked.

'The blond. He looks like Family.'

'The elder?' Sheridan had been given the routine peek at his offsprings' sex and lack of deformity. He wasn't yet sure which was which.

'No. The elder one's heavier, dark. He looks like you. He's Roger. This is the longer, thinner baby.'

'Vliet?'

Em smiled secretly. She said, 'Vliet Reed.'

They brought her babies alternately.

Just from the holding, blindfolded, sightless as a mole, Em could have told them apart. Roger, the dark boy, had a heavier centre of gravity, he cried more lustily, kicking out, relaxing totally when he took the bottle, finishing every drop. The blond baby, Vliet, the longer one who resembled Family, whimpered rather than howled, and never finished. One evening he smiled up at her. 'Gas,' was the opinion of the nurse. Em knew better. She stroked soft white down with her forefinger. Van Vliets could be hard, cruel, yet their smile held charm.

Mrs Van Vliet stood in front of the nursery window gazing at two cots in the front row: Reed male 1, Reed male 2. She rapped glass with her emerald. The dark-haired baby looked up with unfocusing blue eyes. He flailed his arms. Sleeve drawstrings were tied, hiding his hands. The other infant slept on. Mrs Van Vliet glanced from Reed male 1 to Reed male 2 and back, her amused appraisal bearing no relationship to the grandmaternal clucking and cooing around her.

She went to the desk, requesting in her clear voice to know Mrs Reed's room. The head floor nurse, although busy with charts, clasped red hands subserviently, leading the way through corridors that were crowded with visitors to this, the heavy first crop of post-war babies. Em presented her two room-mates to the tiny làdy in the sable coat. Both girls gawked. The head nurse drew green curtains, marking off Mrs Van Vliet's domain.

'The blond one has the family nose,' said Mrs Van Vliet.

'We're calling him Van Vliet,' Em said. 'Vliet.'

'He's prettier.'

'Roger,' Em said, careful not to stammer, 'that's the dark one, he's stronger. And I think smarter.'

The warm smile that Em always had considered Caroline's preserve broke.

'That he is, that he is,' said Mrs Van Vliet. 'You're a good mother, Em. You'll try never to show partiality.'

'They're both mine.' Em's face was fierce.

Mrs Van Vliet patted hospital linen over Em's knee. 'I'm giving them each a five-hundred-dollar bond.'

'Oh Grandma! That's awfully generous. Of course we'll save it for their education.'

'What a serious child it is,' said Mrs Van Vliet, leaning forward to touch her lips to Em's cheek. She smells, Em thought, like spring flowers. 'My first great-grandchildren. Em, truly, my cup runneth over.'

Sheridan took an hour off to drive his wife and sons home. Caroline and Mrs Wynan were in the dinette, where the babies would sleep. Crowded next to the second-hand crib that Sheridan had sanded stood a new Baby Line with cut-outs of frolicking blue lambs. Unhesitating, Em put Vliet into this magnificence. Sheridan laid Roger, who was wet and howling, in the refinished crib.

'It's *amazing* how different they are!' Caroline exclaimed.

'Double trouble,' Sheridan beamed, lighting a cigar, one of the box he'd handed around.

Em pushed at him. 'Not in here,' she cried.

She was always pooped. Yet never could she resist a phoned, 'Is it all right to drop by?'

She wanted everyone to see her pride of sons.

Van Vliets bearing blue-satin-tied boxes descended on the tiny apartment. Omega Deltas flocked to exclaim over the babies and to stare, awed, at Em as though she'd been elevated to a Greater Panhellenic. Beverly Linde (she was very quiet and pale) dropped by with Mrs Linde. Old and new neighbours. Mr Cambro and his employees came by.

There had been a constant stream of company that Sunday afternoon – the twins were almost six weeks old. Em finally succumbed to her weariness. For the first time she left Sheridan in charge of the boys while she dozed on her bed. Sheridan played with the twins on the couch. Vliet somehow toppled down onto the rug. The baby screamed bloody murder while a large bruise promptly rose on his forehead. Em dialled the paediatrician, careless (for once) of expense, insisting on a house call. The doctor pronounced the infant fine, but added that vomiting is a sign of skull fracture and to watch for it.

Em watched. She was still watching at five the next morning.

Sheridan yawned his way into the dinette-nursery. 'Everything okay?'

'He hasn't thrown up.'

'Good,' Sheridan said, both hands on her aching shoulders. 'Now get some sleep.'

She shrugged him off.

'I'll keep an eye on him,' Sheridan said.

'That's what you were doing.'

'You're making something out of nothing, Em. A kid

64

falls off a couch – big deal. Holy God, I fell from a second-storey window.'

'These aren't slum children!'

He looked at her, startled as if he'd been bitten by a shrew he'd mistaken for a tame little mouse. 'I looked away one second, no more, I swear it,' he muttered. 'He's fine. You can't go without a whole night's sleep.'

'Oh can't I? I can stay awake as long as I have to. I'm strong. You don't understand that, Sheridan. You make a lot of noise, but you don't know what real strength is. You think it's war and hitting with belts. Well, it isn't. Strength is carrying on when you want to drop. It's finishing what you start.' Her heart hammered wildly. How could she, Em Wynan Reed, be shrilling this? She was small, drab, female. Sheridan, her husband, male, God's surrogate on earth. I must be out-of-my-head tired, she thought. She focused again on that angry-prune bruise mounding her Vliet's forehead. 'You don't understand, do you, Sheridan? Well, my sons will. They'll understand. Every single thing that they start, they will finish.'

She held a hand to her terrified heart. He's going to hit me, she thought. Instead, he was moving backwards, away into the dark. She was safe from punishment.

So why should she have this pang of loss, this overwhelming sense of disappointment?

The evening after her six-week check-up, Sheridan arrived home with a small bottle of Je Reviens. Her spine was ready to snap in two. Lack of sleep made her bilious. Down there hurt from Dr Porter's speculum. Yet she pulled on her good satin nightie, unworn since the third month of their marriage, dotting her new cologne in the teaspoon-size hollow at the base of her neck. Sheridan waited in bed. His arms circled her, one hard leg pinioning her down, and he didn't say an encouraging word, her name, even. All the time she kept weighing on her personal scales her pain versus his deprivation. He won. Poor Sheridan, months it had been.

He rolled onto his side. She held still until that involuntary jerk which meant he'd fallen asleep, then – quietly – she slipped out of bed, pulling off the torn gown, standing under scalding water until she turned crimson from her neck to her thickish ankles. Through steam she glimpsed a can of scouring powder. She poured some into her washcloth, scrubbing, scrubbing, scrubbing every inch of her small body.

4

Thursday mornings Caroline had no classes.

'I'll sit, luv, and you go run your housewifely errands.'

Mornings the babies napped. Em gratefully hugged her tall younger sister. 'You're true blue,' she averred, and hurried off.

Sheridan needed a shirt. In Thompson's Menswear she was torn between the Sanforized Arrow at $3.75 – Em had faith only in name brands – and the one for $2.50, which was unlabelled but within her budget. She was holding a shirt in either hand when she happened to look to her left, into clear, hot morning. Strolling along Colorado Boulevard was Sheridan.

Sheridan and a girl.

As they passed the display window, Sheridan's hand crept up on the tight blouse. He fingered yellow rayon. Cheap, was Em's first coherent thought. Oh, cheap. They had passed from her range of vision before she recognized the elaborately curled red hair. It was the cosmetics girl from Cambro's Drugstore. Violet or Viola? Did she choose my cologne? Violette, that's it. Em left both shirts on the counter, moving into daylight, squinting after the tall, wide-shouldered man and the redhead with swinging hips. They turned towards one another, smiling, and it seemed to Em those smiles were impersonal and explicit as rutting

66

animals. Dark crew cut dropped towards dyed red hair. An old lady slowed, gazing curiously at Em. Em realized she was weeping right on the sidewalk of Colorado Boulevard.

She managed to get home. As soon as Caroline left, Em poured Je Reviens down the toilet, jerking at the handle. Be fair, she thought, there's no proof. A sharp vision of dyed red hair stung her, and her emotions whirled like the scented water disappearing down the trap. I always let him no matter how tired I am, she thought. And flushed the toilet again.

Roger began to cry, hungry.

She fastened both boys in their low Babee Tendas (purchased with Artie Van Vliet's cheque), sitting on the ottoman, porringers of Pablum at her side. The twins had reached the plump, neckless stage. Roger held onto his spoon as she fed him, according to Gesell and Ilg extremely advanced behaviour. When it was Vliet's turn (his tow hair she'd brushed over her finger into a crest) he turned away, holding up both hands to play peekaboo. Em's back ached, her hands shook, her throat hurt from weeping, but other than that she was fine. She was smiling at her Vliet, wasn't she?

She didn't lunch.

She sat in the narrow, dim living-room. Thinking obsessively. She reached three conclusions:

1. She cared for her sons more than she cared about herself.

2. She cared for her sons more than she cared about Sheridan.

3. She must provide the best of everything for her sons.

After a while she poured herself a jigger of the Southern Comfort that they saved for special company, the first straight liquor of her life, tossing it back with a jerk of wrist as men do in Westerns, snorting and choking as the sweet mash went down. Her stomach was empty. The liquor acted fast, soothing her. She sat on the ottoman, receding chin in small hand, planning.

They ate dinner at the coffee table, as usual, side by

side on the couch, not comfortable, but the best she could do, what with the twins in the dinette. She waited until the Grape Nuts pudding.

'We can't manage here forever,' she said.

'We won't have to, I promise you that.'

'The boys need a room of their own.'

'They do,' he agreed.

'And a fenced yard.'

'I'll put up a basketball hoop,' he said.

Em managed a smile.

'First, they need one of those whatchamacallums?' he asked. 'For climbing?'

'A jungle gym, yes.'

'The kind with swings,' he said.

'Sheridan, you're a good father.'

'Except once,' he admitted sheepishly.

'They're very active for their age,' she excused.

'He scared me shi – to death.'

Em poured coffee from the Pyrex. 'Why not go back to college this fall?'

Sheridan's eyes slid towards her. 'We're talking about a house,' he said uneasily.

'No. The future.'

'That's for sure. Right now we're barely breaking even.'

'With you at Cambro's, clerking, we'll never do more.'

'But can we afford college?' he asked through taut, angry lips.

From her apron pocket she took a used envelope. Down the back ran columns of her small, neat numbers.

'What's that?' He gave his short, abrasive laugh. 'The Gettysburg Address?'

'Here're the boys' bonds.' She pointed. 'Seven fifty for cashing them in now.'

'That's their education money.'

'Another seven twelve fifty a year from our preferred.'

'Em!'

'Plus the GI and –'

'I'm warning you!' His knee jolted up, hitting the low table. Steaming coffee splattered. Em ran for a dishcloth.

'You'll work this summer,' she said, wiping. 'I'll be careful. People manage on the GI. We will.'

'I'm dragging my butt for you.' Sheridan was breathing loudly. 'I might not be up to your fancy Family, but I give you and the boys all I've got and then some!'

'When you graduate, you'll have your pick of pharmacies.'

'You're sucking for a bruise, Em.'

'Nobody's going to hit me,' she said, sipping coffee, no longer calm but pretending calm. 'The house keeps a file of tests and term papers, so if you need help –'

Sheridan was on his feet, crew cut hunched forward, glowering, a bull with the bewildering picks in him. Now, she told herself. Now.

'Or do you have some particular reason for hanging around Cambro's?'

Startled, he blinked.

'I saw you this morning.' The words jerked painfully. 'With. That. Girl.'

He hesitated. 'Girl?'

'Redhead.'

'Where were you?' he asked.

'Thompson's Menswear.'

'Vi and me, we were walking on a public street, so what?'

'That awful hair, that tight blouse!' Em burst out. 'She's so common!'

'Like me.'

'Where were you taking her?' There was a wildness in Em's voice.

'For coffee,' he muttered.

'Why not Mr Cambro's fountain?'

His eyes refused to meet hers. Nasty, she thought, yes, he's been nasty. Earlier she had determined not to weep, but tears oozed under her glasses. Averting her head, she stacked dirty dishes, carrying them past cribs. In darkness she gripped the sink. Em, rocking back and forth, her ancient miseries and inadequacies battling with her new needs, which were the needs of the twin blue-eyed scraps of humanity sleeping in the adjoining dinette.

Years older, she returned to the living-room.

'It's not just a house,' she said. 'There's nursery school, bicycles, lessons, colleges, everything.'

'A nickle cup of coffee, Em, I swear on a stack of Bibles.'

'Don't perjure yourself.'

'You gone crazy?'

'This morning I was. But not now. Not anymore. I thought and thought and after a while the craziness went away.' She sat on the ottoman. 'See, Sheridan, I finally understand about marriage. People say you have to work at it, and that's true. But working isn't enough. Both people have to give. We've made mistakes. Mine was letting you drop out. Yours is her. Now we each have to put in the kitty.' Her face, with hints of wrinkles on brow and mouth, was swollen, the tip of her Van Vliet nose red. 'It's only fair,' she said. Indomitable.

'I buy a girl a cup of coffee, and –'

'This summer you'll bone up. In the autumn you'll go back. And I'll forget.'

His big-knuckled hands dangled. 'Your grandmother,' he capitulated, 'what makes you so positive she'll let us use the money?'

Em wasn't positive. Victory, a forlorn little fire, crept through her veins, though, and she said, 'Grandma won't mind.'

'What if I can't make it?'

'You will,' Em said. 'I'll help you. We'll do it together.'

'She means nothing.'

'But did you and she . . . ?'

'You're my wife.'

A moth thumped at the dark screen, and Em rose, pulling the string of aluminium venetian blinds.

'Did you?' Em mistrusted ambiguities, and painful as the knowledge might be, she couldn't bear not to have it. She needed to feel their exchange was just. 'Sheridan?'

'A wife is permanent. There's all the difference in the world.'

70

And briefly, in a low voice, he made confession. Odours of spaghetti, coffee, Grape Nuts pudding hung in warm air, one of the babies (it was Roger) whimpered, then all was silent, except for a cricket fiddling into the California spring night. Em and Sheridan, wordless, both losers. Em and Sheridan exchanging small, wretched smiles.

Then, in a peculiar gesture, he shook her hand, exactly as a buyer would clinch a deal.

Em, anxious-voiced, inquired of Mrs Van Vliet if she could cash in the bonds. 'But naturally.' The clear voice emerged from telephone receiver tainted with amusement. 'Em, the day I lend you any necklaces, we'll have to get the appraisers in.' She laughed.

Em couldn't see the joke. Admittedly, she lacked a sense of humour, but what was funny about de Maupassant's poor woman drudging her entire life to repay false jewels with real?

By the time Sheridan had graduated from USC's School of Pharmacy, Em knew that his girls were a condition she must live with. Generally they were waitresses or some-such, not the kind her relations or friends were likely to run into, so at least she never was publicly humiliated.

The girls. She didn't understand them. (To be honest, though, she rarely wasted time on painful speculation.) Uniformly cheap, seldom pretty, many didn't even have decent figures. So why? She came to various conclusions. Possibly the girls were Sheridan's way of getting back at her for the Family so awesome, or possibly they took up the slack in bed (what slack? didn't she always let him?), or possibly there was the early imprimatur of his faithless father.

Or – and this one hurt to think – his life consisted of one drab pressure after another, and in order to keep going, he needed a little excitement.

Whatever. It became part of their relationship. After each episode he would confess, his head hunched forwards like a great, truant oaf. Em, using interchangeable phrases, always forgave him. It became integral to their bond. As long as Sheridan carried out his side of the bargain, how could she not? *Noblesse oblige.*

To Em none of this harbingered marital failure. Theirs was, in her opinion, as solid a marriage as any. And as they crawled through that universal tunnel of their time, a GI education overhung with diapers and floored by a rock-bottom budget, they did share what each considered important.

They shared joy in their sons.

5

'Does he yearn to have his own pharmacy?' asked Mrs Van Vliet.

It was a sunny March day two weeks after Sheridan, in rented mortar board and gown, had collected his hard-won diploma. Em and the twins had been summoned to the grey château in Pasadena. Her grandmother's sprawling house always acted on Em's personality as a magnet does on steel filings, drawing from her every atom of self-confidence. From time to time she would reinforce herself by glancing out of the bay window to the sun-dappled slope where her boys picnicked under Geranium's large black supervision. Em and her grandmother were lunching on breast-of-chicken salad.

'Sheridan? I don't think he does.'

'Haven't you discussed it?'

'Mr Cambro's pharmacist has retired. Sheridan's accepted the job.'

'He prefers to work for someone else?' Mrs Van Vliet rarely said Sheridan. Em had pondered if this avoidance signified disdain.

'Mr Cambro and Sheridan get along well.' Em stubbornly, if apprehensively, countered with her husband's name. 'As far as I know, Sheridan's never given a thought to owning his own business.'

Mrs Van Vliet stopped buttering a homebaked roll, her pretty mouth forming a faintly malicious smile. 'Which means you have?'

Em admitted she had.

'And?'

'Sheridan's very bright. He just doesn't come from people used to dealing with money.'

Mrs Van Vliet nodded.

Em took a deep breath. 'Grandma, are you leaving us anything, Sheridan and me?'

'I'm not departing.'

'I didn't mean – Oh Grandma. I'm s-sorry.'

'As a matter of fact, I'm about to rewrite my will. One of the pleasures of age, writing a will. You're testing your wits against the future.' Delicately she freighted chicken on sterling. Chewed. Swallowed. All the time watching Em questioningly.

'The will.' Em's voice faded.

'Yes?'

'C-could . . .'

'Em, I'm no ogre, am I?'

'Could, uhh, if you're leaving me – us – anything, would you give it to the twins?'

Mrs Van Vliet laughed. 'And I invited you here in order to make my donation now!'

'Now?'

'For the great drug emporium.'

Em, knowing how her grandmother held onto possessions, said sincerely, 'Thank you, Grandma.'

Mrs Van Vliet stopped laughing. 'Change your mind, if you want.'

'Sheridan and I don't need anything. The boys will, though. Education, travel. Things the Family has.'

Mrs Van Vliet sat back, examining her eldest grandchild. Em nibbled uneasily on her roll.

'Well.' Mrs Van Vliet raised immaculate white brows. 'Well.' And Em, positive she was being mocked, jerked

73

with surprise as the old lady said, 'Em, come kiss me.'

Em walked around the cherrywood table, resting her lips on beautifully set hair. After she was in her chair again, she asked, 'I, uhh, well – do you think it's unfair?'

'To your husband?'

'Yes, to Sheridan.'

'Em, one cannot be unfair to a husband. Our world isn't set up for the contingency. And as you pointed out, he'll do best without undue pressure.'

'But I haven't discussed this with him.'

'You want your sons to be gentlemen.'

Em reddened.

'Oh, I agree, it's suspect in this egalitarian age,' said Mrs Van Vliet. 'But this worship of the average is our loss. What's happened to breeding, strength, the ability to reach for the highest? Em, don't look like that. To the mediocre, excellence always is a vice.' Mrs Van Vliet set her fork on her plate, her clear eyes narrowing as if she were reading fine print. 'I'll leave the money in trust. The principal to go to them when they're thirty – is that what you have in mind?'

Em nodded.

'Thirty's not too old?'

'No.'

'You're positive?'

'Thirty's just right,' said Em, who was twenty-five.

'The income to be used for education.' Mrs Van Vliet stopped. 'No. That's confining. At your discretion.'

'For camp, travel, lessons, college. Clothes.'

'The amenities yours to bestow.'

'Whatever they need.'

'Whatever you think they need. Em, do change that look. It's an excellent idea. I'm delighted.'

Em couldn't face her grandmother. Oh, that wrinkled, enigmatic smile. Is she delighted because Sheridan won't get any of her money? But Sheridan wants the same as I do. We'd rather the boys have the money. Em's thoughts hesitated. This was true for her, but was it for Sheridan? They hadn't discussed the matter, so how could she be sure? She glanced at tiny, distant figures lit by a shaft of sunlight coming through tall sycamores. Her sober little mind corrected: He wants the best of everything for them.

Em raised her eyes to her grandmother.

'Thank you, Grandma,' she said. 'When the boys are old enough, they'll really appreciate what you're doing.'

Mrs Van Vliet's expression was quizzical, as if by looking at Em she could divine the future. 'I'm sure they will,' she said dryly.

Chapter Four

I

Caroline circled the UCLA quad, her heels coming down sharp on red bricks. With each step her full breasts jiggled pleasantly. On one hip she carried her books. Her free hand clasped a long clipboard.

This was the second Friday in February 1950, a crisp day, chilly as good champagne, with a brilliant blue sky.

'Sir?' Caroline slowed her pace to that of a youngish, round-shouldered man, possibly a teaching assistant. 'My name is Caroline Wynan, and is there any way I can convince you to sign this?'

He stopped, shifting his briefcase, examining the pretty, rose-cheeked brunette. He reached for the clipboard.

> WHEREAS *all employees of the University of California, faculty and otherwise, are obliged to sign the so-called loyalty clause:*
>
> WHEREAS *the clause is in direct conflict with the State Constitution:*
>
> WHEREAS *the clause is not compatible with the freedom necessary to a university:*

His eye flicked down WHEREASES to:

> WE THE UNDERSIGNED *respectfully suggest that the so-called loyalty clause shall not be required of University personnel.*

There were eight signatures, one in red ink.

Thrusting the board back at her, he said, 'I don't have the time.'

Yes, a teaching assistant, a chicken TA, she thought, afraid of losing his job. She held out her pen. 'One second,' she said.

'I'm late already,' he mumbled.

She smiled. 'Then why be chintzy about another *second*?'

'Uhh, very late.'

'Between us,' she said, '*no*body looks at the signatures.' This time a conspiratorial hint of her golden laughter rose from the softness below the undone top button of her red cardigan.

Grabbing at her pen, he signed hastily, illegibly.

'You're not the type,' he accused, and escaped up the chem building steps two at a time.

Reactionary, Caroline thought, her mouth tight. Yet until six months earlier she, too, had stereotyped politically oriented girls as ones who never shaved their fat legs and couldn't get dates. She lifted her hand perpendicular to her face. She thumbed her nose after the disappearing reactionary, chicken, bigoted, and et cetera TA.

Progressive.

Caroline Wynan's new incarnation.

On graduating from USC last June, Caroline had decided to get her master's, switching to UCLA where, not coincidentally, Gene Mathney was working for his PhD in English. On this campus, Caroline had become as one with the Issues. Her commitment was derivative. That is to say, she derived her political views from Gene. Yet not in a phony way. Not unless taking Holy Communion to become as one with God is phony. Caroline wanted to become as one with Gene.

Gene was intelligent, deeply read, with a gift for hard work that is rare in academe. He believed in equality of mankind. Clean Gene. His drawback was he didn't believe in himself. Caroline perceived that she had certain countering qualities: decisiveness, a lively sense of style. And, well, love doth not alter upon alteration finding, or however Shakespeare put it. She loved Gene *exactly* as he was. So she boostered his rallies, mimeoed his anti-loyalty-oath leaflets, contributed to his causes, his friends (all liberal – Sheridan described them as parlour pinkos) were her friends, his causes her causes. They were one in mind and body, both, last April having written *fin* to the frustrations of college love. (She, natch, had been a virgin, and Gene'd had only one other encounter.) According to current mores, therefore, they had become, as Caroline put it, engaged to be engaged. They would be married. One day.

'Genebo!' Caroline cried, waving her clipboard energetically.

He saw her, smiled, and his tall, slender body wove around milling students to her.

She bobbed a curtsy. 'Mr Matheny.'

'Miss Wynan. Fancy meeting you here.'

'I've been patrolling the quad for *hours*.'

'How many did you get?'

'A huge, whopping, record-breaking – are you ready? Eleven!' She showed him her clipboard.

'Mmm, yes, I see.' He pronounced the last two names. 'Euphemia Blittfsk. Conrad Papagadopolos.'

'An exceptionally alert couple.'

'If illegible.'

'Having already tried to sway three thousand and four others, luv, I neglected my routine literacy test.' She took back the board. 'Everybody is totally uninterested.'

'Or terrified.'

'Or both,' she said.

'It so happens, Caroline, you can't be both.'

'It so happens I'm uninterested in and terrified of you. Both.' She tucked the clipboard under her arm. They stood holding hands while students milled around them.

'Forgeries,' she said. 'Those last two.'

Gene's grey eyes blinked.

'I signed for Miss Blittfsk. I signed for Conrad Papagadopolos.'

Caroline often would lie – soon after admitting the truth with a comfortable, lazy chuckle, as if her lies, pedigreed and wittily clever though they were, required too much effort to bring to parturition. Gene never quite got used to it.

He let go of her hand.

'Gene, if everybody's so damn apolitical and apathetic, who, *exactly*, is about to check signatures?'

His grey eyes were – what was that expression in his thoughtful eyes?

'That's where telling the truth gets a girl!' she cried. 'Now you don't love me anymore, do you, huhh, Clean Gene? Now you won't come up to Arrowhead with me, will you, huhh?'

No reply.

She swatted his arm with the clipboard. 'You're refusing to answer on the grounds,' she cried. Another swat, this so vigorously executed that one of her books fell. 'Now see what you've done!' She began laughing. Gene couldn't prevent a smile. He took the clipboard from her, using his teeth to unscrew his Parker 51, drawing thick lines through the two bottom names. 'There,' he said.

'You're too honest. We'll never beat the fascists.'

'Then we won't. Come on, Caroline. The Duquesnes are waiting.' Caroline and Gene, Professor and Mrs Duquesne were spending the weekend in the Wynans' cabin at Lake Arrowhead.

2

Gene idolized LeRoy Duquesne, PhD.

It was Gene's Achilles heel that his lifelong love affair with liberal causes wasn't built on the firm rocks of political belief, but on the misty quagmire of personality. He admired and sought the company of Progressives because they had read *Finnegans Wake* and Kierkegaard and mistrusted anything printed in *Time*, they were always on the side of justice, they dressed casually and enjoyed foreign food and foreign films. They were fanatically tolerant. It was this, their avowed willingness to accept everyone, that Gene cherished most about Progressives. In his deep, thoughtful mind, all men are brothers and basically the same: good.

The goodness of man was no easy belief to hold in the United States of 1950.

Paranoia gripped the country. The insanity had been brought about by the Russians having managed their own (primitive) A-bomb. And words became the symptom of national madness. The red-baiting words of J. Parnell Thomas, words microfilmed and hidden in a pumpkin, words conjuring up subversive influences in the film industry, witch-hunting words of the House Un-American Activities Committee, words of the Far Right printed in the Hearst press. There were screen-writers who merely by exercising their constitutional rights according to the Fifth Amendment never sold another word, there were people who said the wrong word and went to jail.

The Board of Regents of the University of California voted it necessary for each employee to sign words of loyalty: *I am not a member of the Communist Party, or under any oath, or party to any agreement, or under any commitment that is in conflict with this oath.* Near the close of the spring semester, 1949, the regents had made it known that taking this oath was a condition of employment. At the final faculty meeting of the scholastic year, opposition had been fierce, yet for obvious reasons, ambiguously worded. Most professors had refused to be quoted.

The following noon, at an All-U rally, LeRoy Duquesne, Gene's faculty adviser, had stood on Royce Hall steps, speaking loud and clear into a microphone, opposing any and every type of limitation on academic freedom, including the loyalty oath. An act, in Gene's mind, of supernatural courage.

LeRoy Duquesne, at forty-one, was thin-chested and too slight of body for his impressive head, a full professor with a reputation of consequence for his book on Pound. LeRoy Duquesne, therefore, was everything that Gene hoped to become. And it goes without saying that the man scared the pants off Gene. After the speech ended, Gene gathered all his courage, pushing through the crowd of students around LeRoy Duquesne. He could scarcely believe it when his faculty adviser gripped his hand, saying, 'Gene, old son, tonight Hilda's having the faculty wives. Let us imbibe brew at The Glen.'

There, surrounded by students braying out college songs, they fulminated against the Oath, then Gene, burping tap beer, warmed by the glow of proximity to this admirably committed man, heard himself admit his cliché English Department dream. 'Write,' he confessed slowly. 'I did a series of columns on the UN for *The Bruin*. Undergrad stuff. But I want to do the real thing.'

'Journalism?'

'No. Creative writing.'

'Poetry?' There was a warning growl to this question. In LeRoy Duquesne's office, next to his *Ezra Pound: A Critique*, was a stack of different quarterlies, each indexing a poem (#1, #2, and so on, up to #17) by L. Fitzgerald Duquesne.

'Poetry's beyond me.' Gene shook his head mournfully. 'Just fiction. About the ordinary people, little people.' He gave an embarrassed smile. 'My Norman Corwin syndrome.'

LeRoy Duquesne, his territory intact, rubbed the bowl of his Dunhill against his Roman nose, inquiring, 'What length work do you have in mind?'

'A novel.'

'Why not start with a smaller canvas?' asked LeRoy Duquesne with a hint of his lectern irony.

'A novella?'

'A short story. A time-honoured form, Gene, the short story.'

It was well after two when Gene was back under his parents' commodious roof, yet he sat at his desk, two-finger pecking on his Remington:

Troopship
A Short Story
by
Eugene Matheny

And working through the night, he rough-drafted a story of a young Pfc., shipping overseas. Like Gene, the young man had turned down, on principle, a chance at officers' training. Through that foggy May, Gene rewrote and polished 'Troopship'. He did another story. And another. Seven in all. He showed each in turn to Caroline. She thought them splendid. He discounted her opinion. She's my girl, his sense of uncertainty averred, what else could she think?

He did not show his work to LeRoy Duquesne. The professor's good opinion was too important to risk.

For by now the two men were friends.

That summer and autumn, with Mrs Duquesne ('Call me Hilda'), a quiet, exophthalmic little woman, and Caroline, they passed compatible evenings discussing literature and civil liberties.

'You're *not* his friend,' Caroline said once. 'You're his echo.'

'We agree. We're on the same side.'

'He uses you to pump his ego.'

'He doesn't need me for that.'

'Genebo, there's such a thing as having *too* much humility.' And Caroline said no more.

Late in June, the oaths were mailed to university employees, faculty included, with a covering letter asking for a signature. Many didn't sign. A substantial number of non-signing researchers, TAs, junior faculty – in other words those without tenure – were denied reappointment.

And in the autumn of the same year, 1949, the regents issued an ultimatum. Even those professors with tenure would not receive their paycheques if they had not signed their loyalty by 24 February 1950. Or as Caroline quoted the punchline of an old joke, 'No tickee, no washee.'

A special faculty meeting was held in the recently constructed Shoenberg Hall. Before, everyone had been inoculated by fear. Now they were frozen by fear. In the well-lit new auditorium, speakers used two languages. Liberal for image. Non-subversive (apolitical) for the finks surely present. Gene, who had a mathematical turn of mind, kept track of the number of times the matter of withholding paycheques came up. One hundred and eighty-seven times. Nobody, speakers kept reiterating, wanted to back down on so vital an issue as the Academic Senate's Constitution-given freedom to hire and fire. But, they said obliquely. But.

After the meeting, LeRoy Duquesne and Gene crossed the bleak, autumnal campus.

Gene sighed. 'Take the oath or be canned – even with Governor Warren on our side, there aren't enough regents to stop it. God, Germany all over again.'

'I have finally conceded,' said LeRoy Duquesne, 'that it is well within the realm of possibility that there won't be a single hold-out.'

'A few. Us in English. Dr Caughey in History. LeRoy, think one more petition'll accomplish anything?'

'Maybe.'

Gene gnawed a hangnail. 'My feelings about the Oath never've been sound like yours. I mean, I've always nursed a sort of feeling that if we are making this much effort, why not use it to hire coloured and Mexican faculty. But you, you've always seen it as a threat to academic freedom. You've fought the regents on their own ground. That takes tremendous courage.' LeRoy Duquesne kept his eyes on his feet, which were crunching through dry, wind-blown leaves. Gene went on, carefully. 'That's what I don't understand. Today, when they were all backing down, I had this tremendous urge to fight. Me. A TA with no tenure, no nothing. I mean, why should I do battle when everybody's dropping off the bandwagon?'

LeRoy Duquesne had no answer.

'Why should I put everything on the line now, when nobody cares anymore? And when I never cared – for the right reasons, anyway?'

'You're a born champion of lost causes,' said LeRoy Duquesne, his tone implying there could be no more noble occupation. As he bent his impressive head against the wind, he gave Gene an encouraging smile.

Both men understood that without this approval,

which meant so much to Gene, Gene would not have gone to his battered desk upstairs in Royce Hall, and in less than an hour composed his WHEREASES. He and Caroline had circulated the petition, he with thoughtful sincerity, Caroline with high-handed, confident smiles. Both approaches had got terrifyingly small results.

3

Arrowhead is a mountain lake resort about eighty miles north-east of Los Angeles. On steep, hairpin curves Gene's '38 DeSoto boiled over twice. It was dark when Caroline, laughing and gasping into icy air, unlocked her parents' cabin. The men accomplished a small fire. Mrs Duquesne heated her curry, and Caroline produced two raffia-wrapped bottles of Dago red, which for love of Gene she called sour red. After dinner the two women went downstairs to use the chemical toilet.

As their footsteps descended the narrow stairwell, Gene reached for his calf briefcase. 'I've got some material,' he said. He released worn leather. The pain in his stomach was sharp. Sudden.

'Material? On what?' LeRoy Duquesne set down maroon wine.

'I took your advice.'

'About what?'

'The short-story form,' Gene said, pulling out three immaculate sheaves of Eaton's Corrasible bond.

'Three?'

Those that Gene considered his best work. Or rather, his least bad work. 'Each more rotten than the next.'

LeRoy held out his hand.

Gene did not relinquish paper.

'Don't you want a reading?'

'They need more polishing,' Gene muttered.

'I'll tell you about that.'

'They're nothing special.'

'Gene, give me some credit.' LeRoy Duquesne waggled his fingers. Commanding.

Gene, placing his stories in the hairless hand, experienced a sense of release. Sure, he still feared losing LeRoy Duquesne's respect. But he trusted the man. It was the kind of trust rarely bestowed on one human being by another, and then only by a completely decent person like Gene Matheny.

The following morning Gene rose at the first thin light. Caroline slept, the top of her dark head tousling above the quilt. Worry about his literary lacks had given Gene a wakeful night.

Upstairs in the living-room, LeRoy Duquesne was already waiting, a terry-cloth robe wrapping his insufficient body.

'Have you sent these out?' he demanded.

'I thought maybe *The New Yorker*.' As Gene spoke, he realized that his dream of selling to *The New Yorker* was one more English Department cliché.

'But they haven't gone?'

'Not yet.'

'Good.'

'Then they are rotten?'

'We'll work them into shape, old son, you and me together.' LeRoy Duquesne rubbed his hands together. 'Let's start with "Troopship".'

LeRoy Duquesne's talents lay in critical analysis: he could stretch a paragraph on the blackboard and let it twitch, neither dead nor quite living, while he pointed his ferule at character, style, realization of theme, figures of speech. He performed the best damn autopsy in the English Department. Shuffling pages of 'Troopship', his voice ringing with passion, he covered the manuscript with his minuscule, spiky notes. Gene's eyes occasionally would shift from paper to the sculptured features of LeRoy Duquesne, poet, critic, mentor, Progressive, and friend. He would agree, 'That's right.' 'Uh-huh.' 'Yes, the crap game should be deepened into symbolism.' 'Yes, sure, I get it.'

4

The following Tuesday Caroline got a phone call from her grandmother. The right birthday gift for Em, Mrs Van Vliet admitted, had her bewildered. Could Caroline help? And lunch with her?

'Saturday,' Caroline agreed.

Saturday, promptly at half-past eleven, the Daimler drove up Cordell Road. Caroline, feeling blissfully elegant (her pleasure enhanced by a gaping neighbour), stepped into the car as she would a perfumed bath. Joseph, tipping his cap, closed the door after her. 'How was Arrowhead?' Mrs Van Vliet inquired.

'On the way up, the motor boiled over – twice. It snowed the entire time. And Mrs Duquesne insisted on serving her curried lamb – twice.'

'Delightful,' said Mrs Van Vliet dryly.

'Grandmama, remember I told you Gene's been writing about the Army? Short stories? Old luv, you wouldn't believe how good they are. Sensitive. Fine. I cry each time I read them. Well, LeRoy Duquesne spent the weekend criticizing them.'

'Criticize? That has an ominous ring.'

'LeRoy Duquesne's meant to be a *renowned* critic.' Caroline made a face. 'Gene's working like a dog, revising.'

'Does this mean he's given up on the Holy Cause?'

'We're still slaving on the petition, if that's your innuendo, Grandmama.' Very French.

'Will Gene sign?'

'Of course not!'

'Then he'll be dismissed.'

'Faculty firing – there's one little threat I do not believe they'll carry out.'

A hand gloved in French kid brushed light as a butterfly wing on Caroline's knee. 'Caroline, remember those movie writers, the ones who refused to answer the House Un-American Activities Committee? Some went to jail. None'll work again. Ever. The same goes for recalcitrant professors.'

A remark as infuriating as unarguable: Mrs Van Vliet numbered among her friends, Caroline was aware, three regents of the University of California.

They had turned into the heavy traffic on Colorado Boulevard before either spoke.

'Methinks we can work this out,' Mrs Van Vliet said.

'His signing? Gene never will.'

'You two getting married,' Mrs Van Vliet said without lowering her voice. She and Joseph would have considered it a breach of etiquette to hint that his protruding black ears might eavesdrop. 'You've been sleeping together for almost a year.'

Caroline's cheeks burned brighter. Close as she was to her grandmother, she was also a daughter of her time. What girl in 1950 could admit sexual activity? And to another generation?

'God knows I'm no Puritan,' said Mrs Van Vliet. 'But let these long-term romances continue past a certain point and they fade. The girls drift from one affair to the next. Some never marry, some make a bad marriage.'

'Alas and alack for me.'

'Why?'

'You just said he's about to get the axe. How can we afford to get married?' And as she spoke, into Caroline's normally self-assured mind flashed oddly deflating facts: Most of my Omega Delta pledge group are married. Beverly's married and pregnant.

Mrs Van Vliet said, 'We'll find something for him in Van Vliet's.'

Caroline's breath sucked in.

'Why the surprise? Gene has vision, he'll make a good merchandiser, and that's what a market chain needs most.' She gave a chuckle. 'It wouldn't surprise me if he does well. Very well indeed.'

'Why should it? You own half the stock.' Caroline, recovering, bent one leg to the seat, turning to her grandmother. 'He's a sensitive, wonderful writer. A born teacher.'

'We've eliminated teaching. And writing?' Mrs Van Vliet's tone was guilty of malice aforethought. 'What luck your tastes run to expensive red frocks. Apprentice writers are notoriously overpaid.'

'I don't believe Gene could be good in the business.' Caroline's tone echoed her grandmother's. 'He's smart, progressive, creative, the exact opposite of Uncle Richard and Uncle Hend.' Mrs Van Vliet's sons, who alternated presidency of the chain. '*They*'re good at it.'

Mrs Van Vliet chuckled. Caroline's assessment of her two sons coincided with her own. 'Now. Be serious. You can convince Gene.'

'To each his own · disaster area.' Caroline shrugged. 'Sure I can. Bossy from the word go, that's me. But I won't.'

'The idea doesn't appeal to you?'

'It does. Very much.'

'Then?'

'Not for Gene.'

'Let's see if I understand. You want Gene in Van Vliet's, but there you won't respect him?'

'That's about it.'

'Normally, Caroline, you're more straightforward.'

'Van Vliet's just isn't Gene, Grandmama, don't you see that? On campus he can write, do crazy, wonderful things like the petition. He can admire and trust people.'

'Even if he doesn't admire the family, he can trust us,' said Mrs Van Vliet wryly. 'Caroline, listen to me. You're not the little hausfrau sweeping up cookie crumbs like Em. You have style, spirit. You're expensive.'

'Grandmama, why're you playing Mephistopheles?'

'Your happiness is important, very, to me.'

'Then let me be happy.'

'Without the accoutrements, you won't be.'

'With Gene grubbing, I won't be.'

'You don't understand how important money is to women like us,' Mrs Van Vliet sighed. 'I'll have to manage this.'

They travelled the rest of the way to the new Bullock's in silence.

While Caroline and Mrs Van Vliet deliberated over Em's birthday gift, Gene was at his desk in the English Department office, surrounded by empty desks of other TAs and the stale memory of their (possibly) stale bologna sandwiches. He was typing the final draft of 'Troopship' carefully, lovingly, erasing his infrequent typos, blowing away curly dust. He read the story aloud, pausing three times, thoughtfully inking over three sentences. He retyped these pages. He moved to the pigeonholes, folding crisp paper lengthwise into the empty crypt labelled DR LEROY F. DUQUESNE. Pages rustled into a fan. Gnawing a thumbnail, Gene stared for approximately five minutes. He pulled his story halfway out, then hastily pushed it back.

5

'Can't you tell me what this is all about?' Gene asked when he picked up Caroline on Monday night.

'*La grande dame*'s invited us to dine, that's all,' said Caroline, grabbing his earlobes. 'Kiss me, you fool.'

He kissed her forehead. He knew better than to smear the crimson lipstick brushed an immaculate millimetre inside the ripe mouth, a mouth that hinted of the gratification of various healthy appetites. She hugged his rib cage, hard, admitting that although she normally found him most unsexy, tonight there was a full moon, and the full moon invariably brought out the Countess Dracula in her, causing her to yearn after passionate scenes of vampirean lust, floggings, degradation, and your routine bloodletting. All the way to her grandmother's, she babbled.

Parking, Gene asked, 'Caroline, what is it?'

'What's what?'

'The fluster.'

'Can't you tell *per*version when you see it?'

It was rare for Caroline to be nervous. She infected him. Joseph, huge, jug-eared, opened the door. Gene began to sweat. He knew Joseph. Besides, his parents kept an elderly live-in maid. Tonight, though, he realized a butler is a butler is a butler. Mrs Van Vliet took his hands in hers. He felt the outsize gems. Her perfume, he decided extravagantly, was distilled from lilacs grown under rock-crystal panes of a Côte d'Azur hothouse. Normally he enjoyed being with Caroline's grandmother. Tonight she was queen dowager. Joseph passed a salver with three glasses of tawny wine. Gene downed his. And for some reason thought of 'Troopship', now in the agonizingly silent custody of LeRoy Duquesne. He was served avocado salad, a slab of perfect pink beef flanked by tasty roast potatoes and hollandaise-girdled asparagus. An excellent meal that Gene could not taste. He was worrying alternately about 'Troopship' and the vastness of the dining-room. Why was Caroline so nervous? Why was he?

Imari dessert plates were set in front of them.

Mrs Van Vliet glanced at Caroline. Caroline pleated her damask napkin. Mrs Van Vliet looked down the length of table at Gene. 'You're active against the loyalty oath, aren't you, Gene?'

'Pretty much,' he said. 'Yes.'

'Then you won't sign?'

His twitchy stomach knotted. The sixty-four-dollar question.

In theory, of course, he'd told himself he would burn first. Gene, however, was totally self-honest. The implications of not signing, like the *Titanic* going down, had created a disastrous suction, threatening to pull him under. Who would he be if not Professor Mathney, author of critically well-received, non-profitable novels?

Therefore his firmness of tone surprised him as he answered, 'It wouldn't be possible to, no.'

'I see,' Mrs Van Vliet said.

'Not that I'd be perjuring –'

Fragile laughter shattered his reply. 'Gene, Gene. I never believed you were slipping the *Communist Manifesto* to your freshmen along with their Sandburg. Why won't you?'

'The State Constitution says no oath, declaration, or test shall be required of us, so it's illegal. And the end of academic freedom – hiring and firing of faculty after this will be at the whim of the regents.' Abruptly he stopped.

'Go on,' Mrs Van Vliet encouraged.

Gene's long, pleasant face bore more than its customary resemblance to a hound dog. He chewed his thumbnail.

'It's not that logical. I think the Oath is unjust to people who may have done something in the past, when it was legal and feasible. This is ex post facto.' He raised his heavy goblet, taking a sip of water. 'It's even more. The whole thing was started by a bunch of bigots in Sacramento and Washington – Tenney, J. Parnell Thomas, our honourable congressman, Richard Nixon. I'll be damned if I'll sign any paper that sets apart any group of people – whether I agree with their ideology or not – to bolster those hacks.'

Mrs Van Vliet's smile glowed with warmth. 'Gene, I do like you.'

'I'll be fired.'

She agreed.

'I'll have to try my luck at some other campus,' he said with deep uncertainty.

Joseph bore in a magnificent crown of charlotte russe. Mrs Van Vliet shook her head. Caroline, darting a defiant smile at Gene, carved herself a double portion. She was on a diet, she was always on a diet and telling Gene not to let her eat. He took a sliver.

'Teaching,' said Mrs Van Vliet, 'is not the only career.'

'It's the only one I'm trained for, Mrs Van Vliet.' His fork probed whipped cream.

Mrs Van Vliet gazed at him.

And Gene understood the conversation was up to him. 'I don't know what I'm meant to say.'

'Try.'

'By other careers, you mean Van Vliet's?'

His hostess nodded assent.

'I've had no business training. None.'

'Gene, to my knowledge there is not a single graduate of the Harvard School of Business running a supermarket in this area.' She paused. 'The average Californian consumes fifteen hundred pounds of food a year. Van Vliet's job is simply seeing he buys it at the lowest possible price.'

Caroline was watching intently.

Mrs Van Vliet said, 'It's not a pretentious business, ours. The profits are in mills, not pennies. Once I remember my husband debating over some new office furniture. Finally he said, "We'll have to move a million dollars worth of goods to pay for this." And he didn't buy it. Food is the most basic human need.'

Mrs Van Vliet's faintly mocking tone angered Gene. She knew, and was using, his weaknesses. (Or his strengths.)

'You're ringing Pavlov's bell, Mrs Van Vliet.'

Smiling, she bent her head. Through exquisite white hair the skull showed pink. And this was what calmed Gene. For all the imperiousness, wit, wealth, her pink skull proved her mortal.

They returned to the tapestry-hung living-room for coffee.

'Well?' asked Mrs Van Vliet.

Gene realized she'd been staring at him.

'You have no idea what an expressive face it is, Gene.' She paused delicately. 'I take it you intend to make an honest woman out of my grandchild?'

Caroline turned crimson.

Gene, too, felt the blood rising. In those days such a remark, however lightly spoken, wasn't for laughs: it was
cause for a man to pick his ushers and buy the ring. From
one fading tapestry a haloed angel beckoned.

'You'll need a job to support her.'

Gene nodded.

'And selling food,' she said, 'can never bring equal ful-
filment with untangling allegory from the Great White
Whale?'

Gene yearned to follow the beckoning angel into
ancient threads. 'I wasn't thinking that.'

'Something very close, then,' said Mrs Van Vliet. She
set her demitasse on a bow-legged table. 'Los Angeles is
growing. We recently opened two markets in Watts.' A
coloured area, and perhaps the most telling argument
with Gene.

His grey eyes looked into space. This, too, he thought,
is coercion. Caroline, who for once had remained totally
silent, moved to the couch where he was sitting.

'No wonder you were nervous,' he said. 'You'd like me to,
wouldn't you?'

'Luv, she wanted *me* to put it to you. I said absolutely
no.'

They were parked on Cordell Road, in front of her
house. On the radio, Frankie Laine wished to go where
the wild goose went.

'I'd be good at it,' he said thoughtfully.

'Don't be ridic!'

'I would.' He reached an arm around the lightly padded shoulders of her red Ann Fogarty suit. 'Caroline, can
you understand this? I want writing – and teaching – too
much. When you want something too much, you're a
little terrified of it. In business I'd have the necessary con-
tempt. I'd do well, but I'd feel wasted.'

'You would be! It's grubbing. The way my uncles talk
for hours about buying truckloads of toilet paper for three
cents less a case!' She kissed his ear. 'I love you the way
you are.'

'I'd have a job. A living.'

'You'd be a sell-out.'

'You don't want me to?'

'Never.'

'Then I'll stick,' he said.

'Good,' she whispered, and held him with her full strength. He turned his back to the wheel, and they were kissing hungrily. After a few minutes he whispered, 'Are they sleeping, your parents?'

'Like dormice.'

Caroline and Gene, arms around one another, walked through the darkness, pausing to embrace at the back door, she unlocking it, he following quietly into the un-used maid's room. An hour later, smiling and flushed, they emerged. Caroline, rather noisily, unlocked the front door, bidding Gene goodnight.

6

The next morning a note was folded in Gene's pigeon-hole:

After your section come to my office

LFD

Gene stared at cheap, yellow-lined paper. He's read 'Troopship', he thought.

'Come in,' said LeRoy Duquesne, continuing to scan a blue book. Through an open window came the between-class roar. Gene sat opposite the desk. The hubbub quietened. The electric clock rang. Harsh, abrasive. Le-Roy Duquesne's red pencil scratched a grade. 'Troopship' has gone down with all hands, Gene thought, otherwise wouldn't he have dropped a life preserver?

'LeRoy, I'll come back.'

'Wait,' LeRoy Duquesne ordered, picking up the next blue book to correct.

Gene waited. What's the worst thing that can happen, he asked himself, seeking nourishment from his thumbnail. The very worst. He'll say it's garbage. Oh God, God. Gene hunched in the comfortless oak chair. For the first time he understood that the quiet man who cannot sing great paeans, the man who cannot dance to the glory of the gods, offers up his gift on paper. And if the gods find his gifts wanting? Gene's mouth went dry. Another blue book shuffled.

The clock was ticking ten thirty-four as LeRoy Duquesne levelled the corrected stack. Without raising his leonine head, he inquired, 'Are you still working on that petition?'

We're friends, he knows I am, Gene thought, confused. 'Getting no place fast,' he replied, 'but sure.'

'Drop it.'

'Come again?'

'Drop it.'

'LeRoy, I don't understand.'

'Tear the petition in two, in four, in eight. Incinerate the scraps.'

Gene was remembering the autumn afternoon that LeRoy Duquesne had encouraged him. 'You're kidding,' he said.

The professor was paying exquisite care to the packing of blue books in his attaché case.

And all at once Gene understood.

He examined his fingernails. I must stop biting them, he thought tangentially. He lifted his honest grey eyes to LeRoy Duquesne.

'You signed, didn't you?'

LeRoy Duquesne refused to meet his gaze. 'You're one of the few hold-outs in the department.'

'But you've been talking as if –'

'Categorically and unequivocally, I am against any form of loyalty oath.'

'Why sign one, then?'

LeRoy Duquesne glanced around his windowed office, desk, bookshelves, framed degrees. It was no answer, yet it said everything.

'You're one of our best teaching assistants,' he said. 'You'll be a real addition to the faculty.'

'So this is how it's done,' Gene said, unable to hide his bitterness.

'Don't blame me, Gene, for the monstrous times. The country's out of control, and this is only one small part of it. The witch-hunt is upon us, and God help the hold-outs. We'll have martyrs. Historically, there always have been martyrs. The difference is today they'll be denied the dignity of flame or lion. They'll simply be made to appear corrupt and incompetent, both, then thrown out of work.'

'You make it sound inevitable.'

'It is. We liberals are all victims.' At last he met Gene's gaze. 'Either public or private victims.'

The look he gave Gene was of unwilling assassin to victim, of lover who has betrayed love. And in that long, silent exchange, Gene's burden of humanity was compelled to admit the uncrossable rift between conviction and action: i.e., between talking and eating. Gene never had felt closer to anyone in his life, not to his parents or Caroline.

'Gene, listen to me. You won't be hired by any university or junior college. Or even high school. Blacklists do exist. These people aren't fools. They mean business.'

Gene's stomach was in peculiar rebellion.

'What's a signature? This is what you're made for, and you know it. Don't be a fool.'

Gene wanted to reply, *I'm stuck with being one.* But his stomach was churning, and if he opened his mouth he knew a terrible ululation would spurt like vomit from him. He hurried from the office ('Gene,' LeRoy Duquesne was calling, 'Gene!'), moving down the dusty stairs to his desk, hunching in a beam of sunshine, his arms wrapped around his chest as if he were naked in snow.

LeRoy signed months ago, he thought. And the thought was a heavy stone idol falling, crashing on the supportive blocks of his political belief, which was constructed of the fragile human element. LeRoy Duquesne signed before Thanksgiving, he thought. That ties it. He opened his top drawer, mechanically removing three yellow pencil stubs, rubber bands, paper clips, a very clear snapshot of Caroline making a cross-eyed face. LeRoy signed, Gene thought, and his throat clogged with tears, routine tribute to a fallen god.

'Cleaning?' asked Caroline.

He looked up at her.

'Hey,' she said, and despite three other TAs bent over their desks in the big office, she rested a cheek to his forehead, cuddling him to her breasts. 'Wha' happen?'

'The boom was just lowered. Sign or else.'

'Who says?'

'LeRoy. He signed last Thanksgiving.'

'And all this time he's been talking big liberal!' she cried. 'And to *you*.'

'I think I understand. He needed someone to carry the flag for him.'

'Come the revolution, we shoot rats like him.'

'He's got a wife and career to support.'

Caroline held Gene's cheeks in her palms, staring at him. 'Maybe he's right,' she said. 'Why not? It's no lie. You're not in the party. And this *is* what your life's all about. Genebo, the price isn't all that high.'

'Caroline, not you.'

Blue eyes shrewd, Van Vliet eyes. Caroline let her little finger play an eraser across the cluttered desk. 'Listen, what's the rush for us to get married? That's old-fashioned jazz. Your parents'll let you stay in the house. Why don't you just write?'

'Write?' Gene's lips formed the word slowly, like a child sounding out the difficult syllable. 'Write? I went in there thinking we were about to rip apart "Troopship". I was plenty anxious. But once LeRoy started in on the Oath business, I never gave it another thought. Until you mentioned it, I'd completely forgotten I ever wrote anything.'

'Mitigating circumstances.'

'Never. Writing is something you have to care about. Really care. Give total dedication. You can sell out your mother, your father, your wife, your ideals, but you must be serious about one thing. Writing.'

'Gene, you're *good*.'

'And you're loyal.'

'Weren't you published all over?'

'Everywhere. College papers.'

'You never tried the others.'

'Forget it, please,' he said wearily.

On his desk lay books, papers, his *Thesaurus*, his Modern Library *Portrait of a Lady*, clippings of his UN columns for *The Bruin* (these had turned praline brown), slick copies of *Claw*, *The New Yorker* with Hersey's *Hiroshima*, his lecture notes, his looseleaf of ideas for novels, the detritus of years with that intricate blending of smells, must, metal, ripe banana, smells that were familiar and suddenly dear to a teaching assistant who has come to the end of the line.

'Which'll we toss out?' Caroline asked.

'Everything.'

Together they filled two large, institutional waste paper baskets. 'Not that,' Gene said, pocketing the snapshot of her.

She straightened, saying, 'I swear it. I'll leave the minute you bark like Uncle Hend or give the glad hand like Uncle Richard.'

'Caroline, it's what you really want.'

'I know it,' she said. Fishing a Kleenex from her bag, she blew a sob through her nose. 'I'm a rotten winner.'

A chill wind raked the portico. It was one pm, Tuesday, 23 February 1950. The sun was shining. The wind blew leaves and tugged at coeds' long skirts. On Royce steps a cluster of SAE pledges burst into ribald laughter. The chimes started 'Oh, What a Beautiful Morning'. A moment to remember. For Gene knew that although he had stood up for his principles, on a subtler level, at one pm, on 23 February, he had sold out. He was walking away from everything (or almost everything) that he wanted from life. His face was grave. Yet his down-slanted eyes were bright with anticipation. Crossing the quad, he smiled at Caroline.

She did not smile back.

Chapter Five

I

Beverly Schorer curled around herself.

Trapped between sleeping and waking, she imagined she could hear Philip breathing. Sometimes in these dreamlike moments, the three phases of her life merged: she was at the same time a girl, a young wife, and a woman waiting out a divorce to marry her lover. She heard water running in Alix's, her daughter's, bathroom. Beverly pushed herself from bed, glimpsing herself in the mirror. She looked wan and crumpled. Last night was a Business Evening, and (inevitably, inescapably) they had argued, she and Dan. She squeezed toothpaste and told herself not to think about the argument. Instead, she found herself thinking (inevitably, inescapably) about Philip – well, not exactly about Philip, but her guilt towards him.

She had met Philip Schorer about a year after the rainy night she'd broken with Dan Grossblatt. A bad year, but she had dated various boys in the spasmodic way of the forties. Philip was a blind date. As Beverly entered the living-room he rose. Tall, tanned, dark-haired, with perfect features. She had remained in the doorway a few seconds. How could a man be so beautiful? She felt as if she had moved into another dimension. Her skin flushed. Philip was half-Jewish, enough, certainly, to satisfy the Lindes. His father, the Jewish half, owned a small but growing furniture plant. Philip worked with him.

Philip edged his words in a faintly ironic tone that made him sound superior. After they were married, she realized his irony was an act of separation from himself. He wasn't quite sure whether he was scorned for being a mix. This made her feel closer to him. Philip, unfortunately, did not care to be close. They had a daughter, Alix and, two years later, Jamie, their boy. They bought a charming Cape Cod house, a boat – Philip loved sailing, and Beverly learned to love it, too. Yet she was no nearer her husband.

They never argued. Philip, annoyed, would intensify his mocking tone until it was frozen.

To others – and maybe to Philip – they were an exemplary couple. They had been married twelve years that night of the Mortons' big, loud party. The Dan Grossblatts were guests, too. Dan had asked her to dance, and during 'Mack the Knife' had moved in, saying, 'Who can catch up with all this racket? Let's have lunch.' She was about to refuse when he, smiling, traced under her lip as he had years before, and she knew she absolutely must refuse. Must.

Dan took her to the thin-walled bachelor apartment he kept – he made no effort to hide the fact – for 'lunches'. It was rotten. She never before had been unfaithful. Philip was handsome, considerate. What was she doing, her naked thighs clutched around a man who habitually fooled around? It wasn't for many weeks that she was able to accept the simple answer. She wouldn't have been in that position if she hadn't still loved Dan. Love – impossible. Love was veneered with more betrayals than adultery. Love was the enemy. Yet instead of keeping at her easel, she returned to the apartment. Guilty, always guilty. That hot summer and chill winter, Dan would draw acid-green drapes, for a couple of hours closing off her guilts. Beverly had experienced few of the possibilities of physical love. By nature she was a voluptuary, but the times she had elaborated on Philip's joinings, he had lost desire. She bought flowered sheets for the convertible bed, and with Dan on lavender peonies intuited a call girl's skill. Not that it was all sex. They could be as open with one another as they'd ever been. Talking, talking. Dan told her that when, after their break-up, he had left his father's business, his father had ranted in his harsh accent, hitting at Dan with a chair, an old man's terrible weakness. *You'll fail without me*, the old man had screamed. 'I managed to patch things up,' Dan said. 'But after that, you think I could take one penny? When he died – God, I was a mess – I told Justin, my brother-in-law, he should run S&G Shoes. Justin's a *schlemiel*, but what the hell. How could I touch it?' In underwater-green shadows they talked of everything. Except that most guilt-provoking word. Love.

Then, one smoggy afternoon, Beverly could no longer hold back. 'I love you,' she murmured miserably. 'Me, too. I need you with me all the time,' Dan said. His tone angry. The women he once had brought here never had impinged on his sense of family responsibility. DeeDee, whatever else she might or might not be, was his wife, and their two little boys were adopted, which to his mind increased his obligation. He loved them. And Beverly loved her children fiercely. Her bond with Philip, however tenuous the strands appeared, was strong.

So what choice was there? That smoggy afternoon they broke up.

Beverly couldn't sleep. In her bed she would listen to Philip's even breathing, the shape of emptiness filling dark hours. After six weeks Dan showed up, and in Beverly's white-faced presence, confronted Philip with the facts. Maybe Philip had guessed all along. 'Is this what you want, Beverly? Him?' Philip asked incredulously. He was as white as she. Her huge, weary amber eyes closing, Beverly nodded. And two divorce proceedings were initiated.

On leaving S&G Shoes, Dan had moved to California and discovered a business made for him. Land. With unflagging energy he put a hundred thousand miles a year on his car, searching out Southern California for coming areas. He had a nose for it. To buy all the land that he sniffed out required leverage, and while Beverly never quite grasped leverage, she knew it involved one major concept: put up as little of your own as possible. Therefore, Dan syndicated. He got others to put up. His investors, for their cash, received 50 per cent of the profit (in capital gains) while he took the other half for his acumen. Of course future investors required selling. But who was Dan if not Supersalesman? He entertained those in search of tax shelter (acquaintances and referrals both) at

Scandia, Perino's, or LaRue, offering drinks and huge steaks, playing down the success of his previous ventures. The old soft sell. By the time coffee was poured ('Try the cheesecake, it's fabulous here,' Dan would urge), his guests invariably were begging for in. Dan, on Business Evenings, was exuberant as a boy playing football on a crisp October day.

Beverly felt strangers' eyes flicking at her. Dan's girl? DeeDee's successor? An unmarried broad who slept around? A *shiksa*? The years, two children, a Cape Cod house, an interlocutory decree, had altered Beverly not at all. She remained pure of the small retaliatory malice and petty conversation that would have enabled another woman to breeze through Business Evenings.

The worst, though: their arguments, every single one, were tethered, however deviously, to Business Evenings.

And last night's had been a horror. Shuddering, Beverly tied her robe. We're all through, she thought.

She headed for the kitchen.

Jamie was frying rounds of wiener, his beagle, a pedigreed wanderer named Boris, at his feet. ''Morning,' she said. Boris's tail thumped on the brick floor. Jamie smiled. A smile with teeth too large, still serrated, a smile, like Beverly's, that showed the gum, a completely open smile. He wore what he'd slept in, an old T-shirt tight enough to show the ladder of his ribs, and jockey shorts with a tear in the back seam. His arms were gangly, his legs knob-angled, thin, long. At almost ten, Jamie was growing too fast. Philip was a tall man.

The kettle spout steamed – Jamie always put water on for her. 'Thank you,' she said, not quite managing a smile, tipping Nescafé into a mug without measuring, carrying the dark brew to the table. She rested on an elbow, shading her forehead with her hand.

Jamie said, 'I found this baby bird.'

She looked up.

'When I got the paper,' he said.

'Where?'

'The patio. The nest's in the ferns.' He cranked open a

can of Heinz beans. 'Think it'll be okay?'

'Why not?'

'They won't feed it, the parents, if it's been messed with.' His eyes were hazel. In the left iris floated a black birthmark, which gave him a slightly cross-eyed, questioning expression.

'Is that true?'

'I read. I used a spoon, so they couldn't smell me.'

'Clever.'

'There were two others. Ugly, naked, like worms with beaks. Sad. Really sad.'

He'd been sad, really sad, his head out of shape from the birth canal. 'The parents don't think so,' she said.

'They didn't come back.'

'Oh?'

'I hung around.'

'With Boris?'

'Sure, Boris.'

'He's a bird dog.' This time her smile succeeded.

'No, really.'

She got up, giving him a hug, her fingers tightening on fragile, small-boy shoulder blades. 'Really,' she said. 'If you were a bird, wouldn't you stay clear of Boris?'

'I guess.' He nodded, and stirred beans into hot dogs.

'Save some for me.'

Beverly and Jamie turned.

Alix stood in the door, brushing luxuriant, waist-length hair. Beverly's breath caught. Each time she confronted her elder child, her painter's eye marvelled. True human beauty is one of the rarest commodities. Alix. Fine bones, proud tilt of head on slender neck. Arched brows and wide forehead. The slightly full lower lip that rather than being a pouty flaw was the one variation necessary to validate perfection. Of Alix there was no saying, 'She'll be a beauty.' At eleven going on twelve, age of tadpole gawks, Alix Schorer was home free.

Her thick-lashed brown eyes stayed on Beverly as if she were expecting something. Since the separation she always looked at Beverly as if she were expecting something.

Beverly cleared her throat. 'That's a new sweater, isn't it?'

'Uh-huh.' Alix, putting down her brush, opened the cupboard for a bowl.

'Yellow's pretty on you.'

'Oh Mother!'

'It is.'

'Pretty's such a dork word.'

Jamie let his sister fill her bowl – he'd made enough for them both. He ate from the skillet, sitting next to Beverly. Alix leaned against the counter, sweeping neat forkfuls into her lovely, possibly flawed mouth. She swallowed. 'Daddy gave me the money. Boris – scram!'

'Where did you find it?' Beverly asked.

Alix said, 'Jamie, move.'

'The bus hasn't gone up yet.'

'Oh hasn't it?'

'I didn't hear –'

'Which proves you've got earwax.'

'When?'

'See if I care. Be late.'

Jamie ran, leaving the skillet on the table.

Alix turned to Beverly, 'You said something, Mother?' Beverly shook her head.

'I distinctly thought you did.'

'No.'

'Before,' Alix prodded.

'Oh yes. Where'd you get the sweater?'

'Why?'

'Just wondering.'

'It's Daddy's money.'

'Alix, please.' Beverly sighed. 'I can't handle it when you're like this.' She closed her eyes.

'Tired?'

'I didn't think it'd hurt you this –'

'Mother, we aren't in the olden days. Half of everybody's parents are divorced,' Alix stated. 'But you told us that you and Mr Grossblatt wouldn't be late.' (Repeatedly Dan had asked Alix to call him by his first name: she made it a point of filial honour not to.)

'We weren't.' (Ten-fifteen, and Dan's new Jaguar was digging out of the drive while Beverly's shaky fingers were pushing notes into Mrs Elwood's plump hand.)

'Then you're an insomniac.'

'Insomniac.'

'I was trying,' Alix said, 'for humour.'

A heavy rumble shuddered down the winding curves of Maggiore Lane. Alix scrabbled in her mother's purse. 'No change,' she accused.

'Take the ones.'

Beverly watched her children race up the steep drive, Alix handing Jamie his dollar – he tended to forget lunch money and allowances – and shouting amicable insults to her friends, disappearing into the big yellow bus. Jamie, pausing to pull Boris's ear, sitting alone in the last seat.

Beverly, tightening her robe, stared after the bus. It was a time of cold war, of missile crises, and most days there were unscheduled drop drills, children huddling under desks with their arms bent, protecting frail heads from imminent nuclear damage. The bus's roar faded.

Inside, in the maid's room she used as a studio, Beverly angled her easel to the window. On the board was an unfinished pastel, of a baby girl, with a small Kodacolour print of the child tacked to the upper left corner. Sandler Gallery had commissioned the portrait for her. Beverly managed on Sandler's commissions and Philip's child support. She and Dan weren't married yet, therefore she refused the money he persistently offered her. She squinted, choosing a green pastel, filling in background with the flat of chalk. *You're so fucking sensitive, how come you don't marry some starving artist?* Her delicate brows drew together, her soft mouth pulled down. She looked utterly desolate. Soon, though, a problem of highlight involved her.

2

'Beverly.'

Startled, she dropped the chalk.

'You've got something against locking doors?'

'Nothing personal,' she said, picking up the pastel, which mercifully hadn't broken. She didn't have much to spend on supplies. 'Hi.'

Dan leaned against the doorjamb, one leg curled around the other, motionless. Yet from the top of his thick brown hair to shoes that zipped at the side instead of lacing, he somehow managed to appear in supercharged motion.

'About lunch?' he asked.

'S' that late? I've got cottage cheese.'

He picked up a large brown bag with numbers totalled down the side, sniffing. 'Smells like deli. You holding out on me with that cottage cheese?'

She laughed, relieved. It's right again, she thought. Inevitably generous, he'd brought enough for a medium-size bar mitzvah.

Over his thick corned beef-and-pastrami sandwich, he asked, 'I ever tell you about acreage in the Valley?'

'Which?'

'Right off the Ventura Freeway.'

She shook her head. 'I don't think so.'

'A fantastic location for a shopping centre, a good-size one, with two, three major department stores. I've been thinking. Why not a roof over, a mall, and air condition the whole shooting match? Then that damn Valley summer won't keep customers home. Listen, you could have a double decker of shops. And indoor gardens and sidewalk cafés and some sort of recreation for kids. The minute it hit ninety, every broad for miles around would head on over.'

Dan verbally developed each piece he found, building shopping centres and tracts in the air. The land safely his (and his investors') he would begin the search for a hungry buyer. Oh, she knew her Dan.

'Why the scrutable smile?' he asked.

She reached for potato salad.

'Speak up. Who can hear you?' He used his fork to feed her. 'A big one like this, and I'll retire.'

An idea so incongruous – where would all that energy go? – that she laughed aloud, potato trapping her throat, so laughter turned to coughing. He rose, pounding between her shoulders.

'That's for laughing at me,' he said. 'I mean it. No more all-day, all-night shit.'

'I was tired.'

'Otherwise you're big on making friends and influencing people? You love the business, right?'

'Dan –' she started, but he stroked back her hair. 'There's this new invention,' he said tenderly. 'Maybe you've heard of it? They call it the comb. Buzz, you're not tough enough. It's not for you. So I'll put up this shopping centre and we'll have it made.' A sound deep in his throat. He shook his head, aggravated. 'The only hitch is this Alvena Earle. The owner. A crazy woman. She refuses to sell the land – now why the laughing?'

'Your test for sanity.'

'She doesn't have a pot to piss in, and there she is, camping out on Fort Knox. What do you call that?'

'Have you talked to her?'

'Five times. She gives me nothing.' Dan chuckled. 'I'm the one who's crazy. I like the old *meshugenah* – she's an original.' He speared a red sliver of pastrami. 'A prime location like this, May Company, Bullock's, Broadway, all the big ones want in. And with them signed, the little guys trip over themselves for leases. They're the ones who sweeten the deal.'

'How?'

'They pay higher per foot.'

'That's not fair.'

'Who told you life is fair? When I get that piece –'

'If.'

'When,' he said. 'I need it, don't I?' His little finger traced her lip, moving down her throat, parting the Viyella robe, rubbing the tops of her breasts. She heard her own intake of breath and felt the moisture gathering in her eyes – her eyes grew wet, echoing that warm, secret need of him.

'Last night,' he muttered, 'I dreamed of the camp.'

They pulled apart. Silent.

'Come on,' he said finally. 'Let's go to your room.'

On cool, rumpled sheets, she murmured his name, the flat of her hands hard on his back, as he went into her. And after that, there was just the slow, sure thrusting that carried them further and further from thinking about those stacks of skeletal bodies, from thinking that they, maybe, belonged in that vast, muddy hell, from thinking of anything. Under him her hips moved faster.

3

Around two, Dan left, heading for Alvena Earle's land. The San Diego Freeway to the Valley was under construction, Sepulveda Boulevard re-routed onto temporary paving, and stones hailed under the Jag. Dan drove, his mind half on Beverly, the other half working on his financial statement. His divorce had been a bitch. And trust Beverly to drown in guilt. So he let her know the truth, he'd inherited from his father approximately two million, never mentioning that this was in S&G Shoes, which for his own reasons, doubtless half-assed but anyway his reasons, he'd let be managed (or mismanaged) by Justin Winsten, his brother-in-law. S&G stock might have been Confederate bonds. Dan's latest dividend had arrived seven years previously. His own business was good. But there is a joke among land men, three of them drinking coffee and gabbing about net worths well up in the seven figures, and when the waitress puts down the bill, not one can ante up. Some joke. In every deal Dan put up some of his own: always he was land-rich and cash-poor. To pay the first instalment on DeeDee's community-property settlement, he'd been forced into premature escrow on the Lancaster acreage. Each month DeeDee got a thousand-dollar alimony cheque, plus another made out for the same, Michael's and Vic's child support. Dan wrote out three fifty for Aunt Channa's sunlit room at Ocean Park Rest Home. God knows how much Mortie's new disaster in Vegas would cost him. Last week Gary had written: *Dear Cousin Dan, My tuition amounts to ...* This, too, he'd inherited from his father, the ancient Jewish title, Rich Relation, with the duties incumbent thereon. Dan didn't mind. As a matter of fact, the knowledge he'd succeeded gave him a kick.

Except.

There was Beverly. He would glance across restaurant tables to see huge amber eyes remote. A stand-offish expression. He would ache to put his arms around her, at the same time battling a desire to slap her until he saw marks angry-red across her cheek. It wasn't going to work this way. Never. So go climb Everest, swim the English Channel, run a four-minute mile. Find the big one.

4

Dan considered Alvena Earle's undeveloped land, in the heart of the San Fernando Valley, adjacent to the Ventura Freeway, his big one. It would be, he knew, a bargain at a million.

Alvena had no intention of selling. She lived on the property, landlady to the grey field mouse, the jackrabbit, the garter snake, as well as his quarry, the industrious gopher. She had planted trees – apricot, guava, pomegranate, avocado, evergreen, citrus, walnut, and silvery olive. She irrigated with buckets of water. She would toss handfuls of wild poppy seed, and in early spring her land would burn with colour, a molten reflection of the sun.

Alvena had one living relative. A son.

Raymond Earle.

Raymond had been an obese child with the copper skin that comes from an overload of carotene. His eyes slid away when anyone looked at him. His mind worked in strange patterns. Instinctively, other children avoided him. Raymond therefore engaged in solitary vice: ignoring his mother's anathema against refined food, he would slowly consume chocolates filched from a local shop while lying on his back, hidden by rough, almost colourless wild oats. Here, Raymond would consider his classmates' failings, for each child constructing an extensive list of major defects. This endowed him with a sense of Godlike power. In their presence, though, he felt inferior. This baffled him. He, Raymond Earle, was omnipotent, so why, with the others, should he feel small, uneasy, a worm? Superimposed on rustling green overhead, he would see his schoolmates' damned souls writhing in torments, torments that he concocted from newspaper reports of the Nuremberg Trials. He would eat his swiped chocolate, dreaming away the hours.

When he was sixteen, he rose one moonlit night. Taking a box and long, stolen ham knife from under his straw pallet, he hurried to the farthest corner of the lot. From a hidden trap he took a scrawny male jackrabbit, cutting the animal's throat while he devoured a two-pound box of chocolate-covered cherries.

The delicatessen had made Dan thirsty. He asked for water, and Alvena, going into the trumpet vine-covered shack, returned with a glass of muddy liquid. Dan eyed the green flecks suspiciously, but he was dying. Stale grapefruit peelings dashed with pepper, the taste.

'Herb tea,' Alvena said, sinking crosslegged on hard

earth near his chair. 'Made it for Raymond.'

'Raymond?'

'My son,' she explained.

'You have kids?'

'One. Raymond.' Alvena spent words economically.

'He doesn't live with you?'

'Got his own place. Raymond needs the tea. He's liable to haemorrhoids. Eats refined carbohydrates and meat.' Then her leathery skin frayed into a smile. 'Good boy, though. Stops in after his shift Tuesdays and Thursdays.'

Dan was amused. Alvena Earle, strange grasshopper creature, proud of and worrying about her son. Dan was touched. And that always vigilant part of his brain, instinct you could call it, told him something big was about to come off.

Alvena rose, tilting her head. 'Raymond,' she said. 'Hear him?'

Dan heard breeze rustling the avocado branches, the Ventura Freeway. 'Nope,' he said.

But within a minute between fruit trees came a short fat man stuffed into a cheap suit. Raymond was thirty but overweight, and his flatfooted walk made him appear closer to fifty.

'Dan Grossblatt,' Alvena introduced. 'Raymond Earle.'

She darted through the unpainted door. Glancing after his mother, Raymond mopped his brow and asked in a muted voice, 'Mr Grossblatt, what brings you to Mother's hideaway?'

'Didn't she mention why?' Dan was pretty sure she had. Still, who can guess the confidence shared by parent and child?

Ropes protested as Raymond sank into an old-fashioned porch hammock. 'Mother never says much.' He evaded the question and Dan's eyes.

'It's no secret. I'm interested in putting up a shopping centre.'

'Is Mother interested?'

'What's your opinion?'

'She won't sell.'

'How do you feel about it?'

'The matter's not up to me.'

'You have been thinking, though?'

'Yes,' Raymond whispered. 'In my opinion land's at an all-time high.'

Dan's pitch to the reluctant seller. He threw his best curve. 'And who knows how the hell long prices'll hold?'

'This seems like a good time to get out.'

'Why not tell your mother?'

'She doesn't listen to me. Or anyone.'

Dan chuckled. 'Don't I know. I've been here six times.'

'Good. Very good. Excellent. I've certainly got to hand it to you, Mr Grossblatt. You're persistent. No one else has ever got this far with her. You ... certainly are persuasive.'

(There was something too cosy about the hesitation, as if it held an unspoken word. The evading eyes bitched Dan. But Raymond was Alvena Earle's weak spot.)

'I've broken my ass, but she hasn't given me a single opening.' Abruptly Dan stopped. Alvena was returning with another glass of herb tea and a bowl of poker-chip dried apricots.

They talked about Raymond's work, selling kitchen appliances. The swing creaked, the trumpet vine's vanilla scent wafted over to them.

A siren.

Another siren. Warm air groaned with sirens. Peace was shattered. Alvena stirred on her bony rump.

'Must be an accident,' Dan said.

'Idiots on their freeways!' Alvena snapped. 'Racing from nowhere to nowhere. Killing one another. That's their business. But fumes murder everyone!'

'A fact,' Dan said. Excitement suddenly was filling his brain until it seemed the convolutions must explode. His mouth was dry, his armpits wet. Many businessmen rehearse their pitch. Dan always played it by ear. When the key situation arose (and he always knew when), words came spontaneously. 'Carbon monoxide destroys the lungs,' he said.

'Shreds them,' Alvena agreed. 'Exhaust does it.'

'And traps cold germs,' Dan said. Alvena, he knew, considered colds the pimps for heavy disease. 'People in cities have more colds.'

'Direct ratio,' Alvena agreed.

'Also, I read carbon monoxide stunts the brain.'

'Ruins the kidneys.' Alvena.

'How about genetic damage?' Dan tried to remember: had he read this in *Time*'s Medicine?

'Overpowering evidence.'

'What overpowering?'

'Smaller babies. Mothers breathing polluted air.'

'Yeah, that's right,' Dan said. 'However hard you try, who can stay healthy?'

The swing no longer creaked. Raymond Earle was listening intently.

Dan, feeling an idiot, pushed on. 'Every day you hear of more and more cancer. The lungs, the mouth, the throat, bone marrow, breast, prostate. Colon.' He paused. 'Guy I know had a colostomy yesterday. Thirty-nine, and there he is, a sack on him.'

At this, Alvena thoughtfully removed a tiger moth from her sleeve. And then Dan remembered her fear that Raymond might get piles.

'Cancer?' she asked.

'Yep. Cancer,' Dan said. 'And as far as the lungs're concerned, live in this crap and you might as well smoke.'

Alvena stiffened. Raymond rubbed his thumb against his forefinger. And Dan knew he'd gone too far. His second visit Alvena had invited him to sit down and discuss the Mosaic dietary laws, and he'd relaxed, starting to light a Havana. She had turned crimson. He had figured she had suffered an internal haemorrhage, split a gut or something. Snatching the cigar from him, she had stamped it out as if she'd been killing a rattlesnake.

'Nothing's worse than smoking,' she said flatly.

Raymond stood, the hammock swinging drunkenly behind him. 'Time,' he said. 'Mother, I'll see you Thursday.'

Alvena held up a staying finger, popping inside.

Dan rose. 'I'll go with you.'

Alvena returned with a wrinkled brown sack, shovelling in small, dark, dried apricots. 'Here,' she said to Raymond.

As soon as trees hid them, Raymond took from his pocket a handful of Hershey kisses. He offered them to Dan. Dan refused. Raymond peeled foil. 'What's the land worth?' he asked.

'Maybe a quarter of a million.'

'I'd've guessed more.' Raymond popped chocolate into his mouth.

'It's so improbable she'll sell, I haven't checked it out.'

'What sort of shopping centre? A market?'

'And a few other shops.'

'It's an excellent location,' Raymond said. He stopped walking, gazing up at green leaves, smiling as if he saw something infinitely more pleasant than moving patterns of leaves against blue sky. Then he pushed aside a knobby manzanita branch, and they emerged on the street. Behind Dan's Jaguar was parked a dusty grey Ford with a plastic hula girl in the rear window.

Raymond patted Dan's silver paint job. 'A lot of horses,' he said. 'Did Mother mention both her parents died of cancer?'

'They did?'

'Grandmother Bollenbacker died of lung cancer just a year after I was born. And Grandfather died before that. Two years – no, it was three. Cancer of the throat. They left her this land. She nursed them.'

'Which makes this health mania a lot more understandable.'

Raymond sighed a little too dolefully. 'She worries about me.'

'She did mention you had haemorrhoids.'

For the first time Raymond met Dan's gaze. A fine gloss of sweat shone on the fat little man's shaved upper lip.

'Maybe I can help,' he said.

Raymond Earle made Dan itch: there had been his

odd, cosy pause, there were his peculiar eyes. But this was the first progress Dan had made. And he surged with energy to possess this tree-shaded acreage. He needed it. Beverly and he needed it. This land was tangled up with their happiness.

He extricated a card from his wallet. 'Call me,' he said to Raymond. 'We'll have lunch. Talk.'

5

The month that Beverly's divorce became final, she had trouble sleeping. This was different from the insomnia that had troubled her a year earlier, during her futile battle to stay married to Philip. Then she had spent her wakeful nights like a test animal strapped to the table, unable to pass out despite the pain of the operation. Now she would doze immediately, only to waken in minutes, eyes open, muscles tensed. Terrified. Each night she would consider asking Dan to sleep over, then she would think, 'The children.'

On this particular May night – about a week before the wedding – she jolted awake as if hit by an electrical charge, her mind alert, hopping with guilts of every variety. She stared into darkness. And saw, as she often saw, victims of the divorce lined up to accuse her. DeeDee Grossblatt (diamonds and lacquered black hair), whom she'd met only once. Michael and Vic, Dan's adopted little boys, one fat and the other skinny, both now in therapy. Then her parents, eyes dismayed, mouths pursed disapprovingly. Philip wearing his sailing jacket, his face lifted into a superior expression, picking up his children. A Sunday father. And most clearly of all, she saw her son and daughter. Sunday children. Jamie, thin arms awkwardly at his sides. Alix, fixed up to see her father with a full hour's care – and she wasn't yet twelve!

Beverly's hands were icy. She lay in dark silence and found herself composing a liturgical prayer: 'Forgive me for my selfishness. Forgive me for causing unhappiness. Forgive me for ruining lives. Forgive me for indulging myself. Forgive me for being a rotten mother. How can You forgive me when I can't forgive myself?'

Pulling on her old flowered Viyella robe, she went into the hall, which was lit. Both children slept with their doors ajar. She paused at Jamie's room. Her pupils adjusted to the dimness, and she saw him sleeping on his left side, his gangly right arm flung over his forehead. She smiled, a gentle, unconscious smile. Only in dark night moments like these could Beverly admit the unusual quality of her love for her son. Sometimes the depth of this love frightened her. Yet she could not deny it. If a coat of many colours were in style, she would have dressed Jamie in one.

Slowly she walked to Alix's room. She heard the faint, asthmatic whistle. My fault, she thought. It did not enter Beverly's head that Alix had had asthma since babyhood, simply that she was suffering now and therefore it must come as a result of the divorce. Each stentorian breath reminded Beverly of her guilt. She peered through dimness at the head raised on pillows and haloed with huge, purple aluminium rollers. Awake, Alix's mouth and dark eyes were tilted with eager charm. In sleep, a sadness relaxed the open lips. Alix looked her age. Or less. A child. A lovely, deserted child. Beverly sighed.

But say you could go back to before, would you?

No.

Even though leaving Philip has brought much misery?

With Dan I no longer feel that terrible loneliness.

Ahh. A high-minded cause.

I'm not high-minded. I just seem to act. I can't help myself.

Then each time one of them – Alix, Jamie, and yes, Philip, too – suffers, you will suffer.

I know. That's what guilt does.

And while hearing this interior voice – her conscience –

Beverly also was thinking with acute pleasure that in nine days she and Dan would be married. She hugged her arms over her small, pretty breasts. About the marriage she could feel no remorse, only an inexcusable joy. She was happy with Dan, in and out of bed. All his traits, even that bellicosity, delighted her. His warmth, his energy, his openness – she couldn't begin to enumerate his good qualities.

I have a right to happiness.

You do? Even if it brings the reverse on others?

Alix gave a groan. Beverly hurried to the bed, stooping anxiously over her daughter until the breathing eased. Her weary amber eyes were desolate.

They were married in Rabbi Jacobson's office with their immediate families present. The wedding dinner at the Garden Room of the Bel Air Hotel, paid for and planned by Dan, was noisy, lavish, including every age from Dan's ninety-three-year-old, balding Aunt Channa (he supported her), out-of-town relations, in-town friends, and guests of their four children.

Beverly hadn't seen Caroline and Gene Matheny in a couple of years, but whom do you invite to your wedding if not your (once) best friend?

'Dan?' Beverly kept her arm around Dan's waist. 'Remember Gene?'

'Matheny,' Gene prompted. 'We met at –'

'That damn Christmas party. Don't remind me. Is it Professor Matheny now?'

Gene accepted a cheese puff from a waiter. 'As a matter of fact, no.'

'People change,' Caroline said somewhat haughtily. She and Em often speculated how Beverly could ditch a gorgeous man like Philip for one so brash. She waved away the hors d'oeuvres. She had dieted down to rosy cheeks and handsome bones. Her scarlet chiffon was size 8, a Dior, and on her finger glittered the twelve-carat mine-cut diamond she'd inherited from her grandmother.

'I've been with Van Vliet's almost twelve years,' Gene

said. 'I'm treasurer.'

'Some shrink.' Dan grinned at Caroline, then turned back to Gene. 'Some grow.'

Gene couldn't help laughing. He'd lost some hair and gained glasses. 'It's phenomenal how my in-laws recognize true talent.'

'You've given *blood*!' Caroline cried.

'Dan, take care of our friend,' Gene said, leaning forward, kissing the bride, who gave him her champagne-scented mouth without relinquishing her hold on her husband.

When, two weeks later, Dan received the call from Gene, he wasn't surprised.

'I'd like to know a bit about tax shelters,' Gene said. The last two words stumbled over themselves. Dan made an educated guess that Gene, having contracted an early marriage with the socialist ideal, was battling his compunctions: taxation should equalize. Infidelity would not come easily. Dan bit on his cigar, thinking. Gene would be more at ease – more likely to invest in the Orange County acreage – without wives who knew him when. Dan said, 'How about breakfast sometime next week?'

It took four breakfasts for Gene to commit himself, but when he did, he took a larger hunk than Dan had guessed he would. By then the two were friends. Gene's affection was heightened by Dan's open Jewishness, Dan's warmth came despite Gene's (lapsed) Episcopalianism.

One unseasonably overcast morning at the end of July, Gene opened the door of Victory Enterprises. Behind the reception desk sat an excellently made-up divorcée in her late twenties: her hair puffed into a vanilla scoop, she looked like the belle of a singles apartment building.

'Hi there, Mr Matheny.' She smiled.

Gene returned the smile. 'Hello, Georgia.'

He coveted Dan Grossblatt's secretary, but without the edge of lust – Gene, having a good deal of the ascetic in him, did not permit himself to conjecture on any other than the good-natured delights offered by Caroline. Two years earlier, however, he had been promoted from a district manager to treasurer, removing to a carpeted suite in Van Vliet's home office. Standing in the doorway, his chest had swollen with pride. Pinch me, he'd thought, and I'll wake up. At the same time Gene had been baffled by a question: Why was a self-proclaimed one-of-the-little-people so bedazzled by his entry into the upper echelon of management? To shreve himself, he hired as his secretary an efficient, elderly Mexican. Ernestina Saenz's left eyelid drooped, and an almost visible racial chip rested on one squashy shoulder. Gene came to accept his offices as a place to work. He never considered firing his secretary – however antagonistic she might be. This oblation to his early god benefited him. Caroline's uncles, Hend and Richard, would shake their heads, one or the other saying, 'You've got to hand it to Gene. He's the only practising liberal around. Listen, why not let him deal with those labour bastards? One look at this Saenz woman should end any squawks with Fair Employment.' Gene's role was considerably larger and more influential than that of any preceding treasurer.

Georgia touched a pale frond of bangs. Her smile had turned questioning.

'Mr Grossblatt has some papers for me to sign,' Gene said. 'Should I go in?'

'He's in conference. If you'll wait one second, I'll –'

Dan's office door burst open. There Dan stood, one arm around the grey-seersucker shoulder of a fat little man. Dan blazed with unsuppressed excitement. His broad features mobile, his eyes glittering, he introduced Raymond Earle.

Raymond Earle took Gene's extended hand. 'Mr Matheny. Are you connected with Victory Enterprises?'

'Only as an investor,' Gene replied.

Raymond Earle smiled into the distance. Gene shivered. The air conditioner, he decided, was too low.

Raymond Earle said, 'Mr Grossblatt –'

'Dan.'

'Dan. Mother's expecting you tomorrow. At nine.'

'Don't worry. I'll be there with the papers.'

They exchanged farewells. In his office, Dan gestured for Gene to sit, but he himself kept pacing. Dan always had surplus vitality. Today he seemed buoyed by helium. No. Gene remembered his writing days. Be specific. Dan is buoyed by laughing gas. Dan was smiling at the skeleton high-rise going up across Wilshire, rapping his knuckles on the window in time to the hollow clang of a steel-worker. Dan, having a kind of interior exultation.

'Who was that?' Gene inquired finally.

'I introduced you. Raymond Earle.'

'I don't like him.'

'A red-hot liberal prejudging?'

'Once in a while, Dan, the flesh is weak.'

'He won't look you in the eye.'

'He's strange. Creepy.'

'It's the eyes, that's all.'

'I suppose,' Gene said uncertainly.

'His mother's selling me her acreage in the Valley. Prime stuff, right off the freeway.' Dan bounced to teak shelves, filled with awards and trophies, straightening a large silver bowl engraved that Dan Grossblatt was friend to the Big Brothers. 'He talked her into it.'

'How?'

Dan shrugged. 'Probably gave her some line he needed the cash to save his life. She's a health nut.'

'That's pretty low.'

Red exploded on Dan's cheeks. 'Listen, I should ask what he told her? I should interfere? The fat little turd wants her to sell. And I'm the only buyer she'll deal with.'

After a minute, Gene-the-treasurer asked, 'Did you get it at a good price?'

'Half what it's worth!' Dan replied pugnaciously, then he melted. 'Gene, get your ass out of that sling. Take a look.' He was unrolling plans, using heavy ashtrays and paperweights to keep blue drawings flat. The two men stood over the desk, Dan's forefinger moving a vigorous guided tour. 'This is tentative. One thing's for sure, though. Everything under one roof. Like the idea?'

'You've hooked me. When can I put in?'

'No investors.'

'Dan, don't play with me. I'm sold.'

'I'm not giving you a line.'

'But this is big. Can you handle it?'

'Who could?' Dan rolled up plans, snapping elastic around them. 'I'm going into hock. Way over my head.' He handed Gene the Orange County agreement in triplicate. 'Here,' he said.

Gene sat down, pushing up his glasses, reading.

'It's kosher.'

'I always read before I sign.'

'You're a cautious man, Gene.'

And Dan took a cigar from his humidor, prowling the grass-papered office as he lit up. Gene finished reading. With each signature, Dan impatiently removed the stapled form.

'That wraps it up. My last investor in my last syndication.'

'What?'

'After this mall, I'm retiring.'

Gene couldn't prevent a smile. 'To play golf?'

'The way I do business, you need to entertain. And let's face it, entertaining's not Beverly's forte. You might say she stinks.'

Gene considered Beverly's fragile bone structure elegant. Her eyes, to him, held a deep, mysterious sadness which he connected with artistic sensitivity. Mostly, though, he respected her. While he didn't think much of her overpink pastels or those watered-down Chagall oils, he did admire her for scrimping out a year of West Los Angeles livelihood from them. She had borne aloft the banner of art that years ago he'd found too heavy to lift.

'You really can be a prick, Dan.'

Dan, scrawling his name under Gene's, glanced up. 'What?'

'She's a painter, not a housewife.'

'That's news? Gene, why do you think this mall is such a big deal? You know we fouled up once. I'm not going to let it happen again.'

'You're going to alter your entire business?'

'Tell me what else I can do? Yeah, I'm getting out.'

'But –'

'The mall'll bring in plenty. Okay, so maybe I put together an occasional deal, but it'll be gravy, not a living. She won't have to do a thing.' He scribbled his final signature. 'The damn thing should be up already! I hate like hell having her push herself when she should be taking it easy.' He stopped, actually blushing. 'Oh hell. Gene, don't tell anyone. And that means your wife. It's not due until the middle of February. We just found out.'

A baby? To Gene's surprise, his vision blurred and Dan was one huge, shimmering grin. A baby? When Cricket, his daughter, his beloved only child, was four, Caroline had had a pelvic inflammation that made it impossible for her to conceive again. Gene, experiencing a jab of envy, resisted a crazy impulse to embrace his friend, instead making a fist and lightly punching the smooth Italian silk over Dan's biceps.

'Hey, congratulations.'

Dan was still beaming. 'Gene, come to the house for lunch. That is, if you don't object to burned cheese sandwiches and instant coffee.'

'Isn't Beverly working?'

'Why do you think I go home? She forgets to eat. Come on.'

Gene hesitated. 'I'll be intruding.'

'Charge it to business. We'll talk about the Van Vliet's lease.'

'Locations aren't my department.'

'For a technicality you're going to pass this up?'

Gene had to laugh. 'You're one domineering man,' he said.

'Somebody has to goose the world,' Dan said, propelling Gene through the door.

Dan could get 80 per cent financing. He sold off four parcels. If he'd waited he could've got more, but the profit was there and no investor squawked. He borrowed on his life insurance, he borrowed on the boys' trusts, he even borrowed on his S&G stock, he borrowed and borrowed. 'You realize you're taking an insane gamble?' inquired his accountant. 'Once I pull it off, you'll call it vision.' 'Okay, Dan, you're in over your head. But a quarter of a million on a house? Now?' Dan, not a man to live in his predecessor's home, was building north of Sunset in Beverly Hills. 'Fuck off my business. And you say one word to Beverly, I'll kill you.'

So Beverly disliked the house plans for the eight bathrooms, the sunken master tub with Jacuzzi, the two ornamental pools in the enclosed entry, rather than the strain the bills were putting on Dan's blood pressure. She knew Dan was working too hard, but Dan in motion was an irresistible force. Right now he was wooing prospective tenants with the same restaurant chumminess he'd pursued investors.

As often as possible they ate at home. Alix and Jamie would go to their rooms, she would turn on the Gas Company's Evening Concert – low, Dan wasn't wild for classical – and lie on the couch, her bare feet on his lap, while he went over the mall figures. Occasionally he would smile at her.

'D'you think it'll be a boy?' she'd asked.

'Or a girl,' he would agree.

'I can't see you with a girl.'

'Why not?'

'Oh, I don't know. Too masculine, I guess.'

'Buzz, I'll be the strictest old man in town.'

They would smile at one another. Camellia branches would rustle at leaded glass windows, and although there is no working definition of happiness, Beverly knew she was as close to it as any human can get.

She miscarried.

One rainy night in September Dan sped her eastwards to Cedars of Lebanon. Her hands clenched. Punishment, she thought. A sudden cloudburst slashed on the windshield, and Dan was forced to take his arm from around her. The moans, ahh, ahh, ahh, weren't part of her. Punishment, she thought.

A painful miscarriage. She recovered slowly.

6

In the 17 March, 1963, Sunday real-estate section of the *Los Angeles Times*:

MALL TO RISE IN SAN FERNANDO VALLEY

Final plans have been announced for construction of a 550,000-square-foot $15-million shopping centre fronting on Ventura between Cornice and Avianca roads. The 20.5 acres, adjacent to the Ventura Freeway, is said to be worth in excess of $3 million. The shopping centre will be completely enclosed. It is a project of Victory Enterprises and its financial partner, Encino Mutual Savings and Loan.

Dan R. Grossblatt, president of Victory Enterprises, says it is the first such facility on the West Coast. The complex will include a climate monitor – a central computer which collects information on air conditioning, ventilation, and heating – an indoor skating rink, a motion picture theatre, a children's amusement park, a Van Vliet's market, and a Best Western motel facility.

'Bullock's, Broadway, and Montgomery Ward already have signed leases. We have parking for 1,400

cars,' Grossblatt said.

'*This self-contained environment will offer a unique experience to Southland shoppers. We have plans for a health spa and a sidewalk café, a Japanese garden with teahouse, as well as five other restaurants.'*

Completion is scheduled for January 1964.

This Sunday the phones in the new house never stopped ringing. Everyone, it seemed, had read the article and wished to offer congratulations and good wishes. Quite a few offered, 'I've got some spare cash, Danny boy.'

7

The following Monday Jamie had a cold.

He stayed at home. Happily. The move to Beverly Hills had caused Alix no pain. Jamie, though, lacked her social ease. He was New Kid in a different school system. Not that he was picked on. No. He was ignored. He walked invisible through locker-clanging corridors and noisy playgrounds. In gym, when teams were picked, he was overlooked. No teacher called on him, yet he feared the eventuality. What if his voice made no sound? He began to be obsessed with the idea that he didn't exist during school hours – but if he didn't, where was he?

Naturally he never told any of this to Beverly. Naturally, she understood.

He lounged in the sunny, over-equipped kitchen, quartering oranges (good for a cold), reading the sports news, scratching Boris's velvet ears, making tacos. His full, juicy sneezes gave him satisfaction. Around ten that morning he visited Beverly.

Her studio was reached by steps from the kitchen: the architect had incorporated in it all his splendours. Plastic bubble skylights, elaborate storage, a dais for her easel, a marble counter to set up still lifes. Currently on deck, one aphid-infested rose in an Adohr milk bottle. She frowned, using her brush to get to the heart of a rose. Jamie found pastels in one drawer, some rice paper in another. Boris began circling restlessly, giving small yips. Jamie let him out of the back door. The beagle disappeared, Magellan in the many dustbinned alleys of Beverly Hills.

Jamie returned, snuffling into his handkerchief.

'Do you believe in God?' he asked.

His mother looked away from the rose. They'd gone into the matter often. 'Yes. Or Something. I'm not sure what, there's too many definitions. But how could a rose grow?'

'Nature?'

'That's just another definition. People worship nature.'

'I guess most people have Something.'

'Want to go to Sunday school with Michael and Vic?' (Each Sunday morning at eight-thirty, Dan picked up his sons, driving them to temple.)

'That's not what I meant,' he said hastily. He was worried about what would happen when he turned thirteen. Dan was very big on him having a bar mitzvah. His own father was half-Jewish and answered in a funny, stiff voice if you even mentioned religion. After a minute Jamie said, 'I wish I were a bird.'

Beverly wiped her brush. 'Any particular sort?'

'No.'

'Why a bird?'

'I'd fly in the cool air just below the clouds and see everything.'

'I wonder what their eyes do see.'

'Everything,' he said. 'Did you know the diving petrel can fly underwater?'

'Really?'

'I read,' he said. Picking a dark-green chalk, he knelt over rice paper.

After about fifteen minutes, he sat up, mopping his nose. 'Doesn't it get boring?'

'Not for me.'

His eyes questioned her.

'I must have a high boredom threshold,' she said.

'You're good.'

She shook her head. 'No. Maybe that's why I'm not bored. I'm trying to get decent.'

'People buy your stuff.'

'The pastels.'

'Sometimes the other,' he said.

They often talked like this, desultory remarks, maybe picked up later, maybe dropped. It was easy, nothing. But rare.

Jamie turned on his transistor. 'Listen,' he said. 'It's an oldie.'

A nasal voice inquired of a dead teenager, possibly in heaven, if the singer were still beloved.

'Like it?' Jamie asked.

'It's not Cole Porter.'

'Who?'

'Before your time.'

After a while, he wandered away.

After a longer while, someone rang the front doorbell.

Beverly didn't hear. She was deaf to everything. The rose was stubborn about yielding up its aphid-infected heart.

She unscrewed the canvas, turning it upside down to criticize colour and balance. Rotating her shoulders, she squinted. The thalo violet patch in the lower right corner, she decided, should be knocked down. A faraway lawn mower roared. On the marble counter Jamie had left her a sandwich. She ate whole-wheat bread and canned salmon full of mayonnaise, running her tongue over her teeth. A fish taste lingered. I'll clean my brushes later, she thought, and went for milk. Piled on the big kitchen table were yesterday's real-estate sections, six of them, topped by Jamie's transistor grunting out music. A waste of batteries. The sixty-five cents for new ones came from the dollar allowance that Philip gave him each Sunday. With her thumb she twisted the serrated edge of the dial, cutting off a long-drawn-out 'Ugggh'.

'Jamie,' she called.

'Jamie!' she tried again.

Taking the radio, she clattered across terrazzo. Her thongs on the hard surface sounded tropical and slatternly, making her think of magnificent golden trollops wearing only mules, then of the naked freedom of *Olympia,* then the free clarity of Winslow Homer's –

Her feet stopped moving.

Jamie's radio fell. Inside the leatherette case, plastic shattered.

She heard a loud gagging.

All warmth receded. She was ice. The dead dwarf suns of a frozen galaxy were warm compared to her. Ice petrified her blood. Each time she remembered this moment, she would experience this barren, awesome chill. Through the open front door coiled a strand of birdsong. Sunlight jounced from the mezuzah that Dan, two months ago, had nailed to the oversize doorjamb, pronouncing: *'Blessed art Thou ... accept in mercy and favour the prayer of Thy children who gather to dedicate this dwelling and to offer their thanksgiving ...'*

Jamie lay, left side down, one skinny, pale leg twisted under him, a pastel smudge on his right hand. A streak of watery pink drained down his tallow white cheek, a meagre trickle that somehow worried her more than the rich blood soaking his hair. Red streaks pointed across terrazzo. Flies buzzed.

Punishment, she thought.

Philip, what have I done?

In that same instant she was kneeling beside her son, pressing her fingers under his Black Watch robe. The heart was beating. It was beating.

'Jamie,' she said sharply, as if she were angry.

A fly landed on his head, and automatically she flicked. Never move an injured person. Her thoughts skittered frantically. Didn't they say never move an injured person? But didn't they say ambulances could take an hour? Who are they? Jamie's fingers were relaxed, as if he were asleep.

Squatting, she picked him up, not noticing his weight, her only struggle was his limpness. His robe tie fell. He wore shorts. So thin. He. Kicking off her thongs so she wouldn't trip, she lugged him to her car, heaving him onto the front seat: his arms and legs sprawled, and she arranged them, sitting behind the wheel, propping his head against her thigh before she realized she didn't have her keys.

She ran inside, swerving around her thongs and the broken radio, slipping on red, balancing herself before she fell. Where was her bag? Where? When Jamie was two he'd fallen on a Venetian glass ashtray – Philip had held him while the doctor picked out slivered aquamarine with tweezers. Yanking open drawers. Shoving aside books at her bedside, books thumping onto deep white carpet. Where? Idiot! The duplicate is in the desk.

The accelerator resisted her bare sole.

She didn't pause at boulevard stops. An Edsel squealed to a halt, an old man shouted. The fingers of her left hand, some paint-smeared, some clean, gripped the steering wheel. Her right hand spread on Jamie's rib cage. My son, begotten on me by my enemy. The heart, the heart still beats. Her foot pressed to the floorboards. She was unaware of the red brake-warning light, she didn't smell burning rubber. At the Emergency entrance she lifted Jamie, then a man in a green tunic came swiftly at her, taking him, laying him on a gurney. The ice chill had shape now, but she couldn't define it. The stretcher tyres made a *heinie minoosh, heinie minoosh*, the sound once heard in trains, and a nurse called, 'I need information.'

Doors swung shut on the stretcher.

The nurse, separated by windowed counter, mouthed questions. She had a profile like a trout.

A young doctor, an intern or resident, stethoscope in his pocket, came in, leaning towards the nurse. His hair was thin and blond, and he frightened Beverly. After a minute she understood why. He reminded her of Lloyd Rawlings. She had treated Lloyd shabbily by not loving (and levelling with) him. She grew limp with irrational terror. She had been so very callous – would this in some manner harm Jamie? The doctor whispered, the nurse whispered, and Beverly, trying to eavesdrop, caught a word here and there ... Surgery ... Critical ... Massive ...

'Mrs Grossblatt,' the nurse said loudly. 'This is Dr Erland.'

'Is Jamie conscious yet?' she asked.

Dr Erland shifted in his rubber-soled white shoes. 'The surgeon'll tell you. Louis Sherman.'

'Why didn't you say Sherman was here?' the nurse asked.

'Scrubbing. We're in luck.'

'Can I see him now, Jamie, before he goes into Surgery?'

'He's in now.' Dr Erland pressed two professional fingers to her inner wrist, staring at his watch. 'You'd better lie down.'

'I have to call my daughter!' How could I have forgotten Alix? She must be home by now. Alone, home, alone.

'What's your number?'

'Crestview six – No! I have to tell her.'

'All right, all right.' Despite the thinning hair, he looked young and embarrassed. 'But you'll have to use the public phones. Regulations.'

'I didn't bring my purse!'

'Calm down,' he said. 'Doctor's orders.' And fishing under his white jacket, he came up with thirty cents.

She didn't know what she said to Alix.

Alix said to her, 'Mother, cool it. I'm fine, fine. Listen, will you feel better if I'm at Melanie Cohn's? I was going to show her my new pink sweater, anyway. You look after Jamie. Mommy, he is all right, isn't he?'

Dan was out, Georgie told her, but she would do her bestest to locate him. Georgie emphasized by *est*s and *ly*s.

Dialling Philip, Beverly remembered when she'd last been in a hospital – September, she'd miscarried. Dan's son, in embryo. Dead. Now she was in a hospital with

131

Philip's son. She began to shake. Philip's secretary put her right through.

'Where can I find Mrs Dan Grossblatt?' The man in the rumpled grey suit stood at the desk.

'I'm Mrs Grossblatt,' Beverly said. Plastic upholstery had stuck to her thighs, and as she rose, her flesh made a ripping sound.

The man introduced himself. Roehl of the Beverly Hills police. He questioned her. The wrinkles in his terra-cotta face might have been carved with a chisel. She answered him. A lot of times.

He was asking. 'But you didn't hear the bell?'

'No.'

'The boy must have. He went to the front door.'

'Maybe to let in Boris – his dog.'

'You're sure you didn't hear anything?'

'It could've rung. I paint and sometimes I can get pretty involved.'

'Any idea how long he'd been there?'

'Flies were around.' She shivered.

Who, she kept wondering, had reported the accident? Her fingers clenched. She couldn't bring herself to ask. Roehl frightened her. Weren't police a symptom of mysterious perils, the violence beneath surface calm, like that strange pale blood seeping from Jamie's ear?

After the detective left, she again forced herself to the desk. 'Have you heard about Jamie Schorer?' she asked the nurse.

'As soon as we get word, we pass it on.'

A breeze sucked through the stale hospital air. Glass doors to the car park swung shut. 'Philip,' she called. Everyone in the long room turned.

Philip. White shirt, white teeth, and tan. Handsome under pitiless fluorescent lighting. One of those good-life sailing commercials.

He walked towards her easily, as if he was wearing his deck shoes, which he wasn't.

'I got here as soon as I could.'

She looked up at her former husband, again experiencing that familiar feeling, close to hypocrisy, that she'd felt with him during their marriage. (After the divorce culpability had been added.) His dark eyes filmed over. For the first time she realized she was barefoot, in faded Bermudas, and her thigh was bloodstained.

'How's Jamie?'

'They're operating now,' she said.

Philip went to the trout-faced reception nurse. 'Can you tell me James Schorer's condition?'

Eyes admiring. But the same canned message. 'As soon as we get word, we pass it on.'

'I'd appreciate that,' Philip said with a hint of sarcasm. 'Do you have a towel?'

The nurse held out a box of Kleenex. Philip wet several at the fountain, and Beverly scrubbed. Tissue wadded. Scraps clung to her thigh.

'There was so much blood. Oh Philip –'

He cut in hastily, 'Where's Alix?'

'At a neighbour's.'

'Why not check that she's all right?'

Obedient, Beverly walked through crowded corridors to the phones. Inside a booth she realized she didn't know the name of Melanie Cohn's father, and besides she had no dime. The booth door muted clatter. And she heard her own voice. 'Please, it's not fair to punish him for me.' She rested her head on the black box, mumbling, *Shema Ysroel, Adonai elohenu, Adonai echod.* (As much Hebrew as she'd learned as Mrs Grossblatt.) 'Please let him be all right, please, please, please.' If He hadn't helped those others, why should He help Jamie? *Shema Ysroel –*

The door shuddered. The tiny booth filled with rapping blows. Dan. The folding door creaked as he pushed. Beverly's knee got in the way and the door stuck halfway, at the point the light turned off. 'He told me you were here,' Dan said.

She got up. Dan put his arms around her, and half inside the dark booth, she wept into his shoulder. 'Buzz, it's okay, okay.' 'You're so warm,' she gasped. 'Want my jacket?' 'He was lying there, blood all over.' 'Tell me,' he said. And with him still holding her, people moving around them, she managed to, almost coherently.

'And now?'

'He's in Surgery.'

'And?'

'Nobody knows.'

'Somebody knows.'

'The nurse, she told me the operation takes a long time.'

The wide planes of Dan's face were taut.

'The intern said the surgeon's good,' she added.

Dan moved back, staring at her. 'And that's all either of you found out?' he asked. 'Come on.'

In a corner of the waiting-room two young doctors were leaning towards one another, talking through moving cobwebs of cigarette smoke. The nurse clicked on her typewriter. Dan stood at the counter. The typing continued. He rapped on the glass divider. She looked up.

'What's the word on Jamie Schorer?'

'Nothing as yet,' she said, and went back to her typing.

'When did you check?'

'They'll send word –'

'Don't give me that!'

'– as soon as they're finished.'

'My question was when you checked.'

The nurse raised her non-existent chin. 'I told Mr Schorer and Mrs' – she consulted her chart – 'Grossblatt that when –'

'*I*'m asking.'

'I'm sorry,' she answered, her tone implying the opposite.

'Call Surgery.'

The interns had stopped talking and were watching.

'I can't do that,' the nurse said.

'It's easy. Pick up the phone.'

'That's impossible.'

'Look, I asked you not to give me crap.'

'Mr –'

'Grossblatt. Be a good girl. Call.'

Now everyone was watching. Beverly felt a sick jab of embarrassment. But how could she suffer from the world now? Now? Why this sense of alien humiliation now? She heard herself say anxiously, 'Dan, she can't.'

Neither Dan nor the nurse paid attention.

The nurse was saying, 'It's against hospital regulations.'

'So call Dr Abrams.'

The interns glanced at one another, and the taller stubbed out his cigarette reverently, as if Dan had invoked the presence of the Almighty into the waiting-room.

The nurse said, 'Dr Abrams is unavailable.'

'To me he's always available.'

'It's after five. I doubt if he's here.'

'Try. If you can't get him, I'll give you his home phone.'

The nurse blinked, her first betrayal of weakness.

'Tell him it's Dan Grossblatt. I promise, he won't send you back to washing bedpans.'

For a cushioning moment there was silence. Then the nurse expelled a sigh, her mouth ajar, for all the world looking as if she were surrendering to the hook. She plugged in the switchboard, asking someone named Dolores to connect her with The Chief.

Beverly watched Philip's hand arching on green plastic. Long-fingered, smooth, apparently tendonless – Jamie had his hands.

'Dave, Dan Grossblatt here ... Yes ... Not so good. I'm downstairs in Emergency ... My wife's boy, and we can't find out one damn thing ... James Schorer ... I'd appreciate that, Dave.' And holding the receiver against his shoulder, Dan asked the nurse about her typewriter, a new IBM. The nurse, alert and smiling, said she really loved it.

Beverly's hand inched towards Philip's hand. He jerked away.

Dan was talking. 'Thanks, Dave ... Yes ... At least that's good ... Yeah, for lunch.' He handed the nurse back the phone, turning to the couch where Beverly and Philip sat. 'He's in Recovery. A neuro-surgeon happened to be here when you brought him in. Sherman. He's tops. Be down any minute.'

The neuro-surgeon, freckled features blurred with weariness, spoke in medical jargon much as a lapsed priest might use a dead language to cover lack of faith. 'Now in English,' Dan said. The doctor explained the skull is a bowl. A heavy blunt instrument had crashed into this particular bowl, causing a break: splinters had to be removed from the mass. (That's not oatmeal you're talking about, Beverly thought.)

'Well?' Dan asked.

'He's on the critical list,' said the surgeon, looking even more weary.

'When will he be off?' Philip asked.

'We may not know for several weeks.'

Dan said not to stick Jamie in that noisy children's pavilion, put him on Three. The surgeon nodded. 'Private nurses,' Philip said. The doctor's red-veined eye surveyed them (fat fee), then gazed through glass doors at darkening skies (an hour's nap before dinner), saying, 'Why don't you good people rest?'

'Here,' Beverly said, sitting back down to prove she meant business.

'There's nothing you can do here.' The doctor.

'You'll come home and put on shoes.' Dan. 'Later, we'll be back.' He took her arm.

As she and Dan moved across the car park, lights came on. He said, 'Come in my car. Would he have sat all night, so polite and chicken, never finding out one damn thing?'

'No, but –'

'So I embarrassed him. I embarrassed you? Well, I've given a hell of a lot to this hospital. Time and money. Dave Abrams is hoping for more.' Rough pebbles hurt her bare soles and she lagged. Dan slowed, taking her hand. 'Dave invested with me. He did better than with any of his other deals. So he thinks I did him a fat favour.' In the car, she gazed at the single shining star. 'Buzz, they treat you differently if they know you. You get a better room, the supervisor visits, the nurses run their asses off for you – for Jamie.'

Home, he walked two houses north to the Cohns', arranging for Alix to spend the night, he phoned the Lindes, phoned Clara (his and DeeDee's old cook) to come in the next morning. Beverly, to her husband's occasional anger, refused full-time help. When Beverly got out of the shower, he was in the bedroom with two chocolate-covered grahams and a cup drooping a yellow Lipton label. The sloshing, milky tea brought tears to her eyes. Dan refused to have anything to do with the kitchen. Eating in the breakfast area was a major concession for him.

She sat on the bed, drinking and nibbling. 'We were talking this morning, and he asked if I believed in God. Dan, do I?'

Dan sat next to her. 'Yes,' he said.

'But He let those others die?' She had read Camus.

Dan had not. 'Buzz, He's the only Game in town.'

She reached for the wide, warm hand, tugging till Dan lay next to her. She unknotted his tie and undid his shirt, kissing the warm, coarse-haired skin below his neck where the golfer's tan stopped.

He said, 'You'll hate yourself if we do.'

She unzipped her robe. Dampness from her shower patched the white body. She rolled onto her side and her breasts touched.

'You'll hate me,' he said.

'I couldn't hate you. Never.'

'Never say never.' He rested his fingers between her breasts.

'You had pickles for lunch.'

'They're too small,' he whispered, his fingers rubbing gently. 'I'm crazy about them.'

'Dan, help me.'

He helped her.

Chapter Six

I

The following morning in the hospital lobby she bumped into Philip. He was on his way to work, he said, and he'd seen Jamie, yes, the same, and he was glad they had met. He wanted to talk to her. A cup of coffee? They went downstairs to the cafeteria.

'Beverly,' Philip said, wiping the table with two paper napkins, 'a man called Roehl was here ten minutes ago.'

'Roehl's the one who talked to me.'

'Did he ask about enemies?'

She shook her head, mystified.

'He did me. They assume it's a grudge.'

'Then they know what happened.'

'They're just fishing for motives.'

'They must know something!'

'Not yet.'

'But you said –'

'I said they're assuming, that's all.'

'*All?*'

'Beverly, let's stay rational.'

She took a calming sip of the bitter coffee. Staying rational was Philip's goal. He had much of the paraphernalia of a superior husband; he'd never been finical about food, never had made a fuss when she painted (Dan could get impatient), he had taught her to enjoy his beloved sailing, and if he had glanced at his reflection in store windows, this had been a minor vanity that she had found understandable, even endearing. Yet it was *Let's stay rational* that she remembered most of her marriage to Philip. She had realized that logic was the club Philip brandished like a Neanderthal weapon to ward away confusion. (Was he Jew? Gentile? Neither?) Knowing this, though, had not made Philip's voice of pure reason any easier to bear. She put down her cup.

'How's Alix taking it?' Philip asked.

'Fine, just fine. She came home to change. She's wearing that new skirt you got her.'

'I want her with me for a few days.'

'This weekend?'

'Today.'

'But she'll miss school.'

'Her grades are fine. It won't matter.'

'Why? Philip, why?'

'Until we know what happened,' he said.

'Do you think I have enemies? Dan has enemies?'

'Beverly, please.' He creamed his coffee. 'Mother will stay at my place with her.'

A membrane filled her throat. She swallowed with difficulty.

'It doesn't have to be with me. Would you feel better if she goes to Mother L's?'

'Oh God. I'll be so careful.'

'Do you honestly think she should stay in that house?'

'Yes. Yes!'

'You wanted the divorce.' The vein at Philip's temple pulsed. 'Beverly, I didn't make it difficult for you. I could have. But let's not forget the children are mine. Alix is mine.'

Beverly's eyes squeezed shut. An old delivery van had smashed her in the rear, throwing her against the windshield, bruising her face, giving her a black eye, and Philip had come home early from Schorer Furniture. Oh God, Bev, are you all right? Yes, she'd said, yes, her arms tight around his waist, and they, so very young, certainly not knowing of the covenant between parent and child, had fallen to the couch, and Philip, who normally inquired about that hateful thing, had been feeling her body as if it were precious to him, at the ultimate moment calling, Bev, oh Bev.

She opened her eyes and said, 'I'll call Mother.'

The next nine days Beverly spent in the third-floor waiting room. Dan would phone often, and a nurse would run to get her. He ordered full-course meals sent up from the coffee shop, meals that she dutifully picked at. He would pop in a couple of times a day.

Each evening Philip came with Vilma Schorer. The Lindes drove in from Glendale. Through long hours the six of them kept awkward vigil, each in his own manner worrying about Jamie.

Jamie, in his wonderful trellis of bottles, machines, and jars. Jamie, unconscious. Alive.

2

On the tenth morning Roehl came to Dan's office.

After Roehl had finished with him, Dan drove to the hospital, telling the gap-tooth floor nurse he needed to talk undisturbed to his wife. She let him use 310, which was empty and pervaded with the odour of Lysol.

'It's Jamie,' Beverly whispered. 'Dr Sherman's told you something.'

He shook his head, wishing he never had to begin. Dan. A stocky man with driving ability to push people. Yet he never used this power on Beverly. She was too gentle, unique, and there was the matter of the eyes, enormous eyes (now fixed on him) equipped with lasers that cut beyond external, social truths to the heart of truth.

'Dan?'

'First sit.'

She perched on bare mattress ticking. He dragged the chair, straddling it, facing her, leaning on his crossed arms. His head was taut as strings of rubber inside a golf ball.

'He'll be a vegetable,' she whispered. Until now an unvoiced, unvoiceable fear.

Dan shook his head. A nerve twanged, and he rubbed his neck. She rose, massaging with cold fingers.

'They know who did it,' he said quickly.

The massage faltered. Her fingers trembled, and he reached up, holding her left hand to his shoulder. Now. Get it over with. Now. You can't see her eyes.

'It was Raymond Earle. They had no evidence, nothing, but he's on the LA Police Department's blotter, something about cruelty to animals.'

And a memory brushes Dan. Avocado trees, a warm afternoon in the San Fernando Valley, and an odd, cosy compliment. *You ... certainly are persuasive.* Dan lets himself supply the word to fill the hesitation. Jews. You Jews certainly are persuasive.

Go on. Tell her.

'So they questioned him. He didn't deny anything. He said he thought Jamie was my boy.' Dan rose, facing her. 'He read the thing in the paper and imagined I'd cheated him out of millions. Three million, the paper said, remember? He said he was justified.' Dan spoke rapidly. 'The lousy little anti-Semitic turd, I could strangle him and enjoy it.'

'What?'

'He figured I'd cheated him.'

'Not that.'

'He thought Jamie was mine. He knew I had two boys, and –'

'You called him anti-Semitic.' The eyes were that dark, agonized colour.

'Oh God, Buzz! You know me.'

'There must have been a reason.'

'He's an all-round sweetheart.'

'That's not it.'

Dan sighed. 'Just the way he said something. The first day I met him.'

'What?'

'Nothing, really. But something.'

'Yet you went ahead and made the deal through him.'

'Things are lousy enough, Buzz. Forget it.'

'Forget?'

'If I could swap places with Jamie, you know I would.'

The truth, but unfortunately a cliché. Still, how could he let her stare at him like this?

Dan turned away. He heard her footsteps leaving the room. He went into the windowless toilet. Throwing his tie over his shoulder so it wouldn't get wet, he thrust his face under the high faucet, letting icy water strike him.

He found her at the end of the hall, her forehead pressed on the window. A tarnished sun lay small in the overcast sky. Ten minutes he watched her, and she didn't move, though she must have known he was there. He understood for the first time in all the years he'd known her, she didn't want him near her, really didn't want him.

He said, 'See you at dinner.'

Still facing the window, she nodded.

Around six, she phoned. Her mother, she said, had brought Alix, and the three of them were going to that new coffee shop around the corner.

He went to evening services. He said the Shema, remaining on his feet as the Reader began. His father, Dan knew, would consider him worse than an apostate. He drove Saturdays. He slept with his wife at times of the month when he shouldn't – twelve days after her period began, according to Moses, he was meant to stay clear of her. His kitchen wasn't kosher. He hadn't insisted her children get a Jewish education. With uneasy fear that he knew was superstition, he decided these sins would tilt any scale against him. Next to him an old man mumbled into his worn collar. The Reader intoned, 'Blessed are You, O Lord, who heal the sick of Your people, Israel.'

Pray, Dan told himself. Pray for Jamie.

Jamie?

Jamie he loved, the boy had the same gentleness as Beverly. In his heart, though, Dan knew he wouldn't be praying for Jamie. Whatever his faults, Dan was not a man given to self-deception. He would be praying for his wife. He wanted his wife. Would she want him again? Invocations rose in the old-time synagogue. If anything

worse comes up – and there's plenty of possibilities – Dan
answered himself, she won't care to see me, even. Is there
any way I can change this? Change her? Change me? A
circle of questions clutched his throat. He undid the
top button of his shirt, loosening his tie. 'Blessed are You,
O Lord, who hear prayer.'

On Third they waited. Beverly huddled alone in one
corner. She said hi and went back to staring at her broad
gold wedding band. On the table lay a copy of the
Examiner: VALLEY MAN CONFESSES TO STABBING. The others talked quietly. Dan couldn't make sense of their individual voices. He could feel the mass hatred. He watched
his wife twist her wedding band as if it hurt her. They'd
been married ten months, and she was acting as if the
gold had been devalued and shrunk. A well-equipped hell
of any denomination must have exactly such a waiting-
room. Maybe this was Gehenna. No! Gehenna was one
sea of mud with icy rain slashing on shivering skeletons
and over all the indescribable, unforgettable smell. Once
you'd been in that place, how could you take this petty
hell seriously? Oh Buzz, I can't live with this guilt. I
can't live without you. Buzz, look at me.

A little after eleven, Jamie died.

3

Cold hall. Masses of flowers blending into jungle odour.
Young capless rabbi. Her parents and Philip having made
all arrangements, a service as close to High Church as
Judaism can come. The Lindes, Vilma Schorer, Philip,
and her in the Family Room. Vilma Schorer, swathed in
black voile, checking the house through silk curtains.
SRO. (One hundred and thirty-seven of the names signed
in the white-leather guest book were there because Jamie

143

*Schorer was Dan Grossblatt's stepson, Dan drew people,
whether they liked him or not, he drew people.*) '*Or even
the silver cord be loosed or the golden bowl be broken* ...'
*And the skull is like a bowl. Beverly, taking first her
father's dry handkerchief, then his wet one, finally burrowing her face in his shoulder.*

She left with her parents in the limousine. She had
stayed in their house the three days since Jamie's death.
Since Dan had told her. Alix waited at the front door.
Alix had wanted to go, but Mrs Linde had pronounced
a funeral too morbid for a young girl, and Beverly hadn't
been up to arguing.

Beverly kissed Alix. Alix asked if she'd like a cup of
coffee. Mrs Linde said, 'A lot of people will be dropping
by. Willeen's making coffee in the urn.' Beverly kissed
her daughter again, saying she'd love some tea, and Mrs
Linde, firm if pale and red-eyed, said Beverly should rest
while Alix made it.

Beverly sat on her old bed, swinging up her legs. Don't.
Mrs Linde's commandment: Thou shalt not lie on the
bedspread. She folded back Martha Washington candle-
wick. The blanket itched through her stockings.

'Mother,' Alix said, depositing a cup on the bedside
table. 'All those people coming. Think I better change?'

Alix, in stretch jeans and lemon angora, the glowing
quintessence of all-American girlhood. Beverly thought of
Mrs Linde's strained face. 'Maybe your blue jumper?'

'It's home.'

'How about the pink you wore yesterday?'

'It's not dark or anything.'

'It's fine, just fine,' Beverly sat up. 'Alix, are you all
right?'

Alix said yes.

'About Jamie?' Beverly murmured.

'I know what you meant.'

Beverly looked into the luminous brown eyes and found
the familiar barrier. Her daughter wanted reassurance
about a pink sweater and skirt, nothing more. Yet Alix
must be grieving. Alix had been very close to Jamie. In

the teasing, disputatious, often cruel ways of an elder sister, she had spent much time with him. They had shared secrets, trips to the beach, allowances, jelly doughnuts, and Bobby Rydell records.

Beverly said, 'It's impossible ... I keep expecting him to come in – don't you?'

'Mother, drink your tea.'

'Can't you talk to me about him, Alix?'

'I put in a lot of milk. It'll get cold.'

No hostility lay behind the beautiful brown eyes, but no intimacy, either. The door shut.

Beverly needed both shaking hands to hold her cup.

'Mrs Linde. I'll be *one* minute.' Caroline. Outside the door.

'She hasn't slept since we lost Jamie.'

Beverly loathed euphemisms for death. 'I'm awake,' she called. 'Caroline, come in.'

Caroline sat on the organdie-ruffled stool. For a minute the two women regarded one another in the vanity mirror. After Beverly had dropped out of USC to marry Philip, they had seen one another infrequently, yet in the oval mirror, and in truth, their old friendship was reflected.

Caroline took out a cigarette. 'Mind?'

Beverly shook her head.

'For oral types like I, it replaces *le mangez*.' Caroline inhaled. 'Gene and I sat with Dan.'

Beverly said nothing.

'He was crying. Luv, why is it so much worse when a man cries?'

Beverly didn't reply.

'He isn't here *yet*,' Caroline said.

Beverly gazed at the vanity lamp, a shepherdess whose shepherd had been broken when Beverly was ten. Poor shepherdess, widowed lo these many years.

'This is me. Caroline. Nothing if not subtle.'

Beverly said, 'I can't face him right now.'

'Because of that – that creepy weirdo?'

Beverly sighed. 'Caroline, I don't understand why. I just can't. Oh God, it's such a mess.'

Caroline tapped ash into an abalone shell. 'Thinking time?' she asked.

'I guess.'

'How about Arrowhead?'

'You mean that?' Beverly looked up. 'I can use your parents' cabin?'

'*We* can. Package deal. Me or nothing.'

'But – but how can you leave?'

'Gene *told* me to ask you.' An honest lie. Gene certainly would have, if he hadn't been forced to go directly from the funeral to a Van Vliets's board meeting.

'And Cricket?'

'You'll be doing Cricket the big favour. She'll visit Em and be with her twin idols. Well, she favours Vliet, but then so do all us girls.' Caroline's chuckle emerged through smoke. 'One ground rule. You have to promise never, never to use any four-letter words. Especially F-O-O-D.'

'Caroline, thank you.'

'What are friends for?' Caroline stubbed out her cigarette. 'Tomorrow at ten.'

Place is unimportant, Beverly discovered.

A mountain resort is as bad as a city. Two days in the Wymans' cabin blended with collateral darkness. The temperature was below freezing. Caroline lit fires and smoked. And talked constantly to drown the mausoleum silence.

They had driven up in Beverly's car. Beverly dropped Caroline off at Em's. As they pulled up in front of the dinky, shuttered bungalow, Em was turning into the drive. Grocery bags were visible in the back of her station wagon. Em came over. Beverly hadn't seen her since the twins were born. Here was a different Em. Leaner, grooves in the small, carefully made-up face. Her upper arms, though thin, had a faint, dowdy sag.

'There's nothing I can say,' she said to Beverly.

Beverly nodded in lieu of thank you.

The man was a monster, said Em, elaborating on this

146

theme. Then, thank God, Cricket ran out. Beverly hadn't seen Caroline's little girl in five years. Now Cricket's limp was more of a skip. (She had been born with a defective ankle that had been corrected by a series of operations.) She was a few months younger than Jamie, she must be around ten and a half, but tiny, with dense yellow curls and an upper lip that protruded, giving her the tender, unformed look of a baby chick. She hugged her mother. She touched Beverly's cheek lightly. 'Mrs Grossblatt,' she said. Her high, clear voice reminded Beverly of Mrs Van Vliet, dead before this child was born.

The two teenage boys at the front door seemed too large, too vital to have come from Em, or to be contained by the bungalow. Em, beaming, introduced her twins. Vliet, the fair, taller boy, extended his hand into the Buick with a charming, lopsided smile. The dark boy, more solid and strong-looking, had acne on his chin. 'I'm very sorry, Mrs Grossblatt,' he said with difficult sympathy. This was Roger, *Roger's very intense. He's got in mind to be a doctor, and he'll be a good one,* Caroline had said at some point of the Arrowhead torment.

And the other boy, Vliet, the blond, reached for his aunt's Mark Cross overnight case, saying, 'Yes,' with another charming smile.

Beverly turned from the twins. She mumbled something about being in a rush, and sped down a street of repetitive little houses, plans A, B, C, and D, escaping two tall boys, two beautiful adolescent boys, unloading a station wagon.

She drove aimlessly. She found herself on Hollywood Boulevard, and without understanding why, bought a ticket at Grauman's Chinese. Heavy, inert, unseeing, she sat through a Roman epic almost twice before it hit her. Alix! I must see Alix! She was filled with sudden morbid energy, running into the night, dodging tourists who squatted over famous hand and footprints. Alix was with Philip, and Philip lived in an apartment facing the slip of his new forty-two-foot ketch. She drove faster than the legal limit to Marina del Rey.

'Is Alix in bed?'

'Sure,' Philip replied.

'Awake?'

'I doubt it, but –' He gestured politely at a door.

Beverly opened it a slit. For a long time she stared at her sleeping child. Only child, she thought. The energy drained from her.

'Can I fix you a drink?' Philip asked.

She nodded.

'Gimlet?'

In the last two days she'd drunk too much and eaten not enough, she didn't want anything, so why was she nodding?

Philip handed her the stemmed glass. He said, 'Are you ready for our talk?' After the funeral, when he'd come in his dark suit and dark glasses to the Lindes' to pick up Alix, he'd said, *We have things to settle, Beverly, but later.*

'Yes,' she said. Numb.

'You understand what it's about?'

'Yes.'

'Then let's get down to details.'

'Why details?'

'I hate confusion.'

She rubbed frost from her glass, aware of the thwarting distance she'd always felt with Philip, they never had seemed to touch, not even when he was heavy on her, their bodies locked in the moist marital embrace – sweat, semen, and her hungry kisses. Always he was rational and superior, she filled with confusion. And now was the most confusion. She yearned to hold Philip, to feel his once-familiar body in a kind of mourning ritual for their son.

'... likes it here at the Marina,' Philip was saying. 'Beverly, are you listening?'

'Yes.'

'You can be foggy. So for the record. Alix, is, going, to, live, with, me.'

'No!'

'You didn't hear a word. I'm getting a three-bedroom.

And Mother's offered to move in with us.'

'No! Never! I have custody.'

'I'll fight that.'

'Please, Philip, please. She's all I've got.'

'Me, too. And I don't have to explain why' – the pulse in his temple began to beat – 'I can't let my other child live in his house.'

The room's so neat, Beverly thought, battling a tremendous urge to slam down meticulously aligned Waterford glasses. The crystal, she knew, would be an extension of her nerve endings, echoing and crying in pain when they shattered.

'It's my home, too,' she said.

'It won't be Alix's.'

The faint sarcasm. Yet. The beating pulse. Oh, she needed to break those damn glasses.

'If it were just her and me, alone?'

'Alone?'

'Yes.'

The handsome, dark-haired head tilted questioningly. 'Where?'

'I don't know. Yet.'

'But you and her? Just you two?'

'Someplace.'

'I'd rather have her here with me,' he said, polite. After you, my dear Alphonse. 'But alone with you is acceptable.'

'Philip, he was the nicest little boy.'

'We have this straight?'

'Not in Dan's house,' she said.

'Good. That's clear.'

'Yes!' she shouted. 'It's clear! You need to punish us, Dan and me! But it's too late for punishment. It's too late for anything, anything.'

The gimlet splattered and with shaking fingers she set it down. During their marriage they never had shouted. 'Just Alix and me.' Her normal, gentle voice was conciliatory. 'Us.'

Philip's face, still pale, relaxed. 'He was such a nice

little boy,' he said in an odd, rusty tone.

'Phil, it's so terribly empty.'

'Empty, yes.'

She lifted her hands towards him, the fingers separated, entreating. But Philip had a lack, a flaw, a hypodermic of ice embedded in him, and even if Beverly had not left him, he never could have brought himself to share his festering grief. Beverly's face twisted with tears. He backed onto the vinyl-floored entry.

'Goodnight,' he said, opening the door.

She spent the night in an impersonal motel room. There was a scratch pad, and she covered sheet after sheet with convulsive pencil marks that resembled concentration-camp barbed wire. She did not sleep. At seven the next morning she was gone.

Beverly Hills north of Sunset always is quiet: the early mornings are smothered. None of the men is in an income bracket that needs to leave early for work, the gardeners have not yet arrived with sleep-destroying power mowers, and children are not ready to be car-pooled. The slam of Beverly's Buick door echoed. She let herself in, edging around terrazzo, imagining she could see speckles of red, knowing that Clara had scrubbed with the electric buffer. From the direction of the bedrooms came Dan's voice. 'Whozzit?'

'Me.'

The bedroom drapes were drawn. A small amount of light seeped around the top and bottom of heavy folds, but not enough to dim the flame in the tall memorial glass. A *yartzeit*. It occurred to Beverly that in her parents' home and Philip's, too, there had been no *yartzeit*. Ah well, she thought. A sheet had been hung, covering the horizontal mirror. The room was clotted with stale odours: candlewax, sleep, liquor, cigars. A bottle of Scotch stood next to the bed where Dan sprawled, his white shirt unbuttoned to show a delta of brown hair, staring up at her.

'What brings you here?' he asked.

'To explain.'

'After six days?'

Could it really be six days since Jamie had died? 'Yes.'

Dan didn't move. 'I'm not in the market for explanations,' he said. Liquor slurred his voice and a trace of New York clung to the words. Quartuh, Dan would say, not quarter.

Outside, birds sang. She couldn't tell what kind, but their liquid chirping wove a fabric. She sighed.

'All right,' Dan said. 'Where've you been?'

'You know. Arrowhead.' She had phoned from her parents' to tell him she was going with Caroline.

'The whole time?'

Beverly's head throbbed dully, from lack of sleep, she guessed, and a surplus of tears.

'I saw Philip,' she said. 'Then I stopped at a motel in Santa Monica.'

'A motel. That makes sense.'

'Please don't sound like that.'

'How?'

'Reasonable. Sarcastic. Polite.'

He said in these tones, 'Okay, what did you and that prize schmuck talk about?'

'He doesn't want Alix living here.' The words rushed out on an exhalation of fetid air.

'So?'

'I can't let him take her.'

'You mean he wants her to live with him?'

'Just not here.'

'You have custody.'

'He'll go to court.'

'There's lawyers.'

'He'll fight.'

'He'll never get her.'

'He could.'

'Like hell!'

'He could,' she repeated.

'Not unless you go along with him. You agree? She shouldn't live in my house?'

151

'How could I think that?'

'Easy. You blame me.'

'No!'

'Balls. Of course you do. Listen, I sat in that waiting-room the night the news broke. There was a crumb on your cheek, and you looked at me once. The way your parents always've looked at me. Like I'm to blame for whatever's becocked in their world. Then you didn't look at me again.'

The force of gravity had become impossible. She leaned against the chest, the *yartzeit* flame flickered, and black smoke pointed upwards. Jamie, she thought. What difference do all these ex post facto words make?

'Look, if there were any way to apologize, to make it right, don't you think I would?' Dan, his hands dangling between his knees, was watching her from the edge of their rumpled bed. In that bed he had whispered, *This is my beloved and this is my friend.*

'You wouldn't have blamed me,' he said, 'if I hadn't made that one half-ass remark about Raymond Earle being anti-Semitic.'

She had no answer. After a minute he rose, walking unsteadily to the bathroom. She heard the strong splatter of water on water. The toilet sounded, a discreet, expensive flush. Dan returned, zipping his fly.

'If you aren't living with me, you get to keep her, is that the idea?'

'Dan,' she whispered, 'I love you.'

He picked up the Scotch, squinting around it at her. 'Love?'

'I do.'

Putting down the bottle, he moved closer. She could smell the staleness, feel his body warmth, see his expression, chiaroscuro. Dan searched her face. *But my beloved had turned away and was gone. My soul failed me when he spoke, I sought him, but I could not find him: I called but he gave no answer.* She looked away first.

'How can I let him take Alix?' she murmured.

'Schorer can take her about as far – how far can you

throw diarrhoea with a fork? Now. Get the hell out. Get the hell out of my house.'

In a sort of reflex action she fumbled in her bag for her keys, two small ones to the Oldsmobile 88 he had bought her and the heavy Schlage for the front door. She set them on the dresser near the memorial candle.

He followed her down the hall.

'Need money?'

'No.'

'You do!'

'Thank you, no.'

He dragged notes from his money clip, forcing them into her hand. She let green paper flutter noiseless to the carpet. He looked down, then gripped her arm above the elbow, his fingers biting between flesh and muscle to the bone. 'Pick it up,' he shouted. 'Pick it up, you no-good cunt!' And with the flat of his other hand, he hit her full force on the left side of her face. Involuntarily, she reached for his arm, steadying herself. There was darkness, shadows whirling around. His arm, the only steady object in the void. She'd never before been struck, not by her parents, not by her husbands, yet now it was a relief to have a physical dimension to her pain. The world settled. A slow liquid trickled down her nostrils. She ran through empty rooms. Outside, she knelt by one of the ornamental pools, cupping water to her throbbing face. Slowly, redness disappeared in water.

Dan stood over her.

'Here,' he said, giving her his handkerchief. She held it to her nose, rising heavily to her feet.

He stretched his lips, an attempt towards a smile. His strong teeth were even, the result, he'd told her, of long-term orthodontia. 'You'll have a time explaining that eye.'

The pool shivered as a dragonfly touched down. Beverly watched widening ripples, her mind swimming in cross-currents farther and farther from reason.

'We'll find the best lawyers. He won't get her, Buzz.'

Buzz.

The silly nickname. He never said darling, love, sweetheart, always Buzz. He never called her Buzz unless they were alone. In bed he whispered Buzz. A gate slammed, starting a string of mournful puppy howls. Erratically she wondered if she should phone Bel Air Kennels to explain Boris-the-wanderer no longer had a master.

'Come inside. I'll put ice on it.'

She didn't move.

'I've been crazy, Buzz,' he said. 'Six days wondering when I'd see you. If. Know how crazy I've been?'

He put his arms around her. He was warm and she was cold.

She couldn't bear warmth!

She pushed her handbag at his chest, forcing him away. Her heart expanded, her stomach lurched as if she were dropping in an elevator shaft, and bile filled her throat.

She fled.

Down the path lined with voracious birds of paradise she ran, heels clattering on newly paved sidewalk. She didn't pause at Lexington. Her breath came loud. She raced into Sunset, and a red light trapped her on the grassy central divider. Cars swished by. The real Beverly, the gentle, dreamy painter, stood with a hand to her pounding heart, thinking, How I must be hurting him. I can't let it end like this. I'll go back to explain and apologize. Yet the woman with a wild, distraught look, hair in need of shampoo, continued walking quickly south.

4

Five months passed.

Raymond Earle had been adjudged incapable of his own defence, and in accordance with California State

Penal Code 1370, was committed to the state facility for the criminally insane at Atascadero. The walls of Victory Enterprises' Encino Mall rose. And Van Vliet's no longer had alternating presidents, Caroline's Uncle Hend having died in May. During that August hot spell, Caroline and Gene took his widow, Bette Van Vliet, to dinner at Scandia.

As they waited for the captain to seat them, Gene happened to glance into the crowded bar. Dan Grossblatt sat on a stool, one arm around his blonde secretary, Georgia. His hand dangled over a large breast on which a brooch shone like a good-conduct medal. Gene hadn't seen Dan since Jamie's funeral – company reorganization had chewed every minute of his time. Caroline hadn't seen Beverly since Arrowhead – wasn't *that* two days' sacrifice enough for a cheerful hedonist?

Dan, sighting them, waved. The broad face looked puffy. Gene zigzagged through the crush of noisy drinkers.

'Gene, hi. Grab a stool, have some fun.'

'I'm with Caroline and her aunt.'

'Mustn't antagonize the bosses, huhh?' One of Dan's fingers touched Georgia's gold pin.

'What happened?' Gene asked. On Dan's forehead was a large, flesh coloured Band-Aid. A greenish bruise lay under one eye.

'You should see the other guy.'

'Honestly, Dan!' Georgia giggled. 'Mr Mathney, he got the littlest tight and hit a lamp post.'

Dan laughed loudly.

Gene asked, 'How goes it otherwise?'

'What otherwise? Great. Fabulous. The time of my life.' Dan gave him a bloodshot, despairing wink. 'Can't you see?'

Gene could see. And in that awkward minute before he could get loose, he decided this was Save Dan Grossblatt Week, and that friend to all suffering mankind, Eugene Matheny, was elected president.

Which was why he was easing his new, air-conditioned Pontiac (replaced annually by Van Vliet's) through used-car country, peering at fading numerals on run-down units. Number 1043 was a decaying Mediterranean court blanketed with purple bougainvillaea. D, the rear apartment.

Beverly opened the screen door. Chalk smudged her shirt, her brownish hair waved in the soft pageboy of their youth around a face innocent of lipstick. She hugged him. 'Oh Gene, Gene.'

In the shabby living-room she held up a finger. 'One second,' she said. 'I've got to get this shadow.'

She picked up a pastel, stroking lavender onto one of those saccharine baby portraits. He sat in the armchair. A spring came up to meet him. The furniture was awkward, old, but he sensed Beverly hadn't noticed. Almost covering one wall was a vast, unstretched canvas. At first it seemed abstract. Gene realized he was simply too close. Narrowing his grey eyes behind his correction, he saw raised hands, hundreds of pairs of hands, hands of every age, reaching, grasping, pleading into empty darkness. Even though he understood the content, the painting remained mysterious, disorganized, glimmering with something he couldn't quite grasp.

'Yours?' he asked.

'Uh-huh,' she said, still intent.

'It's powerful.'

It was more than powerful. It was desolate. Yet with all the despair, it aroused an odd exultation in Gene. How could Beverly – of the baby pastels – evoke such emotional response?

'That does it,' she said, setting down her chalk, offering him a cold drink. He followed her into a kitchenette, sitting at the breakfast booth. He inquired about Alix. 'Off with a friend to a swimsuit sale. You know how they are at that age. They always need clothes.' And it was her turn to ask after Caroline and Cricket. They talked of daughters and ate cinnamon streusel from a Safeway package ('Sorry, Gene, but there's no nearby Van Vliet's') and drank iced Nescafé. Her face glowed with pleasure, and he put off hurting her. She went for fresh coffee.

156

'It's Dan,' he said.

She put down glasses carefully.

'Beverly, he's cracking up.'

She stared at him. Her eyes, deep and huge, were made to express suffering.

'He smashed his car,' Gene said. 'He's been hitting the bottle. Hard.' *Grossblatt cheated me, so I decided to get even.* Raymond Earle had told newsmen before he was committed. *I thought the boy was his.* 'I don't know how anyone could handle that kind of guilt. And your leaving.'

Beverly stared down at the table. 'Philip won't let Alix live with Dan. If I go back to Dan, I lose her.'

There was something glib about the explanation. Gene had known Beverly too many years. She was never glib.

'Philip's hardly that kind of guy.'

'It's not a gamble I can take.'

'Maybe he would have after, well, after. That's understandable. He was hurt. But not now. He wouldn't take Alix away from you.' He's not that interested, Gene thought, the cold, handsome sonovabitch, he and Caroline having opposing views of Beverly's husbands. 'He wouldn't do anything.'

She stood. 'Gene, that portrait, such as it is, was promised for this afternoon.'

Gene knew a dismissal when he heard one. He started out of the kitchenette. And was confronted by the huge, despairing canvas. He thought of Dan's bloodshot wink. Gene had much quiet persistence. His face assumed that downward-lined, dogged expression.

'At least talk to him.'

'I've tried to call. I never get through.'

Gene digested this. 'Then go see him.'

'I can't.'

'Why not?'

'I just can't.'

'Beverly, maybe you aren't aware of this, but Dan went into that mall for you. I was in his office the day Raymond Earle got him the property. Dan was all keyed up. He said you couldn't take the entertainment end of his business. He needed income, a lot of income. So the mall. He was changing his life to fit yours. If you blame him –'

'Yes, I blame him,' she interrupted in a low, trapped voice. 'Gene, does Caroline still call you Clean Gene? You are. So you won't understand this. Not in a million years.' She swallowed with difficulty. 'Dan's aggressive, he's full of drive, he moves his hands when he talks, he has that wry shrug. He's so very Jewish. That's why I blame him.'

To Gene's recollection, this was the first time Beverly, in his presence, had mentioned Jews or Judaism. She shied away from the subject. He knew it was sentimentality to think of this avoidance in terms of an unbearable psychic wound, yet he, too, had grown up in Glendale. Her confession was against every one of Gene's beliefs, yet he knew she was incapable of wilfully inflicting hurt. He absolved her.

'You're alone too much,' he said. 'Thinking.'

'No doubt about that.' She leaned against the old-fashioned archway. 'My favourite pastime. If Dan weren't so very Jewish, would Jamie be alive?'

'Raymond Earle,' Gene said, 'is a psychopath.'

'There's plenty of them around.'

'Does Dan know how you feel?'

'He's very shrewd about people. And he knows me. Gene, I'm the original anti-Semitic Jew.' She sounded like a child about to weep. Her voice shook.

And then he saw that her body, too, was shaking.

'Honey, what is it?'

'Nothing. I've got these magic pills,' she said, running from the room.

He heard a sharp sound.

'Beverly,' he called, following her. In a shabby bathroom, she stood over broken glass.

'Can you realize,' she whispered, 'how very much I hate me?'

The shaking was worse.

He ran the few steps to the kitchen. 'It's the way you

were raised,' he called, snatching the glass she'd used for her coffee. 'The time, the place. Everything's more open now.' He was back in the bathroom, dropping shrunken ice cubes in the sink, running the faucet. 'Here.'

She took the glass between both hands, convulsively attempting to swallow. In order not to embarrass her, he looked away.

Over the bathtub hung three narrow, unstretched canvases, a triptych of the same man wearing the same murky red clothing. In each, the frail body was knotted differently. Yet the three paintings had the shattering impact of a single pose: a man twisting and jerking as if he were being flayed alive. No pity. No sentiment. It was as if Beverly had recorded the sadism she saw.

And then Gene understood what he should have understood from the large canvas, what he surely would have understood if Beverly hadn't been a friend so many years. However, it requires huge mental acrobatics to revisualize old friends. And Beverly, in this particular, was no longer Beverly.

The slender woman grasping a dime-store tumbler in shaky hands, this woman Gene had known almost half a lifetime, had become, by whatever tragic route, all that he ever hoped and dreamed of becoming.

She was an artist.

It was entirely probable, a great artist, he thought, absorbed in the triptych. She's done it, he thought, turning to her with pathological awe.

'What is it?' she asked.

Confused, he said the first words that came. 'Your work, that's all that matters.'

'I do want to see him.'

'You're an artist.'

The pills, evidently, worked fast. She was shivering, but less. 'Is Beverly Hills out of your way, Gene?'

'He's hurt. He'll hit out. Look, I was wrong. Honey, I don't want him hurting you.'

'Give me five minutes.'

'The portrait –'

'I'll get to it afterwards,' she said, and stepped around him.

5

VICTORY ENTERPRISES
LAND DEVELOPMENT
Dan R. Grossblatt

raised gold lettering spelled. Tucking her bag under her elbow, she used both hands to turn the oversize knob. Georgia looked up. A slow flush rose from tight pink sweater to pale bangs. She resembled an agitated angora.

'Hi, Georgia.' Pretty bunny.

'Mrs Grossblatt.'

'How is everything?'

'Very fine.'

'Is Mr Grossblatt around?'

'He's in conference. He asked not to be disturbed.' Disturb-ed, three syllables. 'For anything.'

Beverly backed out of the office. Trembling, she stared for several minutes at

VICTORY ENTERPRISES
LAND DEVELOPMENT
Dan R. Grossblatt

before taking a deep breath and going back in.

'I'll wait,' she said, sitting on one of the couches.

'He's very tied up.'

'How long?'

'Very. *What do you want?*'

'To talk, but –'

But Georgia had clicked a button, saying crisply, 'Mrs Grossblatt's here. She says she must see you now.'

And Dan's voice clanked through the intercom. 'Be right there, DeeDee.'

Georgia's eyes glittered in twin wedges of triumph. The door opened. Dan blinked, startled. A greenish bruise under his left eye, horizontal plaster above the right. Accident, Gene had said. Beverly glimpsed a man seated in the inner office.

'DeeDee's coming to talk over the boys' school. I'm tied up! You'll have to wait!'

He slammed the door. Hard. Water sprang to Beverly's eyes. Lately, any loud noise dis-turb-ed her. Not wanting Georgia to see, she picked up a magazine, opening it, worrying suddenly that one wasn't enough. What if she got the shakes again? But already she felt as if her blood corpuscles were weighted. Two would have knocked her out. She thought of Gene's face when it started. Nice face, kind, the hair going. Slight, stoop-shouldered now, yet not weak-looking. Always she had liked Gene. Tolerance. Clean Gene. He'd been nice, but oh, how he must despise her. Beverly's fingers clenched the slick paper. What time is it? She wouldn't ask Georgia, wouldn't ask –

'Georgia.' She heard her shrill anxiety. 'What time is it?'

'One-thirty.'

She had asked, unwillingly, twice before Dan emerged from his office with a fat, tanned little man. Bart Cogan, Dan introduced, of Carmel Cogan in Phoenix. Through an over-white smile, Mr Cogan said he was pleased to meet her, truly pleased, and he hoped he hadn't kept her husband too long. Dan said he was sorry as all hell about the interruption, Bart, but hahahaha, you know how these things are. Mr Cogan kept smiling, obviously embarrassed by how these things are. The door closed on him. Both Dan and Georgia were staring at her.

'He flew in to write up the lease,' Dan said, drumming impatiently on his door. 'Come in.'

'Dan, about your calls?' asked Georgia.

'Don't put them through.'

'None, Dan?'

'None.'

Beverly moved past him, smelling cigar and Scotch. She sat in the deep chair opposite his ebony-topped desk. He searched through a turmoil of scattered papers, finding a legal-looking form to read. She stared at his wrist. She could see only the white of French cuff.

'What's the time?'

He cocked his arm. 'Quarter to two. Am I keeping you? I am sorry.' He crumpled the form, tossing it, missing the waste paper basket.

'So?' he asked.

She shook her head.

'Aren't you in a hot sweat to talk?'

'Dan, please don't shout.'

'I'm not!' he shouted. 'Two-thirty I have another appointment!'

'For the mall? It must be almost up. Is it filled?'

'What's it to you?'

'Just interested.'

'Balls!'

'How're the boys?'

'With DeeDee.'

'Did Vic's teeth come in?'

'Crooked. Look. You're here. Fine. Let's get the meat on the rug.'

If I cry I die. Cry and die. Weep and leap. 'Please don't.'

'What're you muttering about?'

She motioned downwards with her hand.

'We'll play it your way, then. How,' he mimicked her low voice, 'are your dear parents?'

You know, she thought, that it's never been right between me and them since I left Philip. She said, 'I haven't seen them much.'

'Delighted they're doing so well. And that prize horse's ass, Schorer?'

'Listen, Dan –'

'Terrific he's so great. And you, anyone can see, are blooming.'

'Have you moved?' she asked.

162

'To the Beverly Wilshire. Why?'

'I called the house.'

'If you couldn't get me there, didn't it enter your brilliant, artistic head to try here?'

'A lot of times. Didn't Georgia tell you?'

His mouth opened, his eyelids quivered. It was as if she had slid a knife through the summer-weight jacket and into his ribs. Georgia had called him Dan once too often. Georgia and Dan. Dan and Georgia. So. She smiled. So. What once would have torn her apart, now didn't mean a thing. Why was she lying to herself? The smile cost her. Oh Dan, she thought, remembering. A wild dove fluttered to the ledge, stretching its wings and raising its slender neck. Dan went to the window, lifting his fingers to rap.

'Don't,' she said sharply. 'It's tired.'

He turned to her. 'So I've been getting laid,' he said, his voice drained of the anger that had ridden it, drained of vitality.

The dove had settled its head under one speckled wing, throat pulsing, ruby eyes turned into the office.

'Do they live on the ledge?'

'It's not my idea of marriage, alone in a hotel.'

'They probably nest nearby,' she said.

'We don't have much community property, but you'll be better off than in that dump I hear you're hiding out in.'

'Across Wilshire there's trees.'

'Get yourself a lawyer.'

'Or maybe it doesn't live around here.'

'You've gotten a divorce before.'

'They fly long distances.'

'Look, I'm trying to discuss something important.'

What is important? Where a wild dove nests? If a sparrow falls? If one twelve-year-old boy dies? Does it matter to Anyone? She had put the question to Rabbi Jacobson and he had replied, *Is it up to Gott to explain His vays to us? Vy lay vaste to yourself demanding explanations?* He smelled of mothballs and had married her to Dan and so knew the whole story more or less. At first he had smiled kindly with stubs of yellow teeth, but as she had grown more insistent that the Lord our God, the Lord is One, is also a runaway Father, he'd become stern.

'I don't remember doves around here.'

Dan shouted, 'Who has time for all this bird shit?'

She tried to block his loudness.

Couldn't.

She heard water pouring. Cool glass was put into her hand. 'Drink,' he said quietly.

She drank. 'It's any loud noise,' she explained. 'Dan, what's the time?'

'Why the worry about time?'

'Alix,' she said, thinking about the bus schedule. She had committed to memory those routes needed for her brief forays. The Hollywood bus left at two thirty-five.

'What's with Alix?'

'Nothing. She's out, and I like to be home when she's there. What is it?'

'Two, about,' he said.

'There's time to talk.' Her voice faded, then returned. 'Dan, do you think it was some kind of punishment?'

He understood. Jamie. 'No,' he said. 'But you do.'

'More than that.' She glanced at the resting bird. 'All my life I've been looking for a meaning, a pattern. I think that's really why I started to paint. Painters and writers are searching for some kind of order. They always have been. Take the writers of the Bible. People always're being punished unto the third and fourth generation. The cruelties of life made some sort of sense if they were punishment by Him, even if for a very remote crime.'

'Take it easy,' he said.

'I'm not coherent? I never am, am I? But think about it, Dan.' And went on, as incoherently, that she didn't believe life is meaningless, she did believe that certain people, certain families, certain groups are pursued by tragedy. She cited the Greeks, and paused, taking a deep breath. 'Groups pursued by tragedy.'

Her fingers pressed down until the nails were purple

shells. 'Would it have happened if we weren't Jewish?'

A gagging noise came from Dan's throat. 'Why I ever made such a half-ass remark.'

'You meant it.'

'Like hell.'

'If I were Caroline and you were Gene, would he have killed Cricket?'

'Look, why don't we knock this off? Raymond Earle is a certified lunatic.'

'Dan?' .

'I make one stupid remark, and you blow it into —'

'If you were Gene?'

Dan sighed. 'God knows.'

'I'm sure He does. But what do you think?'

He sighed again. 'It wouldn't have happened,' he said, and leaned across letters and leases. 'But this is me. On the subject I'm *meshugenah*. Both of us are.' Pause. 'Gene Matheny got you here.'

She heard Gene's name, but it didn't register. Dan's admission had soothed the cranial pressure that had been with her since that afternoon in the hospital. 'It wasn't your fault,' she said. 'It was, but it wasn't.' This made no sense, but when did reason matter to Beverly? 'What is it now?'

He consulted his watch. 'Twenty of three.'

Her muscles coiled and a panic of adrenalin burst through her. The Hollywood bus had left! Five minutes ago, left. Without her. Fumbling in her bag, spreading brown leather wallet. Two ones. For two dollars no cab will take you from Beverly Hills to Hollywood. No way. Dark grasscloth and Dan's bright kudos whirling. Around her. She stood. She must get to Hollywood.

'Hey!' Dan called.

Beige silk pleats slapped against her thighs. She struggled with the knob. Her palm was wet. As the door jerked open, Dan called, 'Beverly!' Georgia was a moment of fake gardenias. Another tug and Beverly was racing down carpeted hall. At the elevator she jabbed her finger on DOWN. Maybe it's a ten and a one, she thought, opening her bag, spilling Revlon lipstick, two zinc pennies, a Kennedy half-dollar, and a used Kleenex. She scrabbled. Dan was helping her.

'What the hell's with you?'

'The bus has gone!'

'So?'

'I told you. Alix'll be home!'

'Then you'll be a few minutes after her.'

'Anxiety symptoms don't work that way. Dan, would you lend me five?'

'For what?'

'A cab.'

'I'll drive you.'

'Your appointment —'

'Screw that!' he shouted. Then, quietly, 'You think I'd let you run around like this? You really think that?' His hand started to reach for her, then fell to his side. Sweat beaded his forehead, darkening the Band-Aid.

In the dim underground car park, their footsteps echoing, he led her to a Cadillac. 'The Jag's at the knackers,' he said.

He did not take out his keys.

'Dan, let's go.'

'I ever get you home late?'

'It's not exactly irrelevant that I can't leave her alone. Please, Dan?'

'Look.' He pointed to the car clock. 'Quarter of. No. Twelve of. Say, fifteen minutes to Hollywood. When's she due back?'

'Half past.'

'So I can talk to you a few minutes without the world coming to an end?'

In the entrance, outlined by gaudy sun, an attendant stretched his arms above his head, circling at his sides, like that drawing of Leonardo's. Beverly exhaled.

Dan took a cigar from his shirt pocket, clipping and lighting it. 'The way you took off,' he said. 'Five months I've been planning exactly how to knock your teeth down your throat. But now —'

'That I'm a crazy lady?'

'Whoever figured you for sane? I'm trying to apologize for being such a shit up there.'

'A first.'

He chuckled. 'Don't think it came easy,' he said. 'Other than that, is it so rough being with me?'

It wasn't. Besides, hadn't she been able to talk to him easily, few holds barred? 'You're the only person left who understands me,' she said.

'Jamie was too young to understand you.'

She closed her eyes.

'Still as bad, isn't it?' he asked gently.

'Worse.'

'Nobody could accuse us of taking it well.' A car drove down the ramp, roaring into a space. 'Did I say something derogatory before? You look good – for a crazy lady.'

He smiled. She smiled back.

'That's better,' he said, resting his knuckles on her cheek, lightly, lightly. 'Buzz?'

The questioning note was clear. He meant, get back together. His features seemed heavier than she remembered, and there was a slackness below his chin. Drinking, Gene had said, and guilt. She could hear Dan's watch, time ticking away on a golden Omega, and he was waiting for her answer.

Dan tapped ash in the tray. 'Worried he'll get her back?'

'No. I'm pretty sure he doesn't want to. He's been very nice.'

After a pause, Dan asked, 'You don't love me anymore? That the problem?'

It was. She didn't. So how could she reply?

'Well, I still do you, Buzz, if that means anything.' Another pause. 'It won't be like it was.'

Like it was. Sadness choked her, and she could hardly breathe. She was thinking of the joy she used to feel with him. Irrecoverable. Unevokable, even. She had been in love with Dan so much for so long: for many excellent reasons had she loved him. Well, Jamie's death broke that up. Our guilt is shared, isn't it? she thought, and our innocence, too? There're too many questions. And the only answer I have is that Dan acted, Jamie died, and now I can't even remember love. Her pupils, enlarged by dim light, rested with bewildered misery on Dan. Smoke hung between them. How had she once seen as perfect, near to a god, this heavy-featured, middle-aged business-man who (like every stereotype in those grotesque Nazi propaganda cartoons) held a cigar in his mouth?

He stubbed it out. His eyes met hers. In the few heart-beats that they stared at one another, she felt as if her silk dress had dropped off. It was not her naked body he saw, Dan, but her naked mind.

Going back betrayed the dismembering price she had paid to come to him in the first place. Going back be-trayed the love she once had felt for him. If she went back she betrayed herself.

Yet she was a passionately gentle woman. Any form of cruelty, even subconscious, horrified her. One moment in an underground car park when Dan read her thoughts, and the die was cast for Beverly.

She reached for her husband's hand, intertwining her cold fingers in his warm ones.

'You'll come home?' he asked. 'You and Alix?'

Beverly nodded.

He started the car. 'Buzz,' he said. 'I'll get to the bottom of those pigeons, I promise you.'

'Wild doves.'

'Doves, then.'

And she searched for an equal pledge of good faith, coming up with something as the Cadillac's tyres squealed up the ramp. 'Alix,' she said, 'doesn't call you Mr Gross-blatt anymore. You're Dan.'

He laughed. He was still laughing as they emerged into the too-brilliant August sun.

And Now

Chapter Seven

I

The letter from Radcliffe came on a Saturday. Alix, who had been waiting for it, got to the mail first.

She took the unopened envelope to her room. In an ell decorated with charming blue-flowered upholstery, a private spot for her and her innumerable friends, she stood, tearing along the sharp edge. She read the letter once. She refolded paper in the envelope, locking it in a lacquer box. As she turned the tiny key, her smile was unhappy yet accepting. She brushed her dark hair. Licked a forefinger to arch her brows. Adjusted her new lime-green sweater. She went out through her private patio, thus avoiding the family room where she could hear Beverly's soft voice and Fat Sam's loud chortles. She drove her Mustang to the Book Shop, moving between paperback racks, stopping to speed-read a paragraph here and there, selecting eight of the fattest, novels all, rapidly printing Dan's charge. Home, she pressed the lock of her door, giving herself up to *Portrait of a Lady*, the longest.

Radcliffe had rejected her.

This she would keep secret from everyone until she was able to recount the facts as a comic anecdote on herself. Rejections are painful to everyone. Rejections shook Alix more than most. To her they seemed the direct result of some personal ineptitude, like a bra strap showing. At this time, 1968, she was eighteen, an immaculate girl, sharply compulsive, and – possibly because of this – she considered rejection inevitable.

Physical beauty, true beauty, is so rare that it might as well be myth. Alix possessed it. Yet when told she was great-looking, she assumed this the routine line handed out to every passable girl. She saw a lower lip too full, hair not dark enough to be black, feet unusually long and slender. She worked constantly on her appearance. Also, she was reputed to be a brain – but then, she let nobody in on the fact that before each test she studied far into the night. By nature she was affectionate. She reproached herself for being aggressive. A natural athlete, she discounted her skill, deciding that anyone who had a mind to could get on the tennis team, say, or ski the advanced runs. She noticed only the rare few better than she.

One thing Alix did give herself.

She caught on fast.

Her most important lesson had come immediately upon Philip's departure. With a child's egoism, she had believed that like the (training) bra strap which other people could see and she could not, she must have done something to make her parents quarrel. She loved her family. The idea that her mother bore full responsibility for the divorce was as incomprehensible to Alix as the quantum theory. On Bellagio Road School's upper playground, she had voiced her belief she'd caused the separation. One of her friends had snickered. Alix had bent over on the green bench, trying to hide her tears. The others, a flock of chickens pecking to destroy a wounded sister, had joined the ugly laughter. Then, miraculously, a voice had whispered inside Alix's head: *Pretend you were kidding*. With superhuman effort she had stopped weeping, somehow managing a laugh. 'Boohoo, boohoo. I mean, my mother's boyfriend couldn't have one thing to do with it, could he?' The laughter continued, but differently. They were with her again.

Alix had learned this: If you were wounded deeply, you joked your way out of it. Brown eyes sparkle, a show of perfect bite. Charming Alix. The façade, yes, oozing confidence. And since the façade is what shows, everyone, including Mother, Father, even Dan (who saw through most people) assumed here lived the golden girl, a Beverly Hills princess of the blood. When the hurt proved too great, there was always reading. Novels never left you in the lurch. Novels prevented you from thinking. Alix drifted on blue-flowered fabric to the formal tranquillity of Jamesian life.

Caroline, Cricket, and Beverly curved around the sofa in the family room.

Caroline and Beverly, like many childhood friends grown to different lives, kept in intermittent touch, seeing one another maybe once a year, maybe less. Alix hadn't seen Cricket since Cricket was a tiny pre-schooler who had napped on Alix's bed, wetting it, in the other house, the other existence.

Fat Sam chased around the coffee table, pulling down his toys. He was almost two. As Alix came in, he galloped to her, lifting his arms. 'Swing,' he demanded. She swung him between her knees. Dan's slanty blue eyes set in a wide Harpo Marx face. Thin. Wiry. Funny-looking little kid. Alix was mad about her half brother. As she swung, she heard Caroline murmur, 'My God. Luv, she is a *knock-out*!' Alix, still holding Fat Sam, pressed her cheek against Caroline's scented pink one. 'I love your suit,' she said and turned to Cricket. 'Welcome.' And Fat Sam shouted, 'More! More!' 'Here's your train, keed.' 'Chug, chug, chug,' Fat Sam puffed, guiding his Tinker Train in and out of legs. Any conversation must centre on him.

CAROLINE: How could he have grown so *much* in a year ... Here, Sam ... No, luv, don't pull ... (The gold chains adorning her red Chanel suit.) Beverly, I don't see how you do it ... (Hint of that enticing chuckle.) Me, I'm too old for this game ... (After Alix removed him.) He's a funnyface.

BEVERLY: Sam, here, play with your keys ... Sit on Mommy's lap ... Oh, it's a matter of adjusting. I always did want to be the senior citizen of the PTA ...

ALIX: Here, Fat Sam, here's a graham cracker ... It's on your diet ... Come on, cut that out. (Caroline's chains still entranced him.) Later, I'll take you to Roxbury

Park and you can pick on men your own size ... (Tickle, whisper, tickle.)

Cricket remained silent. Nearly six stone of girl topped with Orphan Annie masses of yellow curls that she made no attempt to straighten – Alix would have. Small freckled hands relaxed on a nondescript grey skirt. Face innocent as if emerging from babyhood. Was she all that young? No, almost the same as Jamie. Sixteen or thereabouts.

Caroline set her daughter up. 'Cricket, remember Alix?'

Cricket nodded.

'What *do* you remember?' Caroline.

'You had this real pearl necklace.' Cricket spoke in a clear soprano.

'Genuine Add-a-pearl,' Alix said.

'I figured it made you an honorary adult.'

Alix smiled. Even if it weren't mandatory here, she would have smiled. Cricket had delivered her lines with far more grace than she, Alix, could have mustered if Beverly – by some remotest chance – had pushed her. Towards Beverly, Alix felt a dangerously interwoven burden of love and resentment which surfaced in her voice however hard she tried to repress the hostility.

Lupe took Sam into the yard.

Caroline fixed her chains and lit a Chesterfield. Beverly, jogged by Alix, offered refreshments. Caroline would adore coffee, black. Cricket said no thank you, nothing, and Alix – oh, so perfect a hostess – said she didn't want anything either. The women disappeared into the kitchen.

Alix asked brightly, 'Where shall we begin?'

Cricket's grey eyes questioned.

'Catching up,' Alix explained.

Cricket smiled and said nothing, content – it seemed – to watch the maid and Fat Sam in the oversize sandbox. She's young, Alix thought, shy. No-no! Just goddamn uncooperative.

Then Cricket asked, 'Do you have a dog?'

'We used to. Boris.' Alix said. And stopped. Jamie's

dog, she thought. She hoped Cricket wouldn't remember Jamie. Alix could talk of him only to her parents, and then rarely. 'He died full of dog years,' she lied. Beverly had found Boris a wanderer's heaven on an Ojai ranch.

But Alix couldn't let the conversation drop. With anyone new she was in limbo until she roused a spark of warmth. 'That was at the other house. This one's Dan's. He planned it. He plans everything. Talk about your dominant males.' And she told one of her Stories of Dan. Affectionate, with just a hint of derision. Perfect tone for a stepfather story.

Cricket sat with one knee bent, dreamy as a small animal sunning itself. Alix couldn't tell if she was amused. Or even listening. Any of Alix's friends would have had the decency to lean forward eagerly, laughing at the appropriate times.

Alix said, 'Radcliffe turned me down.' What? She hadn't said it aloud before. *Dear Miss Schorer: We regret that there is not enough space on our campus for every qualified applicant.*

Cricket propped her cheek in her hand. Her upper lip protruded, showing teeth as small as milk teeth. Alix felt that warm prickle under breastbone. Contact. She'd made contact. Generally she didn't pay this high a price – complete exposure – but she had made contact.

'Did you get in other places?' Cricket asked.

'Santa Barbara.' Who cared? 'I wanted to be a Cliffie. Generally I get what I want. No-no.' She nibbled a cashew. 'That's not it. Generally I don't let myself want what I can't get.'

'Turndown throws you?'

'Doesn't it everyone?' Alix laughed.

'You don't show any signs.'

'Great surface tension,' Alix said. 'You've got a couple more years?'

'I'm out in June.'

'This June?'

'At Brace Ridge we finish at our own speed.'

'Then what?'

Cricket opened her eyes wider, as if the future were an idea alien to her.

'College?' Alix inquired.

A shake of yellow curls.

'Europe, then?'

Cricket looked more bewildered. She appeared never to have considered that all-important question: Is there life after graduation? Finally she came up with, 'Fool around with my camera, maybe.'

'Then you're a photographer.'

'No.'

'Goddard has this terrific photography department.'

Cricket was watching her.

'Why not college?' Alix asked. 'It's part of the bundle. You know, Add-a-pearl necklaces, Sweet Sixteens, the liberal arts college of your choice – wherever possible.'

'The conventional extras.'

'That's it.' Big laugh.

'Alix, do you know my cousins? Roger and Vliet Reed?'

'Twins?'

'Yes.'

'About twenty-one?'

'Uh-huh.'

'Never met 'em.' Smile. 'Mother mentioned your aunt had twins.'

'They'll be out this summer.'

'Don't they live here?'

'They're at college,' Cricket said, and returned to her thoughts. Or wherever.

Alix buried the silence decently with the new Joan Baez. *Conventional extras* had stung. Alix wanted to be as oblivious as her mother to the material, but the surface is strewn with thingee things, and the surface was where Alix was condemned to live. She was conventional. It bugged her, but she was. She wondered, had Cricket meant to hit a sore spot? She didn't seem the type, but you never knew.

As Caroline revved her Mercedes, Cricket called, 'We'll all get together.'

Don't bother, Alix thought. Big smile.

An acceptance came from Pomona. Statusy enough. Now Alix could joke about Radcliffe's lack of perception.

She paced in step with 'Pomp and Circumstance' across bleachers set up on Beverly High's green lawn, collecting her gold-starred diploma. In the audience sat her Linde grandparents, very correctly dressed (ultra*goyishe*, as Dan said), her father with Grandma Vilma (Presbyterian and not nearly so correct in flowery chiffon), and in the front row, Mother and Dan. One big unhappy family. Afterwards, they clustered awkwardly, kissing her and bestowing keys to a new Mustang, two cheques, and a graduation card handprinted: *IOU 8 weeks in Europe. Father.* Alix hugged and exclaimed and for a few minutes managed to get smiles on their faces. Was each, she wondered, as achingly aware of the missing person?

3

A drab June morning. Alix, shivering, backed up her new Mustang. A circular drive had replaced the walled patio, and she made a sharp right, heading for the street. She was blocked by an illegally parked grey VW mini-bus. She honked. The dented VW didn't budge. She touched her window button, ready to protest, when she saw – sandwiched between two large males – Cricket Matheny.

'Hey Cricket,' she called.

And left her car, to greet her guests. They watched her. On long, friable-looking legs, Alix walked, her heels striking asphalt just firmly enough to produce interesting movements in tank top and white shorts. Who would guess she was self-conscious?

'Alix, this is Roger.' Cricket nodded at the driver, the dark one. 'Roger Reed, Alix Schorer.'

Dark, rough hair and a moustache. Kind of tension. Heathcliff, Alix thought. If Roger's a singer, he drives the groupies wild.

'And this is Vliet.' Cricket tilted her head in the opposite direction. Vliet's hair was pale and sleek. He smiled at Alix, one side of his mouth whimsically down. The twins were opposites. One feature only was held in common. The eyes. The eyes were deep-set and Prussian blue.

'Hi, twins,' Alix said.

Vliet's easy smile came quick.

Roger's slower.

'Hi, Alix,' Vliet said. 'Where're you heading?'

To buy the Modern Library *Anna Karenina*. 'Noplace,' she said. 'Come in and I'll feed you.'

'We're fed,' Vliet said. 'And going noplace, too. Why not come with us?'

She glanced at Roger. 'Why not?' she said. 'Let me put the car away.'

When she got back, Vliet was in the middle, Cricket on his lap. Roger held open the door for her.

'D'you take pills for it?' Roger's voice was husky.

Her lips moved in a wordless question.

'Or is it natural?'

'What?' she asked, unable to look away. Dark-rimmed pupils turned his eyes an even more vivid blue.

'Roger, you'll never carry it off.' Vliet's voice, good-natured. 'Not your style, man, not you.'

'What?' Alix still gazed at Roger.

'The good looks.' His tone was deeper.

To which there was no comeback other than the routine smile.

The minor pass, Alix guessed (correctly) was a first for Roger. It had been excruciatingly awkward. Yet there was something, something with an impact that took Alix by surprise. Her bare leg grazing his Levi's began to quiver. Hastily, she climbed into the mini-bus.

Roger's hands, large and capable, shifted and steered. Fast. He was a lefty. He didn't speak. Neither did Cricket. Vliet and Alix bantered, champion figure skaters making easy patterns across silence.

Alix wanted Roger's attention again.

She didn't know how to get it.

An area Alix never had been compelled to cultivate, what her friends referred to as getting a guy. She had beauty, she had charm, she had males bringing her compliments, admiration, affection. No effort on her part. (Incredible!) To be honest, though, she never had experienced the magnetism that might have made her wish to draw a specific one. Sometimes, generally before she fell asleep, she would worry, was she frigid? And this admitted a greater, more ancient fear. The males nearest her had been banished, murdered. She would sleep on a comfortless credo: It is safest not to let yourself get close to anyone.

They were climbing the landscaped hill towards red-brick turrets and cement-slab modern blocks of UCLA before she ventured, 'Roger, where do you go?' The question, to Alix, sounded pushy.

'Harvard.' Vliet.

The male Radcliffe. Was that why Cricket never mentioned it? Leaning forward so it would be apparent she was talking to Roger, Alix inquired, 'Have much longer?'

'We're graduates is all.' Vliet.

'In what?'

'I just said, Alix, Ha-a-a-a-ava-a-ad.' Vliet.

'Ahhh. A diphthong major.'

'Really.' Vliet grinned. 'I always dig the ones with extensive vocabularies.'

'Pre-med.' This time it was Roger.

Leaning yet further, she asked, 'Going to their med school?' It's so stiff, she thought. I'm floundering, she thought.

'Roger's found us another diploma mill.'

'Where, Roger?'

'Hopkins,' Roger said.

And she – nicknamed Social Alix – could think of no better remark to keep this tenuous exchange going than, 'Are we heading for the beach?'

'How come,' Vliet asked, 'the anxiety about destinations, colleges, the minor details?'

'My environment.'

'Harsh toilet training?' Vliet inquired.

'No-no. I'm a nice three-quarter-Jewish girl.'

Vliet rubbed a careless hand on his cousin's yellow hair. 'Fink,' he said. He smiled at Alix. 'Cricket promised the one-hundred-per-cent genuwine article.'

'It so happens I'm sensitive about that quarter.'

'Who isn't?' Vliet asked. 'Alix, there're days when I could cut my throat for being a Wasp.' He reached out as if to punch Alix's bare, tanned arm, then had to clutch Cricket.

Roger was swerving onto Chattauqua.

There was no way Roger could have seen Vliet's gesture. Yet Alix could swear Roger had cut the sharp left to divert the movement of Vliet's hand. Telepathy? she wondered. Aren't twins meant to have it? They were descending into grey sea fog.

'Anyway,' Alix said, 'with as many parents around as I have, you learn to memorize. Keep the perspective straight.'

'Christ! A broken home, too?' Vliet said. 'For a screwed-up, sensitive, girl, you come across pretty healthy.'

'All cover-up.'

Roger had braked at the entrance to the beach car park. He was watching her. She smiled at him. He stared a fraction of a second longer, shook his head as if hearing unspoken words, and rose up to get change from his Levi's. Choppy waves snarled at brown cliffs: high tide, the narrowed beach was deserted.

'It's a bitch,' Vliet said. 'Come on. Buy everybody coffee.'

'I want to get some gulls,' Cricket said, reaching into the back for a camera. A Nikon, Alix noted.

'Pass, too,' Roger said.

'But it's freezing on the beach.' Alix.

'Great for running.' Roger.

'I like to, too. Especially in this weather.' Alix. She did. Fast and hard, as if in competition. 'After coffee, let's.'

180

'I'm not one for coffee,' Roger said.

'Coke?' Alix.

'Uhhh ...' Roger.

And Alix realized Vliet and Cricket were staring.

'Roger, ever notice the lengths women go to, avoiding being alone with me?' Vliet asked, smiling. Oh, Alix recognized how gracefully it was done, she herself often used a self-deprecating crack to help a friend out of humiliation. Vliet reached across her, opening the car door. ''*Raus*,' he said.

The coffee was bitter, not that it made any difference. Alix, too, wasn't one for coffee. She used the heavy mug to warm her hands. Across Pacific Coast Highway she could see Roger's broad-shouldered back. Hands in Levi pockets, he appeared to be gazing at the dismal sea.

'It's the moustache,' Vliet said.

'What?'

'Don't let the moustache fool you. He's not your type.'

Q (out loud): 'Who said he was?' A (silent): God, she really had thrown herself at Roger.

'I can tell you what's on his mind.'

'Even from this distance?'

'Twins have the power. He's thinking you're not his type. You're too ornamental.'

Alix took a sip of coffee and made a face. Pushy, she thought, how could I have been so pushy? She was furious at herself. And at Roger. Would one Coke have killed him?

Vliet went on, 'He's a practising idealist, Alix. He's sweating out whether 'tis nobler to practise in a poverty pocket or take even less cash on a sea of research.' Vliet wasn't putting Roger down, he was telling the truth in a tone of bantering admiration. 'How's that make you feel?'

'Shallow.'

'Likewise.' He poured her too much cream. 'There. That should bring it up to substandard. I've chosen.'

'Chosen what?'

'My speciality.'

'Which is?'

'Dermatology.' He finger-combed back shining straight hair. ' "Hold still, baby, I'm getting that nasty wart off you." No night calls. Money, tons of it. I'm going to have one helluva practice and join the family. I'm middle class only on my parents' side. I belong with the Van Vliets, or will as soon as that feelthy *dinero* starts rolling in.'

'That a visible scar?'

'Really. Put there by my unique first name and the first million people asking' – he raised his voice – ' "Oh, you're one of *the* Van Vliets? How are you related?" I'd like it known far and wide that Dr Van Vliet Reed enriches his clan. And while we're at this, Alix, I'll let you in on my other major ambition.'

'Which is?'

'To zap every great-looking girl I come in contact with.'

He intended to get a laugh. He did.

Creamed coffee snorted up her nose. For a minute she was helpless, laughing, choking, trying to hide behind a paper napkin. On occasion Alix ran out of control. She fell back into the wooden booth, laughter shaking outwards from the pit of her stomach. Get ahold of yourself, she thought, get ahold, you don't know him all that well to be snorting coffee. Finally she managed, 'And you say, you say you're not an idealist?'

He was laughing, too. Reaching across, he touched her coffee mug. 'Alix, I'm going to.'

'Don't count on it, Van Vliet.'

Chuckling, they sat back.

4

This was the year of Martin Luther King's assassination, the summer of racial riots that took seventy thousand troops to contain, the summer that, right here in Los

Angeles, a .22-calibre hollow-nosed slug scattered Robert Kennedy's brains. This was the summer that Alix's friends were sending closely written postcards out of Europe, Morocco, Hawaii, the summer of graduation, the summer of diaspora. But why make a philosophical deal? Even if the world were imploding, even if every friend she had were camping on her private patio, she would have spent her time with the cousins.

The weather had changed. Sun blazed white and hot. Most days, the four of them went to the beach.

Often Alix would bring Fat Sam. She once had brought another brother, but she never mentioned Jamie. The front door had been open, and fat flies had clustered on bloody terrazzo. Jamie's death went too deep for pain: she never had visited Dan's mall. Her mother had, but Alix couldn't.

Without the baby they body-surfed, each differently. Cricket floated in on small waves. Vliet let the dangerous ones go. Roger, a powerful swimmer, rode only those killers. Alix took them all, regardless of size. Head down, long, dark hair water-whipped to her shoulders, arms flat at her side.

They baked in the sun.

Alix asked, 'Is happiness one giant Pepsi commercial?'

She was asking Vliet. Roger rose up. Though shorter than his brother, a mere six-one, poor midget, his shoulders were heavier, and currently he had a large spot on the left one, caused, Alix decided, by his taste for Hershey bars.

'There are other things,' he said. His eyes were bloodshot from saltwater, which made them bluer, even.

'Seven-Up?' Alix asked.

'Come on, Alix.' He rarely used her name.

'No kidding, I should be brooding about the riots,' she heard herself say, 'and the Middle East situation, and Kennedy and Vietnam and poverty. But let's face it, today I'm happy.'

A wave crashed. Roger's eyes stayed on hers, putting her on the defensive. From that first day, between them there had been this tension that she found exhilarating and therefore terrifying. She ached to hit him in his firm gut with all her strength, he turned her that bitchy. Other girls could afford to be bitchy. Not Alix.

She let sand trickle through her fingers. She *was* concerned about leached earth and Israelis being pushed into the Mediterranean (living with Dan, who could be apathetic?) and war and peace, but at this point wouldn't the admission come off saccharine, too feminine, playing up?

She smiled. 'Besides, what's wrong with Pepsi?'

'To some,' Vliet said, 'happiness is a warm sickle cell.'

'Up yours,' Roger said.

'Anaemia?' Alix asked.

'Roger'll explain.'

'Fuck you,' Roger said. The twins tossed obscenities to one another as amiably as they did a Frisbee, and although Alix could tell no difference in this particular exchange, Vliet must have. He lay down on his stomach.

'All I know,' Alix said, 'is only black people get it.'

Roger eyed her. Grains of sand were caught in his moustache.

She persisted, 'Isn't it a matter of genes?'

To keep silent any longer would have been rudeness. The twins had perfect manners.

'We really don't know,' Roger said. He pushed himself to sitting position. Heavy shoulder and arm muscles worked. He might have come, Alix thought, from a more solid planet, a hard and difficult place that, while not as conducive to ease, was permanent. 'It's a riddle.'

'You enjoy solving them?'

Roger's expression changed completely. His smile, of tremendous sweetness, reminded her of Jamie. He nodded.

'Roger,' Cricket said, 'it's not just that. The gardener's boy, he's why you got the grant.'

Alix stared down at filing grains, wanting to know more about the gardener's boy and how, exactly, Roger Reed had earned a grant.

'Big deal,' Roger said.

'Tell me?' Alix asked.

'A summer job,' he said briefly. His smile vanished and his expression again – or so it seemed to Alix – condemned her.

He wasn't condemning: he was trying to condemn. Her hand propping her face – so luminously bronzed it appeared wet – drew up the lovely dark eye on that side. Dazzling. Unattainable. So Roger was doing something he wasn't proud of, yet couldn't help. Putting her down. He'd done this often with Vliet's toys, belittling them in his own mind until he no longer envied them. (Or the affection that had caused the toys' bestowal.) She's a human being, not a toy, he told himself, and was warmly ashamed but, glancing at her, he decided that nothing he said, nothing he did, could mar the perfection.

'They needed a body to push a broom,' he muttered.

At this Vliet stood, brushing sand from his long arms. Some fell on Alix. 'Roger, time to get food. And quit impressing my girl with how good you push a broom.'

She was Vliet's girl.

They went to see *2001* and they visited one another's friends. They listened to his records. This summer Vliet was collecting the Big Bands – Harry James, Benny Goodman, Artie Shaw. Kay Kayser and Vliet joining in perfect pitch with Ish Kabibble, *Three little fishees in an itty bitty poo*. Breakable, scratchy 78s that brought Dan and her mother, smiling, into the family room.

'Camp?' Vliet said.

'For camp,' Dan said, 'why not play Tiny Tim?'

Vliet riffed his fingers lazily. 'This turns me on,' he said.

Non-negotiable in the currency of truth. Alix knew that Vliet found joy in good music, classical and otherwise: his current purchases came not from strength but from weakness, an abdication of passion in favour of amusement.

When they were alone, she said, 'I never would have

185

figured you so big on kitsch.'

'There's a lot of things we don't know about one another,' he said, for once cold-serious.

'Alix?'
   'Mmmm?'
   'Yes?'
   'No-no.'
'Why?' he asked, kissing her again.

They were stretched in the VW on an old chenille spread. The night was warm, filled with insects and one chirping bird. She liked kissing Vliet. Nothing sex-ridden here, simply a way of sharing affection. She was truly fond of him. His hands moved down her body. She tensed. His touch, it seemed to her, was rough and impersonal. She never could connect his touch with his hands, so rhythmic and graceful.

'What's it you want?' His voice in their metal cave sounded different. More intense. Frightening. 'Tell me, Alix, what you want.'

SHE WANTED HIM TO STOP THRUSTING HIMSELF AT HER!

'Rape?' he asked. 'Seduction? I'll play it heavy, Alix, I'll play it light. However you say.'

She let her lips graze his cheek.

'Beg pardon.'

'Just this,' she said with another brief peck.

'That's white of you.'

'What's wrong with being friends?'

'So that's it. More of a relationship.'

'Why not give it a try, Van Vliet?'

Naturally she wasn't about to let him in on the fact she was an anachronism, the last of the Beverly Hills hold-outs. Virginity might have been swell in Mother's day, but now virtue hath its own reward. A name for being a sexless wonder. She let him touch wherever he wanted, but still, 'No-no.'

Later, in her room, she picked up *Anna Karenina*. The letters made no sense. She kept wondering what in the numerous names of God she was waiting for. Earthquakes, thunder, word from a conveniently placed burning bush? Certainly she wasn't waiting for love. The word, even, terrified her. Looooo-ooooove. It sounded·like a process to melt ore. She liked Vliet, and like was all she wanted. Her eyes focused: *Vronsky's thoughts had profoundly changed. He had unconsciously submitted to Anna's weakness. She, yielding all of herself to him, expected him to decide their fate and agreed in advance to any decision.* Tolstoy, Alix realized, hadn't meant only the obvious sexual yielding. Alix would eventually. She grimaced. Of course she would. But she, unlike Anna, never, never could let herself yield entirely. She wasn't strong enough. Only the strong can afford weakness, and she was vulnerable in too many areas. If a weak person discards her protective carapace, and something shattering happens, she's had it. She's broken. Pieces all over the place. Alix often was praised for her strength. While she knew this was a compliment to her self-erected façade, still, it pleased her. She respected strength, admired it, wanted it.

She read again. *Yielding.*

With a violent gesture, she ripped out the page, crushing it in her fist. Never before had she defaced a book. She lay back on her pillows and thought of Jamie and her father, thoughts drifting to words: gone, forlorn, alone, forlorn, afraid, forlorn, forlorn, forlorn.

5

The next day around noon, she answered the door chimes. Heat hit her like a·slap. Vliet, leaning on the jamb, managed to look cool in stay-press slacks and blue-stripe shirt.

'Why so formal?' she wanted to know.

'I'm taking you to meet Ma.'

She bent her face, laughing into her hand like a Japanese girl. 'C'mon now. I didn't mean that.'

'I did,' he said, eyeing her up and down. Expecting to go to the beach, she was wearing her green-and-blue bikini. 'Pretty fantastic, girl, but not quite appropriate.'

She changed, thinking: I'm not Anna Karenina. I'm that all-time, old-fashioned, full-length-novel tease, Marjorie Morningstar.

The Reeds lived in a tract near Glendale. Acacia roots had buckled the sidewalk, and Alix trod carefully up to the prim little house, worrying that her blue number from Rive Gauche might look as expensive as it was.

'Relax,' Vliet said. 'I've brought girls here before.'

He led her through a cramped living-room which smelled of carnauba wax, opening a screen door into a small, square backyard. A tiny woman in culottes knelt in front of zinnias. A jet flew overhead and she didn't hear them.

'Lady, that position's asking for it.'

Em jumped, turning. Seeing Vliet, she smiled. Seeing Alix, she pushed hastily to her feet. Alix thought: She's only a little taller than Cricket, with the same funny, wiggly nose. Vliet, come to think of it, has the same nose, except it's a perfect fit on him. Mrs Reed looks way older than Mother or Caroline, and those sad, thin, hangy arms.

Vliet introduced them.

'Beverly's girl! Oh Vliet. Why didn't you tell me you were bringing Alix?'

'One of those spur-of-the-moment things.'

'Alix, it's so nice finally meeting you,' Em said. 'I've heard so much about you from Vliet. And your mother was a dear friend of Caroline's – and of mine, too, of course.'

Alix effused in kind.

And Vliet glanced at a window. 'Roger home?'

'He went someplace. I think County General. You know, probably that Dr Bjork.' She looked down at her hands, brown with earth, still clutching the trowel. 'Vliet, where are your manners? Not telling me! Alix, please excuse me.'

As she hurried inside, Vliet grinned.

'Ma's perfectly adjusted to the joys of late-nineteenth-century living.' He sprawled, long legs over the arm of a redwood chair. 'She wants everything proper.'

'With you her work's cut out,' Alix came back automatically. She sat in the shady patio, tucking her mini around her thighs. She was filled with embarrassment. Why didn't I realize Vliet and Roger aren't rich? That first day Vliet said something about being middle class only on his parents' side. Why didn't I let it hit me? I kept mentioning going to Europe. Twice. But so've Vliet and Roger. Backpacking once and in the VW once. Oh God, how I've been flaunting the material. No wonder Roger's forever putting me down. How do the Reeds manage Harvard and Europe and Johns Hopkins for two? How come I'm always so aware of the money angle?

Em returned, wearing a brown shirtwaister that covered her upper arms. 'There's lemonade in the kitchen,' she said. 'Vliet, will you get it, please?'

'Ahhh, the silver-tray treatment for Beverly's girl.' He laughed and went inside.

'I'm afraid we spoiled him,' Em said.

Alix recognized Em's tone as the rich one her parents had used about Jamie. Vliet was his mother's favourite. 'Mrs Reed,' Alix said, 'you have the two nicest sons.'

'Thank you, dear. I think so, too. But I'm partial.'

Em made a small ceremony of pouring lemonade (which was on a silver tray), of passing napkins, offering devil's-food squares.

'Well?' Vliet asked his mother. 'Is she or isn't she?'

'You're terrible.' Em smiled indulgently. She turned to Alix. 'Caroline – Mrs Matheny – said you were a charming girl.'

'She said, "Luvs, she's exquisite! Beverly's girl is the most *gor*jus thing alive."'

A perfect imitation. Em and Alix laughed.

'Mother,' Alix said, 'told me Car – Mrs Matheny used to wear glasses. Now I notice she doesn't.'

'Only for reading,' Em said. 'Excuse me for one minute.'

She went into the house, returning with two large scrapbooks. Wheat-colour pages had come loose, and their frayed edges protruded from brown plaid covers.

'Alix, here's something you might be interested in,' she said, setting the heavy books on the table. 'There should be some pictures of your mother.'

Vliet and Alix on either side, Em turned pages. Grades on penny postcards. Shiny black-and-white snapshots, mostly of the two girls who had inhabited the bodies of this wrinkled woman and Caroline. 'Look. There she is,' Alix cried. Beverly and Caroline (rounder in those days), both wearing one-piece swimsuits, leaned towards one another, forming an inverted V. There were yellowed clippings of Em's triumphs as Panhellenic delegate. A telegram: CONGRATULATIONS ON YOUR GREAT HONOUR, GRANDMA. 'She sent me that when I became president of the house.' Group pictures. The girls, hatted and gloved, looked as if their major ambition were to be forty. The boys, with their dark suits and brutally cut hair, seemed there already. 'Mrs Reed, is that Mother with the sailor?' asked Alix. Em replied, 'Let's see. Yes. Lloyd Rawlings. He was at Caltech, in officers' training. It was taken at our Pink Rose Ball.' She pointed. 'This, too.' An 8x10 glossy of Em smiling up at a tall man whom Alix knew without being told was Mr Reed. Roger resembled him, the same tension around the mouth – or moustache. Em wore a formal with the skirt gathered on either side like a milkmaid's, and a huge orchid pinned on the complicated tucks of her bodice.

'Now I ask you kinda confidentially,' Vliet laughed, 'ain't she sweet?'

His mother laughed.

Alix didn't. She was imagining Mrs Reed all young and happy, possibly wearing that horrendous gown for the first time. Maybe Mr Reed had told her she looked swell as he handed her the corsage. Maybe after the Pink Rose Ball he had tried to make out – neck and pet – although with Mrs Reed this was difficult to imagine. Most likely they'd gone to a drive-in for cheeseburgers while the car radio played those soupy records Vliet collected. Maybe that night Mr Reed had asked her to marry him. To Alix, the most poignant thing was that Mrs Reed had spent the evening without foreknowledge that one day she would colour her hair too yellow, have sad arms, wrinkles grooved in her neck and face. She had lived that pink evening in unknowing joy. Nostalgia for Em's innocence overflowed in Alix. Her eyes grew moist.

Vliet had glanced over Em's head at her, and she didn't try to hide her emotion. Alix never minded showing emotion – if it didn't reveal her inadequacies.

The front door slammed. Roger? Alix never found out.

Em said goodbye. 'Alix, remember me to your mother, will you?'

'Of course I will. Mrs Reed, I really enjoyed myself.' Impulsively Alix bent to kiss Em's dry cheek. Em kissed her back.

'Do come again, dear.'

'I'd love that.'

Em's hand went up, shading her glasses from strong afternoon sun. She said to Vliet, 'Bring Alix back soon.'

As they moved along the Ventura Inbound, Alix said, 'She's a nice lady.'

'Why shouldn't she be? She knows I'm safe.'

'Safe?'

'Unimpeachably. She's executrix of our trusts until we're thirty –'

'Not your father?' Alix interrupted.

'Nope. The money came from her Van Vliet grandmother, and the terms are that it's nothing to do with him. Or us. Oh, to be spent on us, but only at Ma's discretion. Which, if you know Ma, means until the age of thirty or self-support, whichever comes first, no woman can hook us.'

Alix nodded. This solved the financial end.

'She's very high on our becoming doctors.'

'Status? My sons the?'

'Not exactly. Ma considers it total failure not to finish every damn thing you start. Never start unless you're will-

ing to go through with it. Perseverance wins the crown.
Et cetera.'

'Do I detect bitterness?'

'None at all. I'm with her. It's the only way, Alix, to get
it together,' Vliet said. A black-and-white sheriff's car cut
ahead of them. Vliet slowed. 'Did you get the point?'

'About your trusts?'

'Alix, I do wish you'd learn to catch on faster. We have
a relationship. It can't be permanent, but it is sincere.'

'They must have sensitivity training at Harvard.'

He chuckled, taking her hand.

But still she held out.

6

'I'm crazy about this,' Alix yelled, holding out her arms,
whirling in a great circle.

'The beach?' Cricket asked.

The girls, tall and short, were trotting along wet sand,
occasionally splashing through whipped-cream licks of
surf. Cricket's left foot pointed outwards, causing her to
run with a kind of rolling skip.

'This summer and everything about it!' Alix whirled
again. 'I am so HAPPY and RELAXED.' Not a confession she
would have shouted at anyone else, for it implied that
neither happiness nor relaxation was her customary state.
'The seaweed, the jellyfish, the sun, the sand fleas. You.
Vliet.'

'Roger?'

'Roger judges me.'

'That's just his personality. He's not smooth. But he's
strong. And good.'

'Obviously why he's passed sentence. I mean, you
must've noticed he's always chopping me down.'

Cricket had squatted to dig in wet sand. Small freckled fingers uncovered a shell.

Alix sat next to her. Cricket cleaned the pink interior of the shell, lying back to finish the job. She didn't notice that her hair was getting all sandy.

Alix could not for the life of her understand Cricket.

Conversationally, Cricket never shone. As a listener, too, she could fail, gazing off into the distance. If a subject caught her interest, though, the grey eyes opened wide, an ingenuousness that was flattering. But it was her total lack of interest in appearances of every type that boggled Alix. Cricket wore the same denim bikini day after day, she let the fine sprinkling of blonde hairs grow unimpeded on her legs and under her arms. She never carried a comb. When tired, she limped, yet she never stopped any activity in order to conceal this. Also, she must be some sort of brain, graduating before sixteen, but she expressed surprise that Hamlet suffered an Oedipus complex and thought Dostoyevsky wrote *Resurrection*, and, oddest of all, didn't try to cover up these goofs with a clever crack. Alix never was quite able to believe that anyone could be uninterested in climbing the degrees of superiority that make up the human pecking order. So she had decided that Cricket was like water. So transparent she was more complicated than complicated. To Cricket, Alix could confess her failings and feel better. Water quenches and leaves no trace.

She admitted, 'He doesn't like me – Roger.'

'You scare him.'

'Who? Me? Why?'

'Oh, you know.'

'I don't.'

'Look in a mirror.'

'Don't have one at hand. Anyway, why does he have to deal with me like I'm a third-time offender?'

'He's not easy, like Vliet. But he's better in an emergency.'

'For that I keep aspirin on my shelf,' Alix retorted, then thought of Roger's strong supporting arm when she'd been caught in yesterday's wicked undertow. She flushed.

Cricket asked, 'Don't you like him?'

'Aren't you listening, Cricket? He – does – not – like – me.'

'What's that got to do with how you feel?'

'Everything.'

'Remember that first day? I figured it'd be you and Roger.'

Alix laughed a little too loudly, 'But why?'

Cricket raised the shell. A few leftover grains of sand dropped. She blinked. 'I want Vliet for me.'

'Oh Cricket, you snotnose! Quit the teasing. I hate being teased.' She grabbed a small hand, yanking Cricket to her feet. 'Come on.'

When they got back, the towels were unattended. Cricket sat on her frayed blue one, positioning the shell as if she were about to photograph it. Alix, ever conscious of her appearance, decided her back needed more tan. She stretched face-down, listening to nearby transistors and the ever-present mumble of the sea. Where were the twins, she wondered drowsily.

'Hey Vliet!'

Roger's pass was purposefully high, and Vliet had to jump for the striped beach ball. He held it with both hands, running in and out of low-tide wavelets, his long legs pumping high, his hips swivelling in almost girlish grace as if he were running a broken field. Roger, using his high school linebacker form, closed in. Vliet swerved. The ball dropped. Roger recovered. He punted far into the Pacific. The twins raced into the sea, spuming salt-water, pivoting around bathers, simultaneously diving under a small, breaking wave. Vliet reached the ball first, pushing it out. Out again. They swam after a bobbing orange-and-yellow circle, Vliet's long arms and legs moving easily, Roger – a strong swimmer – ploughing doggedly. They gasped, heaved, blew saltwater. Vliet had slowed. Roger, seeing this, churned into a sprint. They were far from shore. Vliet trod water while Roger retrieved the ball, holding it up, Atlas triumphant. Both boys laughed. And with an identical jerk of neck muscles, threw wet hair, brown and blond, out of identical blue eyes. They turned on their backs to float in gently bucking water. Neither had spoken. Since babyhood it had been like this: spontaneously they would break into wild action that was half play and half rivalry.

Roger paddled with his hands, the sun a golden blaze behind his closed eyelids. He had a broad, probing mind. For a few minutes he and his brother had merged. He was pondering if this symbiosis dated back to that other sea, tideless and amniotic, or from some warm primate blood tie ancient beyond man. Roger's human contacts were few and very deep. This one was a miracle. Don't let me always need to win, he thought.

The loss of an inflated beach ball meant nothing to Vliet. SOP. Roger dominated in school, athletics, purpose, areas that to Vliet were of no importance. He, Vliet, wanted the real goods, money, a Porsche with a tape deck, records, the best girls, popularity, and to attain these he would inflict kindness or cruelty with equal indifference. He had many friends. He had no idea how closely he was tied to his twin.

Still, without speaking, the boys turned towards the beach, swimming the butterfly, paired dolphins curving in and out of glittering blue water.

Alix woke. Roger was lying on his stomach two feet from her.

She wanted him to talk to her. She would ask him to. It was that easy. Instinctive moments when the thought is the act are rare in most people. Even more so in Alix. Her life was complicated and full of striving, yet sometimes, without understanding why, she could reach out with no self-consciousness.

'Roger,' she whispered.

His eyes opened. 'What's up?' He spoke as softly.

'Talk to me?'

'What about?'

195

'Just talk.'

'Give me more of an opening.'

'The grant,' she said.

'It wouldn't interest you.'

'I'm asking,' she said, 'as a friend.'

He stared at her, then rolled so he was facing her. Sand clung to his chest and he rubbed at it. 'Not a grant. A job,' he said. 'Bjork got it for me. At County General. He's doing research there.'

'What kind?'

'Sickle cell. I got to be an orderly with his patients. I prefer working with patients.'

'Why?'

He thought a moment. 'When people are sick I feel helpless, impotent. Doing something, whatever it is, to make them better helps me. Nothing noble. Anyway, I met Bjork through this boy –'

'The gardener's boy?'

'Uh-huh. Not our gardener, we don't have one. But he came along in the truck, around the neighbourhood, a nice little kid about eight. Johnny. He was small for his age and he got a lot of infections. He often had these crises –'

'Crises?'

'Bad pain. In his abdomen. The gardener told me he was just a weak child, and they didn't bother with doctors anymore. I sort of guessed what it was.' Roger swallowed as if he had a sore throat. 'Last summer I took him over to County General. That's when I met Bjork.'

'What, exactly, does it mean, sickle cell?'

'Well, normal blood cells are bioconcave. Disc-shape. People with sickle cell don't get enough oxygen, so the cells are misshapen.'

'Into a sickle?'

'That's right.'

'Why the pains in his stomach?'

'Ordinarily a blood cell lives about a hundred and twenty days, a sickled one about sixty. The spleen has to enlarge to absorb all the damaged cells.'

'Can they cure it?'

'Alleviate only. Jesus, do you realize how few doctors can diagnose it, even?'

Her voice below the mumbling sea, she said, 'You did.'

He looked embarrassed, pleased.

'When did you decide?' she asked. 'I mean, that you wanted medicine?'

Roger turned on his back, hands under his neck. Alix was tremendously conscious of dark, thick axial hair. 'So long ago it's hard to remember. Maybe it had something to do with Dad's being a pharmacist. I don't know. I've always wanted to be a doctor.'

'Are you so sure about everything?'

'Jesus, no!'

'But you are about this?'

'This, yes.'

(Later it occurred to Alix that neither of them had mentioned that other embryo physician, Vliet.)

'What're you going to do?' Roger asked.

Try to stay afloat, she thought, shrugging.

'You have a major?'

'I'll find one,' she said. And work my butt off, she thought. 'Roger, it goes without saying, careers turn me off. As the daughter of that famous Beverly Hills housewife.'

'Your mother?' Roger asked, bewildered. 'Mrs Grossblatt?'

'She's known as Beverly Schorer in the art world.'

'She paints?'

'Part-time. Never more than twenty hours a day. She's in the best collections and museums throughout Europe and the US, as her brochure tells us. Including the Guggenheim.' Envy mingled with pride. Ugly, Alix decided. And boastful. 'Roger, face it, you're the fortunate exception with this cosmic goal thing. I'm the rule.'

Bare, heavy legs walked between them, scattering sand. Vliet, who had been sleeping on Alix's other side, woke up.

7

A knock at her door. 'Alix?' Beverly said.

Alix shoved *Arrowsmith* under the chaise pillow and began combing her hair, which she'd just shampooed. 'Come in,' she said.

Beverly, Alix noted, had on her large-eyed expression. Her cheeks were flushed. Shutting the door, she walked slowly to the armchair and sat twisting her plain gold ring. 'I wish I knew how to put this.'

Put what? Faster than a speeding bullet, Alix knew what.

'The Pill?' she asked, smiling too widely.

Beverly's flush deepened. 'I thought ...'

Alix went to her mirror. Drops of water scattered as she passed her comb through wet hair.

'Would you like ... ? Alix, I can't say this properly.'

'Try. Be mod. With it.'

'Please don't make it so difficult.'

'Mother, I'm willing to lay odds there's no easy way. So why not come right out? Do I need the egg killer?'

'You sound, well, so hard.'

'It's an awkward scene.'

'You were such a nice little girl.'

'I wasn't.' In Alix's head a crazed animal ran circles. Circles never end. Why was she so terrified? Everyone, even her mother, expected her to be screwing herself dizzy. But she was afraid. Wasn't that just like her? Well, living on a flat surface makes one afraid of any shadow.

'It's easier for girls now,' Beverly said.

Funny, Alix thought, I was thinking the opposite.

'You won't make the mistakes we did.'

'Father?' Alix stared in the mirror. Her jaw was set. She did look hard. Maybe she and her mother weren't close, maybe that's not on the cards for mothers and daughters but, more important, between them stood the matter of Alix's having a father only a few hours on Sunday. She would fix blueberry pancakes at his place, and they would sail his new Kettenberg. Alix never invited a friend, not even when her father suggested it. Other people would cut into her time with him.

'I didn't mean –'

'Not trying out Father before, was that your big mistake?' Alix asked, surprised how close to tears she was, surprised, too, at her own cruelty.

Beverly sank into blue flowers like (Alix thought) a bewildered doe shot out of season. Alix's animosity always reached this end: her sprayed buckshot drawing Beverly's blood and causing Alix separate but equal pain.

Their pain might balance. But never their guilt.

Beverly's fine features contorted as she sat back in the cushion. I'm a painter, she thought. This parenthetical summing up of identity shivered through her like a freezing wind. In it lay the years and hours since she had found her son lying on terrazzo. The guilts.

Jamie, in all his sweetness, lay under a flat marble plaque. Philip never had remarried – why? Alix. Had she, Beverly, somehow touched Alix into Midas's daughter, the golden girl? Sam wasn't really her baby, but his father's. And Dan? They still shared the mundane things, the rumpled king-size bed (pleasurably), the same toothbrush (four in the holder, but they invariably used the same one), a chequebook, he dealt with her dealers, she went on his rare Business Evenings. But. Dan loved her. And to her, Dan was merely her friend. No more. It's true at times he could get rough, very, but in the circumstances who could blame him? Not Beverly. Her *modus vivendi* (painter) made her guilty as hell.

Most of us hide our guilts in a private safety vault. Beverly hung hers on walls. Her agony burned on unstretched canvas and she rose from the ashes, a phoenix reborn to suffer again. As she gazed up at Alix, pain twisted Beverly, yet in her secret heart she knew she would relive this suffering at her easel and (possibly) manage an oil that some fruitcake would buy for his collection. Perhaps it was this that exasperated Beverly most. What sin, this recycling of life's misery into art! A phoenix, after all, isn't human. And Beverly, of course, considered herself a unique monster.

Alix took an audible breath.

'With everyone else I can say the right thing. Saying the right things is a game. You don't understand, do you, Mother? Well, I just can't play with you. I can't. And I can't be open with you, not anymore. I want to, but I can't.' Her lovely face seemed fuller, childish, pleading.

She reached. For a moment mother's and daughter's long, slender hands clasped.

'Alix, let me help?'

Alix moved away. 'With my sex life?'

'It's always been important to me,' Beverly murmured.

'That,' Alix said, cold again, 'everybody knows. Oh God. Don't you see we can't talk? Okay. Fine. Good. Make me an appointment with a reputable OB.' She grabbed her bag, and hair still wet, ran from the house.

She drove with no destination in mind, and it was without thought that she turned west on Sunset, curving past UCLA, hanging a right on Maggiore Lane, passing the house where once she'd lived. She curved up the hill by older places snuggled into their big trees, coming on the new houses. The sites had been levelled ten years earlier, but she still thought of the overbuilt, starkly modern extrusions as the new houses. Maggiore Lane ended. A thick metal rope stopped her car: FIRE ROAD/ SEPULVEDA WEST/NO TRESPASSING. She parked. Ducking under the rope, she walked along the unpaved ledge cut in the hill. The canyon was filled with late-afternoon shadows: three gulls flew up, their wings turning silver as they touched sunlight. Alix left the fire road, using both hands to scramble up a shale cliff. Pebbles clattered in a small avalanche behind her. She reached a flattened hill-top, maybe a hundred square yards of arid adobe with a few sparse brown weeds managing to grow in the cracks. She held a hand on her pounding heart. Below lay the city, the ocean, and a distant blue-whale hump that was Palos Verdes.

This was the secret place. Hers and Jamie's.

Never had they questioned who had carved off the hilltop, or why. It was theirs, a private domain above the world. The law of the land was secrecy. 'If you bring anyone here, your nose will fall off,' Alix had vowed with pre-adolescent Freudian symbolism. The rule was far rougher on her than him. Social Alix. She'd never been here, though, with anyone other than Jamie. She'd never been here without him.

Pushing her sunglasses firmly up on her hair (almost dry now), she forced herself to seek out the old house. There it was, in the curve of the road. Peaked ell roof, three brick chimneys sheltered by oaks. She thought:

> *That is the land of lost content*
> *I see it shining plain*
> *The happy highways where I went*
> *And cannot come again.*

She tilted back her head. At a point above her eyes a sheer film of atmosphere raced together as if a seamstress were gathering blue sky with her needle. What I told Mother was true. I wasn't a nice little girl. I was a nice little bitch. (It never entered Alix's head that most children aren't nice, merely that she'd been a bitch.) Yet when he lived there, the four of us, I was a person. Whole. Complete.

She looked down at the shake roof, then closed her eyes, thinking, *And cannot come again*, without the nostalgia of the Housman verse, but with anger that hurt her gut. Mother and Dan, she thought bitterly. Oh, wasn't this immature, blaming them? Was it their fault she'd grown into an unhappy ice creature, terrified to get close to anyone for fear she might melt? (Yes, yes!) How much passion and courage she lacked.

Her mother's offer had shoved her into panic. Alix was sophisticated enough to know she was what previous generations had admired. Chaste. But now everyone wore sex-tinted glasses. Movies, books, songs, jokes delegated the non-lascivious to the back streets of womankind. You were meant to be propelled by unhaltable passion. Come to think of it, had anyone described the female end of this unhaltable passion? And what did it have to do with the action on a chenille spread in the twins' battered VW? How dare she question the sex urge, the basis of family life, motherhood, and all advertising? She was un-American. Vliet (and her previous boyfriends) were more than generous to her, an unfallen woman.

She stared down at the shake roof. The house represented a time with Jamie alive, and Jamie alive meant the world whole. Alix whole. She was crying. She cried until her legs itched. Red ants were attacking her. Goddamn ants. Wiping her eyes, she started down. As she passed her old house, she did not look at it.

She began to have a recurring nightmare. She was trying to cross Wilshire at Santa Monica Boulevard, but her legs refused to carry her across the wide stretch. A large truck was bearing down on her. Obvious.

She still could not give in.

8

The 30th of August was hot and, in the late afternoon, sprinklers had been turned on. At a little after eight, cooling Beverly Hills air smelled of damp grass.

Vliet, opening the mini-bus door for Alix, said, 'Got you something.'

'Any reason, like?'

'We've known one another two months.'

'Today?'

'Possibly. Or possibly not.'

The gift was wrapped in maroon velvet flocking and

tied with pink satin ribbon on which was printed: ALIX ALIX ALIX ALIX ALIX ALIX. Under the bow three red roses fanned in full-blown grace. Vliet didn't start the engine. He watched her. She hefted the box. About the size of a book. But too light. Vliet never had given her anything, and this was dangerously sentimental.

Touching his hand, she said, 'Vliet, thank you.' Her voice caught.

'Before you choke up, Alix, why not see what it is?'

'I enjoy anticipation.'

'Really.'

'There's this place on Sunset that does –'

'Did this. Except the roses. They're swiped from Ma. Her last is all.'

Alix touched a petal. Taking care to do no damage, she removed each flower, placing it on the dashboard, bloom towards her. On the last she pricked her finger and paused, sucking the drop of blood. She untied loop-edge ribbon – ALIX ALIX ALIX – rolling it around outspread fingers.

'I'm nuts on unwrapping presents,' she said.

'Never would've guessed.'

'In some ways, it's the best part.'

'That, Alix, is where we differ.'

She smiled, thanking him again, and with a thumbnail un-Scotch-taped, trying not to pull any velvet finish. She folded wrapping into a neat square. The box was plain white cardboard. With both hands she lifted the lid. Shredded tissue.

'What is it?'

'Find out, why don't you?'

Her fingers explored.

Feeling, feeling.

Her fingers contacting only more white shreds. She removed clumps, pulling them apart, keeping the mess on the lid. When she had removed every scrap of tissue, she repacked the box, replacing the lid. Her fingers were steady. Amazing.

'Well, what do you know?' she said. Her voice kept normal, and this, too, amazed her.

'Nothing,' he answered.

'Just what I need.'

'But, Alix, with a fantastic wrap job.'

She nodded.

'It's our little joke.'

'Oh, that I got,' said Alix, leaning over to touch his cheek with her mouth. 'Hit the road, Van Vliet. We don't want to miss Coming Attractions.'

He turned off the inside light, shifting gears. She held the box on her lap. Time. She needed time. Not to examine the depth of her pain – Allah willing, she need never do that – but time to suture the arteries. She was haemorrhaging. It's our little joke, Vliet had said. Me. I'm our joke. A good wrap job and some shreddy paper to poke in. Hahahahahaha. But if that's all I am, why do I hurt so much? Well, he gave me roses. (But what are three swiped roses to a bleeding eighteen-year-old girl who is more ripped up than most and hiding it better?) Suddenly she thought of Roger. He chopped at her, she understood this, out of his own psychological scar tissue. Vliet never had tried to hurt her before. That's what made this calculated. Vliet moves rook to Q4. Check Alix.

They waited in the line of cars at the Olympic Drive-in with its pair of weirdly proportioned surfers painted on the back-of-the-screen entry. An usher flashlighted them to a place.

'Drumstick?' Vliet asked. 'Good 'n Plenties? Popcorn?'

'Please.'

'Which?'

'Whichever.'

He held onto the open door, peering at her.

'Git,' she said.

She watched him go, seeing him above the cars. Alix, you're feeling sorry for yourself. Am I? Definitely. And in a big way. And self-pity is a way of making up for affection that others don't give. Always it comes back to that ancient loss of love. She closed her fist. The lights were fading, and people were hurrying away from refreshment stands.

'Hey,' Vliet said. 'You crushed one.'

'Shame on me.'

He'd got two popcorns. She didn't eat hers. She never could remember what the film was, a genuine case of blocking. After a few minutes he took the full cylinder from her hand, kissing her, a hard, buttery kiss. Open-mouthed, she kissed him back and went from there without anger, hurt, rebellion, self-pity. She felt nothing. If emotions entered the mini-bus, she would throw a fit of drive-in movie hysterics. They squirmed over the back of the seat. He pulled curtains. She was conscious of smells. Dust and Coppertone ingrained in the spread. Rancid butter. Shell Regular. Her Miss Dior cologne. His aftershave. The soap and seawater smells of his chest. Crushed roses. Cleopatra, it is said, used rose petals to close her womb: Alix's was guarded with Mother-bought Ovulen.

In cars around, people either watched or didn't watch the screen. And Alix, shivering, held her breath. 'It's all right, all right,' Vliet said. Flickery Technicolor shadows moving on her, she gripped his shoulders. 'Alix,' he whispered. It hurt less than the raw nerves compressed by her too-tight rib cage. He whispered words in her ear, possibly instructions that she didn't get – didn't want to get – and she worried someone would pass and see through the windshield. Would anyone notice a slightly rocking VW? At the end, it did hurt. So what? Alix wasn't around to notice anything.

'Sorry,' he said.

'Huhh?'

'Half the time I had it figured you were, but the other I assumed you were holding out.'

'And so it goes.'

'Next time'll be better.'

'There's the one advantage of a virgin. She knoweth not.'

Oh God, she found herself praying, please don't let me talk cutesy. German steel cut into her hip. Please, God, help me.

Even without Alix's fear of hormonal deficiencies, she knew from her many friends that nobody should expect the Story of O her first time out, certainly never in a Volkswagen mini-bus at the Olympic Drive-in. And after the empty box incident! Yet for some archaic reason, doubtless brought on by too much fiction, she had hoped she would feel closer to Vliet. She now realized how greatly she'd hoped for affection. Warmth. Instead, she had shivered miles beneath him. Then made cracks. Well, no doubt about it, she thought. Vliet Reed has proved his axiom. Fancy wrap + shredded paper = Alexandra Nancy Schorer. In the next car a very young puppy cried, a spasmodic whimpering. The puppy had been whimpering for a long time.

Vliet kissed her lightly, her hair got between their lips, and he, pushing it away, kissed her again, then shifted his weight. She straightened her clothes.

'All right?'

'Dandy.'

'Sure?'

'Van Vliet, do me a favour. There's nothing to talk about, okay?'

'I admit it.' His easy tenor gone, he sounded as if his vocal apparatus were being worked by machine. 'I'm not exactly proud of the way the deed was accomplished. Christ, the impartial might say it was shitty.'

'Come on, Vliet, the box was a joke.'

'Well, chick, you sure got the point.'

'Do we have here a *double entendre*?'

'Really,' he said. She could feel his muscles relax. He chuckled, and in his normal, casual way, inquired, 'Want me to tell you I love you?'

'If,' she made the obvious reply, 'that's what you tell all the girls.'

He chuckled again and said no more.

A blessing. She was incapable of another word, another syllable. Vliet, lying on his back tapping ash out of the window, began to hum 'Let it Be', a contented sound. But that puppy! Alix, also on her back, not touching Vliet, wished she could cuddle it. How heartless could owners be, ignoring that whimpering?

At intermission they left. After she had unlocked her door, he curved his hands around her shoulders and for a couple of seconds his chin rested on her hair. She voted it most personal contact of the evening.

Chapter Eight

I

Summer, for Cricket, came to an end on the overcast September afternoon when the twins flew to Baltimore. Alix already was gathering clothes for the thirty-mile trek to a dorm in Pomona.

At first Cricket drew into herself. She walked slowly, forgetting what she had been going to do. She would find herself examining her (sometimes) dark-rimmed nails. Everything seemed shadowy. She missed Alix and Roger. She missed Vliet terribly. She would try to evoke the summer, but without the others, without their presence as testimony, the summer faded into an overexposed, out-of-focus, black-and-white print.

Cricket lived very much in the present.

She began to sleep late. After the years of getting up early for school, it was beautiful. She loved her room, the only upstairs in the Mathenys' sprawling Bel Air house. The previous owner, a film writer, needing a place to work, had built this aerie with its circular windows. Most mornings, smog veiled the city in the golden haze of a nineteenth-century sepia photograph: after a heavy wind or rain, though, the air glittered clean, and across twenty-six miles of Pacific, she could make out the purple shadow of Catalina. She would gaze out of the window, dreamily tying the royal-blue kimono with gold-tongued dragons she'd found at Goodwill. Barefoot, she clambered down chill metal rungs which curled like a fire station's. She would get herself an orange. On the kitchen table, her father's breakfast dishes were hidden under the financial section.

The rest of the *Times* was on Caroline's bed. Caroline, propped up by pillows, a mug of black coffee in hand, a full ashtray on the blanket cover, would be on the phone. She would excuse herself with, 'My nestling's down. Call you later.' They would hug. 'I saw Catalina.' 'I know this sounds *in*credible, but we used to see it all the time in the olden days.' Cricket would peel her orange into a paper napkin and snuggle at the foot of the bed, letting tart segments dissolve in her mouth, feeling grown-up as she listened to Caroline describe a party, mimicking the other guests, sometimes unkindly, always wittily. 'And what did you and Tom do?' Caroline would inquire, arch. Tom Gustavsen, pronounced Goose-ta-av-sen, a photography major at UCLA. Caroline knew exactly what her daughter did with Tom. Sometimes Em would phone, reading in her anxious voice a letter from one of the twins. Cricket would scrunch next to her mother, listening. If the postman delivered them a letter from the boys, they would call Em.

Caroline would disappear into her vast, mirror-lined bathroom to ready herself for shopping at Magnin's or Saks. She had her salesladies, whom she gave Christmas presents in exchange for being first to see 'what just came in'. Generally she shopped with friends. Never once did she try to influence Cricket to join them. Caroline considered it her God-given challenge not to impose her dedication to the body (as a pleasure object) on her child. Actually, if she had, it would have been more of a challenge. Cricket, in her small innocence, was incorruptible.

After Caroline left, Cricket would return to the writer's hideaway. His wet bar had been converted to a darkroom. A couple of afternoons a week, she and Tom would take off on a photographic safari.

To Cricket those hazy autumn evenings had the most glamour. She and Tom would visit his friends in their messy apartments around the UCLA campus. I'm old enough to know people with their own places, she would think, awed.

That was the autumn she had turned sixteen.

Cricket stood on wet asphalt at the top of the drive. It was Christmas vacation. Vliet and Roger had been due in last night. Their custom was to drop over the next day.

Rain had stopped a few minutes earlier, and now the sun was out. The silver birch next to the garage was a luminous miracle: opals gleamed at the end of each brown catkin, moonstones caught at each secret bud. The lovely tree gave Cricket a queer ache, as if a bubble were swelling inside her chest.

She was photographing the birch when Vliet arrived. Leaving her Nikon on wet paving, she ran to him. He lifted her, hugging, then put her down. He measured off with a graceful, waist-high wave of hand.

'How come you never grow?' he asked.

With anyone else she would have blushed. Four-feet-ten seemed less than nothing.

'How come you never shrink?' she asked.

He measured her head this time. 'Short-stuff,' he said.

'Where's Roger?'

'Baltimoh.'

'But why?'

'The last minute, and he decided his medical career would be forever screwed if he didn't hit the books.'

For a moment the fresh afternoon dimmed. She missed Roger. But for Cricket it was Vliet's blond hair, Vliet's smile that shone. Since before memory she'd felt this way about him, showing her love so openly that the family, Vliet included, discounted it, like a comfortable chair that one sits on every day and therefore doesn't actually see.

'Where's Aunt Caroline?'

'Christmas shopping and shopping-shopping.'

'The great consumer,' he said. 'Christ, I missed you, Bubble Mouse.' He concocted nicknames for her. Cricket was his invention. She'd been christened Amelie Deane, after her great-grandmother. *But she looks like a little Cricket,* Vliet had persisted.

Inside, she poured him milk, scrambling up on the lower shelf to reach for Assorted Tea Biscuits. Vliet leaned back until the front legs of his captain's chair were raised. He took a crinkly paper of cookies.

'How's Johns Hopkins?' she asked.

'Grinding.'

She wrinkled her nose.

'Really, there's your only description. Meat. Just meat is all. Roger and I share a stiff with two other guys.' He leaned towards her. 'Eau de cadaver.'

She sniffed. 'More like aftershave. Nice. Is Roger really behind?'

'You kidding? You know him. He's gotta be ready to hang up the old shingle. Cricket, he's one damn boil coming to a head. Only for your innocent ears, this, but if the bastard isn't totally horny, I – well, take my word. He is. He's between. Why doesn't he get on to the next dog?' (Roger gravitated to mortal girls with heavy glasses or heavy legs.)

'Ever ask?'

'Ever try for a broken jaw? This is your total uptight situation.'

She nibbled a cookie.

'Being a twin,' Vliet said, 'is only slightly less fun than using a kidney machine. And I'm stuck with him. Not that we're together that much, he being so straight and virtuous and hardworking and honest and sincere.'

'You make it sound bad.'

'Having him three thousand miles away is bad. Ever had that dream, the one where you're at a party and you look down and realize you've forgotten something? Like, say, your pants?'

'Or your conscience?'

'Really.' He grinned, drinking milk. 'That's some shirt.'

She glanced down. She was wearing a navy-and-yellow-stripe T-shirts with CUB SCOUTS written cursively along the yellow. 'Got it at a swap meet. Only fifty cents.'

'I'd've sold you mine for a quarter.' Circling the sleeve, his fingers drummed lightly on bare skin below. 'Sexy you, you sex me up, sexy you,' he crooned like an old-time singer.

He meant, of course, the opposite. Still, she wanted to hold his hand to her and, with this, her happiness shattered. It took her a moment to understand why. Vliet did sex her up. For the first time, her love for him was tinged with carnality. The plain freckled face was suffused with colour. After the autumn, she thought, the loss of innocence this autumn, it's because of Tom. In Tom's place, making love had come about naturally. One minute they had been looking at a proof sheet and the next they were entwined on his Navajo rug. Warm, pleasurable, exciting. Cricket, able to give herself to the moment, was a true sensualist. Yet she did not invest what Tom and she did on coarse, handwoven wool with romance, which, possibly, was why when a couple of weeks ago they had decided to be friends, just friends, they could be. Now she picked Tom up in her car – Caroline's old Buick – to go take pictures, kissing his prickly cheek when she dropped him off.

Vliet took away his hand. He lit a cigarette.

'Where's Alix?' she asked.

'Sweating out an exam. I rise at the crack of dawn, drive through the flood. Buy the woman lunch. Right away she drags herself off to hit the books. Want some?'

Cricket sipped from his milk glass. She didn't envy Alix. But how could she not? In the new circumstances, how not? She was unable to conjure up any emotion towards Alix beyond despairing affection laced with pity. Cricket always had sensed that Alix's perfection was, like the gift of a wicked fairy godmother, a curse. Alix didn't believe in her own beauty, but it turned others envious, catty, awed, surly – obstacles Alix must surmount without realizing why.

Vliet asked, 'And what've you been doing?'

Cricket shrugged. Her doings she considered like her

body. Too small-scale to be of interest.

'Really. You must've done something.'

'Oh, enjoy myself.'

'That activity is no good for growing children.' He leaned back, smiling at her, his feet doing a tap dance under the table. 'Have to get you earning your bread by the sweat of your brow like the rest of us slobs.'

3

'I'm stuck for a drive to LAX,' Vliet was saying through the phone.

The holidays over, Aunt Em must have a 'cold', Cricket decided. She said, 'Pick you up.'

On the way to the airport a funny thing happened.

Vliet started on there's-this-holier-than-everybody-stage-that-certain-adolescents-get-into-causing-them-to-think-they-don't-need-to-do-one-damn-thing-beyond-contemplating-their-navel-fluff.

Stretching his long legs on the Buick's worn carpet, he finished, 'Admit it. To you college is the living pits, and a horde of professors are waiting, for Chrissakes, to corrupt Cricket Matheny from her pure state of intellectual ignorance.'

'You sound like you've been brushing up on your Salinger.'

'But with a grain of truth?'

'A lot of people aren't going now.'

'Don't give me it's a sign of the times, Cricket. It won't wash. Not when I know your IQ's one sixty. Or was the number sixty-one?'

'My parents aren't hassling me.'

'Uncle Gene and Aunt Caroline have the old laissez-faire attitude. Do not interfere with nature's major minor miracle.'

Cricket's small hands tightened on the wheel. Her parents liked her fine the way she was, she knew this, but hearing Vliet say it caused a fuzzy pain on her skin, as if she'd been dumped into scalding water.

'What's wrong with just living?' she asked.

'Listen to what you're saying, willya? No goals, no aims. You're totally, goddamn absolutely satisfied with the *status quo.*'

Of course she wasn't. She knew she was small, plain. Yet at the same time she inherited Caroline's assuredness. She drove the great arcing span to the Ventura Freeway and lifted her chin.

'Nobody chops you, do they, Cricket?' he said, laughing. 'That Lady Vere de Vere in microfilm, it gets me, Cricket, it really does.'

She guided the Buick into the flow of traffic. 'You think I should go?' she asked. She loved him. His good opinion meant everything to her. 'Do you?'

'Just get off that cute little ass is all.'

'Like?'

'How the hell should I know?'

'I've been working.'

'Do it seriously, then.'

She looked bewildered.

'Put yourself on the line,' he said. 'Do it right, finish it, to quote Ma. Don't cop out.' He rolled down the window and threw out his cigarette. He never finished them. 'Maybe you shouldn't go to college. You're too damn unpolluted. Listen, why not head someplace and do the click-click?'

'What's wrong with here?'

'Don't you have any ambition?'

'No,' she admitted sadly. 'None.'

At the airport Cricket watched from the vast window as his plane bumped onto the runway. Her thoughts kept zigging back and forth. Was Vliet right? Had she copped out? Not just on the college question, but all the way down the line? Well? She looked at her jeans – she had found them at the Salvation Army in Pasadena, and the knees were faded a lovely white. A lot of Brace Ridge girls had gone to thrift shops and swap meets. Still ... Was her refusal to visit Saks, Magnin's, and Judy's a means of escaping comparison with the beautiful Alixes? As if there could be comparison!

She had picked photography. Photography is a field where there is virtually no chance of making it. If, for example, she were a teacher, she would be called upon to show how well she taught. But as a photographer she never would have to face up to her own ability, or lack thereof.

She loved Vliet. Yet she wasn't jealous of his parade of Miss Americas, not even Alix. Come on, try a little, she ordered herself. But all she could summon was a kind of dull envy for Alix's competitiveness.

Furthermore, Cricket seemed to be the only sixteen-year-old girl in the State of California who loved her parents, admired them. Worse, was comfortable living with them.

She stepped back and saw herself, one of the crowd reflected in plate glass. A midget, non-productive, a floater, unwilling to enter the ambition game that is humanity's delight and torture. A parasite living on happiness that came to her free as Hawaiian breadfruit. Cricket might be young, but instinctively she understood certain truths. She knew that whatever benefits she would gain from putting herself on Vliet's line, happiness was not one of them.

His words lingered, though, like a flu bug that Cricket couldn't quite shake off.

Several nights later, she and her parents were eating dinner at the round kitchen table.

'I've been thinking,' Cricket announced. 'I'd like to take off, maybe up the coast. Do some serious work.'

Caroline's fork had halted and now was returning un-oiled romaine to her salad plate.

'The coast, luv, to take pictures?' Long pause. 'Then

you can stay with family?'

'I guess,' Cricket agreed. 'Yes.'

Caroline's relief surfaced in her fine laughter. 'We've been *won*dering when you'd flee the coop, haven't we, Genebo?'

Gene's thumbnail was pressed to his lip. Years ago he had broken himself of nail biting, yet at times of stress he couldn't prevent the old reflex of lifting his hand. He looked with searching gravity across the table. Freckles and innocently raised upper lip. Sixteen? My God, he thought, she looks twelve. He could feel the souring of bland food – he'd been nursing an ulcer the two years he'd been president of Van Vliet's.

'All by yourself?' he asked.

'Yes.'

'How far?'

'Oh, like Northern California.'

'She'll be with family,' Caroline put in.

'She'll be driving alone.'

'She drives alone now.'

'In Los Angeles.'

'You're nitpicking. Gene, stop being so *cautious*!'

Gene's glance at his wife, in the non-verbal lingo of the long-married, said, 'We'll discuss this later.'

He *was* cautious. For this reason he'd become head of the chain. When Richard Van Vliet decided to retire, he gathered the stockholders, Van Vliets all, to tell them he wanted to quit and their new man was Gene Matheny. 'You can trust him,' Richard said, thus passing over the two obvious candidates, his own son and his dead brother's son. 'Gene's got vision, but he's not wild-eyed. He's careful. You'll see. He'll double the value of our stock.' And in the two years Gene damn near had. Any man who pursues money, Gene knew, has to have a certain stupidity. And here he was, Eugene Mathney, a pursuant (prisoner?) of the buck. Therefore the stupidest of the stupid. What else could you call a man who wastes his life and ulcerated guts chasing what means so little to him?

In bad moments Gene would wonder if Caroline's jaunty hedonism were a substitute for the regard he'd lost in her shrewd blue eyes that long-ago winter noon when LeRoy Duquesne, PhD, had grounded his hopes. Gene's creative energy had been diverted into merchandising groceries with excessive attention to each mill of profit. He had no respect for his work. Or himself. He was privately aware, as if of impotence, that the markets, which everyone assumed were his pride, were his shame. Yet he was not unhappy. He loved and was faithful to his wife. They had Cricket, the family. Besides, one has to have time to cultivate unhappiness. Gene worked a fourteen-hour day.

He remained a liberal while officiating in the priesthood of capitalism – indeed, for this reason he clung the more devoutly to his early tenets. He believed the finest human is the one permitted to grow up without parental influence. Each child is a *tabula rasa* and must be permitted to scribble his own story. Cricket had been sent to progressive schools. Gene reached with alacrity for his chequebook whenever she verbalized one of her rare desires for more camera equipment. He never objected to the books she read, the photographs she took or bought. When she asked to see *Hair* for her birthday, Gene sat next to her, looking tolerantly through his glasses at frontal nudity and simulated sex groping. A decent, even straitlaced man in his own life, he refused to perpetrate evasions that might alter Cricket's purity of vision. A child developing in its own bent, according to him, was the cardinal responsibility of parenthood. He finished dinner in silence.

En famille they sat in front of the TV for 'The Smothers Brothers'. Afterwards, Cricket gave a yawn and climbed the circular steps to her room.

'The girls all travel now,' Caroline said.

Gene put down the land prospectus he was studying.

'She's only sixteen,' he said.

'They're everywhere. Europe, Asia –'

'Not at sixteen, alone.'

'You know how sensible Cricket is.'

'She's a total innocent!'

'Give me a good, hónest innocent any day. They see far more clearly than us cynical astigmatics.' Caroline removed her reading glasses, making a nearsighted Mr Magoo face, then chuckling.

Gene smiled unwillingly. 'Probably they do,' he admitted.

'Then why don't you trust her?'

'I do trust her!'

'She's a careful driver.'

'But –'

'And we have family up and down every nook and cranny of California. Don't you *see*, Genebo? Like this she can be away from us in a protected environment. Develop her own potential.'

Gene knew his wife was pushing his weaknesses for all she was worth. He also knew that Caroline loved Cricket fiercely, the more so for the operations inflicted on their child's infant body. For these reasons, love and pain, Caroline had vowed never to impose her admittedly bossy self on Cricket. She never would permit Cricket to be smothered under the canopy of protectiveness that is the bane of only children. 'Every night she'll be under a family roof. For heaven's sake, Gene!'

Gene picked up his prospectus. The cautious need more time.

For six days Caroline busily convinced her husband that their daughter should be permitted 'to express herself,' one of his cherished phrases.

Finally, he capitulated. 'She's got to keep in touch every day,' was his condition.

Cricket, unaware of the parental battle, readily promised to phone every evening, to write often, and never, never to give anyone a lift.

In Santa Barbara she stayed with Donnie Van Vliet. She photographed San Francisco while luxuriating in the Nob Hill apartment of Fletcher Van Vliet, who ran the newly acquired Northern Warehouse. She stayed with

Tina Matheny at Humboldt State.

She started home.

4

REVELATION was painted in mysterious Islamic lettering above the restaurant's brick patio.

In Carmel, morning fog is routine, but now, at noon, it had burned away. Oak-shaded crowded tables. Not one vacancy. Waiters and waitresses bore salads and foamy juices, moving calmly to and fro. The bearded men wore white clothes and white headbands to keep back their long hair. The women, too, were in white. Not uniforms. An old Arrow with the collar lovingly embroidered, a pleated Mexican wedding shirt, a blonde girl floating in white muslin, another's blouse patched with crocheted doilies. I must do that with Grandma Wynan's, Cricket thought as she wove her way to a free table.

Her waiter's scraggy beard grew from a narrow face. About her age, she guessed. She mashed her banana into yogurt, eating slowly, luxuriating in white shapes moving in and out of sunlight. She was last at her waiter's station, and he began, hesitantly, to talk.

'I'm Cricket Matheny,' she said.

'I'm Orion.'

'That's an unusual name.'

He ducked his head in an embarrassment that reminded her of Tom Gustavsen.

She soothed, 'But then Cricket's not exactly everyday.'

'I used to be Lance Putnam. You know, Madison Avenue. Here, with the group, we pick a new name. I chose Orion.'

Cricket already had guessed those who worked here were linked, possibly in religion. 'Orion,' she said, trying it out. 'Orion's a constellation.'

'Is it? I just, you know, liked the sound.'

She touched her Nikon, snouted with a new 200-milli-metre lens that was her parents' going-away gift. 'Okay to use this?'

Orion frowned anxiously. 'I better get Giles,' he said.

Giles Cooke, thirty years older than the rest, also wore white. A heavy-set man too short of leg for his massive shoulders, with a greying beard spread across his power-ful chest.

'A lot of people want to take photographs,' he said in a purposefully calm bass. 'I ask why.'

'It's so peaceful.'

'Is that all?'

'I'd just like to try to get it on film.'

'People think of us as freaks.'

His voice was mild, yet she was intimidated – maybe because the mild voice issued from a greying beard.

She flushed. 'But you aren't, you aren't at all.'

'In a way.'

'No.'

'You yourself said we're different.'

'I meant, the place is wonderful, so calm and full of peace.'

Giles sat at the table. He had a scent to him, masculine, yet not tobacco or sweat. He picked up her camera, turning it in thick hands. He didn't know cameras, he said, and this remark, she sensed, was to put her at ease, so she told him about her new lens. He asked about other lenses and exposures. She felt like a young child being manipulated by a clever teacher.

'Do you sell your pictures?'

'I never tried.'

'Are you rich, then?'

'Comfortable,' she said. 'My parents are.'

He returned her camera. 'Go ahead.'

The rest of the afternoon she squatted and perched behind her Nikon. Straddle-legged, she stalked tame white pigeons. Sea fog rolled in, swallowing warmth and light.

Orion asked, 'Giles wants to know, will you spend the night at our place?'

She hesitated. She was on parole, bound by her promise to stay only with family; the fact that she loved her parents made the decision harder. She assessed the fogged patio. White clothes were disappearing into a tall old bus. Well? She'd have to stay in a motel. Wasn't this preferable?

'That's really nice of him,' she said. 'Thank you.'

5

The Chinese compound had been built during the twenties by an eccentric oil millionaire who chose to isolate himself five miles from Carmel Valley proper, his only access a twisting rut that turned to swamp with rain. A white elephant with cheap rent. During Cricket's first visit, seven girls and five boys rattled around in the blue-tile-roofed villas enclosing the courtyard.

The group had started with three members last August when Giles had opened REVELATION. Work and life were integrated as in a monastery. Giles was still formulating the order. Any rule he came up with was obeyed: the deliberate walk, the raw food, the nightly procession from the great hall, white clothes – made it seem like a Chinese funeral. As each law was revealed unto Giles, he would set up a meeting to explain it.

Cricket slept in a vast, furnitureless room with Magnificat (formerly Staci Grant of Orange County). At five came a bronze summons. The two girls rose from their mats, gasping as they washed in icy water, shivering across the dark courtyard to the great, beamed hall. Incense burned. On fleece rugs they meditated for half an hour. Giles then spoke of universal love and peace, his voice reverberating in his thick chest. Cricket had heard it all before, but never so compellingly. The men remained in the hall for Fellowship. Cricket went off with the women to prepare food. At eight the huge verdigris-encrusted bell sounded again. They breakfasted in the courtyard on wheat germ, almonds, raisins, dates, and unpasteurized milk. Nourishment, Orion whispered to her, that must last until six o'clock dinner. The secondhand yellow school bus jounced down the tortuous path. 'When it rains, how do you get out?' Cricket asked. Orion replied, 'Why would we need to? Outdoor restaurants, you know, don't open in the rain.' From the Carmel Valley Road it was a fast half hour to REVELATION.

The bus carried Giles away. He returned with crates of fresh curly greens, crates dripping red of berries, crates of apples, melons, celery. Giles's blade flashed in lettuce and artichokes. Cricket noticed his heavy frame shudder as he re-locked knives in a cabinet above the cash register.

'Why's he locking them away?' she asked Orion.

'He's the only one allowed to use them.'

'Why?'

'They're weapons.'

'Vegetable knives?' she asked.

'All knives're, you know, weapons.'

(The noon rush over, they sat on the patio wall – Cricket had just phoned Caroline to explain she was staying a day or two with new friends.)

'Only if they're used that way.'

'They're symbols,' Orion said.

'Not if they're cutting lettuce.' She had been profoundly disturbed by the way Giles's thick shoulders quivered as if under the whip.

'Every knife, Giles says, symbolizes every other knife. He wants us to kill the violence in ourselves.'

'Kill violence,' she said. 'That's weird.'

'He didn't put it like that ...' Orion's hesitancy apologized even for this mild dispute. 'In each of us there's this murder instinct. Wartime leaders only have to wave a flag and there most of us are with this kill kill kill reaction. We have to rid ourselves of every reminder, you know, of violence, before we can become immune. That's our goal here. To become truly at peace.' He stopped. 'Giles is right. He always is. That's why we obey him.'

Here was REVELATION's first commandment.

Thou shalt obey Giles. They had ended up here because they were lost in the way only bourgeois youth can be lost. They weren't hungry or anything, but something sure was missing. Giles gave them faith, belief, a religion. They were celibate. If, later, they chose to marry, they would come together for the flesh's true purpose only: to create new life. They eschewed knives and leather. They were vegetarian – animals, too, are God's creatures, and anyway, meat-eating destroys spirituality. The work was divided into men's tasks and women's tasks, as the Bible saith.

There are a lot of communes. Cricket, though, never had lived in one. She was entranced. Each morning she rolled up her straw mat, eager even at this unearthly hour to unravel mysteries. She learned that Magnificat, née Staci Grant, willowy, dimpled, and redheaded, had had three (illegal) abortions before she was eighteen, and that Disciple had turned heroin addict in Vietnam. That Orion's life as Lance Putnam had been divided one month at a time between his mother's large home near the Huntington Museum and his alcoholic father's apartment in San Marino.

She ate organic meals, she wore her white Levi's with her Mexican shirt, sat in meditation. Yet even when her ankle ached, she found herself moving faster than the others. She talked in clearer tones. Once, during meditation, she got this crazy urge to shake herself like a wet pup and run noisy, yipping circles around the silent figures.

She would feel Giles watching her. When their eyes met, he would smile. She couldn't award him *loco parentis* as the others had – Caroline and Gene were her anchor people. Yet for Cricket, Giles's grey beard, his powerful build, his age transformed him into a patriarch.

One evening he sat next to her on the bus home.

'I don't see the fancy camera,' he said. 'You have all the pictures you want?'

She had only that first afternoon's negatives. 'I hope so,' she said.

'Go ahead whenever you want to.'

'I, uhh, feel like I'm, uhh, prying.'

'Then you've caught onto our way?'

'You live in peace.'

'And how do we manage it?'

'Everybody shares. You help each other. Synergistic.'

'Amazing, isn't it, how much easier life is when you aren't fighting up the ladder?'

They swayed, jolting. The bus had turned off the road. They moved into purple, folded hills. A pair of quail, crests bobbing, walked unfrightened.

After a silence, Giles said, 'You belong here.'

Cricket had to battle an impulse to answer, *Right, yes, I do belong*. She did not feel this way. Her response came from his depth of voice, his tone of command.

She wondered, as she had before, about Giles Cooke.

Nobody knew his past. Giles believed that former lives have no utility. He had absolved each of them of any past sin, laying on the light penitence of never revealing certain details: these secrets Giles kept hidden in his head like the sacred reliquaries buried under cathedral floors. The past is dead, Giles ordained. We live in the Eternal Now. A philosophy that Cricket, God knows, understood. But Brace Ridge had taught her to question, and sitting next to Giles, conscious of his bulk, his odours, his grizzled beard, she asked herself wasn't Giles the sum of a mysterious former life?

'You belong,' he repeated. And said no more.

6

'You have a good soul,' Orion said.

'Yeah. Sure,' Cricket replied.

They were exploring the hills around the Chinese compound.

'It's true. My head's together enough now to catch the vibrations.'

'You people here are good.'

'We have to work at it. You're there already.'

A peculiar conversation to be having with a shy boy whose rough hand she held as they climbed, especially since it had to be seen in the light of the fact that during the four days she'd known him, Orion reminded her more and more of Tom Gustavsen. Vliet, she thought suddenly, and stumbled. Earth got in the sandal of her bad foot. She wiggled her leg to get it out. Orion steadied her.

'Don't leave,' he said.

'Did Giles say anything?'

'I want you to stay.' Orion's narrow face was tense. 'Yes, he did. We all want you.'

'Because of my soul?'

'Don't laugh.'

'Orion, I'm not putting you down.'

'Just stick here awhile. You don't have to, you know, make any real decision. Not yet.'

Vliet had said she never committed herself. Well, here was her big chance. It was funny and she would have laughed except it would have hurt Orion. Wasn't this place, these people, the last commitment that Vliet had intended? She let go of Orion's hand.

When they reached the crest they were both panting. Orion pushed up his white band, mopping sweat from his forehead. The sky was a soft blue, a patch of early spring lupine echoed this blue, and far below, from blue-tile roofs, a flight of birds scattered. From here they were tiny dots.

'It's so beautiful,' she said.

'Stay.'

The following afternoon she left.

She had been with REVELATION five days, and her decision to go had nothing to do with Giles or Orion. In late morning she called Caroline from a phone booth in Carmel. The sun burned through glass, very hot, but they were a long time.

'Nothing else is new,' Caroline said. 'Oh yes. The twinnies'll be home.'

'Soon?'

'Next week, Em said. They have time off for Easter. God, I *hope* Roger comes this time. Poor Em, she lives for those two beautiful lunks.' Pause. 'Why don't you be home?'

'I will,' said Cricket. ' 'Course I will.'

Chapter Nine

I

They entered the cloud bank, and pine trees came out of the gloom, materializing for one ghostly second before disappearing. Roger flicked on the dims, stopping at the Arrowhead turn-off so they could pile on more clothes. Vliet, a worn, red-plaid shirt, the heavy lumberjack kind, Roger shrugging into a leather jacket with sheepskin bleeding through at one arm, and Cricket – already bundled in three mismatched sweaters – pulling up the zip of an Indian cardigan which hung almost to her knees. Alix thanked God she'd bought her Austrian loden cape – it was old.

As she looped buttons through thick green wool, she said, 'Mother was up here right after –' Abruptly she stopped. She still could not say Jamie's name to anyone except (infrequently) her parents. The violence of her grief repelled her. She kept it to herself, decent, lonely, and raw as a bleeding ulcer.

'After what?' Roger spoke for the first time, almost.

Alix shook her head. Something about Jamie was nagging at her, but she was busy erasing her remark with, 'Oh, after God and before The Bomb. She used to come up with Caroline.'

'Then you have pre-knowledge of the place?' Vliet asked. 'Like memory in a cut cutworm?'

'I pray for it.' Alix clasped her knit gloves together.

'Yeah,' Roger said.

'I do. The three of you, blood relatives, and me the original outsider.'

'Ever try saying something you mean?' Roger asked.

'Hey, it's freezing,' Cricket cried, hauling her small self back in the mini-bus.

At the cabin Roger busied himself with a chemical toilet,

Vliet did things with gas and water pipes, and Cricket was meant to put away groceries, but she was a dawdler. It was Alix who efficiently stocked shelves. Her breath formed clouds. She thought of the ice mansion where Zhivago had written his poems to Lara.

She had noted a stack of logs by the front door. She set rough pine over kindling, struggling to rip a carton with cold-reddened hands, feeding the scraps. She knelt, blowing and coughing. Finally some bark caught.

'What do you know,' Roger said, pausing to unwrap a Hershey. He added the paper to her small flame. 'Fire.'

'Three summers at Trinity, you have to learn something.'

'I never figured you for a Boy Scout.'

She sat back on her boot heels, visualizing the little box house. Trinity was an expensive camp.

'I would've learned from Girls Scouts had I been a member,' she said. Then, without meaning to, added, 'Roger, don't push me. Please?'

'I'm a superior pain in the ass when I try for humour.'

'On the way up, was that meant to be funny?'

He looked uneasily down at her. 'No, not then,' he admitted. 'I'm sorry.' He held out chocolate. A peace offering.

She broke off two squares, putting one in her mouth. He grinned. 'Hey, that cape, I like it,' he said. And went for more wood. She let the chocolate melt in her mouth, watching him. He doesn't move gracefully, like Vliet, she thought, he moves better, with a kind of comfortable strength.

They gathered in front of the fire to eat hamburgers. Afterwards, Roger tilted his head back, drinking Coors from the can. Vliet rolled Zig Zags, passing joints, and Cricket dozed. Alix, keeper of the flame, fire-tonged a log, shifting it. She was riveted to a single fact. Soon, soon, she and Vliet would go downstairs to the bedrooms, she and Vliet together, with Roger watching. Ridiculous, she kept telling herself. Roger knows I'm sleeping with Vliet. Intellectual information, though, is abstract. Having Roger watch them go to a bedroom is concrete, embarrassing and for Alix something far worse than embarrassing. Dishonourable. A log fell, giving up sparks.

Vliet, yawning, said, 'C'mon, Alix. Dance.' Pulling her up, he began to sing 'When the Saints Go Marchin' In', dancing her to the shadowy kitchen corner, dancing her to the windows, putting his arm over her shoulders. Side by side, their hips sashaying in perfect time to his beat, *I want to be in their number*, bumpsy, bumpsy, they danced to the dark stairwell. It was so easy. She should've remembered nothing public was embarrassing with Vliet.

The uncarpeted little room was refrigerated. Alix's nipples puckered into her breasts, and to hide the sad display, she turned her back, hastily dropping on her flannel nightgown. The sheets were clammy cold. Vliet, in old grey sweats, hugged her.

'I've just got my period,' she apologized.

'There's timing,' he said. She held her breath in the icy dark, hoping he would keep his arms around her at least until she was warm. 'Well,' he said, turning onto his back, 'other stuff.'

She thoroughly disliked other stuff, and the disliking made her feel yet more inadequate. Saying nothing, shivering, freezing, miserable, she moved over him and put on a heavy act.

2

Light came around skimpy curtains. She glanced at her small Bulova. Ten past seven. Vliet breathed lightly. Blond stubble showed. His long face was relaxed and his quizzical expression gone. Sleep is more personal than sex, she decided, looking away. She stretched her arms overhead and arched her back. The morning chill was different. Alive. Happy.

She buttoned her robe, pulling on grey woollen socks that, like her cape, had come from *Ach Du Lieber* Vienna, and were too heavy for normal Southern California purposes. She tip-toed out. Upstairs she opened the porch door, gulping mountain-scented ice. Morning sun was brilliant, outlining with black the trees that dropped down to the lake. A small bird swooped directly at her, veering at the last moment. She laughed aloud. Salutation to the dawn, she thought, and waved her arms up and down, dancing sideways along the narrow porch. Fast-moving socks make sweet sluffing sounds.

She heard another noise. Halted.

Roger's hands were touching the top of the door. His T-shirt, stretched like this, exposed a strip of muscular, hairy stomach. Across the faded navy was yellow-stitched WRECKED ROGER'S RAGS. He was smiling. 'Good morning,' he said.

'Not just good. Fantastic,' she replied, too happy to be defensive about her dance.

He breathed big under Wrecked Roger's Rags. 'Isn't it?'

'Want some coffee?'

'Tea,' he countered.

'Me, too. I hate coffee.' She lit the high-legged stove with a match. 'Anything else?'

'I'm going to scramble eggs. Want some?'

'No-no. I'll wait for Vliet.'

Roger was opening cupboards. Finding a heavy china bowl, he asked, 'Don't you eat breakfast?'

'My favourite meal.'

'Unless it's forced on him, Vliet never gets up before lunch.'

'I've never in my life slept past eight-thirty.'

'Me, neither,' Roger replied. He cracked an egg, south-paw. Shell fragments oozed into the bowl.

'Here,' Alix said.

'Eggs are my speciality.' He cracked another. More shell.

'The hands of a surgeon, not a chef.'

Laughing, he surrendered the bowl. She spooned shell from albumen, cracking four more eggs, sprinkling pepper, pouring salt from her palm, measuring in two spoons of icy water, holding the bowl against her robe. Rich melting-butter smells. Bacon crisping in heavy spider. Turn whole-grain bread in old-fashioned toaster.

'A major coup,' he said. 'Everything hot at once.'

They smiled at one another.

She looked away first. For months now, Alix had admitted to herself how she felt about Roger. When he hadn't come home at Christmas, her total misery (undisplayed, naturally) had proved to her what until then she had managed to submerge. She loved him. She loved him, and love terrified her.

She formed a large smile. 'My Beverly Hills exterior hides a Dickensian past. Age ten I was apprenticed as a domestic. Cook, clean, scrub, iron, I learned the household arts the hard –'

'Look, you were the one who wanted me to quit, remember?' The blue eyes were bewildered. 'Jesus, for a few minutes can't you drop the dialogue?'

'Does everything have to be stony-bottom serious with you?'

'When you're funny, I know how to laugh.'

She looked down at her eggs. 'I did do stuff when I was a kid,' she said quietly. 'Mother kept at her painting. Anyway, she's not neat. And here's a terrible confession. I am. So we –' She caught herself in time. Jamie. No trespassing. 'I used to dust between Willeen's Mondays, vacuum, iron. Cook dinner sometimes.'

'Ours wouldn't let us near the kitchen.'

'Let? Mother didn't notice. Artists get involved.'

'Understandable.'

'You get involved, too?'

'Very.' He buttered toast. 'Her painting bothers you, doesn't it?'

'Let me think on that one,' Alix said. She finished her eggs.

'Well?' he asked.

'Well what?'

'Well isn't this a fabulous morning,' he said, biting into his toast, watching her. Butter caught on his upper lip, and he sucked with the lower, watching her.

'I do have a mother-ambivalence thing. I don't mean to keep putting her down. She's very gentle and unique. Other-worldly, sort of. And a terrific artist. Most people think every good painter starves to death in a New York loft. It's difficult to realize a serious artist might live north of Sunset in Beverly Hills. She's going to have a one-woman show in The County. You can't buy that sort of thing. She was into mad rabbis before Francis Bacon and his mad popes, at least I'm pretty sure she was. When we get down I'll show you.'

'You're proud of her,' he said.

'Very. And her talent does bother me. Roger, want honey on that?'

He was starting the last piece. 'Not unless –'

'I'm getting it for my tea.'

'There's a coincidence. I use it in mine.'

They looked at one another.

Touch me, she thought. And her hand inched towards his. Sunlight flickered on her buffed nails. She realized what she was doing. Quickly she rose, getting him a small jar labelled ORGANIC CLOVER HONEY, and nervous about sitting near him, went back to the draining board for a slice of bread, carrying it and her tea mug to the porch. He followed, leaning on the door. She put crumbs on the rail. Wings flashed. Blue jays squawked. 'That one's not getting any,' Roger said. The tension around his cheekbones had softened. His body was relaxed yet solid. She was conscious of her own body, her back muscles, the spring in her thighs as she bent to feed the neglected jay.

Around ten, Cricket, puffy-eyed and yawning, dragged upstairs.

Vliet got up just before noon. He was blowing his nose. 'Terrific,' he said. 'The common cold is with us.'

Vliet stayed indoors. Sniffling, coughing. Irritable.

You'd never know this except for his cracks. They seemed funny, and were, but he would smile until you got the stinging point.

Mornings Vliet slept. The rest of the time he was dispatching his good nurse for soup or hot lemonade or vitamin C tablets. The weather turned overcast. Chill draughts swept through the old cabin.

Alix's time would have been less painful with the other two around.

But Cricket would zip into her enormous sweater and take off, sometimes with Nikon, sometimes without. (Alix would wonder what it was like to be Cricket, never worrying about making conversation, never conscious of hair or clothes.)

Roger spent hours smashing across empty grey water in some relative's Chris-Craft. The rest of the time he was downstairs in his room, alone with the fat medical books he'd brought along.

Breakfast, though, they shared. He would lean towards her, telling her about dissecting a tubercular brain, not gory but fascinating. Vliet never mentioned college. Roger was profoundly involved with every detail of life at Johns Hopkins – even the trivia, like blood counts and protein analyses. She felt the force of his enthusiasm. She listened without impetus to retort wittily.

On the third morning, she inquired what it meant, Wrecked Roger's Rags? The T-shirt, he told her, had been presented by his high school teammates when he'd wrecked his ankle running a touchdown. 'I heard it crack,' he said, and pulled up the right leg of his jeans, showing a scar that extended from hairless ankle to muscular, dark-haired calf.

'At the beach I wondered about that,' she said. 'I didn't realize you were a jock. Did you win?'

'By the six points.' He grinned. 'Otherwise you think they'd've bought me the T-shirt?'

'Roger.'

'What?'

'Christmas I missed you.'

That peculiarly wholehearted smile of his disappeared. 'You melted the butter in the syrup,' he said.

'The pancakes don't get cold as fast.'

'Cold, they're doughy.'

'I needed to see you.'

'I wanted to see you, too,' he said quietly. 'That's why I didn't come.'

'I wrote.'

'You did? I never got a letter.'

'There's the US mail for you,' she said. 'I tore them up.'

'How many?'

'Five. No-no. Six.'

The wind had risen, howling through pine branches.

'I should've sent one of them,' she said.

He chewed.

'Shouldn't I?'

He poured more buttered syrup.

'I didn't quite get that answer,' she said.

'Did Vliet ever tell you about being a twin?'

She shook her head.

'Peculiar relationship,' he said. 'Close, very. Not ESP or anything mystic. It comes from being side by side in your cribs, sharing a playpen, never being apart. Never being alone. You get to know your brother as yourself. There's always him. You don't have to round up a neighbour to play. You're independent, a unit. It cut pretty deep when he started with a gang. People always like him. I'm dull company. We are totally different, but that only makes it more convoluted. What I'm trying to say is, there are ties, ties. Understand?'

'You love him.'

'Yes. But it's deeper and less sticky than that. It's being the same person in two totally different brains and bodies.'

'Kind,' she said.

'What?'

'You're being kind. Letting me down easy.'

'You aren't the type to be let down by anyone.'

'That first year must be heavy on the psych!' she burst out. 'How else could you understand me so well!'

'I only know girls like you have guys waiting from here to there.'

'And from there to here, too!'

'And one of them happens to be my brother and, like you say, I'm a serious guy, so I'd just as soon you didn't phony it up with unwritten letters.'

He might as well have slugged her in the chest. She had retyped each often, and the last had taken her three days to perfect. She felt so lost that she wanted to fold her arms on the battered kitchen table and cry. Big girls don't. Empty, phony girls can't. Alix picked up their dishes. At the sink her chest pains grew worse. I must get out, she thought. Cooped up in this miserable cabin I'm doing and saying all the wrong things. I have to move. A panic of necessity, this removing herself from the scene of the crime (rejection and/or making an ass of herself).

By the time she had washed up the breakfast things, she was able to speak. 'Roger, let me have the keys?'

He looked at her, startled.

'We need milk. Lemons. Stuff.'

'Let me drive you.'

She knew an apology when she heard one. Anyway, it was agree or cry. She got her cape.

The Volkswagen crunched over small twigs scurrying across the road. Alix's period was almost finished, but she felt very menstrual. She had read *Anna Karenina* again, and she remembered, more or less: *Like everyone else, in his past he'd done things that were wrong and that he should have on his conscience. Yet he suffered far less from these wrong acts than from insignificant humiliations.* Humiliations, she kept thinking. Every once in a while she would shiver. Damn him, she would think, damn all three of them.

In the supermarket she chattered inconsequentially. She never let up. 'This brand we use at home. Pure poison ... Believe it or not, Mother's never made a pot of coffee in her life. Always instant. Roger, like Postum? ...

235

What? Never had it? What did your grandma give you when the adults had coffee? ... Think chicken noodle'll cure Vliet's cold?... Smell that? Barbecued ribs. Shall I get some? Why not? ... Hey, there're chocolate cookies. Mmmm, you've had a lot of chemistry. What is it, dicalcimate of glycerine? ... Roger, be a doll, reach up and get those double-A eggs, the extra large. Three boxes.'

'We aren't staying that long.'

'Oh, look! Dried mushrooms. Now, they're good and serious in soup.'

His mouth taut, he shoved the trolley.

The cashier was a youngish woman wearing a heavy sweater pushed up to show thick red arms.

'Think spring'll ever come?' Alix asked with a dazzling smile.

The cashier became Alix's friend. 'Never,' she said. 'That's a darling cape, hon. Get it around here?'

'No-no.'

'You can't never find anything that cute.' She pushed wholewheat bread along the stand, ringing her register. 'You got a basketful.'

'Hungry mouths to feed.'

The cashier said in a stage whisper, 'I could tell right off you wasn't newlyweds.'

Alix laughed.

The cashier rang the total, $23.49. Roger reached for his wallet, but Alix already had her B of A chequebook in hand. 'Now, Roger,' she said dulcetly.

The woman held up Alix's cheque. 'Alexandra Nancy Schorer. One-two-oh-seven Crescent. [She pronounced it Creskent.] Beverly Hills. Have a bank card here?'

Alix shook her head.

'Let's have your driver's licence, hon.' She jabbed a button, examining Alix's licence again. 'Not married,' she said.

'Not in the least,' Alix said.

The cashier glanced at Roger. He turned a satisfying red.

As Roger and Alix emerged, a little girl, possibly she

was eight, pedalled furiously around the car park on a small-wheel, high-handlebarred bicycle. Roger opened the back of the mini-bus, Alix hefted a bag from the trolley.

Tyres squealed.

Thud!

A narrow, wailing cry.

The little girl lay in an acute angle a yard from the overturned bike. The front wheel spun. A man was opening the door of a new green Pontiac. As Alix stared, blood began to spread on the child's pale-blue slacks.

'Oh Jesus!' Roger sprinted.

Alix, dropping the heavy brown paper bag into the trolley, ran after him.

'I didn't see her. Them fucking low bikes! There oughta be a law. How can anyone see 'em?' As the driver spoke, his chin worked.

And all the time the child was emitting a thin, terrible wail.

Roger, flipping off his jacket, knelt over her. His shoulder and back muscles formed a curve, a cave, strong, secure, protective. 'Listen, I'm going to try not to hurt you, but maybe I will.' He spoke quietly, his large hands gentle on the child. 'I have to see the bleeding, okay?' Moving her hips as little as possible, he slid down slacks. Bright red blood spurted from a frail wishbone leg. Pressing the heel of his hand to the depression of inner thigh, he asked, 'You a Brownie? Or a Bluebird?'

The child, now weeping in normal gulping sobs, shook her head. The orange earmuffs, twisted in lank hair, were matted with tears.

'I was a Scout. This is how they taught us to stop bleeding.' Roger glanced up at Alix, whispering swiftly, 'They have diapers in there. Get some. Find out if they have an ambulance or what. A doctor.' And he bent over the child, reassuring.

Alix pushed through onlookers. How do they know, like buzzards, the minute there's an accident? she wondered while another part of her brain efficiently catalogued Roger's order: diapers, ambulance, doctor.

Returning, she found a bigger group and a highway patrolman talking into his pipping motorcycle radio.

'Fold me one,' Roger said. She folded. 'Again,' he said. She did, handing it to him. The wound was no longer spurting, and he held the new diaper to it. The child's face was the blue-white of skim milk. 'Get the spread,' he told Alix. She ran to the mini-bus, returning to cover the child with old chenille. She heard comments.

'Shouldn't oughta allow them low bikes.'

'Hey, isn't that little Bobby Jean Damin?'

'Nobody else.'

'Oughtn't someone call the Damins?'

'Flip did.'

'Poor little Bobby Jean.'

They knew the child. Yet they held back. Roger was young, but Roger had the strength of confidence. They let him run the show. The highway patrolman strolled over to say help would be here directly. In less than five minutes an old-fashioned high ambulance squealed onto the unpaved car park. A grey-haired man – Alix wasn't sure if he was an MD – knelt on the girl's other side.

'There was arterial bleeding,' Roger said. 'But I think the knee's fractured, so I didn't raise the leg.'

'Good,' said the grey-haired man. 'Bleeding's just about stopped. Good.' And he took over.

The ambulance swung out, raising dust, coated people drifted back whence they'd come. Roger went to wash. Alix loaded groceries.

When they were back on the snaking road, she said, quietly, 'You've learned a lot at Hopkins.'

'First-year med students don't get to lay on hands,' he said. 'It's the truth what I told her – Bobby Jean. First aid, learned in Boy Scouts. Anybody could've done it.'

'But none of us did.'

He grinned. 'We already decided you weren't a Boy Scout.'

Alix wanted to apologize for that bitchy, stupid scene in the supermarket. A squirrel, tail raised in a question mark, ran across the road. Roger slowed. 'I don't mean

just physically,' she said. 'You, well, you were reinforcing
her.' It might not be an apology, but it was true.

When they stopped at the peaked garage, Roger
glanced at her, sheepish. 'What do you know?' he said.

'Nothing much, doctor.'

'Yeah,' he said, smiling at her. 'Maybe doctor.'

3

25th April. 25th April. 25th April.

The date shattered her sleep. The date jumped in her
mind. Today is 25 April. Vliet snorted, rolling over, rubbing his stuffed nose in his pillow. Yesterday, making out
the cheque, she had written 24 April 1968, and the writing
had disturbed her, but she'd been too involved with her
brilliant revenge to pursue the question. And the rest of
the time, she'd thought about Roger, nothing else.

25th April was Jamie's birthday. After his death, Alix
had spent the day with Beverly. They would drive to the
cemetery, sitting near the inset black-marble slab:

JAMES SCOTT SCHORER
1952–1963
Beloved son, brother, grandson

A gardener would use his knife, digging out the recessed
metal vase for water, and the two of them would take
their time arranging Shasta daisies; they always took
Shastas because the fluffy white blossoms appeared to grow
naturally from the grass. It was sad yet not depressing.
Her mother didn't have anyone else to go with, certainly
not Grandma Frances, who politely hated Dan, and
certainly not Dan. Anyway, Alix needed to be there,
too. She dressed, shivering, in the bathroom. Upstairs, she
wrote on a napkin:

vliet,

i have to be home.

see you tomorrow.

alix

A curt note that explained nothing. Let it be, let it be. She had no time.

The sun hadn't risen. Grey dawn light invaded the mountains. She hurried uphill, her hands clasped under the cape. Icy air stabbed her lungs. ONE LOUSY DAY IN THE WHOLE DAMN YEAR, AND I FORGET. FORGET! A blind panic filled her. I have to get home, she thought, I must get home! She left the winding path, cutting directly up the embankment. Her boots slipped on pine needles. She used her hands to climb.

Gasping, she reached the two-lane road and trod impatiently back and forth. When finally a car came, it was from the wrong direction. Morning light thickened. Trees soughed. Alix heard a motor from the right. Long before the car appeared, she held up her thumb. An old Chevy, lights on, wipers thwacking half circles on frosted windshield. It didn't even slow. Please, she thought, 'Please!' she shouted, racing down the centre of the road. The Chevy turned the bend. Gasping acrid exhaust, she gazed hopelessly after it.

'Hey, Alix!'

Roger, in his old leather jacket, trotted towards her. A distant car sounded. She moved to the unpaved shoulder.

'What're you doing?' he called.

It was a Ford van. She held up her hand.

He was next to her. 'You don't have to do this,' he said.

A middle-aged couple glanced curiously at them. She jerked her thumb, frantic tears itching at her eyes. The van passed.

'You want to go down the hill?'

She nodded.

'Home?'

She nodded again.

'I'll drive you,' he said.

He drove fast. Thank God, he always drove fast, but anyway her right foot pressed hard, as if on the accelerator. Roger was making a four-hour trip, two hours each way. No-no. Rush-hour traffic. Way longer. She owed him an explanation. They passed Arrowhead Village. A single light shone in the bakery window.

'I'm always with my mother today,' she said. 'It's my brother's birthday.'

He nodded.

'Jamie,' she said.

'Yes.'

'You know I had another brother?'

'Yes.'

Embarrassment at hiding a known fact increased her frenzy. She thought of the way a rabbit dashes through open fields to the warren even though safety demands it remain still.

'Of course you know. One good reason never to mention him.'

'Why should you?'

'Because it's a brilliant secret.'

'We met your mother right after it happened.'

'See? There's genius. Keeping a known matter secret.' She took a gasping breath. 'I . . . it's impossible for me . . . I mean, talking about him. I can't.' But she found she could. 'He'd be seventeen today.' The implications surprised her. She gave a brief, unhumorous laugh. 'He'd be taller than me. Our parents are tall. I've never been able to talk about him to anyone else. Roger, he was really a sweet little kid. He had this funny mark in one eye, it made him look like he was asking you something. Maybe now he'd be playing basketball. He was sort of uncoordinated, but at puberty boys pick up?'

'Generally.'

'He'd have a car and a stereo. He never heard the Stones. Roger, I do appreciate this. Mother lights a candle, a *yartzeit*, that's a memorial candle. Dan says it's not right for a birthday, but she does it anyway. She and I, we go, uhh, this sounds necrophilic, but it really isn't. We go to the cemetery. The one on the way to the airport.'

'With fountains coming down the hill?'

'That's it. And a miracle happens. Mother and I, we don't bicker. It was a senseless crime.'

'Yes.'

'That's right. You know, you know. It was in the papers and on TV and Caroline was up here with Mother, and that's the only kind of secret to have, one everybody's in on. A senseless crime, that means the murderer has his own logic.' Alix could hear her voice, too high, going on and on, but she couldn't stop it. 'Mother thinks it's God's vendetta.'

'Against her?'

'And Jamie, too. For being Jewish.'

Roger said nothing.

'Mother believes. It's in her paintings. She has true belief. God in His heaven is her Enemy. Why doesn't she pick on Someone her size? But she's not small, Mother. She's a very strong lady. And I'm not, Roger, I'm just not.'

'Alix, it's okay.'

'Dan liberated one of those camps. Buchenwald, I think. Aggh!' She was talking very fast now. 'Mother still could be right. In a group the odds are with you. That's what society is, a big group of people acting the same, doing the same, being the same. Most places, Jews are outsiders. Outsiders do get pecked to death.'

'Hey,' he said quietly. 'Calm down.'

'Oh, don't get me wrong. Some of my best friends aren't.'

'It doesn't matter, sweet.'

'Not to me. I live in the age of paranoia. I love my father and he left. I love Jamie and he's dead. Very cold. But you know what happens to a body. When a body. If a body meet a body.'

They were on Rim of the World Highway, and Roger swerved across double yellow lines, braking on a deserted viewing area. Clouds hid the view – the flat agricultural land and cities of the San Bernardino Valley that lay seven thousand feet below them.

She was shuddering. 'I'm fine,' she said, 'just fine.'

'Let go.'

'Let go? This is my high-wire act and I don't use a net.'

He turned off the engine, shifting across the seat. 'We'll make like this never happened,' he said, his arm around her. 'If you want.'

'I forgot,' she whispered. 'Oh Roger, it's his birthday and I forgot.' She wept into his shoulder.

He stroked her hair. His driving glove caught strands and he pulled it off, holding her closer.

She had known she was in love with Roger. What she hadn't expected was that, by holding her to his solid body, he could return her to a childhood place, warm and inviolate, where comfort was possible. The leather of his jacket turned slick. She made no effort to control her tears. She let them stop naturally. She didn't move from the wet, strong-smelling jacket.

'Sometimes that happens when I think of him.'

'Still?'

'Yes,' she said. 'Funny. At first I couldn't. Cry. I figured it was something lacking with me. When we lived in Hollywood –'

'Hollywood?'

'Right after, for a few months, Mother left Dan. She found this funny little one-bedroom and made her living doing baby portraits. I went to Bancroft Junior High and became an instant wheel. I really went at it. The thing had been in the news a lot and I couldn't discuss it, so I did a superb lie job. Jamie became my non-relative. By then I was into weeping. Fortunately we had a garage, unused. It opened on an alley. Nobody could see me. Except a couple of times I saw Dan.'

'What was he doing?'

'Going slow in his car. I guess, checking to make sure she was okay – Mother.' Alix paused. 'Father always was asking how she was. She really was torn up. I fixed her meals.'

'But you couldn't eat?'

'How did you know?'

'It's a classic symptom.'

'A classic bowl of soup took an hour to get down.'

'What were you, thirteen?'

'Twelve and thirteen.'

'But you were looking after her?'

'Just breakfast and dinner. I told you. My major occupation was being Miss Popularity.'

'It's not the easiest age for that sort of trauma.'

'Hey, doctor, are you the one they call Sigmund?'

She could feel his chuckle.

'I meant,' he said, 'what about your anxieties? Didn't anyone do anything to take care of you?'

'Let's go around again. We were each miserable in our own airtight compartment. I didn't let anyone in mine.'

'On the way up, you were thinking about your brother.'

She moved back, looking at him, surprised and a little embarrassed.

'You aren't that inscrutable,' he said gently. 'Somebody should've looked.'

A lefty, he drove with his right arm about her. The musculature of his side brought a drugged weakness, and *carpe diem*, Alix seizing – yielding to – the moment. Was this, she wondered, how Cricket felt all the time? No-no. Who could feel this close to another person short of simultaneous orgasm? (Or what Alix imagined simultaneous orgasm must be like.) He pulled into her drive, glancing at his watch.

'Five of nine,' he said.

'A new world record for rush-hour conditions.'

He cut the engine. They moved apart. His forehead, the end of his nose, his taut cheeks were red. Windburn, she thought, from the Chris-Craft. He got out to open the door for her, but she had it first, and they stood, she holding the inside handle, he on the outside. Across fresh asphalt a single leaf moved, blown by erratic wind.

Her fingers tensed on the handle. 'Letting you in on all that frightens me. It always does, below-the-skin stuff.'

'Subcutaneous,' he said. 'Want me to forget?'

She shook her head. 'But you've seen me ... Naked.'

He pushed the door and they watched it slam shut. In the distance was the pulse of Sunset Boulevard traffic, and nothing but cold morning air separated them. He took the step forward, his arms reaching around her. 'Oh Jesus,' he whispered. 'Sweet.'

She clutched him. No tenderness here. He was her only security and, who knew, if she let go, maybe the universe would evaporate. She could hear his heart, feel his heart, feel him and, a million light-years away, a dog barked.

Against her ear he whispered, 'Know how long I've wanted to do this?'

'How long?'

'Since that first day, when you were getting into the VW.'

'Yes,' she agreed.

They were both breathing irregularly.

'Alix, you did write me?'

'Yes. And I dream about you.'

'You, too?' He was surprised.

'Like this. I wake up when ...'

'Listen, why don't I stay around?'

'Today we go – I told you.'

'Tonight?'

'I can't, it's, I don't know, all confused. Something to do with Mother being with Dan when she was married to my father. I just can't. Roger, first I have to tell Vliet.'

He released her. The warmth on her body faded. She felt weak, bereft.

'When shall I pick you up?' he asked.

'Tomorrow morning,' she said. 'Eight too early?'

'Not at all.'

They examined one another. The dog barked again, thin, shrill, insistent. Tears came to her eyes.

'I love you,' she said. 'Roger, I'm in love with you.' Saying the words required more courage than she possessed. Wiping her eyes, she ran on slender, shaky legs, heading for the side door so she wouldn't have to fumble with her key. Lupe let her in.

4

From the beginning, Roger had yearned for love. It's natural to. And if he hadn't been a twin, if Vliet had been different, Roger would have had affection. But inevitably there were comparisons. Since babyhood everyone had fallen for Vliet's smile, his fair good looks, his grace. Em, scrupulously just as she attempted to be, couldn't help smiling differently at Vliet, speaking to him in a richer tone. Vliet was Family, yet hers. Sheridan, too, favoured Vliet. Roger was bottom banana.

Most children in this situation turn reticent or wild or make trouble or overeat or whatever. Roger, by nature warmer and more capable of love than his twin, was a thoughtful little boy. He turned the matter over and over as he might a piece of jigsaw sky. At last the puzzle fitted. Vliet was more lovable. The answer seemed right to Roger. He didn't become a problem. He simply withdrew from competition in this area.

He was intelligent and a strong athlete. In school he earned respect and authority. But off the line-marked playground, away from classrooms, he was either with Vliet or alone. By the time he was eight he knew he would be a doctor, and this, at the time, made his isolation rather splendid. The marked man of destiny.

He crushed his incipient humour – cracking jokes seemed to be apeing Vliet. His eyes brooded under heavy, dark brows.

His parents he loved from a distance. It was his relationship with his twin, as he'd told Alix, that went marrow-deep. Shorter than Vliet, his bones were heavier. He could – and did – beat his brother at everything, including fists. The dominant twin. This made him protective. He fought Vliet's battles.

Later, he was attracted to girls with thick ankles and

246

near-sighted smiles. Their owl-like glasses roused that protective instinct.

So why did Alix draw him?

With her he felt stodgy, dull, earthbound. She was too quick on the comeback, too physically brave – she rode breakers so huge that she scared him shitless – too exquisite of feature, too smooth-skinned in her bikinis, too immaculate in her tight white pants, too clever, too charming, too poised, too witty, too everything. She had a million friends. She was Vliet's girl.

She must be exorcised.

Accordingly, Roger narrowed his intelligent blue eyes, seeking chinks in the wall of perfection. She had a dead brother whom she lied about in order to keep secret. The lovely, full mouth tensed when she spoke of her mother: a screwed relationship there. When shook, she covered up by using challenging banter. Her shoulder bags stocked as many beauty aids as Cambro's, plus, at all times of the month, a Tampax container. His strategy failed. With each sign of her mortality, he was more ensnared.

Sometimes she appeared to be making a pass at him. This he put down to her bitchiness, which she concealed and which he had ferreted out. Oddly enough, it was this bitch streak that really tied it for him. A razor-sharp, exotically beautiful, Beverly Hills girl.

With all his knowledge of Alix, Roger never suspected she was utterly breakable. This morning, when the diamond wall she had erected around herself had crumbled to the ground, he had felt no triumph, for by now he, too, was an inhabitant of the vanquished city. He had felt her desolation through their heavy clothes. Her sobs had penetrated his body far deeper than he knew.

Em wasn't home. She was, Roger decided, at one of her women's club meetings. (She was with Mrs Wynan.) He mashed tuna with mayo, eating over the sink. *I love you. Roger, I'm in love with you.* If there hadn't been tears gluing the dark lashes, he wouldn't have believed Alix. He had sustained too much injury in the arena of love.

What does she want with a clod like me when she has Vliet? he would have asked himself. But the tears, the shimmering tears, were proof.

Around four Em got home. Roger kissed the top of her dry hair. 'I had to come down to see Dr Bjork,' he said. Now why did I lie? he wondered. Roger was idealistic about honesty.

He helped Em set the table, for once not letting himself notice that what she sipped from her glass wasn't water but vodka. He barely tasted the meat loaf. His mind was full of Alix; he told his parents about his anatomy lab. They responded to his excitement. Sheridan talked about his old college courses, winking once when he mentioned his lab partner had been a snappy Wave veteran. Em, her nearsighted eyes shining on Roger, did not give her husband *that* look. She ran the marriage, and Roger guessed, correctly, that it was her will that made them share a bedroom in a neutered manner. Em drank. Sheridan had other women. Roger and Vliet accepted this, but what they did not know was that their father told Em of each affair, causing her to drink more heavily. They were miserable together. Yet the idea of divorce was so radical to both of them that neither considered it. Loyalty entered into their relationship. As in many stable, unhappy marriages that stick after the children are grown, the Reeds' neuroses had meshed and they held one another up like the supporting beams of a deserted house. Or was the house deserted? Roger, filled with aching tenderness, looked from one parent to the other.

Too high for sleep, he paced the small den that had been his bedroom until he entered high school. Then Vliet – with a nudge to the ribs – had suggested they double up, and turn the room into a den and therefore on-limits to females. *I love you. Roger, I'm in love with you.*

It took Roger time to become aware of the familiar. The wall behind the couch was covered with framed graduation photographs and team pictures. Invariably he and Vliet, two of the tallest, stood side by side in the back row. Shelves enclosed the window, and along the top row stood trophies, mainly his. He reached for a gilt handball engraved with his name and FIRST PLACE. His hand lingered on Vliet's SECOND PLACE. On the lower shelves were carefully dusted books and Parker games they had shared and hadn't touched in years. Anywhere he looked, he was reminded of Vliet. Roger felt as if he were strangling through a badly inserted endotracheal tube.

He pressed down the light switch, feeling his way through the half bath to their bedroom. He stretched fully clothed on his bed. Triangle, he thought. This was the first time he'd bested his twin in anyone's affection. Paradoxically, he was also a loser. Wasn't he his brother?

Bewildered, exhilarated, afraid, Roger attempted to formulate his own Pythagorean theorem.

He held off as long as he could, arriving at her place at seven-thirty. Before he could knock on the oversize front door, it opened. She lit the overcast morning with a red sweater and matching scarf that he'd never seen. He wanted very much to hold her. He plunged his fists into his pockets. Her overwhelming good looks terrified him. He was terrified of losing his brother. He hadn't slept.

'You're early,' she said.

'But you're ready.'

'A behaviour pattern. I'm excessively prompt.'

They walked to the Mustang, which was parked in the circular drive. She got in. He rested his forearms on the open window.

'Hey,' he said. And was silent.

'Something?'

He gazed at the knotted red muffler. He wanted to explain his fears and say he loved her. Instead, he asked, 'You want to meet at the cabin, or follow?'

'Follow.'

'When we get there.' He stopped, his mouth dry.

'Yes?' she asked.

The crimson knot was plump, impeccable.

'Me,' she said after a minute. 'I tell him.'

'You want to?' By this, Roger meant he should.

'I'm a sado-masochist,' she replied. 'Come on, let's hit the road.'

His eyes impenetrable, moody, he pressed down the lock.

5

If a car cut between them, she zipped around. She was glad he was going seventy-five. When she was on edge, nerved up, speeding connected her to reality.

Roger didn't glance back. As they emerged from city traffic, she grew more and more anxious. By the time they passed between uncultivated, yellowing vineyards, angst had overpowered her. Couldn't he have smiled or touched her? Talk about gloom. He was the condemned man without his hearty breakfast. He must have re-evaluated the situation. Or. She grew cold. Maybe there hadn't been any situation. Hadn't she called every play? She had come apart at the seams and he had comforted her, but had his tenderness been any greater than when he stayed little Bobby Jean's arterial blood? Alix had confessed she felt naked, so he'd held her to warm her a little. She had said she loved him. He hadn't replied. Every move, every single move, had been hers. Except his hard-on. Any girl who takes a hard-on as commitment should be judged legally insane.

Before ten, they were at the cabin.

'Hi,' Cricket yawned over her coffee mug. The yellow curls were tangled.

Roger prowled the big room.

Alix went downstairs. The bedroom smelled like sleep. Sour. Vliet's pillow was propped up by the maple headboard. He stared up at her.

Vliet had survived, barely, the roughest day of his life. Yesterday, to the accompaniment of wind howling and a branch falling outside his window, he had been forced into an activity he avoided. Questioning the human psyche. Until yesterday he had considered this the domain of the clergy, shrinks, and other weirdos, he himself sensibly concentrating on ways to get the suede jacket, the trip to Europe, the best girl, a passing grade. Why waste his intellect questioning matters he would need acid to comprehend properly? Unstoned, who has fingered the ties of brotherhood, who has seen the colour of love? Since the first shitty time he'd made it with Alix, he'd wanted to tell her he loved her. Alix, however, preferred to play it cool. One of the reasons he loved her – and love her he did. Until yesterday he had assumed this unvoiced love reciprocal. Vliet never had any reason to doubt his powers to elicit affection.

Two members of the party missing, though. And no toss-up which absence shook him most. His brother not there? His brother, where? Roger was part of Vliet. A strong body buffering (and sometimes buffeting) his. Deep intelligence and heavy textbooks. Shaggy brown hair over (often) brooding expression. Courage (which Vliet lacked). Idealism (another, unimportant deficiency). Roger, intrepid explorer of the birth canal, discovering the continent eight minutes earlier than Vliet. They had been born to a joint fraternal bank account and, while Roger had given this much consideration, Vliet, until yesterday, never had thought about what each put in and what each withdrew. Roger, Vliet saw now, had directed him, given him purpose. Or, as Vliet in his desolation put it, Roger had shoved him into any scene that he, Roger, had wanted. This wasn't entirely true: if Roger had said, *Let's enter a Zen monastery*, Vliet would have cut out. But good, straight old Roger had said, *Pre-med at Harvard*, then Roger had said, *Hopkins*. An MD is transferable into hard cash. So why not? And where the hell was the bastard? Vliet smoked all day, never finishing a cigarette. When an arm is blown off, the full agony doesn't hit immediately, but you sure as hell know you're in bad trouble.

Vliet, in bad trouble, looked up at Alix's serene beauty.

'Don't say a word, Alix, not a word.' His pleasant voice was slightly rough from his cold. 'You and old Roger take off a day and night, you don't have to draw me a diagram.'

'I needed a lift down.'

'And he drove you.'

'That's right.'

'I never expected more. Christ, Alix, I mean, if you took on the both of us at once, they'd have to award you the Purple Heart. You're being wounded in action every time is all.'

Roger's mood had sunk her. She had not thought that Vliet, sitting in judgment from the loose-springed double mattress where they had made depressing oral love once, would be the Reed twin to destroy her. Her arms went rigid. *But I did try. I tried so hard.*

He was watching her. 'And you're telling me this is it?' he inquired pleasantly.

She nodded.

'One thing,' he said in the same whimsical tone. 'You break off well. That's a sensational smile.'

The smile was reflex. She hadn't willed it. But if the smile went, she would start to cry, and the thought of being alone in this draughty cabin with three blood relations and her own gasping sobs was too much. Footsteps, Cricket's light, uneven ones, sounded overhead. The plyboard ceiling creaked plaintively. Vliet stared at her with red-rimmed eyes. The silence between them stretched until she couldn't stand it.

'Vliet, I'm so very sorry.'

'Undoubtedly,' he said. Someone had taken pliers to his chest. He'd zapped his way through *The Los Angeles Blue Book*, the best-looking daughters of the best families, so why should he feel as if a crack medieval torturer were breaking his ribs simply because Alix Schorer was handing him his walking papers? *You love her, ass.* 'Undoubtedly,' he repeated.

'I mean it.'

'Of course you do.'

'But eventually it would have ended.' See what years of practice can do for an ordinary voice, she thought. Not a quaver.

'But why the shit with my brother, Alix? Why with Roger?'

'He's not hung up on me,' she said. The words came from her throat with difficulty. Too insecure to realize Vliet might have any deep emotions for her, she merely hoped her admission would soothe his damaged machismo.

'He gave you this in writing?'

'No signatures, but –'

'Then what brings you to the conclusion?'

She said, simply, 'He's too good for me.'

'Really. On the other hand, he's not blind, Alix. And you are one exceptional-looking girl.'

'Sure. Unique.'

'Absolutely. I gather you are affected by Roger the Good?'

The ceiling moaned again. 'I'm sorry,' she said.

'You keep repeating that, and I'll –' Briefly his mouth contorted, the one physical manifestation of that tyrannical interior squeeze. 'One thing you gotta face, Alix. You and Roger as a couple have a short life expectancy. I mean, he's even less suited than I to the celibate way you prefer.'

Alix's lashes fluttered, her stomach turned frantic. She drew herself up like a lovely, dying flamingo. 'All right, Vliet, all right.'

'Roger's more into honesty than me, Alix. He won't buy the phony panting.'

Humiliation trickled down her back like melting ice.

'He catches on fast,' Vliet said.

'Are we even?' she asked. 'I'm squirming.'

'You're so full of it you're brown in the eyeballs,' he said, blowing his nose. 'Ask Cricket to put on some water. I'll have coffee.'

He began to whistle 'Jesu, Joy of Man's Desiring'. Alix didn't know Bach. They had talked less than five minutes.

They hadn't raised their voices. Vliet had annihilated Alix. Alix had annihilated Vliet. Neither, of course, had let the other know it.

Nauseated, chilled, Alix went upstairs. Roger looked questioningly at her. She refused to meet his eyes. She let the low-pressure mountain water trickle into the pot, and after three matches, succeeded in lighting a burner. 'Cricket,' she said, 'be a real doll, will you? Toss my things in the suitcase when you come down?' Roger had his books. She threw him her key chain. 'Shall we, doctor?'

She held on pretty well, she gave herself points for that. Her expression, she knew, was fine. But the twisting road jagged her.

'Stop!' she said urgently. Holding a hand to her mouth, she ran to a fallen pine, kneeling like an animal on hands and knees, retching up the orange juice she'd drunk this morning.

'That rough?' asked Roger, behind her.

Dreading that anyone should see her – much less Roger – she said, 'No medical assists, please.'

He retreated.

On the outskirts of San Bernardino a freight train moved parallel to the road. They could hear the long, grieving whistle. *Whoooeeeeee.*

'They're piggybacking,' Roger said.

Alix nodded. She was turned to her open window, the breeze rushing glossy dark hair across her face. What Roger could see of her cheek was rounded in rictus. He knew her well enough to understand that this small smile meant DO NOT DISTURB. He didn't know her well enough to understand how distraught she was. For that matter, he was distraught himself. Question marks formed in his brain. He needed to know what had been said, he could guess how Vliet had taken it, but he needed to know.

Alix's stomach remained in an acid knot. By concentrating on her throat muscles she was able to keep from vomiting. Vliet had seen through her. She had exposed herself to Roger, and he had rejected her. She couldn't deal with so much pain. It was as a calming exercise that she started to make a list – she was a compulsive list maker. By the time they climbed the hill where the Kellogg Horse Farm nestles amid green trees, she had a kind of postdated New Year's resolutions.

First, she never again would let her instinct rule her. Others could, but she couldn't afford it. She would keep her distance and be all likeable things to all people. Second. She would work on her appearance. She would get an eyebrow arch at Aida Grey. She would inquire among her friends which hairdresser was currently giving the best cut. She would try Right Bank for new pants. She would start an early tan – without sun, silver foil would do the trick. Third. She would call her friends alphabetically through her red phone book. Maybe have a barbecue next Saturday night. Yes, there's a practical idea. Everybody was home for the break. Suddenly she could see herself moving around the crowded patio, a simpy Catherine Deneuve smirk glued across her face. Oh God, God! That's not what I want. Well, I can't have what I want, and anyway, it terrifies me, loooo-oooove. The external being my destiny, let me win the Miss Superficial of Beverly Hills contest.

To the right of the road, like a vast-winged old eagle, perched County General. Roger glanced towards the hospital. Tired, he drove with his broad shoulders hunched. He can't wait to get away, Alix decided.

'Turn on the Glendale,' she said. 'I'll drop you off.'

'What?'

'A medical library shouldn't have to hitch,' she said with her copious smile.

'Alix?' said Sharon Stein through the telephone. Sharon was an old Beverly High buddy. 'You free this aft?'

Alix sat up. Her stomach muscles hurt. Fifteen minutes earlier she had run into the house, heaving in her toilet long after clear acid had stopped, falling across her bed, weeping. 'Sure,' she wiped her eyes. 'What's doin'?'

'Ronni Bolt' – another Beverly High chum – 'is in Oahu. Her parents have this condoo. My mom was driving me to the airport, but she's got the bug.'

'How long're you going?'

'Eight days. Ever been?'

'Never.'

'There's deprivation for you. It's the grooviest. Hey, I just got this fantastic –'

'– idea.'

'Ronni's been dying to see you. She's for always saying we should get together. Think, Alix. Three foxy ladies on Oahu.'

'What time's the plane?'

The secretary put her right through.

'I thought you were in Arrowhead,' Philip said.

'It was fun. Father, remember the trip to Europe you gave me for graduation?'

'The one you never took?'

'That's the one. Is it the same fare to Hawaii?'

'Much less.'

'Ronni Bolt's parents have a condominium, and Sharon Stein's going.'

'This summer?'

'No-no. This day.'

Philip laughed.

'Father?'

'If it's what you want,' he said. Alix had known he would say that. 'Do you have enough in your account?'

'Six hundred?'

'That should be plenty. But if you need more, call me. Alix, buy traveller's cheques.'

'This'll make two Sundays in a row. Father, I miss you.' Alix should have known better, but she waited for Philip to reply he'd missed her terribly. (Her mother, too, had waited for this handsome, cold – and decent – man to utter words he was incapable of.)

'I have an appointment,' he said. 'Alix, hon, enjoy yourself.'

'Daddy –'

But the phone had clicked.

Sharon's pretty, empty eyes glowed as she described her previous trips to Hawaii. Alix nodded, bemused. With a wonderful sense of unreality she was speeding at seven hundred miles an hour. She was a small appliance disconnecting herself. Far below, a ship lay like a pin in the endless blue curve.

'Alix,' Sharon was repeating, 'what's wrong?'

'Wrong?'

Sharon's forehead went through a repertory of questioning wrinkles. 'You haven't said one thing.'

'Oh, you mean wrong,' Alix said. 'Sharon, ever let a guy in on the fact you're sort of hung up on him?' She spoke wryly, with a trace of self-derision. This wasn't soul baring, but a fine joke on herself.

'I don't believe it! I – do – not! Alix most beautiful, Alix most cool, Alix most popular.' Alix had been voted these by their graduating class. 'Alix in love? Impossible!'

'Possible.'

'My God – at this late age, it can be fatal.'

Alix shivered.

Sharon had had her moment of vindictiveness. She put her hand on Alix's. 'Hey, you're ice,' she said, her plump little body twisting in the awkward half stoop that plane design requires, turning off the air nozzle, pulling down a blanket. 'Here.'

Alix clasped her freezing hands under acrylic. 'Have you?' she asked. 'Told any guy that? First?'

'Everybody has,' Sharon replied. 'Who?'

'Nobody you know. I've been dating his brother.'

'Oh that one. The Safeway twins.'

'Van Vliet's,' Alix said. 'He's a really beautiful person. Very idealistic and strong. He's at Hopkins, too. Sharon, he saved this little girl's life. He's very stable.'

'But he hasn't said he's hung up on you?'

'You've hit the teensy problem. He isn't,' Alix said. 'Now what?'

'Oh, keep coming at him. Make excuses to phone him, see him. Be subtle, but keep pushing, know what I mean? The important thing is to keep his attention.'

'Does it work?'

'Either it does or it doesn't.'

'But it's the only way?'

'You'd know it is,' Sharon said, 'if you were human like the rest of us.'

At Hawaii International, Ronni, a pert redhead, greeted Alix with hugs and kisses and cries of delight. Alix responded in kind. Ronni had a couple of men in tow, the short one, deeply tanned, Alix didn't quite catch his name, took her mother's blue overnight case, and Alix must have made the right responses at the right times, because he was laughing. They walked miles through the terminal, at one point mingling with a planeful of Japanese tourists. They crowded around the baggage slide.

'Alix,' said Sharon, sweet, dumb Sharon, 'Alix, let's go to the john.'

Alix realized she was crying.

'Got change?' she asked, wiping her eyes.

'For the john?'

'For the phone.'

Sharon, Ronni Bolt, and the two men donated silver.

Alix direct-dialled the Reeds' number. On the first ring Roger answered.

'Where are you?' His voice was subdued and not by distance.

'Hawaii.'

'So your mother said.'

'There's a flight back in two hours. Pan Am 8.30. It lands at seven-fifteen am.'

'Uh-huh.'

'Roger?'

'Yes.'

'You sound strange.'

'I'm not exactly alone.'

'My car's at the airport but, Roger, will you meet me?'

'What? I can't hear you. We've got a rotten connection.'

'It's because I'm crying.'

'Don't do that.'

'I said, will you meet me? Please? Roger, this is pushy and not very subtle. But I love you.'

'I feel the same.'

'You do?'

'Isn't it obvious?'

'No-no. I'm very insecure.'

'I am, too,' he said, his voice lapsing into its normal huskiness. 'Tell you about it at seven-thirty.'

6

Laguna is forty miles south of Los Angeles, and the Nautical Motel is a mile and a half south of Laguna. The original ship-fronted building, circa 1938, is level with Pacific Coast Highway. The white cabins, which ramble down a cliff planted with pink Martha Washington geraniums, become newer and more expensive as they approach the beach. On every door hangs a life belt with a red-painted name. Roger and Alix picked the First Mate's Bunk, it was on the street, cheap, and had a kitchen area: Alix wanted to fix their meals – 'play house,' she said. As far as her family knew, she was in Ronni Bolt's Hawaiian condominium. Roger had told his parents he was visiting a friend for the six days until he must fly back to Baltimore. Neither considered telling the truth. Couples their age lived together, God knows. But Roger and Alix were middle-of-the-roaders – imprinted by previous bourgeois generations, they were what their elders referred to as good kids. Their evasions were not hypocrisy but form to assuage parental mores.

They awoke at the same time, on their backs, naked, her left calf under his right, his arm across her stomach.

'Alix?'

'Mmmm?'

'You awake?'

'No-no.' She was stroking his shoulders. 'You've got a bump.'

He felt. 'Yes,' he said. He traced her collar bones. 'You're totally different.'

'From what? A spot?'

'You look tall and sort of . . . sort of . . .'

'Horsy,' she supplied.

'Awe-inspiring. But you feel small. Soft. Like a little kid.'

'Ahh, flat-chested?'

'Let me – No, sweet, not at all.'

'Now you'd have a terrific bod if you could clear up that post-adolescent acne.'

'My diagnosis is too many Hersheys,' he said. 'What do you weigh?'

'One sixteen.'

'Five-seven?' he asked.

'Eight and a half. Why? Is this a complete physical?'

'I'm trying to understand you.'

'Maybe it's best if you don't,' she sighed.

'Hey, don't shut me out.'

At the same moment they rolled towards one another. 'I never realized you'd be so fragile. Breakable.' He finger-walked her spine, cupping her shoulders. 'Sweet, you did break there, sort of, didn't you?'

'Yes.'

'The second time,' he said. 'Not the first.'

She tugged his moustache.

'Right?' he asked.

'It's embarrassing.'

'I'm the one with anxieties.'

'It never happened before.'

'That you didn't?'

'You do have anxieties,' she said. 'The other way round.'

'Seriously?' he asked.

'I have this major problem.'

'You don't.'

'I can cross it off my list?'

'Yes.'

'Roger.'

'What?'

'Nothing. I like the sound of it. Roger. Roger.'

'When your mother told me you'd gone to Hawaii, I wanted to cry.'

'Did you?'

'Some.'

Her lips touched his eyelids in turn. 'I'd never've guessed on the phone. You were very suave.'

'One thing you never can accuse me of.'

They chuckled into the darkness.

'Where'd you get the money?' he asked.

She rubbed her cheek in his neck.

'I want to know everything about you,' he said.

'My father. It's a graduation gift.' Moving her palms down his sides, she whispered, 'Was I okay?'

'A post-mortem?'

'You know, on a scale of one to ten?'

'You're really asking, aren't you?'

'But you don't have to answer,' she said.

'At the end I was sort of out of my head. I never imagined it could be like this.'

She whispered. 'Me, neither.'

'But being with you, holding you now, is as important.'

They listened to the sea, small waves sucking at a foggy night, and after a while he held her hand to his chest. 'If I had one moment,' he said, 'one out of my whole life, this would be it.'

They walked downhill to Laguna. She needed groceries. Ralphs' was closer, but she insisted on Van Vliet's. A tremendous number of men (and quite a few women) turned to look at her. But how could drivers in a resort town gauge Alix from the rear? Roger, lagging back in the spirit of research, decided it was her walk. Long-legged, free and easy. Catching up with her, he dropped an arm around her shoulders, saying, 'You're a Maserati.'

'What?'

'The guys all look at you.'

'That, let me explain, is a sport. It is called girl-watching. Every girl is watched by every male under ninety and over nine.'

'We don't spot the Chevies,' Roger laughed.

Before, she had turned him heavy. Now, she made him light. He had brought his *Bloom and Fawcett* to bone up on histology. For the first time in his life he was unmotivated and the book stayed shut.

They would walk for hours on the empty, iodine-odoured beach, talking. Pleasure rippled through him each time he uncovered a similarity. Oddly, there were quite a few. They both strove after perfection and grades, they delighted in physical action, enjoying sports as fierce competitors. They used Pepsodent and favoured the sourest green pippins. They were intelligent, full of vitality, and both had suffered childhood allergies. When Alix told of her asthma, they were sitting on the sand in front of the Laguna Hotel, but he held his ear to her breasts to find out if she still had rales. Jealous of and guilty towards Vliet, he avoided mentioning his brother. When he told her about his old girls – there were three – she fired questions, afterwards demolishing each of them with the facts. He protested that they were nice girls. She threw a rock at him, the rock was grey and had holes from a species of boring seaworm. He ducked. 'Jesus, Alix! That could've been a concussion.' 'What's the matter? Haven't you learned how to treat one?' He saved the stone in his pocket. Thursday it rained, and after lunch they went back to bed. He could hold off no longer. Through taut lips he asked if his brother were the first. 'The only,' she sighed. Rain anointed the roof. He put his arms and legs around her.

'Want to talk about it?' he asked.

'No-no,' she said.

And with uncharacteristic hesitancy, began to. As an adolescent, kissing didn't repel her, she said, it scared her to death. How come she never got those hot little urges to move on to phase two, three, and etcetera? After, uhh, well after, she had been really terrified. She had fantasized a hush-hush trip to learn intercourse in the clinical St Louis clinic of Masters and Johnson. She had to fake it.

'With you I never fake it – I can't. It's always nice, very nice, but ...' A long silence before she whispered, 'Darling,' in a voice so inaudible that even though they were wrapped around one another he had to strain to hear, 'it doesn't always work, only sometimes.'

Here was a truth very few women would dare confess. And Roger appreciated – overwhelmingly – that Alix trusted him enough to tell him what he already knew. When it worked, this delicate, squirming passion of girl with her high coital cries shook his entire being. He held her, just held her, until the rain stopped, several hours.

She was protective of her mother, her father, her brothers – alive and dead – even Dan, and when he mentioned this loyalty, she jammed him with hip, brittle Beverly Hills chatter. Her own goodness humiliated her.

Roger felt as if he existed in a rising point of discovery, and while he ached to learn more, he didn't want the point to move in time. He hated her small gold watch, which was their only clock. How can a man with a scientific background hate time?

7

Friday, their last full day, was cold, with a sharp north wind. After breakfast they walked along the beach to a huge outcropping of rocks. The tidepools. Heads close, they knelt to examine tiny sea creatures in the impermanent pools.

Roger said, 'I'm transferring to USC.'

Surprised, she blinked. 'Oh?' she said. 'Well, there's a

goof. For the MCAT you only scored above the ninety-five percentile in all four categories. How do you expect to hack it in one of our really phenomenal West Coast medical schools?'

'Alix, I know it's not as good as Hopkins,' he said. 'But I've been thinking a lot. About us.'

'Me, too,' she said. 'And I bet there's even an undergraduate school in Baltimore.'

A gust of wind snapped her hair onto both their faces.

'In Baltimore,' Roger said, 'there's Vliet.'

'Vliet. Let's see. Isn't he the one you didn't go to Harvard Med School because of? And you could've gotten in with only three years of pre-med?' Tenderly she held his face between hands that were orange and purple with cold. 'I already messed it up between you. I want to make it right.'

'How'll your coming to Baltimore do that?'

'Here, you'll be separated.'

'Someday the umbilicuses have to be unwound.'

'I don't want to be the responsible party.'

'Alix,' he said, looking at her, putting his hand in icy water. He let the fleshed petals of a sea anemone close around his finger.

'As symbolism goes,' she asked, 'isn't that a mite heavy?'

'I'm the one who brought up the subject,' he said. His tone, perversely, was filled with gloom.

She gave him a sharp look. 'Oh, the prognosis isn't all that rough.' Her tone, too light. 'We'll both make a satisfactory recovery.'

'Do you believe that?'

'Take a peek outside Hopkins. Real life can turn you cynical.'

Her voice remained light. From the set of her mouth, though, he knew she was thinking of her parents' divorce, of her mother's separation from Dan. Love is a highly perishable commodity, she was thinking.

'I'm nothing,' he said, 'if not steadfast.'

'Steadfast. Let's see. That means six months.'

'You really can be a bitch.'

'We who play it cool, we are the survivors.' She gave him that dazzling smile.

Roger pushed himself up. On cautious feet they clambered over barnacled rocks. More than barnacles lacerated Roger. She had every right to be bitchy, he decided. He should be insisting he come out here, not let her move to Baltimore. Yet his dilemma involved not only the quality of medical education but also his brother, so he said nothing. When they came to the edge of rocks, he jumped six feet into sand that stung his ankles. He reached a hand to her. Ignoring his help, she landed easily.

'When,' he asked, 'are you going to tell your parents?'

'About the transfer? Tomorrow. I have to move fast to get enrolled someplace this semester.'

'You'll get reactions.'

'Roger, face it.' Alix used that infuriating tone of banter. 'So long as the sex is decently under the blankets, nobody'll say a word.'

Tell her you'll come back here where it'll be even more decently hidden. 'Your father –' he started earnestly.

'He pays. He'll tell himself he's putting in for a better school. And Mother – well, she gave me The Pill.'

'When?'

'Last summer. To save me from making the same mistake she did. To let me make my own mistakes.'

Roger sombrely considered her use of the plural before he asked, 'Dan?'

'Screw Dan.'

It never occurred to Roger that any problem might come from his parents: he was a male, and even as far as his mother was concerned, sex was permissible to males. Who she thought they were meant to have it with, Roger never had ascertained.

'And nobody's going to say anything that we're – what's their expression? Shacking up?'

'Dummy. We're playing it their way. Separate addresses, the same bed.'

'For as long as a week or two,' he said with a painful degree of cruelty.

'Oh, give it a semester,' she said. Suddenly she laughed. 'Shacking up! There's a terrific description. I mean, a lean-to and lots of grunting. No wonder you don't sound all that eager.' And she punched his arm. Hard.

He feinted, as if to hit back, she dodged, hitting again, he feinted again, and she started to run. He put his arm around her, forcing her into a hard trot. He could hear her jagged breathing at his side, but he didn't slacken his pace. Climbing steps, they counted in unison, gasping out fifty-three. They fell, panting and sweaty, across the unmade double bed. Their minds exhilarated and clear from running, they began to make love, violently at first, becoming more and more tender.

'Always been such a stud, Roger?'

'There's a loaded question.'

'Know something? You don't believe it when people are rotten.'

'What's that got to do with being a –'

'You don't believe I could use you and dispose of the wrapper.'

'Could you?'

'Will you listen to the point I'm making? You get all mean and bewildered when people aren't as decent as you are.'

'Alix –'

'That's me. And I was there, remember, in Arrowhead. I saw you with Bobby Jean. You cared, Roger, cared. And don't tell me you helped the gardener's boy because he was black and currently relevant. Another case of caring. You waited for Vliet. I've never met anyone else who puts himself out for decency and caring.'

Embarrassed, delighted, and guilty because he was so much less than she thought, he said, 'Sweet, I'm hardly Jesus Christ.'

'For that you'd have to be Jewish.'

He laughed.

'I did get nasty back there,' she said. 'You were making noises like you didn't want me. Why am I so damn vulnerable with you? It scares me. I mean, do I jump from the Beverly Wilshire roof on the day you don't want me?'

'I'll love you until I die,' he said.

It wasn't the remark a young man of absolute integrity makes. Roger hadn't intended it. He had meant to say *I love you*, which he could with honesty. *I love you* is present tense. *I'll love you until I die* is something else again. A promise, an obligation. Roger had dedicated himself to the admittedly archaic concept of behaving at all times with honour. The only thing that stopped him from being a prig about it, as Alix had pointed out, was his sullen bewilderment when he (or others) didn't live up to his principles. He never made a commitment he couldn't keep, even on a social level. A large seabird bumped into the window. They looked up. Alix saw Roger's expression.

'I painted you into that,' she said. 'Roger, tomorrow I have to explain about the transfer to Father. Come with me?'

He kissed her shoulder. 'Won't that be obvious?'

'I have this thing for both of you. I'd like my Oedipuses to meet.'

'To show which you're sleeping with?'

'For a Phi Bete, Roger, you really aren't very brilliant. Can't you understand? This has nothing to do with sleeping. I am changing schools. A little fast, maybe, but a simple transfer. This semester I enter fabulous Baltimore College – wherever it is – and in the fall, Hopkins.'

'Both in Baltimore,' Roger said. 'Where I am.'

'A connection Father won't let himself make.' (Alix underestimated Philip here.)

'I guess they'll all know,' Roger said. 'Once you're there, it can't be a secret.' A secret, anyway, that Roger was ambivalent about: it was his basic honesty versus his desire to protect Alix from criticism. He felt even more unworthy that she was making the transfer.

'Stop brooding,' she said. 'In fond parental eyes it'll be another Andy Hardy boy-girl thing, not the CBS Love Affair of the Week.'

He gave her a long, tender kiss.

'Father has to know first. For gross reasons,' she said. 'He pays the tuition.'

8

Philip lived in a new two-storey apartment in a new part of the marina. They arrived the following morning around eleven.

'You're home early,' Philip said to Alix.

'A couple of days,' Alix replied.

'Weren't you enjoying Hawaii, hon?'

'It was fabulous. Thank you, Father.'

'Why didn't you ring? I'd've picked you up.'

'My car was at the airport. Roger hitched out to meet me.'

Philip glanced over her shoulder. 'So you're the twin,' he said.

'No-no. Roger's *the* twin.'

They shook hands. Roger noted that Alix's father was tall, an inch or so taller than he, around six-three and, since it was Saturday, wore informal white ducks and a boat-neck striped shirt, a cinematic man smiling at him with gleaming teeth.

'Come on in, Roger,' he said.

Philip appeared to sense he should let Hawaii go, and in the living-room (a two-storey window overlooking a fortune in masts) he began a conversation about UCLA basketball and Lew Alcindor, a topic that was easy enough, yet Roger kept shifting in his chair. He tried leaning back. The seat felt uncomfortably short. He dreaded hearing Alix lie about the transfer, he ached to blurt out the truth. She carried her coffee mug to the couch near her father.

'The thing of it is,' she said, 'I'm not going back to Pomona.'

Philip tilted his head as if he were afflicted with otosclerosis and in need of a hearing aid. He said, 'The English Department's good at Pomona.'

'Great. At ripping apart my favourite novels.'

'Alix, are you saying you're dropping out?'

'No-no. I wouldn't do that. There's this other school I found.'

'Oh?'

'Baltimore College,' she said.

'Baltimore,' Philip echoed. His deep tan was fading to putty colour.

Roger gazed out of the window. A red-and-white sail moved along the finger of water. From this comfortless chair he couldn't see the boat, and the sail might have been a stage prop pulled by ropes.

'Well,' Philip said, 'there's plenty of time to think about it.'

'There isn't. I'm transferring this semester.'

'That's impossible.'

'Not if I start now.'

'Your dorm fees and tuition are paid.'

'They'll refund the dorm.'

'I'm afraid, they, won't,' Philip said. His separation of words was faintly sarcastic.

'They will,' Alix said. 'I'm pretty sure, Father.'

'No. It's in the contract.'

'Maybe if I apply for the refund before –'

Philip rose. 'We can discuss it tomorrow.'

'Daddy –'

'Alix, later.'

Roger stood, his arms dangling awkwardly at his sides.

'But we must talk if I'm going to enroll now.'

'You aren't, hon. So there's no rush, no rush at all.' And he extended his hand to Roger, saying it had been a pleasure. Roger, flushing, took the outstretched hand.

As Alix kissed her father goodbye, she was smiling. So

was Mr Schorer. Affectionate. Serene. Roger wondered if talent for concealment was a hereditary trait, like the excessive beauty, like sickle cell.

Earlier they had decided to go from her father's to his home so he could, if possible, check in with Vliet. They headed for Glendale.

'Look,' Roger spoke first, fifteen minutes later – they were on the San Diego Freeway, carving into the Valley. 'I shouldn't have been there.'

She raised her dark glasses, looking at him.

'The association with Baltimore was pretty strong,' he said.

She kept watching him.

'You're the one who said to keep the sex under the blankets,' he muttered.

She replied, pleasantly, 'Say you weren't there. He would've assumed I'm under them with Vliet.'

This was his father's Saturday off. The house smelled of bacon, and his parents were eating late-lunch sandwiches in the breakfast nook. Roger introduced Alix to Sheridan.

Em, after her initial greeting, did not offer bacon, lettuce, and tomato sandwiches, or even coffee. She didn't look up.

She couldn't look at Alix. Vliet had come home from Arrowhead to announce he was dropping medicine. Then (after a certain amount of what Sheridan called inter-ference from Gene) Vliet had made it public. The entire Family now knew that Vliet was not finishing Johns Hop-kins but going to work in Van Vliet's, a training pro-gramme, Gene called it, but Vliet would be less than a clerk! And who was to blame for all this? Em and Sheridan together had ferreted out the few known facts, discussing the matter exhaustively: they had come up with an answer. Alix. Alix was to blame. And after this discovery, Em knew she hated the girl now standing in the doorway, hated her for so many different reasons that she, Em, couldn't begin to sort them out. Alix obviously had slept with both her sons – and who knew how many

270

others? Alix was a tramp. Alix had caused a split between the twins. Alix was too beautiful. Alix wore her pants too tight and her skirts too fashionably short. Alix's mother, although a former friend, was an adulteress, a divorcée, and married to a man Em couldn't abide. Alix was a Jew – this normally wouldn't have bothered Em, Sheridan yes, but not Em. Alix had caused Vliet to drop out of Johns Hopkins. Alix had stopped Vliet from finishing what he had started. Alix had made Vliet unhappy and Roger happy. In Em's distraught mind it wasn't clear which of these last two was worse. In either case Alix was a tramp. Roger was a serious boy, and maybe, over Em's dead body, would end up trapped into marriage with Alix. Alix Alix Alix. Em's mind was a weighted mass of loathing that never could hurdle her high standard of fairness. She couldn't stand being under the same roof as the girl.

'Roger,' Sheridan said, 'why not take Alix into the living-room?'

Alix flipped through a *Reader's Digest*. Roger stared at the sports section. He read the same paragraph ten times and couldn't remember a word. The back door opened and closed and he saw his father sit in the redwood chair that faced the garden. After a few minutes Em came to the door. Her lipstick was too bright. Both Roger and Alix stood.

'Roger,' Em said, looking only at him. 'Vliet brought down Alix's suitcase.' Her voice was icy. 'It's in the front cupboard. You better put it in her car for her.'

'Thank you, Mrs Reed,' Alix said.

'Where's Vliet?' Roger asked.

'Aunt Caroline's,' Em replied with more frost.

'Alix was in Hawaii,' he said. The truth being in part a lie, stumbled out.

Em's fingers plucked at her skirt seam. 'Roger, your father wants to talk to you.'

'Now?'

'I'm sure Alix will excuse you for a moment,' Em said and hurried back to the kitchen.

271

Roger went out to the patio. Mid-afternoon sun hit full, a hazy, reddish light. He sat on the edge of the barbecue bench, looking at his distorted reflections in his father's dark glasses.

'Your mother,' Sheridan said without preamble, 'doesn't want Alix here.'

'Sir?'

'I think you heard me.'

'It's more a matter of understanding.'

Sheridan's jaw tightened. The resemblance between father and son increased. 'You know your mother, Roger. Her line of reasoning should be apparent.'

'Mother likes Alix. Vliet's had her over several times.'

'She's what we used to call a real tomato.'

Roger stood.

'All right,' Sheridan said. 'You're too old for me to tell you what to do.'

'But why doesn't Mother want Alix here?'

'Roger, you've never been stupid. Don't start now.'

'Dad?'

'You want it spelled out? On the simplest level, then. Your mother believes that for the past six days and nights you've been with Vliet's girl.' His tone questioned.

The muscles below Roger's eyes grew taut.

'Well, if you boys want to share, that's your business. But your mother is old-fashioned.' Sheridan paused. 'Around the house I'm old-fashioned, too. Take her anyplace you want. Just not here. Not with us.'

Hypocrite, Roger thought.

'Your mother's upset. I've never seen her so upset. And I don't need to remind you how you go to college.'

The trusts. 'No, you don't,' Roger said, adding, 'sir.'

'Roger.' Sheridan took off his dark glasses. 'This hasn't been much fun for me, telling you. I – well, I feel close to you, son. I'm proud of you. You understand?'

'I understand,' Roger said. His mouth tasted like salt.

As he opened the mothball-hung front cupboard, he found himself remembering a dim time when he'd had an attack of enuresis and his mother had rubbed his nose in the sheet: for the same crime she hadn't punished Vliet. Another time his father had taken off his belt to punish him for borrowing Vliet's bike without permission. A rush of other memories, all on a single theme. They always loved him, never me. I'm jealous, Roger thought. Stupidly, childishly jealous. At the same time, he felt unlovable, unworthy. He lifted Alix's suitcase.

They drove a few blocks in silence.

'Roger.' Alix tilted her head at him. 'What's the medical term for being hooked? I mean, I don't think I can go another minute without a McDonald's burger. That wondrous machine-shred lettuce, the limp pickle, the sesame-seed bun.'

Without replying, he headed for the nearest McDonald's.

She doodled with her malt straw on the cement table, not eating, talking lightly of the demographic impossibility of the billions of hamburgers that a sign proclaimed the franchise had sold. Roger hadn't bought himself anything. He felt as if he were choking. He kept seeing his mother's face. Under the powder it had been slack-muscled, as if a malignant melanoma were eating her. He, Roger, had caused the melanoma by taking Vliet's girl. At the hospital he'd seen people dying of cancer. Oh hell, he thought, crushing a napkin to wipe Alix's doodling, probably she just missed her pre-lunch pick-me-up.

'She drinks,' he said.

'Who?'

'Mother.'

'We each have our little crutch. Mine happens to be these hamburgers. Roger, get me another?'

'You barely started that one.'

'It's cold,' she said, pushing it away.

'They were so damn negative.'

'They wanted to finish lunch, that's all.'

'How was Mother with you before?'

'I never interrupted her lunch,' Alix said lightly. 'And I'm dying for a hot burger.'

'I want to know.'

'She's always a nice lady. Stop making something, Roger. I really would love another. Humour me?'

Silent, he went to the order window. He handed her the hamburger.

'We need to talk,' he said, sitting opposite her.

'I have been. Incessantly.' She unwrapped the grease-proof paper and smiled. 'Nice and warm. Thank you.'

He knew she had far more problems dealing with rejection than he did. But for once couldn't she at least help him try to cope with these infantile regressions? Deal with his jealousies of, and fears that he was forever separated from, his brother? Did she have to smile a smile that was impenetrable as bullet-proof glass? He needed to get through to her, he needed to in the worst way. She smiled again, nibbling. 'Delicious,' she said, and began to talk about the franchising of hamburgers. Roger considered what pain he would need to inflict to force her to emerge from this smiling banter. What cruelty? What would wound her most? He despised what was going on in his brain, yet he clutched the idea with bulldog tenacity. He knew – Hadn't she herself exposed her weakest point to him? He watched his mind fight the ultimate misogyny.

She deposited the hamburger, gnawed slightly, in the waste paper basket. 'Doctor, you just saved a life. Thank you.'

'Anything's better than this,' he mumbled.

He sped along Los Feliz Boulevard until he spotted a motel: $5.50 WITH TV AND COFFEE. He swerved, tyres skidding. She waited in the car while he paid.

'Jar their teeth, why don't you?' she said. 'Bring up the suitcase.'

'Humour me. Shut up, why don't you?' He spoke viciously, but his mind was numb.

Without a word she climbed cement steps.

No attorney could ask for a more clear-cut case of rape.

Streetlights came on as they pulled into the circular drive.

She was staring ahead with that slightly glazed smile. Her expression hadn't changed since they left the motel. He was getting more and more terrified. Each time he'd started an apology he'd been halted by that smile. 'Alix,' he said, this time intent on carrying through. But Sam burst out of the house. He wore faded blue pyjamas that were twisted, fastened on the wrong snaps.

'Alix!' he yelled.

'Fat Sam!' she yelled back, jumping out of the car to lift her little brother. Beverly appeared. And Alix, still holding Sam, retold the Hawaii fiction, and Beverly murmured how kind it was of Roger to meet Alix, very kind. He wondered how emotional he'd come across in last week's phone call.

'Stay for dinner,' Beverly invited.

Roger looked at Alix. She was busy refastening snaps on a wiggling small boy.

'There's plenty,' Beverly said. 'We'll have a welcome-home party.'

'For me? How lovely.' Alix kissed her mother.

'Thank you, Mrs Grossblatt,' Roger said, and lugged in suitcases, one from Arrowhead, the blue one with the Pan Am sticker. 'Where do these go?'

'The service porch.' Alix nodded to the left, not looking at him. She hadn't looked at him since they'd left the motel. 'Fat Sam,' she said, 'gotcha a nothing.' In Laguna she'd browsed for hours for the right book, a Dr Seuss. She and Sam disappeared.

Beverly and Roger were alone, drinking Scotch, when Dan's key unlocked the front door. Beverly explained that Roger had met Alix at the airport, and Dan gave Roger a glance, inquiring, 'A few days early, isn't she?' and went into another part of the house. Roger heard Alix's faraway laughter before a door shut. Beverly said did Roger mind, but she had to finish up in the kitchen. Roger was left alone with his acute anxieties. Dan returned, switching on Walter Cronkite. The 'Seven O'Clock News' seemed to last forever.

Alix emerged. 'Dinner,' she announced.

'Roger,' Dan asked as he sat at the head of the table, 'why were you the one to meet Alix? Why did you drive her down from Arrowhead?'

'He was available,' Alix replied.

Dan examined her. A stocky, greying man, his face heavily lined with concern.

A Mexican maid brought food to the table. Alix, Roger could tell, had made the salad. Cold and crisp, raw mushrooms, red pepper, and thin-sliced apple with romaine, light oil-and-vinegar dressing. The rest of the meal was imperfect, and he attributed it, correctly, to Beverly.

'Dan,' Alix said, 'aren't you going to ask me how was Hawaii?'

Dan forked a slab of overdone rib roast. 'How was it?'

'Fabulous.'

'Weather good?' Dan asked.

'Rained.'

'All the time?'

'That I was there. Mother, why don't you put it in later?'

'I never can figure how long when it's frozen.'

'All the time it rained?' Dan.

'For my entire visit.'

Dan set down his knife and fork. 'So what did you do?'

Alix smiled. *When I'm shook I hassle him,* she had told Roger. *I can't help it, I don't want to, but egging him on's a conditioned reflex.* From the way Dan's neck turned red, he didn't need much egging. High blood pressure, Roger diagnosed.

'What's that supposed to mean?' Dan.

'Oh, you can have fun when it rains.'

Dan propped his chin on his hand, gazing at her. His rolled shirt cuff fell back to expose heavy-veined forearms. 'I'm not sure I've got this. If you had such fun, why did you leave early? How long were you there?'

'Two hours.'

'Perfect short vacation.' A roughness, a faint New York hectoring, had moved into Dan's concern. 'And the rest of the time?'

'Laguna.'

'Alone?'

'Should I've been?'

'If we're talking about the same thing, yes.'

'Well, well, well.'

Dan turned on Roger. 'Where've you been the last six days?'

'Laguna,' Alix said.

'I thought it was your brother,' Dan said, softly, dangerously.

'It was,' Alix said. 'Past tense.'

'Roger seems like a bright boy. Why not let him do his own talking.' To Roger. 'Laguna, how was it?'

'Dan! Please,' Beverly said.

Dan turned to his wife. 'I should think you'd be interested when your daughter and her friends tell you what they're doing.'

Beverly cut her meat. Her hand shook.

'Leave Mother out of it,' Alix said, sharp.

'It was the best six days of my life,' Roger said quietly.

'*Mazeltov*,' Dan said.

Alix said, '*Mazeltov* means –'

'I know what it means,' Roger said. 'Alix, I'm the one you've got it in for, not Dan. So knock it off.'

Startled, she looked at him. Her eyes seemed to grow larger, more luminous, and he felt his lips move. Then she blinked. Took a sharp breath. And he knew that by revealing her complicated neural patterns, he had pushed her too far. He had pressed the final jolt in her day of electroshock.

'But Dan's so interested. And so quaint. In his day, nice Jewish girls didn't do that sort of thing, not until after they were married.'

'Alix,' Roger said, trying to stop her.

'See, Roger, that's what made everything okay. The marriage ceremony. After that you could do it. With whoever.'

Beverly turned crimson. Dan's face seemed to swell.

Alix was on her feet. 'Mother, I'm so very sorry. Please,

I didn't mean that.' Briefly she rested her cheek on her mother's head. A moment of glossy black hair spilling onto light brown. 'It's a fine roast beef, a fine welcome-home party. Mother, listen, I'm not going back to Pomona. I'm going to Baltimore. And I have to go to the toilet. Mother, excuse me. Dan, I'm sorry.'

As she left the room, Roger's shoulders quivered with an involuntary spasm. Relief. It's on, he thought, I don't know how, but it's still on. He relaxed against the leather of his chair.

'Baltimore?' Dan turned. 'You go to Johns Hopkins the same as your brother?'

'Yes, sir.'

Above broad cheekbones, Dan's eyes glittered like blanched almonds. 'Again, *mazeltov.*'

Roger, weak with his reprieve, couldn't be angry. 'Would you like some answers, sir?'

'What the hell do you think I want?'

'All right.' Roger's forehead creased soberly. 'I've liked her always. And she me. But she's a little too spectacular. And I'm very stupid. And by then she was Vliet's girl, so I sort of avoided it. Last week she somehow forgot her brother's birthday.'

'It was very dear of her, coming down,' Beverly said. 'Roger, you don't have to tell us this.'

'I want to, Mrs Grossblatt. I hate all the sneaking around. But we thought it was best, covering up. It's not possible, though. Anyway, she misses him, Jamie. I don't think you understand how much. And forgetting the day restimulated all the hurt. She started to cry.'

'Alix?' Beverly asked.

Roger felt his eyelid twitch. 'It made how we felt unavoidable. I mean, her being so shaken. But before, uhh, we got anything going, she wanted to tell Vliet. It was rough on her. She panicked. She did go to Hawaii. As soon as she got there, she called me. I met her at the airport and asked her to come to Laguna with me. It was – I told you. The best six days of my life. Then today.' Roger sighed. 'I'm the one who should be transferring. It

278

would've been easiest. But Alix is a very giving person. Even if it does embarrass her, she is. She decided to come East. And today, today.' He sighed again. 'Her father said he wouldn't pay for any college near Baltimore. My parents weren't exactly cordial to her. And then I – Oh Jesus.' Briefly he closed his eyes. 'Mrs Grossblatt, I'm sorry. I shouldn't have told you this, should I?'

The chandelier glowed on a not-quite-pretty woman with creases radiating from amber eyes. She appeared soft, reticent, compared to her shining child. But Alix is more fragile, Roger thought, far more. Beverly smiled at him. A remote, gentle smile that he sensed was not for him but for old times' sake, and he filed away the question: Was Alix's mother the only one capable of remembrance or was she the only one with something worth remembering?

While Roger talked, Dan had been drumming his knuckles.

'And so she's off with you?'

'Yes, sir.'

'There you are, Beverly. Cards on the table. Your play.'

Beverly said to Roger, 'Alix has always done everything well. Easily. She's wonderful with people. Poised. Happy. That running to Hawaii and flying right back. I just don't understand.'

'She doesn't want you to understand, Mrs Grossblatt.'

'I don't know her, not at all.'

Roger knew her. Someplace in this large, overdone house, she wept.

'There's a john?' he asked.

Dan jerked a thumb in the direction of the front powder room, and Roger, saying, 'Excuse me,' went the opposite way, towards the bedroom wing. Neither Dan nor Beverly noticed. They were staring at one another.

Roger was in a spacious hall with lighting bubbles inset in the ceiling. The doors were closed. The walls covered with paintings. Here, in the windowless heart of the house, were Beverly Schorer's mad rabbis. Hung in the Guggenheim. Strictly non-representational daubs of black, streaky reds, touches of white rising upwards. Roger glanced at a painting and was trapped. Humiliated by his outburst, worried because he didn't know any way to apologize to Alix, depressed by his actions, this painting dragged him a million miles farther down, into chaotic, agonizing questions about evil that he didn't have to ask. Hopefully, would never have to ask. Turning away, he concentrated on which door to try.

Dan's voice. 'Well?'

'When she left for Hawaii, she was excited, happy. That is, she seemed happy. Dan, I can't remember her crying. Not since she was a baby. She never does.'

'Alix? No.'

'She's my daughter, and I don't understand her. Terrible, terrible. He understands her.'

'You mean you're going to encourage it?'

'He's different from Vliet. I don't know. He's less sure of himself, but more settled. Serious. And there's something very decent about him, sweet almost.'

'Sweet? Decent? Understanding? Oh balls! Don't be so fucking sentimental!' Pause. Calmer. 'Listen to me, Buzz. So we've all had our reasons for spoiling her every step of the way. New cars. Any clothes she wants. Two-hour trips to Hawaii. One week in the mountains with one boyfriend, then it's off to Laguna with the other. Now she's decided to shack up with this Roger. Well, her father won't foot the bills for it and, for once, I'm with him!'

'That's holding money over her.'

'Like hell!'

'Yes.'

'So what if we are? If she's decided to be a fuck, let her go be a fuck on her own!'

Mad rabbis spun. Roger's fists clenched. He realized that Alix had pushed, especially with that last crack, and she shouldn't have slapped their sex life on the table with overdone beef, but to Roger the words (even though said in exasperation) were unforgivable. Roger was not quick to blame. Or to forgive. He never was able to forgive Dan for saying the words.

Beverly murmured.

'Buzz, it's not different now. She's a beautiful girl. Charming. Brilliant. She's got everything. We can't let her throw it away. For once we'll try to do what's right for her, not what eases the most guilts.'

Roger moved along the hall. A cut-off that way. He opened a door and was in a vast, gold bathroom. Another door. Blackness and the smell of the lotion she used on her hands. His pupils adjusted and he saw her on the bed. Closing the door, he inched through dark, pushing over something light, a waste paper basket possibly. His leg touched the bed, and he dropped, kneeling, pressing his face to hers. Her cheek was hot and wet.

He said inside her ear, 'Know how much I love you?'

'I resent how much I love you.' She exhaled through her nostrils, a snort he felt. 'The Love Affair of the Week, and they're making it all dirty. Roger, what did your father tell you that jarred you like that?'

He couldn't tell her. He probably never could. A rejection on this level, he knew, could destroy Alix. 'Hey,' he said, 'I think your mother's about to foot your bills.'

'No!' she said, too loud, considering she had her cheek pressed to his. 'Roger, I do not want her money. I do not want any of their money.'

'What's the other choice?'

'It's called work. I'll get a job.'

'Doing what?'

'Don't hassle me, please, not now. They will kill us. Or me, anyway. I'm sick of being a chattel. I have to do this on my own, otherwise it'll never be right.'

More or less what Dan had said.

She patted the mattress. 'Join me.'

And Roger free-associated. 'If I get on the bed and anyone opens the door, they'll assume I'm fucking you.'

She pulled away. 'Oh, hasn't this been one great big joyous day! Before, *we* made love. Now, *you* fuck –'

'Rape. Oh Jesus, Alix, please listen, please, look ... Sweet, please?'

She cradled his head. 'Don't, Roger.'

'Why not? You are.'

'It's just not Gentile,' she said, kissing the tears under his eyes. 'I got all mixed up and I froze. Your Frankenstein's too good. I froze with you!' she said in horror.

'You were meant to ... Alix, tell me how to ... I'm sorry ...'

She knelt, facing him, her hands moving over his quaking shoulders. She could be tender, Alix, and this tenderness in a sharp, quipping girl would always take him by surprise. She whispered endearments, she held him, she comforted him.

After a few minutes he rubbed his face in her neck. 'I better get home. Face Vliet.'

'That's the worst for you, isn't it?'

A rhetorical question. She reached out and a tall lamp went on. He blinked. Her eyes were wet, the lashes glued in points. He followed her to a corridor with louvered cupboards on one side and an elaborate washbowl on the other. He watched her splash water on her face, brush her teeth, her hair, finger white under her eyes, plum colour the lids. In Laguna she hadn't used make-up. She licked a mascara brush. He defied anyone to guess she'd been weeping.

He looked at his reflection. He defied anyone to guess he hadn't. He threw water in his face, blotting with the same tiny blue towel she'd used.

The bubble lights shone down on them, a harsh, honest light, and Roger ran his palms down her sides, cheating a little with his thumbs at the roots of her breasts, cheating again at the rounded pelvic bones. She was right. They couldn't live another day like this. They couldn't risk it again. Alix wasn't a naïve girl. She was fully aware that she was giving up inexhaustible clothes behind louvered doors, quilted upholstery, the open-end bank account, all items of considerable importance to her. She was committing a vast generosity.

'I always wanted to be a doctor,' he started.

'What else is new?'

'But there're other careers.'

'What? Who said anything about dropping medicine?'

'Me.'

'Then shut up.'

'I can't let you work.'

'Roger, you're very beautiful, but also you can be a stodgy crock, and right now you've got me all confused. So will you please shut up?'

Filled with love and guilty relief, he had his arm around her as they went back into the dining-room. Dan stared over chocolate ice cream at them. Roger kissed Alix's forehead goodnight, a public act which shamed him because it seemed to him defiant. Vliet, he thought, Vliet could carry it off.

9

He parked Alix's Mustang across the street from his house. He was unable to communicate with his parents as if nothing had happened. He was equally unable to face Vliet. The living-room lights went out. Then others. Finally the one in his (and Vliet's) window. Roger waited forty minutes before he went in. He moved silently to the kitchen, finding a bottle of Smirnoff's – his mother's crutch – and in the den nursed it until either he fell asleep or passed out.

'Up,' Vliet was saying. 'Up!'

Venetian blinds clattered. Sunlight blared.

'Off your ass,' Vliet said. 'We've got a handball game.'

Roger cleared the back of his throat. Pain and the flavour of vomit reverberated along his sinus canals. Holding his forehead between his palms, he asked, 'What's 'a time?'

'Almost seven.'

'Why're you up?'

'To get your shit together.' Vliet dug gloves and shoes

from the cupboard. He saw the bottle. 'You did a job?'

'Alix,' Roger said quickly, 'she's coming to Baltimore.'

Vliet gave Roger a look that Roger couldn't fathom. 'We better settle up before they're on us. Get off it.'

'I'm dead.'

'Nothing like handball to jolt the adrenalin.'

They drove through sleeping Sunday streets towards the pseudo-mosque that was the Glendale Athletic Club. As usual, Roger was at the wheel. Vliet lounged back (they were in Alix's Mustang), a peculiar expression of decision moulding his face.

Vliet lacked his brother's mental force and physical stamina. God knows, he was no idealist. There aren't many Rogers around. But Vliet, from conception, had been tied to his lacks. He had adjusted magnificently. He let Roger propel them through infancy and into various schools, with sports in season. It was a terrific situation. Vliet saw himself as a member of the royal family, free to enjoy himself while an equerry (Roger) handled the grubby coins of decision. There's a fly in every ointment, though. And Vliet's bug was that the royalty role he envisioned was that of the champagne-head princeling who appears briefly but winningly in the second act of a campy Lehar operetta.

He shortchanged himself. He was very similar to the father of them all, the original Hendryk Van Vliet who had crossed the Isthmus with his spices, yeast powders, mercenary instincts, and ambitions. Vliet's easy blond looks hid these tougher traits from everyone, including himself. And here was a talent he had down pat. He could hide from himself.

One emotion he couldn't hide. He loved Alix. Of course – as he'd equivocated with himself these last six embittered days – he loved her for all the surface reasons. True, true. (But what did this have to do with anything? All Vliet's life, people had loved him for the wrong reasons.)

He could get his own way with anyone. This uncanny ability Vliet used as a social asset, along with his tennis game, sense of humour, and holding of the best grass. When the chips were down, though, he could put his skill to purpose. And today he needed to cut himself loose from Roger. He also needed *not* to cut himself loose from Roger. He wanted the twinship intact, and he wanted to be sprung. Vliet watched small, decently kept houses slip by. He would have to lie, show his superior cool, use a touch of malice – he'd been there before. And with Roger he had the advantage. He knew every button. Take your time, was his advice to himself. Don't rush it.

Accordingly, they played for fifteen minutes. Vliet, panting, served from between red lines. 'Twelve-five,' he said. 'There's no problem where she'll stay.'

Thwack.

'Huhh?' Roger missing the easy lob, brushed sweat from his baffled eyes.

'Thirteen–five,' Vliet said. 'I mean, you do plan this the healthy way? Share quarters?'

'There's a vacant single in the building.'

'Why not just change room-mates? I'm not going back.'

Roger let the ball echo disconsolately against the back wall. 'What?'

'I'm staying in Los Angeles.'

'You're – You mean, you're dropping out?'

'Christ, the man's a deductive genius.'

Roger turned to get the plum-size ball. All the years of spontaneous joys and perplexing rivalries, the shared Parker games and Tom Swifts and classes coming to an end as he'd feared. Sweat chilled him. It was a moment rather like death. He wondered if Vliet felt this terrible finality. I could ask, he thought. Shrugged. Vliet would come back with a quip, not the truth.

'Rogerboy, you cold-cocking the game because I'm up on you?'

Soon it was 21–7, Vliet. Game.

They collapsed, panting, knees up, bare wet shoulders resting against stucco. Vliet retied the red shoelaces that, he said, grabbed his opponents by the eyeballs.

Roger said, 'You're quitting because of me and Alix.'

'Really. Why else?'

'Well, why?'

Bodies gleaming, white shorts grey where sweat had soaked, they examined one another through identical Prussian-blue eyes. Roger was inside Vliet. Therefore Vliet switched the subject.

'I've made up my mind. Hey, Roger. What rocks you most? I have a mind –'

'Vliet.'

'– or I made my mind up myself?'

Roger's hurt was too obvious.

'It can't come as news that you've made every life choice,' Vliet said.

'Me?'

'Christ, you want baseball, I head for the dugout, the year you decide it's basketball, we go to Johnny Wooden's Summer Camp. You opt for football, I suit up. You want Ha-a-ava-a-ard, I hit the books. You've always been into medicine, and there I am, looking at spit on a slide. Rogerboy, face it, we've lived in your straitjacket.' He tossed Roger the ball. 'Now serve.'

Roger served. 'Zero–zero,' he said.

Vliet's slighter, longer body bent into a return. *Thwack thwack thwack*. Vliet's red-laced shoes moved with Fred Astaire eloquence, but anyway the volley ended with Roger's slamming his heavy muscles into a return to the right rear. Vliet couldn't get it.

Roger burst out, 'You wanted medicine!'

'As a means, yes, a means of making the bread, Roger. Now will you serve?'

Roger clutched the black handball. If this separation were a kind of death, Roger never truly had accepted death: to him death might always be battled off – if only there were better drugs, more surgical know-how, something.

'For Chrissakes,' Vliet said, 'it's not exactly news that I'm no idealistic crapshooter.'

'Who is?'

'You. Now will you the fuck serve?'

Roger served. He was hung over, his head burned with pain, but how could he give up? Vliet placed the ball in the left corner, an impossible shot that somehow Roger, with a lunge of brawn, got, placing equally well. Vliet missed. Roger grabbed the ball, holding it in his gloved left hand. 'You've put in five years. Five years! Think.'

'Six days, Roger, and think is all I've done.' Six Christ-awful days when Vliet couldn't avoid being plugged in to himself. Six days he wouldn't live again, not for every Porsche in the line. He fingered back his pale, wet hair. 'The decision's firm.'

'You can change it.'

'Down there, boy, down. You fail to see we have one additional factor in our relationship. You're no longer omnipotent.'

'Omnipotent? You have all the friends. Mother, Dad. The Family. Any girl –' He stopped.

Vliet gave him a smile that only Roger could have known was painful.

'See?' Vliet said. 'You think you've done me the shits, and you don't have shit in you. So you can't bulldoze me, not anymore. I'm free.'

They could hear muffled sounds of the adjoining courts. Vliet's cover-up smile had awakened in Roger a dim pre-school memory. Peal after peal of night thunder, and two little boys stretched under a cot. Vliet had been terri-fied, not Roger ... Roger ached to grab his brother by his long, sweaty neck and shove him onto the twelve-thirty TWA flight. But Vliet was right. Vliet had him.

Roger tossed the ball, smashing a serve. He won the second game. They rested.

Roger asked, 'What'll you do?'

'Uncle Gene's about to play nepotist.'

'Waste your life in business?'

'Roger, you haven't had your psychiatry rotation yet. So here, in simple layman's language, is the answer to problems of sibling interference. Up yours!'

Roger won the third game. They had played according to historical precedent. The first game was won by Vliet, rarely the second, and Roger always endured to win the third.

In the shower room, stripped naked, Vliet said, 'Roger, quit frowning. I like the markets. I'm named after them. I belong in them.'

'You never wanted them before. It's got to be Alix.'

Vliet could feel a tearing, as if Roger had ripped adhesive from his burned skin. Why the hell does he have to be so damn right? And so fucking persistent? Vliet turned an old faucet. The loose head sprayed ice water on him. He jumped back. For one moment he considered giving in to habit, doing what Roger told him, losing all that he, with Cricket's help, had struggled for. Then he thought of being a third, broken wheel in Baltimore.

He said, 'Sure it is. I mean, you've swiped my girl. Fantastic-looking, heavy on the charm. Still, strictly between brothers, sackwise, she's not that —'

Roger ended the sentence with a heavy fist in Vliet's gut. Vliet slid on cracked wet tiles. The water, hot now, hit him full force. They hadn't fought physically since they were thirteen.

'Oh Jesus! Vliet, I didn't mean that.'

Vliet didn't inquire what his twin had meant. As Roger's fist flew, murder had lived in his eyes.

They showered in adjacent stalls.

Vliet turned off his faucet. 'Roger?' Getting no answer, he reached around and turned off Roger's shower. 'I didn't mean to put you in a bind. But Ma's in a high-grade sweat. Not only have I quit, but quit in front of the entire family. I've been absolved, though. She lays my crime on Alix.'

Roger's mouth tightened. 'I know.'

'You didn't hear 'em in the bedroom last night. Ma was so bagged she forgot to be quiet. Or fair.'

'Dad gave me the message.'

'Good. Then you won't be tempted to spell out your new sleeping arrangements.'

Roger towelled across his back, jerkily, angrily.

'Christ, though, Roger, you don't help things. It was our last night. Couldn't you have showed? Or at least called? Ma fixed shrimp cocktails, the works.'

'I had to stay with Alix.' Roger winced. 'She's not going to college.'

'What's this?'

'She's getting a job.'

She never would for me, Vliet thought. His mind, unused to his new jealousies, couldn't rationalize this one, so he blocked it. 'How come?' he asked.

'For one thing, her family isn't interested in her coming near Hopkins.'

'They won't pay for the finest medical attention?'

'Look, I feel rotten about it.'

'You're too serious, Roger, and I fear for you. This is a psychotic situation. Last night I heard several allusions to the cutting off of funds.'

'That money's ours!'

'Not until we're thirty. So for once, forget you're so damn honest.' Vliet glowered, miming Roger's fury, then he grinned and held out his long hand.

Sheridan had insisted they shake after every small-boy tussle. Naked, patched with wetness, the brothers clasped hands.

'I'm sorry,' Roger said. This was part of the ritual.

'The hell.' This wasn't.

'I'm out of my skin about her.'

'No kidding? Who would've guessed? What an actor!'

Suddenly Roger smiled. 'Hey, it's okay, Vliet?'

'Sure.'

'Okay, okay!' Roger slapped his towel at his twin. Vliet snapped back, and the two ran, towel-flicking, through shower and locker rooms. Three sedately togaed elders frowned disapprovingly: the Reed twins were grown men, large men, they made too much noise, they took up too much space, and someone should tell them to cut out the horseplay.

So Vliet, with well-concealed pain, had done what he

intended. He was free of his brother, yet in a peculiar way still part of his brother. A week ago he wouldn't have believed it possible. But then a week ago he hadn't given a fart.

Chapter Ten

I

A week earlier in Arrowhead, right after Alix had explained to Vliet that they were through, Cricket had listened to the Mustang backing up the hill. She had tightened her yellow afghan around herself. Grandma Wynan had knitted this for her pram, and Cricket, preferring the old and familiar, was comforted by the stretched wool.

Vliet came upstairs. He was pale. This made his sharp-tipped nose seem redder. Without speaking, he went to the pot that Alix had put on the stove, making himself Nescafé, sitting on the couch to drink. Finishing, he tossed back his straight, silky hair, drumming his fingers on his thighs. 'My old lady and my brother, yeh yeh yeh,' he sang in a raucous Beatle imitation. 'Not no other, yeh yeh yeh.' He broke off, his eyes desolate.

Here, Cricket thought, must be the ultimate daydream, the purest fantasy. A mountain cabin, Vliet in urgent need of comfort, and she the only one around to give him comfort. So why did she only feel this grey echo of his despair? This juvenile awkwardness?

'I'm going to get some pictures,' she said, scratching a spot on her jeans, watching the whiteness flake under her thumbnail. 'Is your cold better? Will a walk kill you?'

'Let's give it a try for the grandstand.'

The chill north wind had swept away clouds. It was a brilliant azure day, with white ruffling the out-of-season emptiness of Lake Arrowhead. Along the cold, sunny lakeside path moved two shadows, a long, striding one, a small one trotting rather like a toy poodle keeping up with a borzoi. It took them a silent half hour to reach Edgewater Cabins. The windows were still boarded.

Here Vliet stopped, sneezing violently.

She said, 'We better head back.'

Returning, he started to talk. Briefly, he tore into Roger. 'He's just lost himself the Albert Schweitzer Award.' Vliet's major efforts, however, he reserved for Alix. He demolished her every small vanity, ripped into her charm, exposed how spoiled she was. 'A narcissistic phony,' he called her. 'Roger goes for slob chem-major types, the pathetic ones. How can he mix with her?'

'She's vulnerable.'

'As a cutting diamond,' Vliet said.

'She's not how she seems.'

'If you say so. And since you've got this child's unbiased eye, how long do you figure it's been going on?'

She stooped to get a pine cone. He slowed.

'How long?' he persisted.

She examined the cone. It was a sugar pine with one side crushed.

'Let's not go mute here,' he said.

'Remember at the beginning?' Cricket's head was bowed. 'Roger made that joke about good-look pills?'

'Yeah, not like Roger. You're right.'

'And then at Christmas you said he was in a fierce mood?'

'With good reason,' Vliet said. 'And her? Alix?'

'Always, too.'

'Sure. Why else start with me?'

'You went after her.'

'Terrific, really terrific. According to you, then, Cricket, all the time she's been hot for Roger, she's been making it with me. And you call her vulnerable?'

'She's just very complicated.'

'Why not try another description? Like cold-blooded bitch.'

'Vliet, what's the point? It's over.'

'I know, I know. She told me – is it an hour already? She kisses off well, Alix. She has the perfect goodbye smile.'

'She's covering up.'

Vliet took the cone from Cricket. He hurled it into the lake. 'Go play with your damn Barbie dolls!' he snapped.

'They're something little kids can understand!'

Sunlight scoured his face to almost impersonal pain. He was striding fast again, and to keep up, Cricket had to run. Her left ankle turned out. He loves her, Cricket thought, he really loves her. The Nikon banged painfully between Cricket's breasts. He didn't any of the others, but he does Alix.

After dinner Cricket tried the half lotus she'd picked up at REVELATION, one foot extending towards the fire. Her navy sock was worn. The big toenail shone through thinned wool.

Vliet, on the couch, sipped wine. That afternoon they had driven to Arrowhead Village, where, even today, he had taken his time, choosing the best in his price bracket, Louis Martini Cabernet Sauvignon. He poured himself another glass, then spoke, maybe their first words in an hour. Cricket possessed a unique gift of silence.

'Roger carried us both,' he said. 'And here I am, chopped off. O-F-F.' Vliet put his glass on the rug, stretching his long fingers, playing on an imaginary keyboard. 'The Gold Dust Twins apart, the Bobbseys separated, Humpty and Dumpty broken. Where does that put me?'

Cricket reached out to hold his hand. Shaking her off, he continued his slow, imaginary playing.

'What am I gonna do from here on in?'

'Finish Hopkins,' she said.

'Why?'

She didn't answer. She had no answer.

Vliet laced his hands over his Irish knit sweater. His eyes were closed. He saw, splashed in red paint inside his cranium: FREEDOM IS SLAVERY. Until now, he had handed over his free will to Roger. But this morning Alix with an easy smile had cut the invisible cord. Even when Alix and Roger were through (and Vliet never doubted that day soon would come), the cord of fraternal trust never could be reknotted. Yesterday Vliet had been filled with unwanted analyses. Today Vliet was in terror. Eyes closed, nasal passages clogged, mind slightly woozed on red wine, he lay in acute terror. He was experiencing a text-book case of the anxiety of freedom. Absolute freedom corrupts sanity absolutely. It is the root of more mental evil than money. Until now, Vliet wisely had handed his freedom over to Roger. Now, though, his decisions were his to make.

After ten minutes he said, 'Like hell I will!'

'Will what?'

'Can't you follow a conversation, Cricket? I'm not going back to the Mecca.'

'Where'll you finish?'

'I won't.'

'But –'

'But. That's what's scaring the shit out of me. But Roger always pointed the way. But. He's the one who wanted to be a doctor.'

'You never did?'

'Well, for mercenary reasons,' Vliet admitted.

'That reason still holds.'

'Christ, there's other ways. A million. So many ways you could go bananas.'

'Narrow down,' Cricket said, giving advice learned at permissive Brace Ridge School.

'From infinity?'

'You have to start someplace.'

He thought a moment. 'Garbage collection is out. So there's infinity minus one.'

'Keep going.'

'I don't want more school, so cancel nuclear biology.'

'Infinity minus two.'

'Not much interest in midnight cowboying.'

She giggled. 'How about law?'

'That's not what I call positive thinking, Cricket. I just told you. No more school.' And his voice broke. 'Get me, willya? The same guy who lectured you so magnificently on goal pursuit. Cricket, what the hell am I going to do?'

He wasn't asking anything as simple as career advice. His arm went out in the involuntary, pleading gesture of a prisoner hearing a harsh sentence. She reached for his hand. This time he let her hold it.

They stood at the foot of narrow stairs, her room to the right, his to the left. He pulled the string of silver beads. Icy darkness. Spooked noises. At night, she remembered, one's hearing is more acute – part of the circadian rhythm.

'Move ass to bed, Cricket,' Vliet said.

Cricket's face grew hot, her heart pounded. Her lack of possessiveness never had meant she didn't ache for Vliet. Tonight, she thought, tonight. For Cricket, time was a sort of mobile geography, different places she would visit only once. This particular moment would recede and she would float to another inlet. Tonight never would be on the map again.

'Come with me,' she said. Darkness (and circadian rhythm?) made her voice too loud.

He said nothing.

'Or I'll go with you.'

'Being alone is the living pits, but ...'

'But you're drunk.'

'I'm straight-line sober. And Cricket, aware of this juicy, schoolgirl crush.'

'So?'

'I can't take advantage.'

He couldn't leave, either. Stretching his arm to panelling, he leaned over her. The silence was taut as a dam before it breaks. Unendurable. In that moment their silence communicated, far more than words could, the violence of his new-learned anguish, the full impact of her love – yet for all this love, had she not understood the extent of his pain, she would have let the matter drop. As it was, she knew he needed her. Or rather, he needed comfort.

Thighs weak, face burning, she said, 'How's it taking advantage if I want to?'

'Ever hear the term "using"?'

'This isn't.'

'You're my cousin. Christ, who needs to be more of a turd than's necessary for survival?'

'You aren't, Vliet.'

'Like hell I aren't. And besides, you're twelve.'

'Sixteen.'

'Eleven.'

'Sixteen.'

'I think of you as ten, and I'm what matters.'

'It's not as if it's firsts.'

'No?'

'No.'

'That I can't argue, Cricket, but I'm pretty stunned.'

'One night,' she said. 'Only tonight.'

He gave a peculiar choking sigh.

'It won't alter anything between us, Vliet. I promise.'

Snap, snap, snap. Vliet never hid from Cricket. And now his nervous, snapping fingers made a sound defenceless as a child's forlorn weeping.

'It'll be like we slept in our own beds, Vliet. Tomorrow we'll be the same as ever,' she whispered. And could speak no more. She listened to his fingers. She heard her heart. Circadian heart, she thought.

The snapping halted.

'Cricket, don't let me. Don't.' His plea held bewilderment, pain, and fear. Then, suddenly, he laughed. His breath stirred the warmth of Louis Martini wine onto her face. 'Check this, willya?' His tone now mocked. 'Me with the good fight when we both know the last thing I want is to be alone.'

She groped for his hand. In that sad, dusty chill, their fingers twined, his long and damp, hers childsize and trembling. They felt their way along shellacked pine to her room. His had the double bed. That bed, however, was occupied. Alix was in the cabin, palpable as if she slept in the room on the far side of the stairwell.

Cricket reached for the light.

'No need,' he said.

Darkness suited Cricket. She never had been self-conscious, but now she kept thinking she was a slob-pathetic type. Too short. Plain. She yanked sweaters over her head, skinning off jeans. She heard a button fall, rolling on boards. She paid no attention.

He held back clammy sheets to receive her.

She traced the skin of his shoulder, he brushed away her fingers. She kissed his chin, he jerked his head. He moved onto her. Surprised, she struggled. But he had her pinned down, his body paying no attention to hers. I'm being used, she thought, exactly as he'd said. Fury burst through Cricket, a sexual outrage that she'd never experienced. Don't, her brain shouted, and she almost yelled it aloud. DON'T! With Tom, always it had been mutual. Tom Goose-ta-av-sen. And I didn't love Tom. She found herself moving, but Vliet was a runner, sprinting alone, uncaring. She could smell his sharp, mustardy sweat, the soured wine.

Vliet was experiencing a frantic brutality alien to him. Alix's rejection, Roger's defection were a gangrenous wound. The body under his was merely a vessel into which festering pus could explode.

Maybe ninety seconds and he was rolling off her, getting out of bed. The other mattress creaked. Neither had spoken. Neither spoke now. She curled on her side, making herself smaller.

A groan awakened her.

'Vliet,' she said into the dark.

Muttering.

'Wake up!' she said.

A low, wordless cry.

She padded across frozen night, crowding next to him. He was shuddering. Cold sweat covered his naked skin. By osmosis, his night terror reached her.

'Huhh?' he mumbled.

She moved her hand gently down the damp trough of his spine. 'Shh.'

'Cricket?'

'Me, yes.'

He sniffed violently. 'I was killing Roger.'

'A nightmare.'

'Then he was murdering me with his fists. He can,

Cricket, he can.' Vliet's thumb rubbed her cheek. 'Hey little cos. You rescued me in the nick of time.'

He reached under the bed, finding a pack of Chesterfields that he must've stashed beforehand. He took a long time lighting up. In the yellow flicker the line cut by his crooked smile was deep. He looked drawn, ill. He looked as if he were getting over far worse than a cold. Shaking out the match, he inhaled deeply. 'C'mere,' he said.

She moved over, aware of biceps, muscles hard below her neck, aware of contiguous bodies. She had forgotten the misery of impersonal sex. She watched the glow of his cigarette, thinking of the bonds of warmth, familial affection, shared memory that joined them. And separated them. She understood the sense of vocation that leads a woman to a convent. The religious feel they are joined to, yet divided from, God. They consider their lives a bridge to gap the distance to Him. Cricket, the drifter, knew she had similar purpose. She would live only for Vliet. Even to her the idea was ludicrous. Puppy love, crushes, adolescent yearnings are very funny. (Yet who laughs when a young postulant in white cuts off her hair and takes her vow?) Vliet stubbed out his cigarette, turning on the pillow, nuzzling her cheek. 'It's one of our small-size Van Vliets,' he said.

'I am?'

'Really.' He touched her breasts in turn. 'Full and nice here.'

Dazed with pleasure, she whispered, 'You're beautiful.'

He kissed her lightly. 'We shouldn't let it get personal, we shouldn't. Cricket, Cricket, it is you?'

'Me.'

His fingers traced down her back. 'Remember? I picked cactus from this.'

She began to tremble.

'You were one,' he said.

'Three.'

'Two.'

'Three,' she whispered.

'Three, then,' he said, kissing her, the kiss turning inside out, and they started to make love, side by side, easily, gently, her hands floating on him, and he rambling about the cactus, yes, here the cactus. Caroline had driven Cricket and the twins for a day at Uncle Hend and Aunt Bette's ranch near Palm Springs, and Cricket, wobbly from one of the operations, had fallen, spiking herself on a cholla cactus, and Vliet was the only one she'd let use the tweezers to remove painful spikes. I love you, she thought over and over, maybe she said it, she kissed sharp collar bones and lightly fleshed chest, their breathing the only sound, their sweat-glazed bodies protected by their mutual grandmother's quilt stitchery, and they were moving luxuriously as if they had had a lifetime's carnal pleasure of one another, and when it finally came, that mingling of flesh, fluid, nerve ends, and self, it was through her muscles. There was odd tenderness in such culmination. Vliet never before had been able to permit it, it was too unguarded, but this was Cricket merging around him. Cricket held no danger, no shadows, he trusted little Cricket, ahhh ... trusted ... Their breathing quietened slowly. Through frost-edged windows shone huge mountain stars, a glittering that had travelled atomless eternity to reach a tall, elegantly handsome man with a nose like a Viking ship, who held a tiny, freckled girl with the same nose and blonde golliwog hair.

'You're a small snail,' he said.

'I love you.'

'You said a few hundred times.' He kissed her.

'It's no crush. I love you.'

'I encourage you.' He strummed on her shoulder. 'Cricket, recognize?'

'No.'

'Should.'

'What is it?'

'For you I chust composed. I vill call it der *Moonlight Sonata*.'

'You mean everything to me,' she said, rubbing her nose in his neck.

'There's one thing.'

'What?'

'Not to give you a swollen head, but that was topnotch stuff. And now it's very cosy. Really. I could stay in bed with you forever.' He curled, yawning, around her. 'You're my small snail.' Another yawn. 'Small snail.'

2

Cricket transferred food into cardboard cartons. There were soups and chili, packages of cookies and crackers, an unopened two-pound jar of unprocessed honey, cellophane-packed dried mushrooms, eggs. Most of the purchases made by Alix four days earlier.

Vliet slept downstairs. Cricket moved slowly, the soft upper lip a dreamy curve. She set a bottle of White House dressing on Hostess Twinkies, crushing them. She wasn't caught up by anything that Vliet had said (*I could stay in bed with you forever*) or by the way he'd acted (tender, gentle, and yes, loving). She had promised last night wouldn't exist. And if she couldn't exactly keep this promise, well, she could come pretty close. For Cricket, as for small children, once a yearned-after activity is in the past, it takes on a mythic quality. For her, last night already had transcended what is real.

Vliet, shaved and immaculate, came upstairs, giving her his standard smile. Except Vliet, a night person, wasn't good for smiles until his second cup of coffee.

''Morning,' he said, smiling into her eyes. 'Packed?'

'Finishing up.'

'We're set, then.'

'There's the beds. I'll do them while you get the toilet.'

'First my coffee.' He moved to the stove. His lopsided smile definitely was lasting too long. A white-toothed reminder: your promise.

She hurried downstairs.

She folded Alix's stuff into Alix's case. Except for a faint perfume, the clothes were as they had emerged from the tissue of an I. Magnin box, where, according to labels, most of them had been bought. She stripped beds. She ended up in her room.

'Ready?'

She jumped. Vliet lounged at the door, smiling at her. She let the quilt (they had shared it) slip, then hastily refolded it.

'Practically,' she said.

'No rush.' He lit a cigarette, letting it dangle. 'Hey, little cos, you've got milk on your upper lip.'

Reddening, she licked a finger to her mouth.

'Just for the record, say something.'

'I don't know what.'

He gave her a long look and walked to the bed nearest the window, sitting, extending his legs. Sunlight polished hand-sewn boots.

She said, 'If you mean – That didn't change anything for me, last night.'

'How could it, Cricket?' He smiled. 'Nothing happened, last night.'

She shoved more dirty linen in the pillowcase. She was confused, hurt. Obediently she had sponged away his moist, affectionate coupling as she would jam from a blouse, and if a faint mark, no longer quite real to her, stained her memory, well, she wouldn't wear that side. She didn't understand what it was that he wanted from her.

'Must you,' she asked, and her voice trembled, 'keep grinning like that?'

'Get off that damn high horse! What're you trying to hold me to?'

Camera slung around her neck, duffel over her shoulder, afghan under her elbow, Cricket headed for the door.

'I didn't mean ...' Vliet's voice came apart. 'I'm sorry. Really. Listen, you're a good, generous, smart little nip-

301

per.' Dragging on his cigarette, he discovered it had gone out. He dropped the butt in his palm. 'But you're ten –'

'Sixteen.'

'– and for the sake of argument, let's say I hadn't slept in my own bed.'

She turned away.

'I might have said things, done things, I couldn't mean. No way I could mean them. You're too young. You're my cousin. You're not – you're not my type.' His voice had that odd, toneless quality. Despair, she thought. 'Tell me, how do you figure I'd feel every time I see you?'

'Vliet,' she said, 'today's today.'

'For you. Not me. If I'd behaved in a way that led you on ...' He paused, relighting the cigarette. 'I'd feel lousy. And people cannot face those they feel lousy towards. I wouldn't be able to come into the same room with you. Understand? We couldn't be in the same room.'

She leaned against the battered tallboy.

'You mean too goddamn much,' he said.

She avoided looking at him head-on. What was it he wanted? Cricket had the tendency of openly generous people to imagine the motives of others were cleverer, more cerebral than her own. She never could realize that in general the elaborate circumlocutions they used were to justify their own triviality. She stood silent, weighted down by the heavy duffel.

'Cricket,' he muttered, 'it's gotta be the same, you and me.'

'But it is.'

'I am so screwed. Lost. I couldn't take it if things changed with us. Can't you see that?'

And finally she did see. Vliet wanted her to behave as he had. A bit much. He wanted her to let him know she was playing his game. At first she had ignored last night, so how could he assume she was ignoring it?

'Know what?' She forced cheer into her voice.

'What?'

'That's what,' she said, brightly nodding at the lumpy pillowcase.

And he, rewarding her with his fine, uneven grin, swung the makeshift laundry bag over his shoulder. 'Off, off and away.' Relief sang in his voice.

She followed him upstairs. Her shoulders were hunched, her face drawn. She looked like a shy child who has been coerced by grown-ups into performing at one of their parties.

3

A low-pressure area had formed over the Pacific. The next day, around eleven, rain started. As Cricket came out of her bathroom, she heard Vliet's voice. He must've been telling Caroline a joke because as Cricket circled down her stairs, Caroline's golden laughter rang.

'Cricket,' Vliet said. 'Let's drive.'

Caroline's laughter ceased. 'It's pouring cats and dogs. *She* has wet hair, and *you*, luv, have a cold.'

'The VW's well caulked.' Bending, he kissed his aunt's pink cheek. 'Mmm. Only nymphomaniacs should use that perfume.'

Silent, Vliet drove to Topanga Canyon, snaking between mountains dead with tumbled igneous rocks. At the summit, he pulled over. Leaving his door open, he whirled gracefully around the mini-bus. When he got back in, rain had darkened his hair, his Irish sweater smelled woolly.

'Why the skipping?' she asked.

'Don't be dense, Cricket.' He palmed water from his cheeks. 'That was a rite of thanksgiving.'

'For what?'

'For the first time in twenty-four hours I've been free from speeches about hauling ass back to Hopkins. Ma and Dad never stop. And the minute I set foot in your place, Aunt Caroline's on me. She's what gets me down.'

'It doesn't sound like her, even.'

'Ma must have her brainwashed.'

'They were on the phone hours this morning.'

'Before Uncle Gene left?'

'Daddy?'

'Eugene Matheny, president of all the Dutchmen.'

'Funny. I never think of him like that.'

'Don't give me your mental lapses, Cricket. Was he around?'

'Part of the time.'

'Well, that ties it. And I was going to talk jobs.' Vliet stared at rain-bleak mountains. 'Cricket, when we discussed my future, we overlooked the obvious. Groceries. The markets've always smelled good to me.'

Vliet did question her father about business, often, but Cricket never had been positive whether the interest was genuine or Vliet was simply being *simpático*.

'Well, so much for lost causes.'

'He'd side with Mother, yes.'

'Think the condition could change?'

'Maybe,' she said with great uncertainty.

'Any ideas how to get it to?'

She shook her head.

'I'd be in your debt.'

'Daddy would never go against her and Aunt Em.'

Vliet dropped by the next afternoon when he knew Caroline would be out shopping. For an hour he was a stand-up tragedian. Cricket listened to his acid one-liners about his parents, his biting monologue on Alix and Roger. She offered milk and sympathy.

In the kitchen, he asked, 'Did I mention Executive Employment Placing?'

'No. Were you there?'

He downed his milk. 'This morning.'

'Any luck?'

'When I told 'em I wouldn't do heavy lifting, they were stumped. They are going to have a genuine problem with me.'

'You're a Harvard graduate.'

'Sure, and with a name like mine, I should have it made. But ...'

The next afternoon was a repeat, with more emphasis on the day's fruitless visit to Executive Employment Placing.

If you are being worked, there inevitably must come the moment when you realize it. At this point, one is meant to experience hurt, then anger. And refuse to let it continue. In truth, if you look up to the worker, when the fact hits you, you are flattered. Who, *me*? *I* can help *you*? This flattery gives a tremendous high, like winning at craps: you can't lose. Every throw will come up seven or eleven. You tackle forces normally you wouldn't dare. Afterwards, you'll remember and be a little proud, or ashamed, or unbelieving, but at the moment, you wade in, saying and doing things that you'd never say or do for yourself.

God knows, Cricket wasn't a fighter. She let events shape themselves. Certainly she never had fought Gene, and she never even suspected that Caroline sometimes did it for her. She loved her father for his slow way of talking, for the few loyal remaining strands brushed across his scalp, for being decent, for being her father. She never could understand his involvement with the heavy black ledgers and stacks of paper that he strewed across the den table every night.

As soon as she grasped the situation, though, Cricket – for her knight of the currently doleful countenance – entered battle with her father.

She opened fire at bedtime, when Caroline was in the bathroom washing her face, a two-minute soap massage followed by thirty counted splashes followed by a lengthy slathering of four different anti-wrinkle emollients.

'Vliet's not going to be a doctor,' Cricket said.

'That's all I hear.' Gene, in faded flannel pyjamas, was winding his watch.

'He never wanted to, Daddy.'

'Nobody gets that far without an affinity.'

305

'Roger's got the affinity.'

Gene admired Roger's drive, honesty, strength of character, but always he'd been caught by Vliet's humour, his quirk of smile. It was Vliet who made him laugh. Gene was ashamed of loving the less worthy boy. He set his watch on the mantelpiece. 'Vliet's grades are fine. There's no reason for him to drop out.'

'Roger and Alix.'

'Oh?'

'They're going together now,' Cricket said. 'Didn't Mother tell you? It's what decided him.'

'He should come up with something more profound.'

Cricket gazed at him.

'All right,' Gene sighed. 'A girl's as good as a loyalty oath. But Vliet's had a hundred girls, all beautiful. He'll recover.'

'He hates Johns Hopkins.'

'That, surprising as it may seem, isn't crucial. A lot of men hate their schooling.' Gene opened a door to what once had been the adjoining bedroom. Caroline recently had converted it into a vast cupboard lined with shelves for bags, sweaters, shoes: there were racks of varying heights for blouses, dresses, long-gowns. I work all day, Gene thought wryly, for unequal distribution of women's clothes. He wasn't blaming Caroline, but himself. This, this was how he had chosen to spend his only life. He shut the door.

'Know what I wanted to be?' he asked.

'A professor.'

'A writer, too,' he corrected.

'You worked on the UCLA paper.'

'Not a journalist. A real writer. Novels. I started with some short stories. I never had the nerve to send them out.'

'Daddy, that's sad.'

'I'm not telling you this for sympathy.' Gene paused. 'The family tell me I'm a success. What do you think?'

'Yes. No. I never wanted to do anything, not really. I don't know.'

'Well, I'm not. Success would've been those books with my name on the jacket. And you know why I failed?'

'The Oath. You wouldn't sign it. You lost your job.'

'That needn't have stopped me from writing. The truth, Cricket, is, I ran away. I thought I wouldn't be any good, so I ran away. I quit.'

'Daddy, give Vliet a job.'

'Haven't you been listening?'

'You're trying to tell me he should keep on at college. But you're wrong. He's not like you. He's more, well, commercial.'

'Commercial? That's all the more reason for him to keep going. A Beverly Hills specialist makes far more than I do.'

'Under any conditions, he's not going back.'

'Honey, don't encourage him.'

'It's what's right,' Cricket said.

'Your aunt lives for those boys. Did Mother ever tell you the story how Aunt Em arranged with your great-grandmother to put her own inheritance – the money she would've had – in trust for the twins? They aren't wealthy people, and then they were in a very tight spot. She made a tremendous sacrifice. The boys're her life. Especially Vliet. She's beside herself.'

'What about Vliet? Isn't it his life, too?'

Gene chose not to reply.

The following morning Cricket woke after he had left. She pursued him to the Assyrian fort that took a full block of Pico Boulevard. Van Vliet's Warehouses No. 1 and No. 2, and home offices. There, across his gleaming presidential desk, Gene admitted that Vliet was personable, great with people, intelligent, and – most important – his frame of reference was money. 'He adds up to the compleat executive.' Gene stopped, his face concerned. His resemblance to a faithful hound had not abated. 'Cricket, honey, tell me what it is? What's wrong?' Just then, Mrs Saenz buzzed. Time for his next appointment. 'We'll go into it later. But about Vliet, I can't. Your mother'd flay me. Em's mental on the subject.'

Hearing muffled voices in the front hall, Em tilted her wrist with a practised movement. For years now, her dishwasher hadn't run without liquor, the vacuum cleaner had needed a shot. Em's use of alcohol almost never reached the visible stages of jollity or despair: her nipping was a deadener of subliminal frustration. This, though, was too much.

It was unlike Em to be bitter. Yet she couldn't help thinking of the comfort – cash – she had denied herself and Sheridan, of how hard she had worked, making sure the twins got well-balanced meals, finished their homework every night, and went to Sunday school, never quarrelled but stayed close to one another as their carefully fitted Stride Rite shoes strode up the path to success. Now all this was wasted. Em had no idea what had happened at the cabin, but in her bones she knew at the bottom she would find Alix. Somehow the girl was ruining Em's life. However much Em drank, she couldn't anaesthetize herself against the pain. Her sense of justice took a permanent break. I can't bear to see the girl. Never, never, never. Em deposited her glass next to the water carafe that contained vodka.

Cricket opened venetian blinds, admitting strips of greyish light. How young she looks, Em thought, and let her fingers torture her brow.

She whimpered, 'Light hurts.'

Cricket readjusted cords.

'It's my migraine.'

'Want an icebag, Aunt Em?'

'No, thank you, dear.'

Cricket sat on Sheridan's bed. 'It's Vliet,' she said.

(A minute ago, when Vliet had let her in, he had been wearing his dark suit. She had inquired why. 'Congratulate me, that's why. Executive came through. I've got this position with A&P – providing I change my name to Wladislas or something.')

'I've got to talk to you about Vliet.'

308

Em's wrinkles deepened. She shot her niece, whom she loved, a look of fury. 'He's in his room. Listen.'

They listened. Bouncy, scratched music. For an instant Em's expression softened. 'It's "Getting Sentimental over You,"' she said. 'He's packing.'

'He's not.'

Em gripped her forehead again. 'Please God, you never get migraines. As you leave, dear, close the blinds properly.'

Cricket drew a breath. 'I'm not going yet,' she said in her clear voice.

Em turned her head, moaning.

'Listen, please listen, Aunt Em. Vliet's graduated from Harvard. He's never been in trouble. Everybody likes him. The family loves him. He's a success. You're a success.'

'I don't hear you!'

'Aunt Em, he's going to work at A&P if you don't let Daddy give him a job.'

'He and Roger are very fortunate! Uncle Sheridan never had their advantages. They never have to scrimp. There's money for them to finish the best medical school.'

'Please let Daddy.'

Em, perfumed in Vick's VapoRub to drown any aroma of alcohol, pushed to sitting position, her long-sleeved dress momentarily trapping her. 'You listen to me, you!' The voice, precariously on edge. 'There's one thing I want. Only one thing out of life. And that's for my sons to have the best. And for that, they must persevere. And that, Cricket, is why I don't hear you!'

'Vliet enjoys business –'

'It's that terrible girl!' Em cried, her voice over the edge now, rasping, drunken, hopeless. 'That Alix!'

And, eyes closed, she fell into pillows.

Cricket ran for the icebag.

'What in the name of God did you say to your aunt?' Gene wanted to know.

'What did she tell you?' Cricket's voice shook. Her scene with Em hadn't worn off. It was the same evening, and Gene, in his navy robe, had just climbed circular steel to her aerie.

'A half hour ago we had our annual sisterly eye gouging.'

'I'm sorry.'

'Em called to say she'd had a terrible migraine which you'd aggravated into the mother of all headaches. Oh, she didn't really blame you. Mostly she ranted about Alix.'

'She really has it in for Alix.'

'But she did feel you were meddling in affairs that didn't concern a child. Your mother isn't one to take this lying down. She countered that Em's overgrown lunk was harrying you. One thing led to another. And it came out you'd told a heinous lie. Vliet is starting at A&P.'

'It's not a lie.'

'I know.' Gene patted his knee. Loving him, never considering deeper hang-ups, Cricket sat. 'Listen,' he said. 'I don't have to mention we're both delighted with you, do I?'

She hugged him. Parental esteem, or lack thereof, never had been a problem with Cricket. She knew they loved her.

'Now, honey, tell me what's wrong?'

She left his lap, picking up a proof sheet. Film shot in Arrowhead: tiny pictures on slick paper showing Roger in Cousin Sidney Sutherland's new boat.

'I called Vliet back,' Gene said. 'He told me it wasn't an important offer, but he was taking it. So I told him to go see Don.' Don Dalton, the barrel-shaped head of Van Vliet's personnel. 'Don't put him in the training programme.'

The battle was over.

She'd won.

Cricket clutched the proof sheet. Before each of her operations, a nurse would suck on a little rubber tube to get blood samples. She'd won. So why should she feel this slow draining?

'You didn't mention me?' she asked. 'To Vliet?'

'What? And let him know my daughter makes my business decisions?'

'Thank you.'

'Cricket, let me help you.'

'You have, Daddy.'

'Since you got down from Arrowhead, you've been different. You're not you. You don't push this way.'

'Must be the family determination coming out.'

Gene didn't smile. Thumbnail pressed between bottom incisors, he examined her. 'Whatever it is,' he said slowly, 'we're here when you need us.'

'I feel terrible about Aunt Em.'

'She'll forgive you. In time, even me.'

'But not Alix.'

'No, not Alix.'

He kissed Cricket goodnight. After he had disappeared down the stairwell, she stood at the dark circle of windows.

An owl lived in the hillside sycamore. *Hoo hoo hoo.* When you win, you lessen the other person. She had shrunk her father. And somehow herself. And that was why she felt this crazy siphoning. Family determination? *Hoo hoo hoo.* Sighing, she got in bed.

'I never could do that again,' she whispered. 'I can't fight.'

Her seventeenth birthday was on 10 July. She had slept with Vliet at the end of April. By her birthday she'd known for some time it was fight or run. So run it was. She thanked God the ice had been broken last year. (Cricket didn't have enough savvy to know she also should thank Him for making her a daughter of liberal, upper-middle-class Californians in the late sixties. She was not on drugs, she had graduated from high school, and therefore on the Mathenys' socio-economic level was considered a job well done. Despite her parents' trepidations – and they had plenty – it was an article of their faith that from here on – if they loved their child – it was hands off.)

Gene took in the Buick for a complete overhaul.

Caroline, reeking with Interdit, hugged her small daughter goodbye, slipping her a fifty to augment the wad of traveller's cheques. And Cricket was off, as Caroline put it, 'to take pictures around Carmel, she'll stay with a group of friends.' This explanation was received with commiserating sympathy. Who in Caroline's and Gene's circle didn't have a child bent on some oddball way of life?

4

1. *Love your Spiritual Father as you love life.*
2. *Incline your heart to the teachings of your Spiritual Father and obey him in all matters.*
3. *Share all that you possess with the family of your Spiritual Father.*
4. *Cast off your old life and dwell in the current of the eternal now.*
5. *Harm not your body by food, drink, or knife.*
6. *Eat not the flesh of animal nor fowl nor fish.*
7. *The man and his woman are .united: let nothing separate them.*
8. *Come together, O man and woman, only when forces of physical, mental, and emotional love are in perfect harmony.*
9. *Harm no person, including your own self, with knife, deed, or word.*
10. *Dwell in peace with those in the home of your Spiritual Father that your days may be happy and long.*

The commandments had been etched on a panel of the great hall. Below, a pottery vase half as tall as a man was filled with branches dangling reddish berries. A scorching afternoon at the end of July. Thick walls kept out the heat. Giles sat on the only chair, tugging his greying beard, while Cricket, on a tatami, explained her predicament. She called him Giles. 'I'm not Giles now,' he interrupted. 'Daughter, call me Genesis.' 'Genesis,' she said, and her voice receded. The pungent odour of sugar bush drifted around them.

'Your folks,' he inquired, 'do they know?'

She shook her head.

'Why not?'

'They'd get me an abortion.'

He leaned forward. The skin above his beard showed craters from long-ago acne.

'They love me,' she said. 'They'd feel it was best. They'd insist. I can't fight them. I'm not good at fighting. They'd talk me into it, I know they would. That's why I came.'

'What'll you do with the child?'

'Keep it.'

'Here?'

'Yes, here.'

'And the father?' asked Giles – no, Genesis.

'He doesn't know, either.'

'He'd've insisted, too?'

She could visualize Vliet sidestepping fatherhood gracefully: *Cricket, keed, for Chrissake, this isn't downtown Dresden with the B-29s on the way. There's this very good man. Clean and safe.* And after that, he would not be able to force himself into a room with her.

'He don't care about you?'

'He's my cousin. It's impossible. He loves me, too, but I'm like a little sister. Not his type.' She nodded. 'He'd insist.'

'Ever think how strange? The world out there loves with a knife.' Genesis spoke with the impersonal rancour he always used on life beyond this sanctuary. He paced, short, thick legs coming down heavy on old boards. His footsteps reverberated through Cricket's seated body. 'In crises,' he said, 'a person can't accept revelation.'

'But this is the only place I have!'

'We need to resolve all past conflict before we're free to become.'

'Then I can't stay?' Her question, high-pitched and anxious, travelled through shadows.

He came back to sit in his chair. 'Not as one of us,' he said slowly. 'But you can stay.'

'Thank you.' Her muscles were limp with reprieve. 'Thank you. I'll pay.'

He glanced up at engraved wood. *Share all that you possess.*

She flushed. 'I'll work.'

'Got your camera?'

She nodded.

'Customers at REVELATION sometimes ask about us. The way we live. There's quite a few who're curious, and never mind why. Others, though, are sincere. The words I come up with can be taken wrong. Sniggered at. But a photograph – people don't laugh at a photograph.'

How he hated to be laughed at! She said, 'I'll get across the feel of REVELATION. I'll try, really try, Genesis.'

'After, you'll be one of us.'

'Thank you.'

'One thing, daughter.' He raised a thick, warning finger. 'Don't mention the baby.'

This, also, she remembered. He snipped secrets from people to wear like amulets against his leonine chest.

'There will be no way to hide it,' she said.

'When the time comes, I'll tell everyone.' The words were spoken as law. Fond and paternal, but law.

She dug from her bag the keys to the Buick, her traveller's cheques, her wallet with the scented fifty-dollar bill, her Union Oil card. These she turned over to Genesis in accordance with commandment No. 3.

Genesis himself had burned the commandments into wood. As REVELATION had grown – and now there were thirty-one members, plus four girls including Cricket in a state of limbo – he had formulated an orthodoxy.

Like Jesuits, the group was obedient to a centralized authority. Genesis. For each minor decision he had a rule, for every act a regulation. They knew at five they would be washing with ice water, at eight they would eat their uncooked breakfast, they would bob a head to greet one another. Sundays, women sewed at the long table while men would take turns reading aloud from Hesse and Gibran. People instinctively yearn to be told what to do – if only to have something to rebel against. These offspring of America's upper-income bracket had found their old lives chaotic. They had been excused from working. College classes had been liberated from roll-taking, not obligatory. Each day had been a desert and no signpost to help them cross it. In REVELATION the Select (as members now were called) had crept into the immutable freedom where there's not a single decision to make.

Unaware of time as a little cat, Cricket drifted around tables and into the kitchen, getting the restaurant on film. One time she snapped Genesis with his knives. 'Don't!' he barked. For once, his chesty gravel voice was out of control. As penitence, she took him with arms akimbo, eyes thoughtful under white headband, a very fine shot, and borrowing her car plus three dollars of her money, she drove to Monterey and had the picture blown to poster size. She presented it to Genesis. Delighted, he hammered the poster to a wall. That very day a customer requested a copy. Genesis had a dozen printed, selling them for five dollars each.

Carmel Valley turned from grey-green to rich, late-summer brown. Cricket's pregnancy never localized into a lump. Beneath the loose white clothes of REVELATION her body appeared to have spread into adolescent pudge, and she had no difficulty keeping her promise not to tell. She felt fine. Fine. Doctors were anathema here, but she remembered reading about calcium and so drank quarts of raw, unpasteurized milk. Her only craving, sunflower seeds. She cached them in her pockets, and her small white teeth were forever cracking papery shells. She bounced through the daily trip to Carmel until she had well over a hundred rolls, then she set up her developing equipment in the never-used butler's pantry of the Chinese compound.

To make a print, light must pass through the negative onto light-sensitive paper. Cricket experimented with a technique called dodging, covering a place to keep it lighter, thus darkening the background. She redid the poster chiaroscuro like a Rembrandt. Genesis, delighted, had these printed.

She wasn't in the restaurant that overcast Friday morning in early October. Neither was Genesis.

That was the morning the Select found *Murderer!* slashed in heavy black paint across Cricket's work. The patio buzzed like a disturbed apiary. Who had printed this slander? Who in this uptight resort, who in this un-enlightened town? One by one, they were drawn to trace jagged lettering. *Murderer!* Just before the lunch trade arrived, Orion tore it down.

They drove home in blue-hazed twilight. Genesis sat in the great hall. Everyone halted on the veranda. At last, Orion, breathing in audible gasps, extended the ripped poster. Genesis stared. His bearded face turned terrible and still, as if he were viewing a Gorgon. They shrank back. His heavy footsteps echoed across tile paving. The door to his room slammed.

Nobody spoke. Finally, one of the women went to the kitchen house. The other women followed. After dinner both sexes gathered in a circle of lantern light talking about the guacamole pie they'd eaten for dinner, the morning fog, the ways to seat more customers. Anything except *Murderer!*

Cricket huddled alone on the dark steps of the hall. Orion straining his eyes, went to her. He thought he loved her to desperation. That he didn't was a technicality. She was the first girl he'd ever felt relaxed with.

'Come be with us,' he said.

'No, thank you,' she said.

'Is it, you know?' he whispered tenderly. Orion alone had noticed she was pregnant. She had bound him to secrecy for Genesis' sake, amen.

'Uhh-uh. No.' Cricket put her lips to her bare upper arm, the way children extract comfort from their own flesh. 'Orion, we don't know Genesis. Who he was or what he did.'

'What's the difference? He's shown us how to live.'

'But it's almost like he's making a movie. We're actors and he's directing us. We don't know the script, or if he's improvising, or what. Or even the kind of movie. I haven't told anyone about the baby, and without him to focus in, nobody's even guessed. Except you. People don't see unless he tells them to see. Don't do unless he tells them to do.' This remark, she realized, set her apart, so she added, 'I write one letter a week. Call home once a week – and I miss them so much. But I do what he tells me. We all do. What if he told us to ...' She couldn't finish, but the meaning was clear. *Murderer!*

'If that's how you feel, you better move right on out,' said Orion. The harsh, cold disciple. He left.

The others went to their rooms. She didn't budge.

Footsteps.

'Here,' Orion said, dropping a handful of sunflower seeds in her lap, forgiving her her trespasses.

She cracked one, her tongue seeking the tiny kernel.

He said, 'Shouldn't you go to a doctor?'

'We here don't use doctors.'

'Now who's following?'

'I'm very healthy.' She was. Besides, she hated gyn visits. Dr Porter had said maybe she was too young to stay on The Pill and that he would fit her with an IUD. Putting off her appointment had been Cricket's contribution to the population explosion.

'Women all the time go to obstetricians.' Orion's heresy went muted into darkness.

'Not in other countries.'

'Maybe you better tell your parents.' His implication: They'll get you to some kind of medical care.

She shifted her weight.

'Cricket?'

She said nothing.

'Eventually they'll have to know.'

She knew this. She just didn't think about it. Afterwards her avoidance seemed inexplicable – but when had she worried about the future? At the time, she decided the boy sitting next to her was a real worry wart. He cared, though. 'Orion,' she touched his bony wrist. 'Everything's going to be great. You'll see.'

Genesis stayed in his room the next day.

And the next. They didn't dare knock on his chipped red-enamel door. Anxiety settled under Chinese roofbeams and in the salty air of the restaurant. The Select once again were open to the slings and arrows of choice. Arguments bubbled everywhere.

On the fourth morning, it was Magnificat's turn to sound the rising gong. Cricket woke to grey light. Magnificat slept with one hand under crinkly red hair. 'Oh shit!' she said when Cricket nudged her. 'I'll do it,' Cricket said, and Magnificat retorted, 'But you aren't one of the Select – oh hell! Big deal who hits the damn thing.'

The deep note came then. It seemed to hang forever in the cold dawn.

Magnificat jumped from her tatami, performing the ritual she'd neglected the past two mornings. Long red hair flapping, she touched warped board with her palms. 'I am of the earth,' she intoned, 'I am of the earth.'

Genesis stood on the veranda. His robe was fresh, his beard and hair damp with combing. Everyone stopped at the foot of the steps, waiting for him to open the doors of meditation. When they were assembled, he moved his hands, a flat, benedictory gesture. 'Today,' he said, 'we aren't meditating. We won't open the restaurant. We won't eat. This day is for searching.'

And he sat on the highest step.

Awed by his reappearance, filled with apostate guilt, aware of reverting to their old contentiousness, they understood how those Israelites had felt when Moses tramped back from Sinai. Meek, they sat where they were. On dew-slick tiles. Genesis gazed down at them. He could sit for hours like this, erect as if a yardstick were against his spine.

His voice came from deep in his barrel chest. First he spoke of the unique gift of the moment, then he shifted to former lives. Throw off your past, he said. 'There isn't a thing that ties any of us to our old, evil selves, not if we don't choose to be bound.'

He gazed at each one. When it was Cricket's turn, her breath caught. The hypnotic brown eyes seemed to pull her from herself.

'What is the greatest fear a little child can have?' Pause. 'That he's not loved. Each time his father hits him, each time he sees someone getting an extra cookie, he's thrown into that lack of love. Rejection. He wants to hit out. The child grows up. He forgets the reason for his terror, but he keeps hitting. I've seen men killing over nothing, but it wasn't nothing. It was that lack of love. We each have it. It moves us all.' Long pause. 'I am going to tell you about Giles Cooke.' Third person. This man has no connection with me.

Orion straightened a leg. Genesis stared at him. Orion was still.

'Giles Cooke was born in Oklahoma, on a dirt farm. His folks were poor, and a great Depression had fallen on the land. And there was a drought. No rain. Dust, dust, always that crumbling, dried-out earth which wouldn't grow corn or any green, living thing. The house was kept shut tight, but dust filtered in little lines under doors and windows. Dust was Giles's first memory. Dust and going to bed hungry. A brother was born. Giles's mamma fed it a bottle and cuddled it, gave it love. Love. One day it got a fever. The next night it was dead. Remorse burned in Giles. So often had he wished his little brother dead, he was sure he had killed him. His mamma cried all the time. And his daddy ran off. His mamma took Giles to San Diego – she came from there. No work any-place, and she took up with sailors. She'd leave Giles at his aunt's teetering off in her high heels with some sailor. She'd be gone days. At ten Giles joined a gang. They were older, but he was tough and quick and he had a switchblade knife. If they wanted money, the gang found some drunk sailor on Main Street to roll. Giles saw these sailors not as human beings but as something on which to avenge himself. Jumping them, he felt like God's punishment. The war came. Giles stood in line to enlist in the Army.' Genesis wet his lips. His red mouth shone in his greying beard. 'He was a commando. He could knife a man with no more feelings than a butcher slaughtering a steer. He was a fine soldier. He killed nine Germans. He earned medals and citations and the war ended.'

'Amen,' said Orion.

'In 'forty-seven he got into a fight with a man who beat him at poker. Not because the man had cheated him. No. Because the man was rich. Giles envied him his Caddie and wad of notes. The man had a knife, too.' Genesis pulled his robe to show his right shoulder. A long, pale scar ridged from the heavy neck to the base of the arm.

Shocked whispers.

'The man died. A coroner's jury said Giles, the war hero, was acting in self-defence, and let him go. In 'fifty-nine he cut a fat little shopkeeper because he coveted the man's wife. The man died. This time Giles was convicted of manslaughter. He did time. This isn't seeking pity for him. But all his life he'd been lost, lonely, and the cancer of envy had eaten him. In Chino, for the first time, he looked into his soul. A pock-marked, ugly soul.'

Magnificat gave a long sigh.

'When he got out, he went into the desert. He lived alone in a shack outside Indio. Thinking, always thinking. He came to realize his soul was ugly because he'd been living in pain. Because of his own pain, he'd inflicted pain on others.' Genesis stopped and took a minute before going on. 'One day there was a sandstorm, a bad one that scoured paint from cars. Giles took off his clothes and stood in that gritty gale until he was bleeding. He submitted to physical pain until he was rubbed down to his own damaging pain.' Genesis gazed at them, his heavy grey brows pulled together, a stern look, a reminder that each of us has committed a treachery so great that we fear to pull it from the darkness of our own mind. 'Afterwards, he washed his blood away, he drank cool water. And he laughed. Trees are torn to nakedness in the autumn. They are reborn each Easter.'

Magnificat sobbed aloud.

'And I was reborn to a world of love. We can each have our share of that love. Love is possible for everyone.' His gravelly voice choked.

Now they were all weeping. He descended the shallow steps. Everyone hugged him, hugged one another, then, linking hands to form a chain, they wound into the great hall, reading the commandments in unison, a vaguely theatrical ceremony that caught in the throat. They didn't go outside until the setting sun had touched flat clouds with red.

Orion followed Cricket. 'Been thinking about the doctor?'

'What?'

'We were talking the other day. When it comes, there's gotta be a doctor.'

'Why?'

'All I know is in movies women have complications.'

Cricket, also, had learned obstetrics from problematic on-screen birthings. But she knew, too, that throughout time women have borne healthy infants without the benefit of the American Medical Association. And Cricket was Cricket. Never having suffered a queasy morning, how could she imagine any difficulty? Indian squaws had gone into a bush alone, emerging with neatly wrapped papooses. She and her baby, they would be naturals.

'You're so little,' Orion fretted.

'I'm pure Sioux.'

And she went back to brooding about Genesis.

5

Her doubts about Genesis lingered through the next day, Sunday. In the afternoon she went out alone, climbing the same hill that she and Orion had climbed last spring. A north wind pushed cobbled clouds and moulded her loose grey poncho to her abdomen. Seen like this, her pregnancy was very apparent – for any who chose to see.

She was afraid. Why? Why? All yesterday and this gloomy morning the Select had repeated how beautiful was Genesis, a truly beautiful man, he had risen through many hells to rebirth, a fancy, Dantean phrase which Genesis himself had originated. Cricket's wide-set grey eyes saw with a stubbornly innocent vision. The child might love her emperor, but always she would note that he didn't wear snappy new clothes – or any clothes at all. She couldn't forget the dead. A poker-playing Cadillac owner, a fat little husband. Nine anonymous Germans. (In war, though, it's kill or be killed: should soldiers count?) Genesis was reborn. Fine. Yet Cricket saw, too, that eleven men no longer brushed their teeth or tasted fresh bread. They were dead.

She climbed faster. Her thighs spread as if she were on skis.

All at once light drained from the hills. There was no bird sound. The eternal insects were silent. A lizard darted into chinquapin. She halted. Gazing around at motionless, empty hills, she thought of autumn, a season of death and dying, autumn, time of repentance.

Killing, she thought. Killing.

Lightning zigzagged. The electric smell of ozone, then thunder rolling. Cricket's heart hit the sides of her rib cage. Usually storms didn't frighten her. Now, though, she was terrified. And, oddly, this fear had nothing to do with Genesis or killing. This fear was irrational –

Monster X chasing her, the Unknown breathing down her neck.

She raced pell-mell down the hill. Lines of rain hit her, immediately gluing her hair to her head, reaching under her poncho. Her sandals were deep in mud.

Another lightning bolt strafed the hills. The thunder's nearness panicked her. She saw the oak. She didn't watch for roots.

As she fell, instinctively she protected her stomach with her hands. Her head slammed against the exposed root.

Stars.

She really did see stars.

She lifted her head. Pain shot through her right eye. She touched the orbital bone. A lump already was rising. With difficulty, she pushed to her feet.

'Jesus Christ!' Orion forgot the rule against blasphemy. A yellow slicker held over his head, he'd come about fifty feet from the peak-roofed entry gate to search for her. 'What happened?'

'I tripped.'

'You sure did. You're covered with mud.'

'Do I have a black eye?'

'I can't tell – yes. Your forehead's grazed.'

And taking her hand, he led her to Genesis' room, where necessary bandaging was done. Rain drummed on roof tiles, rain rushed in gutters. Genesis examined her and turned on the tub. The faucet was barely audible in the rain.

Cricket's wrists ached. The wet poncho gave her trouble.

'Here, daughter,' said Genesis. 'Let me.'

Asexual and kind, he helped with her mud-sopping clothes. Cricket wasn't physically modest. Still, she was pretty glad Orion had been dismissed.

'Hey.' Startled, she looked at Genesis.

'What is it?'

'My stomach. Everything's all weird.'

'How?'

'Tight, sort of.'

'Does it hurt?' he asked, his voice concerned as he helped her into the high, claw-footed tub.

'No, not exactly. Genesis, nothing should be happening for two months.'

'You're fine,' he said. His deep voice resonated with certainty.

The tautness ended. He went into his room, leaving the door ajar. She moved her grazed hand, rippling warm water, distorting her small, round body.

Clean, dry, she stretched on his mat. The blankets smelled of him. He plastered adhesive and gauze to her forehead. 'There,' he said.

This time her veins and arteries froze. Orion, bringing her a glass of milk, stared at her, his face whitening.

'What's wrong?' he asked.

'My stomach.'

'Shouldn't she, you know, be in a hospital?' he stammered apologetically.

Genesis straightened the wick of a fat candle, holding it to a coal. 'I've birthed plenty of babies,' he said.

They looked at him.

'In the desert,' Genesis said. 'One a breech.'

'But this is early,' Orion said.

'About that,' Genesis smiled in his beard, 'there isn't anything anybody can do. Son, in this rain we're stuck. You question too much. Have faith in the now.'

Cricket closed her eyes, breathing deep. Lamaze and yoga, she'd heard, are alike.

'Again?' Genesis asked.

'Uh-huh.'

'Next time, let me know.'

She did. He went back in the bathroom, soaping his hands and arms.

Orion watched in the doorway. 'Maybe ...' He hesitated. 'If we go real slow, maybe we could make it to Monterey.'

Genesis blotted his arms. His face rocklike, he gazed at Orion. Commandment No. 2: *Incline your heart to the teachings of your Spiritual Father and obey him in all matters.* 'Son, we need your help.'

She let herself go with the pain, she followed the pain like an old-fashioned waltz partner, dipping and bowing and whirling with the pain when it was with her, relaxing when it wasn't, pain and she moved together in the dance of birth. 'There's a good girl,' Genesis said, wiping her forehead, avoiding the bandaged square. Candles flickered and she and pain were away, arching and prancing across every dimension, including time. Rain beat windows. Orion disappeared and returned. The smell of olives. Genesis poured oil on his hands, deliberate yet charged with energy like an actor just before the curtain rises.

'Push,' he said.

'Push!'

PUSH.

KEEP PUSHING.

NOW!

Her body was being torn in two, her partner, pain, dragging at her from either side. Ripping, tearing her right up to the rectum.

'Good girl.'

And an infant mewed as he was laid on her stomach to expel the afterbirth.

'Never had one come this quick.' Genesis chuckled. Scissors glinted on thick purple cord.

'Isn't he awful small?' Orion asked.

'He's a fine boy.'

'What about eyedrops?'

Genesis didn't reply. He was sponging the baby, wrapping him in two clean, handwoven napkins, laying his bird weight in Cricket's arms.

This was no fantasy infant. This was a person. Her son. His eyes opened with bewildered, unfocusing acceptance. They were very dark blue. Pale hair, thin and flat to the throbbing skull, formed a perfect widow's peak. The tip of his nose had a miniature Van Vliet knob. His mouth opened in a pink yawn that wasn't even. He looks like

325

Vliet, she thought, Vliet and a baby duck.

She held her forefinger to his palm, and his fingers curled, they were like tiny pink worms. How could such threads of flesh grasp so tight? However bad things get, she thought, whatever goes wrong in the world, these fingers make it okay by me. An expression of awe came into her face. She looked up at Genesis. He nodded.

'It's always a miracle,' he said. His eyes were wet.

'Thank you,' she whispered.

Genesis blew out most of the candles. The room was filled with wax odours and something salty, ripe, that Cricket thought of as *human*.

'Have a name?' Genesis asked.

She touched a finger to incredibly soft, white hair. 'Van Vliet,' she said.

'Like the markets?'

'Yes,' she said, thinking that tomorrow she'd explain.

'There's a name he won't keep.' Genesis bundled the towels he'd put under her. 'In the morning we'll show him off.'

'What's the time?'

Genesis peered at his old Benrus. 'Eleven-thirty,' he said. 'October twelve. Van Vliet's a Libra.'

The three of them smiled.

'Tomorrow,' Genesis said, 'we'll have us a Libra party.'

'Thank you,' she murmured. And thinking of the joy her baby would bring to the Select after their time of doubt ... *for unto us a son is given* ... Cricket fell asleep, a smile on her dry lips.

Waking, she reached next to her.

The baby was gone!

She pushed up on her elbow. A single candle flickered. In shadow, Orion hunched over his knees, scratching under his white headband.

'Where's –'

'Genesis took him to the hospital.'

'Hospital?'

'For a sort of, you know, check.'

'Genesis wouldn't. Anyway, he couldn't. Not in the rain.'

'It stopped.'

This, Cricket realized, was true. The drumming accompaniment to her pain was gone.

'What for?' she demanded.

'He was small, premature. Maybe he needed eyedrops.'

'That stuff bugged you, not him!' She tried to get up. Her knees wobbled. She sat, an abrupt, coltish movement.

Orion sat forward to pull the blanket over her.

She pushed it away. 'What's wrong?'

'Nothing.'

'Genesis wouldn't go to a hospital unless – *what is it?*'

'He was having a sort of, you know. Breathing problem.'

'Breathing?'

'Cricket, cut that out.'

She was struggling up. 'When?'

'Twelve-thirty or so. It's been a couple of hours.'

'How did you get Genesis to?'

'Me? He just took off. Come on, Cricket, get back in bed.'

She was leaning on Genesis' wooden trunk, struggling to open it, bending over, pushing aside credit cards, wallets, snips of paper with undecipherable writing, a small glossy she'd made of the poster negative. She fished out the Buick keys.

'Which hospital?'

'You can't even stand.'

'I am standing. Genesis wouldn't've taken him if it weren't – which?'

'Peninsula Community, I think. Come on, Cricket, hey, please. You can't drive.'

In the end he drove, inching cautiously through a continent of mud and dark. Cricket huddled towards the windshield, peering in headlight beams for a stalled bus.

As they turned on the Valley road, she fell back exhausted. And saw herself. Gauze above her eye, wearing Orion's dirty poncho, doubtless leaking through her sanitary protection into unzipped Levi's, white ones at that, searching a cold, wet night for her newborn son. Melodramatic. Sad. And neglectful to the nth degree.

Suddenly Cricket had a picture of the baby's grandmothers. Together over a sisterly cup of coffee in the Mathenys' decorator-decorated kitchen, her mother's head back, throat moving with chuckles, a cigarette near her rosy cheek, Aunt Em's carefully lipsticked mouth nibbling Bailey's coffee cake. Whatever people said about women their age (and people said plenty), certain things they had done right. Very right. If, by some chance so mathematically remote that Cricket couldn't believe it, either had found herself illegally pregnant, she would have insisted on marriage, no matter what, and twenty years ago would have been in St John's, surrounded by floral arrangements. The hypothetical infant would have been kicking in its incubator under the watchful eye of a private nurse, with a pair of top paediatricians consulting nearby. The baby would have been in excellent hands. The baby would have been fine. Because women their age had worked at making it fine. Aunt Em had given up her inheritance. Cricket imagined her own mother, in a different way, had sacrificed equally. They had been careful of new life. They never would have been shiftless where a baby was concerned.

How could I have come here? Genesis doesn't believe in doctors, and I knew it. How could I have had my baby here? A single headlight blazed at them, and a motorcycle vroomed by. Orion said something. She didn't hear him.

6

A medical scale was shoved into one corner of the windowless cubicle, a green bag stamped PENINSULA COMMUNITY HOSPITAL lay against a stretcher piled with cartons.

Cricket had been led here by a wrinkled lady. Dr Esteban, the admitting physician on Emergency, as she'd introduced herself. Cricket decided if she catalogued Dr Estaban's wrinkles she wouldn't have to listen to that voice going on about premature births. The wrinkled doctor would make a fine subject, especially if you had a good flat light. Wrinkles at the corners of the eyes formed a geometric pattern, the brown cheeks were rippled like wet sand, canyons cut the forehead. One odd thing. The face wasn't old. Why? The eyes. Yes, that's it. The eyes are clear. Sharp. Young. The voice stopped.

Cricket said, 'He wasn't blue.'

'Noncyanotic,' the doctor agreed. 'That's what I've been explaining. Other things can go wrong.'

'Would he have made it,' Cricket concentrated on wrinkles under young eyes, 'if he'd been born at the right time?'

'He wasn't.'

'Or here?'

'He wasn't.'

'Then, with a private doctor?'

'I am a Fellow of the American Board of Surgeons.' Stiff.

'It was raining and all muddy and I got careless, running. I fell.'

'Any baby can be premature.' Gentler now.

'If he'd been delivered here?'

'He was very small. Cricket, the odds are against preemies. However much we do, they sometimes die.'

Die.

There. One syllable. Die. Nobody could cancel die by thinking about wrinkles. Die. Everything else had been small talk. Die, that's the point. Die. An ugly sound grew, bouncing from windowless walls.

Cricket raised her hand to her screaming mouth, her small teeth fastening on the pad below her thumb. The doctor pulled at the hand. Cricket bit harder. She felt nothing. Dr Estaban struggled, the awkward yankings of a woman retrieving her lamb chop from a toy poodle. A carton fell from the gurney. The doctor slapped Cricket's cheek. Hard. Cricket let go.

She got the needle. Her hand was stitched.

She came to slowly.

'Awake?' Genesis. Blurry white.

'Sort of.'

They were curtained, maybe from a ward, maybe a room. Whatever, the place was empty. Silent. Genesis didn't speak for a long time.

'I shouldn't of brought him here,' he said finally in that rejecting bitterness he used when telling of his former life.

'It's not your fault.' It's mine, Cricket thought, and numbly added, 'The odds are against preemies.'

'Who says?'

'The doctor.'

'Doctor! That Mex woman? Then why did she work on him? To prove she's wiser than God?'

'She tried.' Cricket rolled over. Everywhere ached. 'You did all you could.'

He rose. 'Come on, daughter. We'll go home.'

'Genesis, I mean it. You were really great.'

'You'll be better there.'

'No,' she said. 'I can't go back.' An unplanned decision that once spoken became irrevocable.

'This was a mistake. It's the last time I do anything against my belief.'

'I just can't.'

He gazed down. She floated in the brown depth of his eyes, remembering how gentle he was during the birth, the encouragement of his voice. But she shook her head. No.

'Death is part of life,' he said.

Her lips trembled.

'Fill yourself with revelation,' he said. 'You'll be able to accept it.'

She stared out of the window. The storm had cleared all softening haze. A cruel blue sky.

'It's their drugs,' he said.

After a while he said, 'Don't come back, not today. But daughter, silence is a jail. Talk to me.'

So, uncaring, she asked, 'Why'd you register him as Van Smith?'

'It seemed best. You're connected to the market people, aren't you?'

'Yes.'

'How?'

'My mother.' Her hand throbbed. The sharp pain strung through nerves to her forehead.

'And your father, what's he do?'

'President.'

'Of all the markets?'

'Yes.'

'And the cousin, the one you're protecting?'

'He works there, too.'

'But you're with me.'

She guessed from his tone that he felt he'd replaced one secret of her life – now deceased – with another. But she would have given him her background anytime he'd asked.

'You'll be with us again.' The curtain ballooned and he was gone. No goodbyes. Just *You'll be with us again*.

At four Dr Estaban released her. 'Go home and get right into bed,' she ordered. The shift was changing, and nurses bustled in nylon uniforms. Cricket's yellow mop was too vivid, too alive around her bloodless face. She moved slowly, woodenly. In the waiting-room Orion hurried to her.

'What happened to your hand?' he asked with hesitant, condoling embarrassment.

'I hurt it.'

The room was empty except for a middle-aged woman with hard blue veins knotting tan legs. She was staring at them.

'You meant that?' Orion asked. 'About not coming back?'

She nodded.

'Then Genesis says you should have these.' And he

handed her her car keys, Union Oil card, American Express folder – this he opened, counting eight twenty-dollar cheques. (The rest she'd signed for Genesis.) He gave her the full, worn wallet. The fifty was still there. 'Your camera stuff's in the trunk.'

'Thank you.'

He moved at her laboured pace down the corridor.

'You really hate REVELATION that much?' he asked.

'It's a kind of symbol, that's all.'

'Of what?'

'Everything I did wrong.'

'Like?'

'You worried,' she said bitterly. 'Not me.'

A skeletal old man in a hospital robe shuffled by.

'Worrying's not how you operate.'

'Well, I should've.'

'Cricket, it's too brutal. Don't think any of this.'

'How can't I?'

He gave a nervous cough. 'Look, in my whole life I never met anyone else who, you know, rings true all the time. Even Genesis the other day. Well, you're the only one. Come on, quit beating yourself.'

He pushed open the heavy door. Fog had rolled in, greying the Buick. She started to take off his poncho.

'Keep it,' he said. 'A present.'

She managed a smile. 'When I get home I'll write.'

'Okay, I am a worrier. Can I help it if I care? Cricket, don't drive for a couple of days.'

'I won't. I can't.'

'Where'll you stay?'

'The nearest motel.'

She found a Best Western and slept for eighteen hours.

In the next block was a Sambo's. She ordered their inevitable pancakes and a breakfast steak. An orange ball of tiger butter oozed over the steak. Her first meat in months. She didn't reach for her knife and fork. She knew a mistake when she smelled one. That odour of charred, dead flesh! Dropping dollar bills, she escaped.

The next morning her breasts ached. She dozed feverishly, dreaming that the baby was clutching her finger. Waking, she would find her other hand curled about the finger. Her sweat drenched the sheets. The squat black maid was concerned. 'Took like this, you should be with your mamma. How old are you? Thirteen?' 'Seventeen.' 'Don't look none of it. Let me fetch in something for you.' Cricket gave the friendly, garrulous old woman money for Kotex, graham crackers, milk. She kept the milk carton on the ledge outside the bathroom. At twelve every day the owner, in a flowered muu-muu, would come to collect. On the eighth day, the twenty-first of October it was, Cricket had no cheques left to sign.

The fever had broken. Her breasts no longer ached. She unwound gauze from her hand. Black tags on pink scar. Dr Estaban, she remembered, had said to have a doctor take out the stitches. Cricket used her nail scissors.

She examined herself in the washbowl mirror. The yellowish discolouration under her eye was gone. She looked exactly the same.

Of course she wasn't.

First Vliet, then Genesis had inflicted secrecy upon her. In this all-beige motel room, the feverish hours had coiled around her. The net result? Van Vliet Matheny, no longer in her uterus, lay firmly embedded in her mind. A secret belonging neither to the past nor the future, but always current. I'll never, never be able to talk about him, Cricket decided, turning from the mirror. The door to total frankness – especially with her parents – was being locked by the good old key of guilt. I just can't discuss him, she thought.

She drove south on 101, passing towns with conquistador-haunted names, Paso Robles, San Luis Obispo, Santa Barbara. Light faded, traffic grew thick. She was home.

There are easier ways of growing up.

Chapter Eleven

I

A man, given happiness, either can accept it or he can hold up his gift to the light, searching for chinks. The chink seeker is not necessarily ungrateful. Often he is the man with a strong sense of ethics.

Roger, in Baltimore, had both medicine and Alix.

Yet he was, as Alix variously put it, 'Straight', 'Fantastically decent', or 'Out of the nineteen-forties'. Living with her wasn't enough. He needed to marry her.

Marriage was out. Impossible. The Reeds' letters and phone calls never admitted Alix, thus Roger knew his mother had in no way altered her position. Married, he wouldn't receive Em's neatly written cheque, his trust income. The records in the bursar's office proved he could afford Hopkins, so a student loan was out. God knows, they couldn't manage on what Alix made.

Another chink here. Alix's job. On arriving in Baltimore, she knelt over the Sunday *News American*. ' "Help wanted, women. No exp. nec." – hey, that's me!' And when Silver Fork on Madison offered her work, Roger was sure she got a perverse joy in writing to both parents: *i'm gainfully employed as a counter girl*. Roger got no joy, perverse or otherwise, when she zipped into that short, skimpy uniform. He disliked her working while he was in college. Their set-up was all wrong.

Yet they were very happy, and Roger knew it.

So did Alix. She shared none of his compunctions. To her, marriage guaranteed no permanence – hadn't she watched her mother slip in and out? Her job lacked status, true, but the tips she pocketed in her blue-and-white uniform, the cheque she was handed every two weeks, liberated her.

The Grossblatts or Philip Schorer would stop in Baltimore 'on the way to New York'. Alix would invite them to dine at the apartment. There was a warning in the lovely smile which halted questions – even from Dan. Roger could smell guilt oozing from his own pores. These evenings generally precipitated one of their rare arguments.

His own parents he didn't see until the end of his third year.

Em wrote: *Dad has his vacation the last week in May. We plan to be in Baltimore.* Alix, while not in on the full extent of the Reeds' hatred, was aware she would be *persona non grata.* She hied herself to New York, staying in the Winstens' lavish Essex House apartment. Gloria Winsten, Dan's sister, arranged for men to show Alix the town.

Roger was terrified that Alix might prefer one of her Manhattan guides. He loathed himself for succumbing to cover-up. He couldn't respond to Em and Sheridan's pathetically open delight in seeing him. He wanted to, but he couldn't. Unable to admit he was living with Alix, he kept repeating her name, as if by hammering the two syllables into his parents' eardrums he could overpower their minds and hearts. Sheridan or Em would change the subject. Em, though, would find herself looking into her son's hurt eyes. Em, yearning to be fair. But how many mothers could find justice for a girl who had switched from sleeping with one son to another, for a girl who had cut a favoured son from his education, who prevented the lesser but still well-beloved son from flying home – even for Christmas? Each time Roger said, 'Alix', Em's thoughts would erupt like Krakatoa. Under make-up her small face would mottle. She either would get a headache, weep, or order another vodka martini, 'Straight up, please.' Finally Sheridan, who agreed with Em's prejudices, took Roger aside.

'We aren't interested in your shack job,' warned the father. 'And Roger, I advise you not to do anything stupid.'

They departed. The week had cost Roger and Alix. Cost them plenty. Alix never told Roger precisely the mental cost of that week. In New York she had panicked. What if Roger, exposed to his parents, were infected by their hatred of her? What if he decided he didn't want her? What if? What if? Smoothing on new eye shadow and smiles, she charmed the dates Mrs Winsten produced. In that single week, three men swore undying love. Two proposed, and the third, a recently burned divorcé, offered a trip to Bermuda. Alix did not believe a word. How could she? She was such a mess, so ugly. She fell prey to any witty, smart shop. By the end of that week she had spent $897 on clothes. Floors and walls weren't meeting properly. Sidewalks slanted at an alarming angle. She had shattered into a hideous swarm of anxieties. And on her return, Roger bickered with her constantly.

He didn't understand why he picked on her. He couldn't help it. She would respond in that bantering tone which further infuriated him. A chain reaction, continuing until somehow they were clinging miserably to one another, his breath moving strands of her silky hair.

The recuperation period lasted that entire muggy summer. By then, Roger had a reply of sorts to his conscience.

A ring.

Since their engagement could not be public, the ring had to carry more weight than an ordinary engagement ring. Furthermore, or so Roger decided, it must be presented in a meaningful place, their root place. California.

September brought his surgical rotation. After that, in the middle of October, came his break.

'Alix, let's go to California.'

They were in the plant-hung breakfast nook. They lived in the same cruddy apartment he'd shared with Vliet, but you'd never guess it. Alix had worked miracles.

She put down her spoon. Her throat tightened around fruit salad. For her, California was the state of families and therefore taboo.

'Using what for money?' she asked. Neither was frugal, and Alix's round trip to New York, including all those desperate clothes, was being paid off monthly by her Bank-Americard.

'My cheque,' Roger said.

'It'll cover fares. What'll we spend for food? Where'll we stay?'

'San Francisco,' he said. 'With Cricket.'

(Cricket, for reasons that had not seeped through her infrequent communications, two years ago come Thanksgiving, had enrolled in San Francisco Institute of the Arts and, as far as Alix could tell from pencilled notes, was doing as she always had done, moving through life with her camera slung around her neck, no male or ambition in sight.)

'Roger, accept it. For us, family reunions are total disaster.'

'It won't be a family reunion.'

'What then?' she asked.

'I haven't been to California in more than two years.' Alix had been – she'd flown to Los Angeles, weeping, for her Grandfather Linde's funeral. Roger said, 'We won't see any parents.' And under his starched white medical-student jacket was the familiar hunch of broad shoulders.

He's spent a lot of time on the idea, Alix thought. She said, 'Only Cricket?'

'Just Cricket,' he promised.

2

The first person Alix saw in San Francisco Airport was Vliet. She halted at the end of the landing corridor. Her face turned pink. She was back in mountain gloom, the odour of sleep, Vliet on a double bed blowing his nose and whimsically telling terrible truths about her major phobia. Roger, you lied, lied, she thought. Then amended: But Roger never lies. She glanced at him.

He was staring at his twin, the grooves between his eyes coming and going, alternate expressions of joy and bewilderment. For a moment neither brother moved. Years and a continent might have separated them, yet each had remained part of the other's interior landscape.

Vliet, one hand on the low barricade, vaulted into the crowd, swivelling his way upstream. 'Hey, runt. Hey, shorty, hey.' Vliet punched his brother's arm. 'Hey, surprise.'

'Vliet ...'

'All you medical students are the same. Over-emotional.'

'Two and a half years. What're you doing here?'

'I was in the neighbourhood.'

Roger socked Vliet, faking, and Vliet hit back. Two tall men clowning. Roger in worn jeans. Vliet's light hair an impeccable curve touching the collar of his well-tailored jacket.

'Pardon me,' a fat man said, swerving his briefcase around them. All at once Roger hugged his brother, kissing him on both cheeks in the French style. An airport embrace. Awkward. Not quite spontaneous. Yet as they parted, identical pairs of deep-blue eyes were blinking back tears.

After a minute Vliet turned to Alix. She formed a smile. *That's a great smile there,* he'd said.

Now he planted a kiss on her forehead. (Nice cologne, she thought, I'm glad Roger doesn't use cologne. I cannot be with Vliet, I cannot.) 'The celebrated waitress,' he said.

(Roger's eyes have tears. They phone one another all the time, they write. For a few hours I can carry it off.) 'The celebrated executive,' she said.

Cricket was calling, and they went through the gate. More hugging. Next to Cricket lounged a tall, actressy brunette: her thin body and large, weary eyes conveyed a type of smouldering, bruised sexuality. Vliet introduced her. RB Henderson.

'For Chrissake,' Vliet said. 'You people're jamming traffic. How can anyone get off the damn plane?'

They started walking. Beyond glass walls jets taxied.

Vliet dropped an arm over RB's shoulder. He said, 'A friend of mine –'

'Me,' RB said.

'– has a place that's not being used. It's ours for the weekend.'

'In Carmel,' said RB.

'Carmel?' Cricket turned away. 'I can't.'

'Are freebie weekends bad karma?' Vliet asked.

'I have work.'

Vliet pantomimed guffaws.

'I do,' Cricket said.

'This, little cos, is Friday. Nobody works weekends.'

'A batch of film to develop.'

'The Puritan work ethic won't wash, not for you. So be a good little kid. Quit interrupting.' He ruffled her bright curls.

For a second, misery glimmered on Cricket's face. The others were too trapped in their own emotions to notice. Except RB. And she, yawning, turned away. They were at the baggage slide.

'Well?' Vliet asked Roger.

Roger reached for a backpack, then turned to Alix. 'Sounds good to me,' he said to her.

A weekend? No. Not a weekend. A betrayal. He had promised. No family. Only Cricket, small, harmless Cricket. Vliet knows all about me, Alix thought, Vliet has my number, Vliet surely sides with his parents, the Montagues. Oh God, doubtless Cricket, kinswoman, does, too.

Alix turned to the other outsider. 'RB, won't so much company hassle you?'

'Who's going to be there?' RB stretched indolently. 'Me, I've got a six o'clock call tomorrow morning.'

'My friend the starlet,' Vliet said. 'The four of us is all. For old times' sake.' He smiled at Alix.

They both had tears, Alix thought. I can make it. I have to. 'For auld lang syne,' she said.

They dropped RB off at the Fairmont. Cricket, for

reasons she didn't explain, lived on the Berkeley side of the bay, and they double-parked in front of an elderly frame house until she emerged lugging a straw satchel.

In the airport car park, Roger had whistled at Vliet's silver Porsche, and Vliet, tossing him the keys, had said, 'Be my guest.' Roger drove fast. Warm air blasted through open windows at brothers laughing – Vliet was saying this month he'd been made district manager in Orange County, seven of Van Vliets' least profitable markets. 'Three of them could be closed tomorrow, except for the leases. We'd still have to pay the damn leases.' His half-humorous put-down did not hide his enthusiasm. Cricket curled quiet on the narrow back ledge. Alix, next to her, was taut in every muscle. She was waiting for Vliet to turn in his bucket seat and throw the first stone.

Pastel subdivisions were behind them when she finally looked around. How, Alix wondered, could she have forgotten this ultimate California landscape? Bluer sky, brighter sun, cattle grazing somnolent in pools of shadow from live oaks – trees that were black against lion-brown hills. Then they were tearing across one of the green valleys that feed the country, whizzing by car after glittering new car in which every passenger was tanned, youthful. How had she forgotten this fertility and motionless heat, freeways shimmering like great rivers, this land in thrall to a quest for the Fountain of Youth? Here, everything was newborn. Hostage to the future. Alix tried for less literary concepts. Found none. She had missed California a lot.

She was almost at ease when they reached Carmel. 'Stop,' Vliet said. A beamed cottage set far back on a brick patio. They went through a comfortable living-room to the bedrooms, and Roger set their backpacks in the one with a king-size bed.

'RB's divorce settlement,' Vliet explained. 'Not bad for three unconsummated months. He's Loomis Henderson, the director.'

On the patio they drank Vliet's margaritas. 'To your new job,' Roger toasted. 'Hey, Vliet, why're you up here?'

'To see you,' Vliet answered. Right, right, he'd driven up for the weekend. 'That's a big trip,' Roger said. Vliet, dropping to one knee, flung out both arms. 'I'd walk a million miles for one of your scowls, buddeee.' A perfect Jolson. The twins threw back their heads, howling with laughter.

'Now,' Vliet said, 'for the real reason we're gathered together.' He turned to Roger. 'Cricket's got your gizmo.'

'How'd you find out?' Roger demanded.

'Easy. She told me.'

Roger turned to his cousin, 'Cricket, how come?'

Vliet asked, 'Isn't that the point?'

'No,' Roger said.

'You're off your bird. You want it public. Under the circumstances, I'm as public as is available.'

Alix said, 'How about letting me in on this?'

Cricket, having dug through ravelled straw, held out an old velvet ring box. Roger sat on the end of Alix's chaise, opening it.

An antique ring. Huge cabochon garnet with a star of diamonds surrounding a pearl. Oh lovely, Alix thought, perfect.

'It belonged to our great-grandmother,' Roger said.

'Whose is it now?'

'Yours,' Roger said. 'Sort of.'

'Explain sort of.'

He opened his hands.

'You'll have to be more specific,' she said.

'For that,' Vliet said, 'you'd have to know our great-grandmother.'

'A trifle late, yes?'

'Great-grandmama,' Vliet said, 'spent her declining years figuring how to take it with her. Finally eliminating that happiest of possibilities, she tied it up so nobody else could have it. Her jewellery – and this was one acquisitive old chick – goes to her female descendants.'

'Which eliminates me.'

Cricket put down her untouched margarita. 'Some things were set aside for Grandma Wynan's branch. Not

Mother or Aunt Em, but their female descendants.'

'Until we have a girl,' Roger said, 'it's yours.'

'Cricket's,' Alix responded. Even the dead in Roger's family denied her.

'Rather have a new ring?' Roger's voice was hurt.

He's gone to monumental trouble for this one minute, she thought. She said quickly, 'It's beautiful.'

'I wanted you to have something that's family besides me.'

'I love it.'

'You'll have to have it sized,' Vliet said. 'Hey, Roger, remember anything about her?'

'Just she smelled good.'

'She did? Well, she's reputed to have had these tiny, aristocratic hands.'

'One thing about me,' Alix said, extending her left hand. 'Skinny fingers.'

Venus shone in a lavender sky and Roger slid on the ring.

Vliet said, 'Welcome to the family, dear Alix.'

Cricket, her plain little face glowing, hugged her.

And Roger put his arms around her. 'Sweet, you're freezing.'

She was. As the ring touched her finger – cold – she had shivered. A nightmare flash. This wasn't hers, this never would be removed for Roger's daughter. On some unknown day, in some unthought-of manner, she'd have to give it back. She said, 'I better get my sweater.'

Roger went along.

Vliet watched his brother slide the glass door shut, watched as Alix – doubtless thinking them invisible – turned to his brother. Seen through a glass dimly, Vliet thought. I deserve an Emmy. Best supporting actor in a continuing drama. Today's is a sterling performance. I love her, my brother I love, and there they are. They weren't kissing. Their bodies were meshed, his legs around hers, his shoulders curving about her: he seemed to be protecting her. There was intense passion about the embrace without any of the thrashing contortions that generally reward a Peeping Tom. Depression overpowered Vliet. Normal, he thought, under the circumstances. He forgot his friend-and-brother role. He let his face relax.

Cricket, who had been watching him, looked away.

3

A few minutes later they emerged. Alix buttoning a lemon cardigan.

'It's my dinnertime,' Vliet said.

Alix said, 'We better get some food.'

'Out,' Vliet said. 'It's celebration time.'

'On me,' Roger said.

'On me,' Vliet said. 'Where?'

Alix turned to Cricket. 'Didn't you work here one time, in a health-food place?'

That Cricket had worked in Carmel, that she had lived with a group, never had been secret. Only her son had been secret. This is inevitable, she thought.

A quiet hubbub of year-round regulars filled the patio. Vliet pointed to a free table, and Cricket trailed after the others. Candlelight flickered on handwoven napkins (her son had been wrapped in one) that were heavy with sea damp.

Orion, behind the antique brass register, saw her. He frowned. She remembered his worry over the unexpected. Then his face melted into pleasure. He hurried over. His chest and shoulders had filled out, and his pale beard, though still scraggy, no longer was tentative. He grasped both her hands.

'See? Father Genesis was right. You're back.'

She pulled away. 'For a weekend.'

'That's all?'

'All,' she said. And introduced the others.

When – at last – Orion went to give their order, Vliet leaned forward, saying in a stage whisper, 'Everyone catch that? The boy's ape for our Cricket.'

A customer hurried by, almost dousing the candle. Cricket protected the flame with her hand. She rarely talked about herself. Who was interested? Other than Caroline. Caroline would inquire eagerly, 'Anyone *new*, luv?' There had been seven – no, eight others – since Vliet. The longest tenure belonged to the most recent – Carl Werkhausen, a gentle, round-shouldered Berkeley linguistics major – it had ended only a few days ago. She still lived in Carl's place, she still liked him. She liked all of them. And it was this continuing affection that disturbed Cricket. How could she be willing to lend this one a ten, be able to introduce that one to a girl? For her, sex (invariably fine) was a gold coin disappearing in a deep lake, leaving wider ripples of the original friendship. Any older woman, hearing of this, must be shocked. Caroline, secretly, was. To Cricket – unclouded by value judgments – her ability to remain friends was simply a bad sign, the final proof that misery, excitement, and love still centred on Vliet. A loves B who loves C who loves D, she thought. Hopefully C and D will live happily ever after.

Aubergines and quiches arrived, huge portions bubbling with cheese and giving off a steam of garlic. Alix leaned towards Roger. 'I don't have a knife,' she said. 'They don't use them here,' Cricket said, and a passing waiter remarked, 'Knives are weapons.'

Alix, Roger, and Vliet shared glances.

They ate hungrily. 'Crazy as loons,' Vliet said. 'But man, can they cook!'

People Cricket knew came to welcome her.

'Where's Magnificat?' she inquired. 'Our women don't work anymore. They stay home,' Orion answered. He laid the bill down. Vliet and Roger grabbed. Roger won. 'No charge?' he said.

Orion gave Roger his worried smile. 'It's, you know, for Cricket.' He pressed red-knuckled hands on the table. 'Come on Sunday,' he said.

344

'Thank you,' she said. 'Is Genesis around?'

'At the back,' Orion said, glancing at the other three. 'He wants you to bring everyone.'

Cricket thanked him again. 'Okay to talk to him?'

Orion stacked plates. 'Tonight he's not one with the world,' he apologized.

She was surprised. Always Genesis had been their grey-bearded pivotal point, his deep voice tying them with comforting orders: Except for those few terrible days, he'd always been at one with their world.

The four decided to stroll off their organic dinner. At a pretty little Ocean Avenue shop, Alix paused to turn a revolving paperback rack. Roger, arms clasped around her waist, his body pressed to her back, watched the titles.

Vliet and Cricket continued along the narrow brick sidewalk.

'Even if the boy's ape about you, that bunch give me goose pimples,' Vliet said.

'Why?'

'Why? Don't you get the resemblance? Really, I swear to God, it's old Charlie Manson revisited.'

The bricks had sunk. Cricket stepped cautiously. 'When I lived here, nobody had heard of the Mansons.'

'Okay. But there's a point here. Cricket, believe me, counter-culture isn't necessarily better culture.'

'I know it, Vliet. You don't have to think you're playing iconoclast.'

A fat man was smirking up at Vliet and down at Cricket. Vliet fixed him with a superior Van Vliet look. The man turned his bullet neck, hurrying by.

'I love it when you put in those five-buck words. Someday you'll have to tell me how you know these freaks.' Vliet ran a friendly hand across her shoulders. She stepped away. 'Listen,' he said. 'Father Geritol, or whatever he calls himself when he's in this world, I bet he believes he's the Second Coming. And what's with this segregating women just for sex?'

'No sex,' Cricket said.

'None?'

'Well, for having babies.'

'You're kidding! Should I kneel or something? For procreative purposes!'

They walked a couple of minutes.

When Vliet spoke again, his voice was sober. 'You see only the good, little cos. But Christ! Can you imagine Ma or Caroline living with a bunch like this? Creeping around in whites, talking about cutlery as weapons? Maybe they aren't Mansons, but this is a cult. A cult. C-U-L-T. Caroline and Gene would file joint heart attacks if they knew you'd lived in a place like this.'

The reason she'd lived here — procreative purposes — made her walk faster. He kept up.

'That's what's wrong with today's set-up,' he said. 'Some young people assume that any group who live other than the normal life-style belong in the Greater Galilee area.'

'You eat one dinner, and –'

'And get that murderous glint out of your eye, Cricket. I'm worried about you.' He looked down at her. Concerned. If Vliet was concerned, the handsome, whimsical face got an expression that charmed. And was meant to charm.

'It's not necessary.'

'They want you back.'

'No,' she said, 'they don't.'

'Hey, what's wrong?'

'Nothing.'

'Then why so?' he asked, pulling down the corners of his mouth.

'I'm not.'

'You can tell old Vliet.'

She was silent.

'What sort are they?'

'Mostly middle class, like us.'

'Not me, not like me. And what does that mean — mostly?'

'Before, Genesis was sort of wild.'

'Hairy wild?'

'I guess,' she said.

'Sunday's out.'

'I have to.' They stopped at a red light. 'Genesis, he was
... very good to me ... helped me a lot.' The light
changed. They crossed. She asked, 'Let me have the
Porsche. I'll only be a couple of hours.'

'No.'

'Please, Vliet?'

'If you remember, I was invited.'

'You'll go?'

'Not willingly.' The smile went up on one side, and the
lower lip, the tender lower lip, moved forward in the
centre. 'I don't trust you in their clutches is all.'

4

Indian summer and Carmel Valley sweltered, but cool
shadows filled the north side of the porch. Here, on
Chinese boards worn silky, sat Cricket, Alix, Roger, Vliet,
and Orion. Genesis had not put in an appearance. The
Select came and went. There were over twice as many as
the last time Cricket had been here, maybe eighty, with a
ration of three women to each man, plus an even half
dozen babies under a year old. Cricket's friends relin-
quished their monastic calm, hugging her. And Magnificat, redheaded Magnificat, Cricket's old roomie, was
saying with dignified pride, 'Now I'm Mother Magnificat.
Father Genesis and I were married May first.' Cricket
kissed her friend, since May elevated to the blessèd.

'It's good to have you here again,' said Mother Magnificat as she departed.

The Select gazed at Cricket with shining eyes as if expecting her to announce something. What? I'm going to
stay?

Roger had been looking at Orion. 'Your hair,' he said.
'It wasn't tied back the other night, was it?'

'No,' Orion replied.

Roger held his finger in front of his own ear. 'Had this long?'

Orion touched the fleshy scab on his cheek. 'Six months, about. It's nothing.'

'Ever bleed?'

'Uhh, yes.'

'How often?'

'Couple of times. Father Genesis cured me, you know, with salve.'

'Mind if I take a look,' Roger asked, zeroing in. 'A doctor seen it?'

Orion gave Cricket a pleading glance.

She explained for him. 'They don't believe in doctors.'

'This must be looked at,' Roger said. 'Right away.'

'Father Genesis'll make more salve,' Orion said.

'No. A dermatologist.'

And Mother Magnificat returned, circling the court, hand-woven white blossoming around her lanky legs. 'Cricket,' she said. 'Father Genesis is waiting for you in the great hall.'

Boughs of St Catherine's lace, dried to a delicate rust, filled the altar vessel. Genesis propped his grey beard in a thick hand, looking silently at her. In the underwater light his eyes never seemed to blink. He nodded at the tatami by his feet. She sat.

Why did he seem so different? It was hard to say. Was she seeing him as Vliet (and Alix and Roger) would? Or had he changed? Take this not talking. He'd done it before. But for the first time she was grasping that it was planned showmanship. How he imposed his will on others. The disloyal thought made her uneasy. She crossed her legs, pressing the sole of her right sandal into the opposite jeaned thigh. She inhaled his familiar odours.

And she stopped questioning his disparities. She was remembering. Not wanting to, but remembering. Sharp-edged pictures of the birth, the hospital cubicle, emerged as if she had developer in her brain. The cruel minutes of her life. At this point, Genesis began to speak. She didn't hear words, simply the rumbling voice.

He leaned down to her. 'You mustn't, daughter.'

She came to, her hands tightening on her ankles.

'Live in the Eternal Now,' Genesis said.

'I try,' she said. 'I do.'

'You aren't now.'

'He was born here.'

'That pretty boy, the tall blond, he it?'

'Vliet,' she said. (How long had Genesis watched them? Had he always spied, adding to his deck of secrets? How could she think this way about someone who had been only good to her?) 'Yes.'

'And he doesn't know?'

'Nothing,' she said.

'Why didn't you tell him?'

'I couldn't. I couldn't tell anyone.'

'There's no point,' Genesis agreed. 'You're back.'

'For the afternoon,' she interjected hastily.

'And you hurt?'

She nodded.

'This isn't enough time,' he said. 'Give me more time.'

It was a command.

After a moment she said, 'I'm in college.'

'College!' he snorted. He gazed up at the commandments. 'Last year I went down to Guatemala. Some villages there haven't been touched. No corruption by outsiders. They followed the ancient ways. Pure Maya. I studied their book. *Chillam Balam*. The Maya was great while we grovelled in caves. Peyote taught the old ones. It still teaches.'

'Carlos Castaneda,' she said. 'Did you try acid?'

'Acid is chemical. It burns the brain. Peyote is natural. With it you see beyond the horizon, hear voices of trees, know everything. Peyote is from before corruption. Yes, I tried it.' He laced his fingers, tensing his powerful forearms. 'It's become the central fact of our lives.'

'Cricket,' Vliet called. 'Hey, Cricket!'

They turned.

Vliet was peering in, his fingers curved around the door-jamb. 'You in here?'

'Yes,' Cricket said.

And Genesis said, 'Come in.' Another order.

Vliet, followed by Roger and Alix, moved forward, silhouettes in the dimness. Cricket made the introductions. Genesis examined each in turn.

Vliet looked up at words burned into wood. 'The Big Ten?' he asked.

'For us,' Genesis rebuked quietly, 'they aren't a laughing matter.'

'I wasn't laughing. Really. I'm interested.'

'It's our Rule.'

And in the ensuing awkwardness, Alix said that the compound was fascinating, and had some China buff imported it board by board? Ignoring her, Genesis turned from Vliet to Roger, who also was studying the etched panel.

'Why no knives?' Roger asked.

'Knives kill.'

'And cure,' Roger said.

'Also,' Vliet said, 'they're handy at the table.'

'They're for killing,' Genesis said, his tone purposefully mild.

Vliet said, 'Cricket, I'll buy a trip to see that weaving.'

'Oh yes, the backstrap looms,' Alix said. 'I never have understood how to work one.' She glanced at Roger.

Roger said to Genesis, 'I'd like to talk to you, sir.'

'See you outside, then,' Vliet said, extending a hand to Cricket. 'Upsy daisy.'

Genesis was watching. Cricket's eyelids fluttered, then she took the hand. Vliet pulled her up. Genesis stared at the door after they left.

To Roger the hall seemed warmer, and he thought of wiping his forehead but decided against it. Genesis' chair threw him off-balance. It was the only furniture around, and either Roger sat on the mat, as Cricket had done, a disciple at dusty, bunioned feet, or stood in front of the older man, a suppliant. He managed uneasy compromise. Half squatting, he rested his back on a panel.

'They couldn't get away fast enough,' Genesis said. 'Why did you stay?'

'It's Orion.'

'What about the boy?'

'He's got a lesion on his cheek.'

'Lesion?'

'An abnormal scab.'

'You a doctor?'

'Medical student. Fourth year. I'm pretty sure it's basal cell carcinoma. Cancer.'

'We don't believe in doctors.'

'He needs one.'

'I put on herb poultices. Ointment.'

'You don't cure cancer with applications.'

'Then it can't be cancer. I cured it. The bleeding stopped.'

'A scab's formed twice, but the bleeding'll start a third time. That's the pattern with basal cell.' Earnestly Roger leaned forward. His thigh muscles pulled. 'If this is caught early enough, his chances are fine. There's a terrific hospital for the Peninsula.'

'No.'

'It won't be any problem. We'll drive him down. The clinic's free.' Roger wasn't sure if Peninsula Community Hospital had a free clinic, and it didn't matter. He'd pay. With what? Who cared? He'd borrow from Vliet.

'He's not going to no clinic, free or otherwise.'

'Isn't that up to him?'

'He won't go,' Genesis said, crossing his arms and looking away. A dismissal.

Roger didn't move. He was remembering an autopsy, a man younger than himself, manila tagging the brown arm, water flowing along canals in the cement, water under and around Death. Younger than he. Roger had felt nauseated, as if he'd taken a beating. Death was an affront to his own healthy body.

'If it's what I think,' he said, 'there should be complete surgical excision.'

'And you told him?'

'I told him to see a doctor.'

'Well?'

'He said you've cured him.'

'I have.'

'But you aren't qualified –'

'They come to me,' Genesis interrupted, 'to find a way from their pain. I show them a road, nothing more. Knives aren't part of the road. Nature is.'

'This won't cure itself.'

'He gave you his answer.'

'He's been brainwashed.' The dim air began to pulsate in front of Roger's eyes. 'Is it really such a big deal to you, sir?'

'The cutting, you mean? Yes, it's a big deal to me. And to Orion. The boy believes in our way. Faith, that's all that matters when you come right down to it. Faith.'

There was silence. Roger told himself to keep calm. He could hear faraway voices, and somewhere in the hills, a quail's fluty call. 'Oh Jesus!' he burst out.

'We don't blaspheme in this place.'

'Maybe it'll be a biopsy, nothing more.'

'You've got one idea in your head.'

'Yes, curing.'

'No. The knife.'

'He needs a doctor. It isn't important what I –'

'Mutilation,' Genesis said.

Roger felt an echo of pain in his own cheek muscles and wondered, foolishly, if the blotch had moved to his face. Alix said he took disease personally. 'I can't let you do this!'

'You can't?' Genesis asked quietly. 'Can't you just.' He raised an arm, chopping down. Old Testament prophet with black belt invokes Divine wrath. The violence of the gesture contradicted his mild tone. It was funny. Neither the young nor the older man noticed any humour.

Genesis said, 'We do not mutilate ourselves.'

Roger jogged down shallow steps, he strode across blue tiles. At the dust-coated Porsche, he spat the bitter taste from his mouth and waited for the others.

When they were driving through unpaved ruts, he asked, 'Know what that scab is?'

'On Orion's face, you mean?' Cricket grabbed the seat in front of her as they bounced over a pothole.

'Basal cell carcinoma,' Roger said.

Vliet whistled. 'For sure?'

'I haven't taken a biopsy, if that's what you mean.'

'Your word's fine with me,' Vliet said.

'He needs surgery.'

'They don't believe in –' Cricket started.

'They have faith, not doctors!' Roger shifted gears. 'To me, Orion looks like he's got more anxieties than faith.'

'It's like a real religion to them,' Cricket said.

'He'll have to lapse for a while!'

'Listen to yourself, Roger, will you?' Vliet said.

'We have to get him to that hospital.'

'I don't suppose you've given thought to one minor matter,' Vliet said. 'This is none of your damn business.'

'Whose is it, then?'

'Orion's. Genesis's. Christ, what assy names. And this Genesis is one guy I'd just as soon not tangle with. The man's a power-hungry banana.'

'Psychotic with schizoid delusions.'

'That's your considered opinion?' Vliet asked.

'Yes.'

'Good. Then you know enough to stay clear.'

'You always were chicken,' Roger muttered.

The sunbaked path twisted. Roger made a sharp left. Tyres squealed, dust rose.

'Easy there. It's not paid for yet,' Vliet said. 'Roger, listen, will you? Thou shalt not, it has definite implications. It implies that there's a heavy chance people shall. We don't need to be told *not* to do something unless there're possibilities we will do it. Strong possibilities. We put up rules, Roger, because we're afraid certain impulses

353

will get the better of us. It's pertinent, this business of knives. In my view, this old fart's afraid he'll use 'em. And once he starts carving, he won't stop until he's cut up all the piggies.'

'Vliet!' Cricket's voice was sharp. 'You've got Manson on the brain.'

Alix leaned forward, gripping Roger's shoulder with her left hand, the one with the garnet, and he held the hand to him, his thumb stroking the delicate line of knuckles. Her touch soothed him, and he was able to think. A winged bug hit the windshield, leaving a creamy bruise.

'In Hopkins,' he said, 'we use the Moes Technique. You remove a little each day so you can stain and fix the slides. The pathologist knows exactly what came from where. You know when your borders are clean. They probably aren't using it here.'

'We'll never find out,' said Vliet.

Roger asked, 'Is the cottage available a few more days?'

'Christ, I'd forgotten. You never give up, do you?'

'How can I?'

'Easily.'

'Vliet.' The voice had its old dominance.

'All right, all right, help him, you upright, bullheaded bastard. Get that crew after your ass.'

'Do you want me to call RB?' Alix asked.

'I'll do it,' Vliet said.

'Hey, Cricket,' Roger said over his shoulder. 'You talk to Orion. You're his friend.'

5

'They don't give appointments,' Cricket said. 'Roger had to hack at them. This afternoon at three-thirty.'

'I can't make it,' Orion said.

'Why? The rush is over.'

'I'm in charge of the register. There's money to be
ounted.'

It was eleven-thirty the following morning. Monday.
Around six, Vliet – yawning prodigiously – had left Car-
nel for Los Angeles, and the spell was broken: the
eculiar unity that each of the four had feared never in
his world could return, had, only to be shattered by the
arly Monday *vroom* of a Porsche motor.) REVELATION
vould open for lunch in fifteen minutes. Orion was fold-
ng napkins.

Cricket set her round-nailed forefinger on the stack.
Remember? You told me to get a doctor.'

This, their first reference to her son. Orion gave a
ervous little cough.

'You were right,' she said.

'I'm the only one allowed in the register.' Pride tainted
is apology.

'By then you'll be through.'

Orion glanced towards the sheltering oak. A pimply
man poured honey from a five-pound can into a glass
itcher. Bees buzzed down from overhead branches.

Orion said in a low voice, 'Father Genesis, he's
hanged.'

'Yes, I thought so.'

'He's, uhh, firmer. If you don't keep the Rule, he be-
ieves, uhh, you don't belong with the Select. He's right,
f course. If you don't go along with what we believe you
hould . . . you shouldn't . . .'

'He'd throw you out?'

Orion sighed. 'He could.'

'I don't believe it.'

'Listen, Cricket, this is the only place I ever belonged.
Here, my head's together. I owe it to him, Father Genesis.
My life, you know, depends on his life.'

'You honestly, truly think he's that different? He'd
end you away?'

'I can't take the chance.'

'The scab's bad,' she said.

'How?'

Cricket's grey eyes were direct. 'Roger says skin cancer.'

Orion clenched a napkin. His hands turned white.

'Taken care of,' she said, 'Roger says it's the most curable kind, skin cancer.'

'How's he so sure what it is?'

'He's sure you've got to be examined. Orion, Roger's always been into medicine, he really knows what he's talking about.' This last she said with a bubbling hint of enthusiasm.

In one respect Cricket was a fink. She was an out-of-sight-out-of-mind-person. She didn't miss people – except Vliet and her parents. She wrote a few letters. She wasn't much on putting in long-distance calls to old friends. Reunited, however, she was immediately hooked. As Roger, whom she loved with sticky familial bonds, had stepped off the plane, she had seen him as beautiful, exciting, strange. All weekend she'd been dazzled by how fine a human being he was, by the two strands of white in his thick brown hair, by his medical knowledge, by how easy he'd become (Alix's influence). Cricket trusted Roger completely. Orion's untreated pathology had become as shaking to her as to Roger.

Orion was pushing back his hair, fingering the raised mound.

'They'll run tests, Roger says.'

'If you break the Rule, you walk over everything REVELATION stands for. You betray Father Genesis.'

'He'll understand.'

'No way.'

'Roger says, put off, it could be too late.'

A bee landed on the table. Orion brushed it away, then stared pleadingly at her.

'Cancer?' he whispered.

She knew she'd won.

'Community Hospital,' she said. 'Go to Emergency at three-thirty. Roger'll be waiting for you.'

He nodded blankly.

She kissed the air near his cheek. 'Blame me,' she said.

'Or say Roger pushed you. Blame Roger.'

Five. The beach was deserted except for noisy gulls. Cricket, barefoot, walked on cold sand. Chill seeped into her bone marrow, forcing pain through her ankle, bringing her to a limp. After a while she huddled near a large rock, gazing at the purple line that drew the horizon.

Orion was in hospital, in professional hands, and she wasn't thinking about him. She was thinking about Vliet. These past two years she had seen him on holidays and at family gatherings. Sometimes he'd phone: 'There's this G-rated movie, let's take it in.' He treated her, as always, like a cousin-sister, a little kid. She, as always, loved him in every possible way.

Her thought processes blurred. *Once on a high mountain we lay down ... Small snail, he said, topnotch stuff ... From this came another person born into Genesis' thick hands ... The Van Vliet nose, our baby had it, and perfect, tiny fingers ... dying, die, death ... The most meaningful hours of my life, and not Vliet nor Mother nor Daddy know.* Cricket kept her secret for one simple reason. Guilt. It was alien to her, this ungovernable flood of self-recrimination, self-hatred, sorrow, grief, blame. She had been solely responsible for a life. She had let her son be born too soon. She had therefore let her son die. If one has a whole orchard of guilt apples, one might not be struck dumb by taking a single bite. I just can't deal with it, Cricket thought.

She shifted so her spine rested on rock, and went back to Vliet. *Saturday lunch, club sandwiches, and he asked if I had boys after me in San Francisco. 'Nothing serious,' I said, smelling the bacon in his sandwich. 'I didn't figure you were serious, Cricket. Still, a little puppy love is important in growing up.' And I smiled because he was smiling, and he fingered mayonnaise from the corner of my mouth.*

Cricket leaned forward to massage her ankle. She noticed a brown pelican one-legged on driftwood. She took off her lens cap. The shot would be too red. Late-

afternoon sun photographs too red. But that big beak!
Just look at that wondrous beak! Heavy wings rustled
Cricket trotted after the pelican. Blonde curls standing
up in the wind, Cricket forgot all past griefs and raced to
capture a bird from an endangered species on Kodacolour
X.

6

After Roger and Alix had dropped Cricket off at the
beach, they went directly back to the cottage and now
were on the patio chaise, Alix curled facing Roger, she
reading *Swann's Way*, he on his back with one finger
twined in her hair, his free hand holding the *New England
Journal of Medicine*. Next door, Janis Joplin wailed: *I
keep pushin' so hard, an' babe, I keep tryin'/To make it
right to another lonely day*. Roger set the magazine on his
stomach to negotiate one-handed page turning.

He chanced to look up.

Genesis was leaning on the gate, thick arms akimbo on
sequoia planks, watching them. Roger jerked to sitting
position. And understood the taboo that ancient kings
had put on gazing at the royal person: he felt part of himself, part of Alix, had been stolen. Besides: 'How'd you
know where to find us?'

'Won't you come in, Genesis?' Alix said far more
smoothly.

Roger, standing, repeated the invitation, adding 'Sir'
rather sullenly. A mechanism to hide his sense of under-
handedness. 'Orion's in Peninsula Community Hospital.'

I keep pushin' so hard, sang Janis. Kozmic Blues.

Roger turned on the yellow light. 'The growth has to
be removed tomorrow morning,' he said.

Genesis said nothing.

'He'll stay a couple of days. Go see him. He's terrified
about your reactions.'

The gate creaked. Genesis had moved his arms. 'So you did take him.'

'I met him there.'

'But you arranged it?'

'Yes.'

'When I had him cured.'

'The biopsy showed it malignant. They're going to have to cut some ear cartilage to get it all. The prognosis is good, though.'

'What gave you the right?'

'Me? It was the matter of his need.'

'Christ on His cross,' Genesis said, 'is the man who has relief stolen from him.'

Roger's heart was pounding. Logical and rational, he never was quite able to believe that others didn't share these qualities in some degree. He never could conceive that a blind spot was truly blind or that mental quirks and aberrations were real. On his psychiatry rotation he'd been positive that the other students drew on vast knowledge while he, hopelessly ignorant, was reduced to talking common sense to his patients: he'd given himself up as a psychotherapeutic disaster area and was speechless when Dr Haries, handing him a Styrofoam of coffee, had inquired if he'd considered making this his speciality. Some shrink he'd be! Separated by a gate from a psychotic, he nursed an angry suspicion that the man was putting him on.

'That nodule,' he said with forced patience, 'took months to grow to that size. It ulcerated and bled and you used ointment. It scabbed, but it would have scabbed anyway. Scabbing's not cure. Eventually it would've bled again, scabbed again. Grown. Spread. Destroyed him.'

'You've destroyed him.'

'Sir, at Peninsula Community Hospital they'll explain better than I can.'

And Alix put in, 'We'll drive you. We've got some paperbacks for him.'

Genesis' mouth moved in his thick beard. He said, 'The boy can't be one of us.'

'What?' Roger's head jerked.

'He's mutilated.'

'After surgery, later, they'll do a little plastic work. It won't show much.'

'They've already cut him, haven't they?'

'A biopsy.'

'So you've already taken him from us.'

'You mean you're punishing him because he's getting treatment for cancer?'

'I'm not the one to punish.'

Roger's fists clenched. 'What do you call it? Reward?'

'Go ahead. Laugh.'

'I'm not.'

'You people laugh at everything that doesn't fit your ways. Well, let me tell you, there's a better way than you ever dreamed.'

'None of this has anything to do with basal cell carcinoma.'

'Our Rule is a cathedral. You can't take away one of the foundation blocks. The building will topple. We obey every part.'

'If you'd ever seen anyone die of cancer, you wouldn't.'

'I've seen men die.' Genesis squinted one-eyed at Roger as if he were a crack marksman (Giles Cooke had been) sighting along his M-1 rifle. 'Vengeance is Mine, saith the Lord.'

The quiet words seemed to hang in the pale dusk. Genesis didn't say goodbye.

His footsteps rang, and the darkness swallowed a middle-aged man, the type sometimes seen in California, loose shirt, beard invariably whiter than long hair. *Time keeps movin' on.* Alix pressed back a cuticle. Roger picked up his journal. Moths thumped on the yellow lightbulb. *I keep movin' on but I never found out why.*

'Brrr,' Alix said finally.

'Cold?'

'Him.'

'He's an infuriating bastard.'

'He's more than that.' She hunched her shoulders to prove a shiver.

In the kitchen she took off her ring, washed her hands, and bent in front of the refrigerator searching for hamburger. Roger kept the door open, taking out a bunch of celery.

'Look,' he said, rinsing two stalks, 'if he weren't basically all right, Cricket never would've lived here.'

'I guess,' she said, pouring Lawry's Seasoned Salt on round meat.

He put one of the celeries in her mouth. She bit. Chewed.

'Roger, I keep thinking of the man who killed Jamie. Peculiar, isn't it, how the mind works? I relate every nut in the world to him.'

Chapter Twelve

I

On Roger's graduation day, Alix slid into their mailbox a card: Roger S. Reed, MD. Roger, holding the small key at the double row of boxes, flushing with triumph touched the letters.

'Engraved,' he said.

'Nothing but the best, doctor.'

She'd had the card made for this one occasion. Before seven the following morning they were out of Baltimore He had been accepted as an intern at Stanford Medical Center. 'California,' he said. 'Home.'

Across a continent of tender early summer they drove the rear window of her four-year-old Mustang obscured with her clothes, the floor jammed with his Bausch & Lomb binocular microscope, books, journals, the trunk gorged. They had figured on taking it easy, but as they left the city limits, there was Roger's foot gunning down. They travelled Route 66 remembering their years in Baltimore bursting into spontaneous laughter at phrases humorous to them alone, they tuned in to local radio stations. 'Oh remember that one?' Alix would cry. Roger would describe incidents that proved he should go into internal medicine, thus becoming a specialized GP in a rural area They would eat soggy A&W hamburgers in shimmering heat, drink shuddery-cold 7-Ups at Texaco stations. They marvelled how endless was the Midwest, they dived into motel swimming pools, stretching on unfamiliar mattresses to make love with bodies that smelled of chlorine Home. They were going home.

In Phoenix they stayed at a rundown court, walking to a café they'd spotted a few blocks back. A moonless night the stars were huge.

'Look,' she pointed up. 'There's the Big Dipper.'

'And the Little Dipper.'

'Which?'

He held her fingers towards the sky. 'There. See? Those three stars make a handle.'

'So they do.'

They passed a boarded-up garage: in the shadows a cat darted, eyes glinting as if battery-operated.

'How's the country with you?' he asked.

'Or a poverty pocket.'

'Country's better for kids.'

'How many are you counting on?'

'Lots.'

'Ever hear of Zero Population Growth?'

'I'm old-fashioned. We've got good genes. I plan to teach you the constellations and keep you pregnant.'

'About those night calls?'

'I'm healthy.'

'Very.'

'Say two boys and two girls?'

'What if it's four boys?'

'We'll keep trying.'

She didn't really believe in the babies. It was as if Roger were telling her the story of some girl on one of those distant pinpoints of light. She was cool from a recent shower and numb in the flesh from twelve hours of driving. She was very happy. How simple it sounds, she thought, as he held open the screen door for her. How easy.

2

The house on Kings Road in West Hollywood was like an ancient, extremely ugly woman. When others in her generation have died, she no longer is considered in terms of looks. She is a relic of the past, unique and irreplaceable. Therefore precious. The house, old only in Los Angeles terms, was built just before the twenties in a style that the architect probably had called Gothic – else how could he have justified the ells, useless gables, the tower, the narrow, stained-glass windows that caught sun and kept out light? This anachronism was centred on two large lots. It was protected by dagger-topped iron rails and hidden by a bushline of lemon trees. Later, it would be called a handsome old estate, a former gathering spot for Los Angeles society, a secluded mansion.

Secluded it was.

The neighbouring houses had been levelled. On either side, foundations were being dug for hundred-unit apartment buildings. Soon, soon, salvager and wrecking crew would fall on the old place. Its owner, Mrs Dormin Van Vliet, great-great-aunt to Cricket Matheny and the Reed twins, was dead.

'I don't see why they want to come here,' Orion said. 'Your aunt and uncle live in Glendale. Alix's parents must be, you know, someplace around.'

'Beverly Hills.'

'Well?'

'It has to do with the family situation.' Cricket hooked her knees over the back of the sofa. A warm evening, she wore cut-offs. The horsehair upholstery felt like a brush on her bare legs. 'I'm neutral territory – Alix wrote that.'

It was almost eleven and they were in the little downstairs library.

Three months earlier, Cricket had called Sidney Sutherland – he was probating the will of his late mother-in-law – to inquire about the place, which enchanted her. Could she stay? Cousin Sidney had replied, 'Until the estate's settled – that is, if it's okay with Caroline and Gene.' Of course it was.

Orion had been here since last Friday.

He had travelled to Los Angeles in one of REVELATION's secondhand school buses. Genesis, Magnificat, and their entourage of Select males were at Magnificat's sister's

364

home in Hollywood. Orion had phoned Cricket: 'Okay if
I crash with you?' In the ensuing time he had explained,
more or less, how things were with him. Bad. (Although
this he never verbalized.) His face appearing thinner, he
had told her that after he'd left the hospital he'd not been
allowed in the Chinese compound or to work in the
restaurant. He had rented a room in Carmel, working at
Taco Bell. 'I can't be one of the Select, but Father Genesis, he's been very good, he lets me hang around.'

Orion sat on the Bokhara, clumsily sewing a button on
a white shirt. Though no longer bound by the Rule, he
followed it, wearing only white and never trimming his
hair or beard.

'Where'll they sleep?' he asked.

'Aunt Raphaela's room.'

'Creepy.'

'Why?'

'You said she died in there.'

'You don't want them, do you?'

He pulled. Thread snapped. He licked the end, concentrating on passing it through the eye of his needle.
'Roger interfered,' he mumbled.

'Helped.'

'Wrecked me.'

'Paid most of the bills.'

'He did?'

'It's lucky he saw you when he did.'

'Lucky?' Orion stared at her with outraged eyes, as if
she'd congratulated him on being the sole survivor of a
hydrogen holocaust. Then he went back to threading his
needle.

'Look, I understand,' Cricket said, touching his arm.
'It's hard for you to be with him.'

'Impossible.'

'Then move in with the Tadovitches. They won't mind.'
The Tadovitches, a Czech couple who had worked for old
Mrs Van Vliet, had remained in their garage apartment
as caretakers. The garage was a replica of stables and, like

real stables, had been placed as far as possible from the house, way at the back of the property. 'You won't be around him.'

Orion bent over his sewing.

And Cricket understood. A choice. He wants me to choose. Him or them. By now she was used to this male egotism: former boyfriends – not that Orion fell into this precise category – asking favours they never would have considered asking but for warm, moist sharings. She stood.

'I'm going into the kitchen. Want something?'

He shook his head.

'Milk? Or the bananas are just right.'

'Thanks, I'm not hungry.'

She padded barefoot, circling the loose board, opening one of the golden-oak doors of the built-in refrigerator, shaking Altadena certified raw milk, tilting back her head to drink.

She took the plastic bottle with her.

'Cricket,' he said slowly, 'come back to REVELATION.'

'It's bad for me there. Like you seeing Roger.'

'You're different. You're a serene kind of person. You'll get over it.'

She took another gulp, holding creamy milk in her mouth.

'It's not like you're doing anything,' he said. 'You dropped out of college.'

She hadn't dropped out. She had oozed out. Most semesters she'd ended up with maybe five units. Five hours a week. Last semester she had stared at registration forms. How dumb, she had thought. And torn papers into her waste paper basket. She'd driven back to Los Angeles, asking Sidney Sutherland for housing. She had a trust fund, not inherited like the boys' but set up by Gene with no strings. It paid her $1,800 a year. Without rent, she managed fine.

'Is it so great for you?' he asked. 'Are you so happy?'

'Pretty much.' Except, of course, when she thought of her guilt. For it was a great guilt. And at this moment very much with her.

She bent to a cabinet below empty bookshelves, retrieving a blue nylon sleeping bag. She yawned elaborately. 'Mind?'

He retreated as if she'd shouted. The commandment of celibacy ruled him yet.

She unrolled the bag on the horsehair sofa. She thought. She zipped herself into the bag. She thought some more. A family of raccoons lived under the avocado tree and one of them rustled by. Cricket, thinking, unzipped the bag, pulled on a chenille robe, felt her way upstairs. Darkness never frightened her. (Orion, on the other hand, flicked on the Tiffany wall brackets wherever he went.)

'That you, Cricket?' Orion's voice came anxious from the room that had belonged to Dormin Van Vliet, a tiny man with hairy nostrils and a pacemaker in his heart who had departed this life from St Vincent's and therefore, according to Orion, could have left no haunting ghost.

'You really want me back, don't you?' she said.

He switched on the light. 'Father Genesis would be pleased,' he said.

'There're things you never can repay. Genesis took me in, he helped me have the baby, he's always been good to me. But that doesn't stop me from seeing stuff.'

'What?'

'He's become bitter.'

'He has cause.'

'And look at the way he cut you out.'

'I disobeyed the Rule.'

Cricket ran a finger along the rosewood dado. Examining accumulated dust on her fingertip, she asked, 'If I go back, will he let you in again?'

'I'm not sure.'

'But you think so?'

Orion's scraggy beard worked. 'He wants us all to live the Rule.'

The Rule. Goosepimples formed under Cricket's swapmeet robe. Yesterday Genesis had come over. He had sat on the low wall of the terrace with Magnificat at his feet, leaning her red hair on his knees. The other Select, crosslegged on flagstone, had gazed devoutly up. Genesis had spoken of civilization doomed: *Those who have accepted* REVELATION *shall survive*, he had rumbled. According to Genesis, humanity was divided in two parts – the hundred or so who belonged to REVELATION and the billions of doomed. He had crossed his bricklayer arms, prophesying the end. Roger and Vliet, both, had called Genesis a nut. He probably was. (But doesn't a prophet have to hand over his sanity as collateral until the world is proved round, man related to the ape?) Genesis had said, *Who do you think will survive? The killers of animals, the men who knife other men? The workers in gun factories? The Nixons and Congress? The fornicators, adulterers, sodomites? Surely before God builds His new world, these, too, must pass.* Under a balding forehead that had sojourned in prisons, the eyes had glowed. It was the eyes that got Cricket. Eyes searching, peering, probing, gazing into the sun. Peyote, Cricket had wondered, does it affect the eyes?

'He's hooked on this doom thing, Orion.'

'If Ralph Nader says the human race has had it, people believe him.'

'I didn't.'

'You should,' Orion said.

The next morning he told her he was taking off.

She knew he had no friends in the city and was untrusting of his parents – across town in their separate San Marino homes. He had no one else to stay with. 'I'll take you over to meet the Tadovitches,' she said.

'So I can stick around here and listen to you tear apart Father Genesis?' His voice was cold, hateful.

'I wasn't.'

'What were you doing?'

'He's become so different.'

'See?' Yet more cold and hateful.

Over eggs, though, he relented. 'Father Genesis doesn't want you to change. The others have to.'

'Orion, does he really think he can alter the world?'

'He has to start someplace.' Orion pushed away his half-eaten eggs. 'I'd give anything to get back where I was. I'm so lost, so terribly lost without him.' The *him* sounded capitalized.

'But where'll you stay?'

'It doesn't matter.'

3

They arrived that night around eight, hot and grimed with grit from the Mojave Desert.

'Wow,' Alix said. 'Built by the Addams family.'

'Van Vliets,' Roger replied, reaching for the bell.

As his finger hovered, the door was flung open. A huge shadowy cave engulfing one small, freckled girl. 'It doesn't work,' Cricket said, hugging Roger. 'Doctor, doctor, doctor.' And she turned to embrace Alix. 'Come in,' she said. 'I've got aubergine casserole. Or would you rather shower first?'

'Shower,' they cried in unison. And laughed.

Wet-haired, they sat at the kitchen table, devouring Cricket's casserole, mopping up tomatoey strings of cheese with whole-grain bread, the radio behind them giving Elton John while Cricket, without innuendo, transmitted family news.

'Vliet's flying down,' she said.

'He's not here?' Roger asked.

'No. Seattle.'

'Seattle? He didn't write me that.'

'Saturday night he should be in.'

'Tomorrow?' Alix asked.

Cricket nodded.

A June breeze played with ivy on the gable. The big kitchen was cool, the big old house comfortable. Secure.

They smiled at one another. Three already were home. Tomorrow they would be complete.

Alix woke before Roger. Covering his bare shoulders, she went to the window. She stared into the green of the huge old elm, leaning forward, delighted to find a nest on the branch below her. From tangled hedges birds sang. A dog poked his yipping snout between boards of the service yard fence. The Tadnitzes, wasn't that what Cricket called the caretakers? Must be theirs.

'Alix?' Roger mumbled drowsily.

'They've got a Doberman.'

'Wha'?'

'The Tadnitzes have a killer dog.'

'Tadovitches,' he said. 'Buster. He belonged to Aunt Raphaela, and he's, let's see, around fifteen. Very gentle.'

'Obvious cover-up.'

Roger folded his hands under his neck. 'Today,' he said.

'What about it?'

'We tell 'em.'

'Tell who what?'

'Our families. That you've landed a self-supporting MD.'

'Not to put you down or anything, but self-supporting is hyperbole.' She sat on the bed.

'I won't be paying tuition,' he said. 'I'll earn like you earn.'

'You've got some complex about that.'

He said, 'Thursday.'

'Then what?'

'It takes three days to get a licence, and –'

'Roger –'

'– we're due in Palo Alto next weekend.'

'I mean, let's keep it nice and slow and easy.'

'It'll be more like a wedding down here.'

'Wedding?'

'What do you think I've been talking about all year?'

'Hopkins,' she said.

'Look, in Phoenix we agreed.'

'Phoenix. I remember Phoenix distinctly. You promised screwing would take up the slack between night calls and astronomy lessons. Oh God! And this was such a beautiful morning.'

Sunlight moved patterns on the comforter. A minute passed. Another.

She said, 'Not that I'm afraid.'

'What of, sweet?'

'Everything. Them. Us.'

'It doesn't matter what they say.'

'To me it does. Always.' She sighed.

'This cover-up, I hate it,' he said.

To Alix, marriage was a handleable concept – in the future. The remote future. Right now she feared it would gum things up: any change (especially one formalized in the presence of family) might well ruin them. Roger, though, all along'd had this archaic feeling he was doing her dirt, and ringing her finger with gold was his way of handling his problem. She made a small, sad grimace. 'Thursday,' she assented.

He took her hand, the one with antique garnet that she wore in trust for their future female infant. Awkwardly – it wasn't Roger's style – he kissed her palm, bending her fingers around his kiss.

Her lips parted and after a moment she stretched on the bed next to him, and they began exploring one another. They moved dreamily, as if time had forgotten them. Leaves filigreed shadows on their naked legs, a faint smell of must inhabited the bosomy old bed, the Doberman gave a series of yelping barks. Alix drew a long, trembling breath.

'Alix,' Roger said.

She opened her eyes.

'Forsaking all others, keep me only unto thee as long as we both shall live.'

Her pupils were huge, mysterious.

'To have and to hold,' he said, 'from this day forward.'

'Roger,' she whispered.

'With my body I thee worship.'

371

'Darling?'

'What, sweet?'

'Without you, I don't exist.'

'Or me without you. Ahh?'

'Yes yes yes.'

Later, they stood together under the lion-mouthed shower head. He fingered soap on her neck.

'I seem to have bruised you.'

She felt. 'Mmm, there?'

'Yes.'

'Kiss.'

He kissed. 'With this kind of injury,' he said, 'you better rest.'

'Tomorrow, then?'

'One day,' he said. 'Don't we deserve one day home without their hassling?'

So they didn't phone the Grossblatts or Philip Schorer. They didn't take the Glendale Freeway so the Reeds could congratulate their son the doctor. Later the Reeds would blame this omission on Alix. They would put the blame, as they always did, on Alix.

4

'Cricket,' Vliet said, 'you always huddle in the smallest room.' And bore his Taittinger into the living-room. He made ceremony of the opening. The cork, gratifyingly, popped to the ledge that ran along the north wall. He poured champagne into the ragtag of glasses that Cricket had dug up.

He raised his green tumbler. 'To Dr Reed.'

They drank.

'And to me.'

'For what?' Alix and Roger asked at the same moment. Vliet, bowing with a click of heels as for a Heidelberg duel, said, 'I was in Seattle getting it together. Regional manager. Fifteen outlets is all, but mine to lead.'

There was hubbub. Roger pounded his brother's shoulders. 'Hey, Vliet, hey.' Alix kissed his cheek. Cricket gave him her artless smile.

Only RB Henderson didn't react. RB had picked up Vliet from the airport – Vliet had phoned asking her to, although he hadn't seen her since borrowing the Carmel cottage: he had the ability to drop and pick up girls as easily as he traded in his sports cars. RB's legs remained stretched to the ottoman, legs so slender that sharp ankle bones stood out. She continued to smoke with yellowed fingers. Alix wondered that anyone so devoid of emotional response could be an actress. But undeniably RB Henderson was an actress. The film she had been shooting in the Bay Area had sealed her reputation as an actress. This, the year of *One Step, Two Step*, an incision of changing American sexual mores. RB's ex, Loomis Henderson, had directed *One Step, Two Step*, casting RB in the role of vulnerable young wife to a middle-aged tycoon, eliciting from her every ounce of bruised sensuality.

'Got us some music,' Vliet said, going to his car, returning peeling cellophone from Handel's *Messiah*.

Roger groaned.

'Medical men are notorious for their lack of culture,' Vliet said. 'Where's the stereo, Cricket?'

'My room,' she said. 'The library.'

He called, 'Your needle's shot,' and sacred music came into the old house.

Comfort ye, comfort ye my people, saith your God. The music blended with their voices and they accepted it and were oblivious to it, all except Vliet, who from time to time cocked his head with choruses that the others didn't hear. RB, curling one foot, sipped from her glass. Cricket watched Vliet as he talked to Roger.

Vliet was all keyed up. 'The youngest regional manager,' he said, circling to pour more champagne, 'unless you go back to our late, revered Uncle Hend. Smell a whiff of nepotism?'

'To answer that, I need more information,' Roger replied.

'What's wrong with a few hereditary favours?' Vliet asked.

'Daddy said you got the promotion because you're a shrewd merchandiser,' Cricket put in. 'And hardworking.'

'Hardworking?' Roger chuckled. 'Vliet?' In school Vliet had been a notorious goof-off.

'He made Orange County profitable.'

'No kidding,' Roger said. 'So quickly?'

Vliet smiled, triumphant. This rivalry-love thing had been with him all his life. He never had baffled over it as Roger had. Yet the brothers were so intertwined that each had problems telling a victory over the other from a defeat. Even now, Vliet yearned to throw himself – as he had as a kid – into a spontaneous wrestling match which he must lose. Christ, where's the rivalry in self-immolation? he thought. That Cricket had let his brother in on his success delighted Vliet.

'There you go, Cricket, ruining the playboy image.'

He stroked her arm. She pulled away. Her small, freckled face turned pink. She loved him, and Vliet knew it. (Oh, he called this love a hung-over crush and he'd been successful in blocking that Arrowhead night. In his own way, though, he cherished Cricket. He sensed that Vliet Reed would be diminished if at some future, unbelievable hour, this small, plain girl quit loving him.) Her love was part of him. Roger was part of him. And in a painful way, Alix Schorer was part of him.

Alix rested her head against Roger's shoulder. 'To our self-made man, another toast.'

RB said languidly, 'With this.' And from a Virginia Slims pack, she took a joint, lighting it, offering it around. Alix, Cricket, and Vliet dragged. Vliet handed it to Roger.

'Pass,' Roger said.

RB drew a square with her forefinger, giggling. Either grass worked on her instantaneously or she'd popped something with her champagne. Vliet turned the three records, turned them again, Alix rested her head in

Roger's lap, in the hall the grandfather clock chimed elaborately, and it was after ten when the door knocker banged.

Vliet said, 'Stuff that damn thing!'

'Anyone could smell,' Cricket said, rising.

'So if it's the law, don't ask 'em in.'

Cricket floated on Septembral odours. They couldn't see the front door, they could hear *Lift up your heads, O ye gates*. And Cricket's clear voice.

'They're all here,' she said.

Mumbling.

'Yes, Roger,' she said.

Mumbling.

'Positive it's okay?'

Mumbling.

'Then come on in.'

Cricket returned, followed by Orion. He greeted them, was introduced to RB, refused champagne and/or grass, sat on the floor helping himself to cubes of jack cheese.

'No, no problems.' He was answering Roger.

'Recurrences?'

'None.'

And to Cricket's surprise, Orion lifted a frizz of hair. Normally he kept the scar hidden. Roger looked closely at the patch of smoothness. 'Fine,' he said.

Orion let the hair drop.

'Had it checked out?' Roger asked.

'No.'

'It looks fine, but you should.'

'Did you graduate?' Orion asked.

'This week.'

'So now you're a doctor?'

Vliet laughed. 'The lowest form. Intern.'

Cricket was watching Orion. His thin face was different, but she couldn't pin down why. Something within him had withered and something else had flowered, and she knew only that under the sparse beard Orion was different.

'And you?' Roger asked. 'What've you been doing?'

'Working.'

'Where?'

'Oh, round Carmel.'

'But everything's fine?'

'I'm not in REVELATION.' Orion bit into pale cheese.

Roger said, 'Look, if there's some way I can help?'

Alix, now sitting, put her lips to his ear. 'Easier on you, doctor,' she whispered, 'to stay a bit more aloof sometimes.'

'I'm going back,' Orion said.

'You are?' Cricket exclaimed. This, then, the difference?

'There's one thing and I'll have squared things.'

'With Genesis?' Roger asked.

'And the Eternal Now,' Orion said.

'For some reason,' RB said in her tired voice, 'this scene plays a trifle hazy.'

Vliet replied, 'It's complicated – unless you're among the initiated.'

'Principals front and centre,' she said.

Orion asked, 'Are you an actress?'

Vliet, pouring final drops from the third Taittinger's into his and Roger's glasses, emphasized, 'RB Henderson.'

Orion blinked, bewildered. In his former life RB had been an unknown. The Rule proscribed movies, radio, magazines, television.

Vliet said, 'Famous star of famous films.'

'*One Step, Two Step*,' Cricket explained.

'Oh. That one,' Orion said, examining RB. The advertising campaign had been extensive. The logo used on billboards and in newspapers was RB, nude, half turned, bending to adjust a sandal.

'What'd I tell you?' Vliet was laughing. 'Nobody recognizes you with clothes on.'

Everyone laughed. Except Orion. None was drunk, none stoned, they were happy, and so they laughed. Cricket, with ash down her T-shirt, Vliet's hand resting lightly on Roger's shoulder, and Alix, her head again on Roger's lap. RB flexed her toes, which had maroon nails. Orion sat a little apart.

'You guys going to be here long?' He glanced at Vliet, then Roger.

'I'm sleeping over,' Vliet said.

'We are?' RB looked up from her toes.

'Wanta break up a family reunion?' Vliet asked.

Her shoulders raised. Either way, the narrow shoulders said.

Cricket looked at Orion. 'Why?' she asked.

'It's late. I figured I'd go to bed.'

'You're staying here?'

'If it's no problem.'

And Vliet said, 'Problem, man? In our great-aunt's mansion are many rooms.'

5

On the sagging, cracked court, Roger and Alix played hard, for the first time using their new rackets, aluminium ones Alix had bought as part of Roger's graduation hoard. Winning the match, he flung himself, panting, on semi-mowed grass, gazing up at the elm that shaded him from eleven o'clock sun. 'When the house goes, the trees will, too,' he said.

'Progress.' Alix wiped his face with a towel. 'It's sad.'

'After the others get up,' he said.

'Then what?'

'We'll go see our families.'

'I guess.'

'Which do you want first?'

'Yours. Get it behind us.'

'I'll hold your hand,' he said. He was smiling, but he meant it.

'Pants or skirt?'

'Sunday,' he said. 'Better wear a skirt.'

'I'll shower.'

'After you, then,' he said. And went up with her to get his *Atlas of Anatomy*, pausing on his way back for Cricket's radio. He stretched under the elm. The Dodgers were playing a double-header in Shea Stadium.

Cricket ate dry granola. She was in the living-room, and through open windows came Sunday sounds: water running, a baseball game, Buster barking.

Orion came in. 'You never sat here before.'

'It's too large,' she said. 'Want some?' She extended her bowl.

He shook his head. 'It's no smaller now.'

'There's people,' she said. 'People make a place all cosy.'

He sat on the rug near her. 'I guess you're wondering about last night?'

'You had made it clear you couldn't be with Roger.'

'I changed my mind.'

'You're, well, different.'

'How?'

'It's not easy to explain.'

'High?'

'Not really,' she said.

'No, you wouldn't say someone who's taken the sacrament is drunk, would you?'

'Peyote.' She set the half-empty bowl on the couch. 'Orion, you really are going back?'

'Yes.'

'I'm glad,' she said. 'Really glad.'

Some cheese remained from the night before. He took a cube. 'Alix is beautiful.'

Cricket nodded.

'I don't think I ever saw such a beautiful girl.' As he spoke, uncertainty flickered on his face.

And it was then that Cricket realized the difference. This, Orion's one sign of uncertainty since he'd returned to the house. Last night, for the first time since she'd met him, he'd been neither hesitant nor shy. He had not clawed at his beard or equivocated or worried into apology. He had been sure.

'How did Genesis tell you?' she asked.

'We talked. Alone. For a long time.'

'And he understood how terrible it's been for you?'

'Yes.' Orion slid a finger under hair that covered his scar. 'There's acts of contrition.'

'What?'

'Oh, nothing.'

RB sat naked on the edge of the carved rosewood bed that had belonged to Dormin Van Vliet. She was brushing her lank brown hair. Pausing, she held up a strand for examination.

'They're splitting,' she said.

'Who's splitting?' Vliet called from the adjacent bathroom where he was using his Remington Electric.

'My ends,' she said.

Noisy shaver to his cheek, Vliet looked through the open door at her. Unwrapped, the body proved disappointing. The knobs of her spine were purplish. The body, to be frank, was breastless, pale and scrawny. The cinematographer on *One Step, Two Step* had genius, her ex-husband had genius, and possibly in a role RB projected genius. As it was, here sat a flat-chested ectomorph chick with split ends.

'I shouldn't've stayed,' RB said. 'I've got this publicity deal at one.'

'No sweat. We'll be there.'

'Two's fine.' She yawned. 'Sunday, who's up before two? But, Vliet, these ends.'

Orion said, 'Okay to use the phone?'

'Sure.'

'It's not a toll or anything.'

She heard him dial, she heard him say, 'Let me talk to Father Genesis. It's Orion ... Father Genesis ... Yes, it's for the good ... I understand ... The only way ...' And so on. Sunlight cut through dusty leaded windows that soon would be broken by a wrecker's crew.

He returned. 'Thank you,' he said. For some reason his gratitude sounded like an apology.

'Welcome,' she said. 'Orion, have some breakfast.'

'Not yet.'

'Sure?'

'Sure,' he said, squatting. He put both hands to her cheeks and gently, very gently, kissed her. His beard was soft, his lips cold. This the first and last time Orion – Lance Putnam – would kiss her. She heard footsteps coming down the hall. She felt Orion's breathing, and she thought of Genesis on that terrace, his mouth a purplish wound gaping amid grey hairs as he spoke of destruction. Orion pulled away.

'What's that for?' she asked.

'It's something I wanted to do, always.'

'Why didn't you, then?'

'It's against the Rule.'

'And now?'

'Now everything's going to be right,' Orion said.

Vliet buttoned the fresh blue shirt he'd had in his flight bag. RB continued brushing lank hair.

'That Orion's one creep,' she said.

'You should see the rest of them.'

'There can't be more.'

'Hundreds. All purer than St Augustine,' Vliet said.

'He's a creep.'

'So you said RB.'

'I know your cousin sometimes limps, but . . .'

'Even a basket case can pick and choose?' Vliet asked pleasantly.

RB shrugged, unmalicious, uncaring. She held out a clump of hair so she could see it. 'Shit. All these ends. I've got to condition.'

'Why?'

'Splits make me nervous,' she said. 'Are you getting my conditioner or aren't you?'

'I wasn't quite sure that's what you were after.'

She yawned.

'What's your pleasure?' he asked.

'Wella Balsam.'

'Maybe Alix has some.'

He knocked on the back-bedroom door and Alix answered. Sashing a long yellow skirt, she regretted she used whole milk on her hair.

'She wants a name brand, and I have to get the damn stuff. Tag along?'

Any excuse to put it off, Alix thought. 'We do need dinner,' she said.

They went downstairs to the sunny, weed-filled garden.

'I'm going to pick up some groceries,' she said to Roger.

He held a finger to his place in the heavy book. 'I want to go over this again, anyway,' he said, rubbing a tiny emerald insect from his shoulder. 'When you get back I'll be ready.'

She gave him a too-brilliant smile and forgot to kiss him goodbye. Vliet opened the screen door for her.

'And now?' they heard Cricket say.

'Now everything's going to be right,' Orion said.

Vliet pointed at his cousin. 'We're off to Chalet Gourmet,' he said.

'Join us?' Alix said.

'No, thanks,' Cricket replied.

'Yes,' Orion said.

'Why?' Cricket.

'Why not?' Vliet said.

'Cricket,' Alix said, 'let's barbecue tonight.'

'Would a Van Vliet's please you?' Vliet asked. 'No way as elegant, but you do have stock in the company.'

'Go.' Orion pulled her to her feet.

'But –'

'I'll scramble myself some eggs.'

'Alix made pancake batter, and I could –'

His face convulsed and he turned to the empty, baronial fireplace. 'Please go!'

'What is it?' she asked.

But there was Vliet grinning down on her. 'We need

someone to push the basket,' he said.

Cricket picked up her sandals.

They went out to Vliet's car, an Austin-Healy, getting in gingerly because the leather was hot. Sunday. Kings Road was free of its weekday racket of hammers, saws, cement mixers. Vliet steered his new car around hillocks of sand fronting a huge construction in the raw lumber stage: SINGLES/NOW LEASING FROM $185/SAUNA/STEAM-ROOM/THREE RECREATION ROOMS/NIGHT TENNIS. 'Not to mention night screwing,' Vliet said, turning onto Santa Monica Boulevard.

Cricket was bent, buckling her sandal, otherwise she would have seen it. The old school bus swerving onto Kings Road.

6

Vliet pulled into a Jack-in-the-Box. 'I need my coffee. Ladies?'

'Milk,' Cricket said.

'A root beer for me,' Alix said.

He parked in the shade of the building and they leaned against the car. Cricket swirled her straw in the milk carton. Vliet and Alix bantered. Every word she said was filler to distract her from this afternoon's torture sequence – the meeting with Roger's parents.

In Chalet Gourmet Cricket watched lobsters lumber over one another. Trout flashed in a nearby tank.

Vliet waited with Alix at the meat counter. Frilled lamb chops, opaline-white veal scallops, impressive pork, ruby roasts set like great jewels on a velvet bed of parsley. A high-class operation for a high-class trade, Vliet thought. He pushed his playboy image, the image of a guy to whom things came easily. This covered the sweat. But. When

Cricket or anyone called him shrewd, Vliet felt as if he were passing. He was unaware that from those he called the Dutchmen he'd inherited a knack of blue eye for seeing each turn of profit.

The huge porterhouses he'd selected were being wrapped. 'And we worry,' he said, 'about getting the optimum cuts per carcass.'

'But now Seattle will have large steaks?'

'More cleverly wrapped is all. But I do covet the luxury end.'

'I could acquire a taste for it, too,' Alix said.

'Alix, you always had a taste for it – thanks.' The butcher was handing over a heavy white package.

'My Beverly Hills background?' she said. 'Is that what gets your parents?'

Vliet pushed the basket over carpeting. He had dated Miss September, he had dated a novelist who promoted her best-seller by being more pneumatic than Miss September, he had dated three models, one of them nymphomaniacally inclined, he had dated a stunning philosophy doctoral candidate who popped Ritalin, he had dated RB Henderson – this had got him in Joyce Haber's column. These women roused in him the same emotions as fine tailoring. They looked great on his arm. Nothing they said or did could pierce his cool. Alix was by that barrier. And the last thing he cared to do was get into a discussion, however oblique, about her relationship with his brother.

They were at the vegetable gondolas. Vliet cupped a bright cos lettuce in one hand as if hefting a bowling ball. 'Consider,' he said. 'This was in the fields yesterday. If it were ours it wouldn't be at the warehouse dock yet. Tomorrow it would be reloaded and – maybe – maybe trucked to the market. The lettuce in a Van Vliet's is four days old at the youngest.'

'Is it that I'm not Elsie Episcopalian?'

'I got you the first time,' he said. He dropped a cellophaned English cuke in the basket. 'You're here to shop, girl.'

She picked up a pomegranate. 'Or I'm living with him?'

Vliet bagged something round and purple, a red cabbage maybe, or an aubergine.

'What?' she asked.

'Alix, are you buying that or fondling it to death?'

She dropped the pomegranate in their basket. 'I'd like to know. We're going there this afternoon.'

'White of him to drop by.'

'We,' Alix said.

'I think, Alix, you'd better reconsider.'

'It's already settled. We're getting married this week.'

He jerked as if he'd woken with a painful charley horse, though why her announcement should affect him this way, he didn't know. Christ, no surprise here. She was smiling as if she expected him to say something. So he said, 'Congratulations.'

'Thursday. Vliet, you have to be down here.'

'Are they invited, too, my parents?'

'Why do you think I've been giving this questionnaire? Of course they are.'

'If I were you, then, I wouldn't play it so up front. Let Roger visit alone. At best they think of you as a working girl, an independent contractor. Let Roger go alone. They care for him, they care a lot.'

He hadn't meant to be cruel. He disliked cruelty – unless it got you someplace. She had provoked him into it. But she continued smiling as if he'd said something not exactly funny but wry.

'He wants me along.'

'Roger the bulldogger,' he said. 'Well, be braced for the worst.'

'I am.'

'Good,' he said.

At Sav-on they stopped for RB's Wella Balsam. The car park was full. 'I'll run in,' Alix said. She fled the little car. She was thinking of volcanic eruptions, earthquakes, atomic warfare, pestilence – where were those apocalyptic horsemen who showed the world in its proper perspective?

7

The front door was open.

Choral music flooded from the house, assaulting the open car. Hallelujah. Hallelujah! HAAAAAAAAAAAA-LLLLLLLLLEYYYYYYYYYYYLLLLLLLLLUUUUUUUUY-AAAAAAAA, the Vienna Academy Chorus filling the smogless California day. Buster yipped violently, a small tympany counterpoint to the amplified voices. HALLE-LUJAH.

'Funny,' Alix said. 'Roger wouldn't have that on.'

'No,' Vliet agreed. 'RB either. And Christ, listen to that volume.'

Handel, lucid, airy, rejoicing, transparent, with woodwinds, oboes, bassoons, harpsichords. Loud. Loud. *For the Lord God*, repeated the sopranos. *For the Lord God*. Handel had written for more powerful castrati voices, but these recorded twentieth-century women sang their staccato blocks of triumph, the music soaring into an ear-shattering universe.

Cricket stared at the open door. Her face had gone ashen. Lord God, Prince of Peace, let it not be, she thought. Don't let it be. She couldn't force herself to think what it was that she prayed God not to have happened. A chill rested on her skin, it was as if the temperature had plunged to zero. She was sharing the bucket seat with Alix. Leaning across the perfumed girl, Cricket jerked at the door handle, swinging over crisp yellow piqué, bumping long legs, spilling bagged groceries. Then she was skimming over brown lawn, music battering her, HALLELUJAH, her big toe cracking against a sprinkler head. She almost fell, but regained her balance. As she climbed front steps, one two three four, her toe began to bleed.

At the door she stopped.

Inexplicable forces had propelled her from the car.

She had been unable to slow her momentum. Now she stopped. She could go no farther. Knees flexed slightly as if she were readying herself for a parachute jump, she peered into the dim hall that was the interior of the tower. The amplified oratorio might have been a river in full flood, raging towards the sea, battering, pouring, hammering, sweeping, destroying everything in its path. Terrible, mindless voices. Overwhelming. Warning. Voices stopping her. Vliet was brushing by, and Alix. She saw them stop at the living-room. Alix, suddenly white, held onto the carved entry. Vliet tensed, his mouth opening.

Over the music, she could hear Alix's shrill 'ROGER!' Saw a lift of yellow skirt, long slender legs fleeing to the end of the hall, door flinging open.

Vliet sprinted towards the butler's pantry.

Cricket waited, not knowing which would scream first, knowing only that one would scream. The music, a cruel tidal wave, poised in balance, waiting to drown her.

'Roger, ROGER!' Vliet's peculiar, hoarse cry skimmed above choruses like a bird over that tormented river.

Cricket's soft upper lip for once was pulled down over her teeth. The muscles under her eyes quivered. She stood some time before she could force herself through sound into the Gothic house that had been built by her great-great uncle. She did not glance into the living-room, she went stiff-legged to the library, raising the needle, taking the record from the spindle. She bent ringed plastic until it snapped. The raw edge bit into her chest.

She moved to the hall, reaching for the phone.

8

Alix was poised on the terrace, scanning the overgrown garden, one hand shielding her eyes, when she heard the hoarse cry, 'Roger, ROGER!' She wheeled, racing to the door at the far right. Hinges had been pulled, and she struggled before the spring gave.

Full midday sunlight came through rusty screens, glinting on broken pieces of a green tumbler. The day's heat filled the room with a gluey warmth. Cabinet doors had been flung open, and across three of them was rusty printing. The doors were old-fashioned oak. One would have to look carefully to make out capital-lettered words.

Alix did not look, carefully or otherwise.

In the arch between service porch and large, airy kitchen the stepladder-stool had been kicked over. She swerved around it. The heavy black frying pan was upside down on linoleum, and the pottery bowl she'd used for mixing pancakes was on its side on the stove. Batter had dried on the porcelainized top, dribbling down the oven door. These pale stains were a relief.

They relieved the various reds. Blood.

The sunlit kitchen was drenched with blood. Blood pooled on linoleum and on the hardwood floor of the butler's pantry, it had been tracked to make paths from various doors, yet – strangely – only one shoe print, near the sink, was clear. Blood formed a long curl, a brown question mark pointing to the service porch. One of the dirty breakfast plates had been impressed with a maroon handprint – it resembled the hand medallions that kindergarteners make from clay as Christmas gifts for parents. A dishcloth had been used to wipe blood, then been crumpled on the table. Everywhere crimson, rust, maroon, dark plum, every shade of red. The warmth made the smell overpowering. Ripe. Salty. You could taste that red smell.

The two bodies were sprawled like life-size dolls sewn from red cloth.

RB, naked, thin arms flung up over her head, lay on her back. Wounds cut a spaced line down her torso. Her shift, borrowed last night from Alix, white eyelet now splattered with red, hung from the cooler knob.

Roger's T-shirt and shorts were soaked red. Cuts

marked his arms. His clenched fists were drawn up as if he still battled his attackers.

Naturally, none of this was real. When Alix read, she willingly suspended belief. Now her belief took off for points unknown. She had seen Orion neatly dead in the living-room, and she had not believed in that. So how could she believe in this? Roger couldn't be on worn linoleum. There was no way he could be lying here, a Raggedy Andy dipped in Rit, not when he was due to report to Stanford Medical Center next Saturday, not when this morning he'd played tennis and eaten from-scratch pancakes doused in Log Cabin, pouring more syrup on the bottom one. *Have to do something about that sweet tooth*, he'd said. She'd left him a little more than an hour, so how could she believe? Her breath made an angry, denying bubble. She dropped to her knees, crouch-ing over him. She did not know she was repeating his name. His chest is warm, she thought. He's warm, yes. Warm equals living. He is warm, therefore he is.

Vliet was already hunched on the other side of the body, grasping his twin's wrist. His first two fingers moved frantically. He lifted the arm, holding it against his chest, and his fingers continued their worrying. After a minute he set the wrist down, carefully. It was if the arm had been severed from the body and he wanted to get it positioned right. His brother's blood made a maroon pattern. Vliet's shirt's an abstract, Alix thought. Mother should get a load of it. Here we have the latest Beverly Schorer masterpiece awaiting frantic bidding. Vliet tried for pulses at the groin, at the neck. He looked up.

'Nothing,' he whispered.

'There must be!'

'No.'

'Otherwise he'd be cold,' she insisted.

'Not yet.'

'We've got to get him to a hospital!'

'No point, Alix.'

'Now!' she ordered. Their heads were very close. She could see tiny bubbles of sweat on Vliet's forehead. Red wires crisscrossed in his eyeballs.

Vliet bent his ear to Roger's chest, then he raised his head and said, 'No' again. With his second and fourth finger he closed Prussian-blue eyes. That's what they do in movies, Alix thought, he's seen too fucking much celluloid to behave rationally.

'Hurry!' she snapped. 'They need to do stuff right away!'

'His vital signs –'

'You with your two-thirds of a year of Hopkins! They inject right into the heart, don't you know that!' She jumped to her feet. 'I'll get the fire department.'

'Approximately six quarts,' he said.

'What?'

'That's how much there is in the average adult male, Alix. Blood.'

And it was then that her consciousness admitted the blood. That is to say, her mind darted with thoughts of blood. Amazing. So much from two people. And in the living-room, Orion's blood. A sea of blood. The red sea. Each blood cell has a spiral that codes every secret of the entire body. Blood ties, blood kin, blood enemies. Blooded is what happens in English novels when a hunter kills his first fox. Each month flows blood from every woman born. A crime may be committed in hot blood or in cold blood. Roger stopped that little girl's blood in Arrowhead, what was that child's name? He knelt over her and pressed his hand like so. (Alix pressed her hand on the largest wound. The flesh was limp and sticky.) In olden times doctors were called leeches because they bled their patients. Leech Roger Reed, MD, has type B. Six type B quarts is all the average adult male has.

Howsabout your average pre-adolescent male?

(She and Melanie Cohn walked home from Hawthorne School, gradually dropping off the others of their crowd at various large houses that got larger as they walked north. They talked about Richard Chamberlain and how sexy he was, and Melanie, who was in love, really in love with JoJo Buberman, wondered if JoJo didn't look just a teensy bit like Richard Chamberlain, and Alix agreed. Visions of JoJo with his own TV series danced in the cool Beverly Hills air. It was slightly uphill all the way, but they chattered and the long blocks went quickly. On Melanie's floor they devoured scoops of fudge ripple and Cheezits, listening to Melanie's new single. *I wanna hold your hand*. 'My little brother's sick,' Alix said finally. 'I better get home.'

When she walked onto the patio, she saw the front door was ajar. Strange. Boris rushed out, whining circles around her. 'Wassamatta, boy? Wassamatta?' Boris yipped and slunk into the yard. Then she noticed her mother's car was gone. She was in the enclosed patio, a funny halfway point, not inside, not really outside. A nervous breeze rustled through bare new landscaping, touching the recently transplanted olive tree, shaking the birds of paradise. They look like orange vultures, Alix thought, shivering, clutching her books closer. She edged slowly around the pools. About five feet from the open door, she called, 'Mother! Jamie!' No answer. But Mother's always here when we get home. Besides, Jamie's got a killer cold. Everybody's left me, Alix thought suddenly, not just Daddy, everybody. She wanted to race back to Melanie's house, noisy and alive with three bickering younger sisters and a huge, comfortable black maid. But Alix, new in school, had set up a reputation for being hip, and how would hipness jibe with this baby fear of an empty house? They've left, I'm alone forever and ever, Alix thought. She called again, 'Mother!' Flies rose, circling the open door. Alix got a sick feeling: something awful had happened and it was her fault and she deserved to take the blame and deserved to be left alone forever. She took three tiny steps. Now she could see her mother's ratty thongs, and next to them, Jamie's transistor. Broken. He never took care of his junk. Alix did. Compulsively. The flies had settled on some funny brown marks on the terrazzo. Alix was inventing reasons to take her back to Melanie's when the phone rang, a thin sound of life from the dead heart of the house. Alix raced inside.)

390

Huge, lazy houseflies buzzed. It took Alix a heartbeat to realize the music had stopped. When? Awhile ago. Vliet was sitting back on his heels much as a Zen monk would. He did not hold his hands to his contorted face. He wept openly.

A strange, cold fury towards Vliet burst in Alix's stomach. He ought to be functioning. Roger would be, she thought, Roger would know what to do, Roger never sits on his Adidas weeping. Vliet's always been shallow. Weak. He rose, walking unsteadily towards the ugly half-bath off the service porch.

Cricket was there. She made no sound, but her face, white under messy curls, turned a pale, tentative green. Her freckles appeared three-dimensional. She moved to the cooler for the shift, letting it float over RB's torn, naked body. Eyelet, already marked, blotted up red.

The sound of retching. A toilet flushed.

Roger, help me, Alix thought, and tried to lift him. Tell me, please, darling. How can he? He's dead. She didn't believe this thought.

'I'll call the police.' Vliet had a cloth at his mouth. Tears oozed from his eyes. 'Get them over here.'

'I already phoned.' Cricket was crying, too.

In the human mind is something rather like a Dutch door. When reality becomes too painful to accept, the bottom half closes. A sort of partial amnesia to reduce the horror. This was happening in Vliet and Cricket.

Alix, having lost more – everything – the top door, the door to sanity, had begun to swing. She stood, carefully adjusting her skirt.

She was not crying.

Chapter Thirteen

I

The elder policeman was rotund, florid, with bushy, peaked grey eyebrows, the stereotype Irish cop. The younger, though fair-skinned, by feature, was obviously Mexican-American. They noted that a red Austin-Healy, licence number 850 DIW, was parked in the courtyard with its motor running and both doors open. An overturned grocery bag seeped milky liquids onto floorboards. In the background a dog barked their arrival.

The two men, drawing their handguns, started cautiously for the open door.

Almost immediately the elder returned on the run to use the radio.

Within ten minutes patrol cars filled the entry, their sirens drawing a Sunday crowd in shorts, muu-muus, swimming trunks, and bikinis from nearby apartment buildings. The media converged. Routinely, police calls are monitored. Working press and Sunday indolent alike were kept beyond the iron dagger gates. Overgrown citrus trees limited their view. Each time a police officer came in sight, questions were shouted. A network helicopter circled overhead. As the hot afternoon wore on, the old house shuddered with its final burst of activity. Patrol cars, a fire department rescue unit, an ambulance, three members of the county coroner's office were admitted. A team of detectives. More uniformed police. News cameras whirred and clicked. And finally Dr Thomas Noguchi, Los Angeles County's chief coroner, arrived. The crowd buzzed his name with satisfaction.

It was a big case.

Reporters beyond the pale put together snips of information. Extrapolated. And news bulletins interrupted Sunday afternoon programming: 'What appears to be a ritual mass murder took place this afternoon in a secluded

West Hollywood mansion. Victims include RB Henderson, star of *One Step, Two Step*. Miss Henderson is the
former wife of the film's Oscar-winning director, Loomis
Henderson, Dr Roger Reed, a member of the Van Vliet
market clan, is reportedly another victim. Possibly three
others are dead. For details tune in at five.'

Dan, freshly showered from golf, had turned on 'The
Game of the Week.' He caught the full interruption.

'Again? Oh God! Not again.' Paling, he moved on the
colour Zenith as if to shake a denial from it by the tubes.
'But how? How? They're in Baltimore.'

It had been decided to do the preliminary questioning in
the house rather than at police headquarters. Cricket was
questioned first, Alix second. The plainclothes detective
with the wandering left eye sat opposite Alix in the breakfast room. There was a wedge of dust on the heavy Tudor-
type table. Fingering it away, she answered concisely.

'We were gone a little more than an hour. An hour and
fifteen minutes at the most. We had something to drink at
Jack-in-the-Box, we shopped at Chalet Gourmet – then
stopped at Sav-on.'

'When you returned, did you notice anything unusual?'

'Yes. The front door was open and the stereo was tuned
very loud. It was music that Roger never normally would
listen to.'

'Or the others?'

'I don't know about them.'

'Where were the bodies?'

'The same place. Orion was in the living-room. RB and
Roger were in the kitchen.'

'There were signs of struggle in the kitchen, but Lance
Putnam – Orion – doesn't appear to have put up a fight.
Did you rearrange anything in the living-room?'

'No-no.'

'Did you see anyone else here?'

'Nobody. Oh, wait. There's the caretakers, the Tadovitches.'

'They're down in Vista for the day. With their son. We

checked it out.'

'Oh. I didn't know. While I fixed breakfast Roger let out their dog and played with him.'

'Did he lock him back up?'

'He had to so we could play tennis.'

'Are the bodies exactly as you found them?'

'Vliet and I tried to see if we could help Roger. We moved him, sort of.'

'And that's it?'

'I think – yes. Cricket covered R.B. Her shift was off.'

The voice and face were calm. Shock, the wall-eyed detective later told his assistant, the beautiful one's in shock. It wasn't shock. Alix was a decimated army that has not yet surrendered: the mortally wounded cry in a dark charnel-house alone, for every available force has been dispatched to the front. She concentrated on externals. About those three crumbs under the table? She retrieved them while answering: 'What was your relationship to Dr Reed?'

'I love – I mean, I lived with him. We were going to be married.'

'I have to ask this.' The left eye wandered, but the right looked kindly on her. 'You understand, Miss Schorer, don't you? It's my job.' He coughed. 'Was there anything between Dr Reed and Miss Henderson?'

'They hardly knew one another. She was his brother's friend, not exactly Vliet's girl, but sort of.'

He nodded. 'That's all for now,' he said. 'Is there anything I can do? A car to take you home?'

'Home?' She pronounced it as she might a foreign word. 'No-no. But thank you.'

He led her into the octagonal hall, saying, 'Mr Reed?'

She and Vliet stared at one another. They had not spoken since he'd vomited. The B-type blood pattern had rusted on his shirt. A flashbulb popped on his dark glasses. 'Mr Reed,' the wall-eyed detective repeated. Vliet moved silently into the breakfast room.

On the bottom stair, two uniforms sat smoking. Another pushed dust into an envelope. Someone else knelt, exam-

394

ining a bloody footprint. 'Hell, it's probably my own.' And a fat sergeant, eating a glazed doughnut, used the phone. 'Honest to God, Myrt,' he said into the receiver, 'I seen less blood on Okinawa. I mean it. A real battleground. So? Tell 'em I won't be able to make it. No, I don't know the hell what time.'

Across the eggshell paint in the living-room was scrawled, rusty, bloody: VENGEANCE IS MINE SAITH THE LORD. A sheet covered Orion. Standing on the couch, a photographer aimed downwards. *Pop flash.*

She circled a man reading a magazine. She pushed open the kitchen door. A policeman was pulling a Baggie onto RB's hand. A sheet covered Roger. As she started for the sheet, a tall detective came at her, saying, 'Sorry, honey. You're not allowed in here.'

'Why?'

'We're working,' he said. 'Is someone coming for you?'

'I'm waiting for the phone,' she said. 'When can I see him?'

'Later. Look, while you're waiting, why not change your clothes?'

In the bedroom she found a man powdering with grey dust. She locked the bathroom. She stood under the lion-head shower. Icy jets pricked her unfeeling skin.

2

They came for their children.

First the Mathenys. Caroline, erect, lipstickless, and arrogant, swept by police. Gene, his face set, pale, followed. They shed tears with Cricket in the small library – the police had set it aside for family. Vliet came out of the breakfast room. Gene left Cricket to put his arms around Vliet, then Caroline pressed herself to her tall nephew. Always they had been close to the twins, and

395

since Vliet had been in the business he had taken on filial status. He let himself be embraced. His arms were at his side and his hands trembled.

Then the Reeds. Upon seeing the remains of her son, Em opened her mouth and let sound come, peal upon peal of sound. Vliet hurried to the Austin-Healy, handing the bottles of Louis Jardot to Gene to open, and Em drank lukewarm wine that had been bought for steaks now never to be barbecued. She gulped one glass, two, three, then sank into the horsehair couch, Sheridan's arm around her, Caroline – kneeling – patting her hand. 'My poor luv, my poor luv.'

A woman stuck her pretty, raddled face around the door, announcing, 'I'm Lance's mother, Mrs Putnam.' Cricket, wiping her eyes, went to her.

A bald man wearing tennis shorts – he was older than any of the parents – after identifying the dead woman as his former wife, RB Henderson, clutched his round stomach and began to weep. He was comforted by a bearded man who identified himself as David Froude, Mr and Miss Henderson's agent. They left immediately.

Caroline had learned the value of social trivia. At times like this, homely actions can be the glue that holds us together. She suggested Mrs Putnam and everybody needed some of Vliet's wine.

Beverly and Dan arrived last. Kings Road was jammed with police and press cars, and Dan got as close as he could, leaving his car – with keys – in the middle of the road, shouldering aside onlookers, reporters, and police. He and Beverly didn't know if Alix were alive, dead, or in some hideous limbo between. They knew only what Dan originally had heard. The same message came five times over the car radio, KNX and KFWB. Beverly, pale, large eyes wild, could have posed for Tragedy. As they came through the open door, Alix descended the stairs, passing through afternoon sun that illuminated the landing. She wore clean white pants, a pink French cotton T-shirt. Her long combed hair shone in the sunlight.

Beverly moved towards her. The stairs were wide. Alix

evaded Beverly. 'Mother,' she said. 'I was about to call you.'

'Alix. Oh my God!'

'I'll be right back. I have to see Roger.'

Neither he nor RB was in the kitchen. Chalk outlines replaced the bodies. A small group of plainclothesmen, drinking Cokes from bottles, surrounded these outlines.

'They've been taken downtown,' said the detective with the wandering left eye.

'But they promised!'

'Dr Noguchi's orders.'

Alix turned to Dan. '*Make* them let me see him.'

Dan said to the lieutenant, 'They've already left?'

'Dr Noguchi's orders.'

'Then come on, Alix,' Dan said. 'Come home.'

'I have to get my things.'

And followed by Beverly, she ran upstairs. Dan questioned the police.

Beverly sat on the bed, watching her daughter meticulously fold a man's denim work shirt. Alix looked normal. Which is to say beautiful, which is to say every male in the house had stared as she passed. Her voice was normal, even to the faint bickering note that inevitably permeated their conversations. She moved normally. By this normalcy she rendered help superfluous. The huge tree engulfed the bedroom in premature dusk. Alix smoothed Roger's clothes, folding at the proper creases.

Beverly watched, her eyes dark. Her joy at finding Alix alive was melting into something else.

She sat on this high bed where Alix had slept (and, Beverly guessed, made love) with the dead boy. Dead, she thought. The unreachable place, death. Jamie, she thought, I've been in the environs myself. Roger. And specific and clear. Beverly remembered a dinner table and the dead boy explaining, intent and embarrassed, yet the blue eyes remaining steady: *She doesn't want you to understand, Mrs Grossblatt.* A sweet, serious boy. I'd hoped ... Dead. At least I had Alix. What has Alix got? These worn clothes. (My God, Beverly thought. Euripides could write the family chronicle. Our story as told to.) Why can't she show grief? Why won't she let me help her? Why can't I force her to let me help? I have to help.

Alix now had two piles. Male. Female. 'The rest's in the car,' she said, opening the cream American Tourister she'd bought when she entered Pomona, packing the male clothes and two large books. 'His *Anatomy's* in the yard,' she said. 'Don't let me forget.'

'I won't,' Beverly promised.

Alix opened the top drawer of the old bureau, checking. The middle drawer stuck. She yanked. The bow front stood firm.

'Don't worry,' Beverly said. 'If you leave something, Dan'll send for it.'

Alix wedged the drawer open, inching it forward. Empty.

'Mother, take these?' she asked, handing Beverly a flat make-up case and three pairs of sandals. She went into the bathroom to make sure the faucet wasn't dripping.

'Do you want Dan to get the suitcase now?'

'It's Roger's stuff. It's the Reeds',' Alix said. 'Is Father in town today?'

'I'll find out.'

'Would you, Mother?' And she moved the carefully packed suitcase a little. 'I'll finish here.'

Philip Schorer, sailing home from Catalina, had heard nothing of the murders. As he unlocked his door, the phone rang. Beverly's low voice rushed at him. 'Oh Philip. Thank God. I've been dialling and dialling. Alix needs you. She needs you so.'

After Cricket had said goodbye to Mrs Putnam and the fat, ruddy man that Mrs Putnam had introduced as 'Lance's father', she remained at the door. One of the squad cars was manoeuvring out of the jammed court-yard, a sweat-drenched policeman directing the effort. In the hall, just behind her, a kneeling man brushed dust on the floor. He was talking to a photographer. 'Sixteen stab wounds, can you buy this, in a pattern, like buttons, down her?' Cricket had been questioned first. She had answered questions numbly, without thought. 'The guy, the doctor, he took a long time. He must've put up a real fight. They weren't so damn neat with him.' 'Yeah, all them arm wounds. And that head!'

In Cricket's grey eyes were two points of perplexity. She looked like a child taking a difficult test. A breeze from the open door ruffled her yellow curls. Of the three survivors, only Cricket – who loved Roger and cared deeply for Orion – had the capability for the moment, even a dark, satanic one. It was she who had thought to cover RB. As Orion (and Dostoyevsky) would have said, a pure soul. 'They really contused the poor bastard.' Cricket bit down on her lower lip, leaving a sharp semi-circle.

She walked with a slight yet visible limp, passing the library, passing Mrs Grossblatt at the phone. She went into the kitchen. Five men were deep in conversation. One of them was the detective who had questioned her earlier.

Before you speak, words are nothing, blank as unexposed film, meaningless. After you speak, words are irrevocable. At the moment of sound they are action. 'Lieutenant,' she said. 'I have to talk to you.'

The five men turned.

'Miss Matheny,' said the one with the strange eye, the lieutenant, 'whatever it is, you better discuss it with your father.' He spoke respectfully. This was a big one, no ordinary murder, and he didn't care to blow it.

'About a lawyer, you mean?'

'Adequate counsel,' he agreed.

'I don't need one.'

'Why not talk it over with Mr Matheny, anyway?'

'There's no reason. I mean, you have to know this.'

They were all staring at her curiously.

'Alone,' she said.

'The breakfast room, then.'

Cricket nodded. I am voice, she thought.

'And how did they behave this time?' The questioning

across the Tudor table had been going on for ten minutes.

'I told you. The same. Peaceable, very. Docile. Except Genesis.'

'Giles Cooke, you mean?'

'Yes.'

'How was he different?'

'It's like he'd gone sort of crazy. He thought he was here to save the world.'

'How was he planning to do that?'

'He said there had to be a complete change in morality. His idea was that for the world to be right, most people would have to die.'

'And he was going to kill them?'

'He never said that.'

'But it was implied?'

'Not exactly.'

'He never said he was going to kill anyone?'

'No. But he had.'

'*What?*'

'He'd killed people.'

'When?'

'In the war and –'

'So did quite a few of us.'

'– after.'

'Oh? How many?'

'Two men.'

'Then he's got a record?'

'Uh-huh.'

'And you knew this, Cricket?' By now he had dropped the Miss Matheny. 'Before?'

'Not until the second time I stayed at REVELATION.'

'How are the others involved? Drugs?' (The police had found 4.2 grammes of marijuana, machine-rolled into cig-arette form, as well as traces of cocaine, in RB Henderson's bag. When Cricket had gone into the kitchen, they were discussing whether this were a drug case.)

'Involved? I guess Roger was.'

'How? Drugs?'

'Roger never used grass, even. Last year Orion had this

400

funny scab, and he – Roger – got him into a hospital. It was skin cancer, and he was operated on. Genesis hates knives and cutting. And doctors.'

'Then you think this is retribution?'

'And a warning to others.'

'That fits in with the writing, yes.' Pause. 'Reed and Putnam, okay. Why Miss Henderson?'

'I don't know. Maybe she was here, that's all. Maybe she was the kind of person he wanted the world rid of.'

'Why leave out you and Mr Reed and Miss Schorer?'

'We weren't around.'

'You realize the charges you've made, Cricket?'

'Yes.'

'Are you willing to testify?'

'Me?'

'You.'

'In front of him?'

A long pause.

'I'm trying to understand you, Cricket. It's not easy. Why a girl from a good family like yours gets mixed up with a bunch like this.'

'All right. If I have to.'

'Here. Take my handkerchief.' The detective opened the door, calling, 'Get Mr Matheny, will you?'

Alix, clothes piled to her chin, stopped at the open door of the library. The group might have been posed by a quattrocento painter. Em, the focal point, wore a sleeveless blouse – maybe she'd been gardening – and the slack of her arms was flattened across her bosom as if she cradled an infant. Caroline had an arm around her sister's shoulders, attempting to draw the dyed head to comfort. Sheridan, his seat drawn to the couch, hunched towards his wife. In an almost identical position, Vliet held out a glass to his mother. He had changed his shirt, but not his pants.

Em glanced up.

She saw Alix.

Em's pale-blue eyes were bloodshot, the upper lids red,

the lower puffed and purple. For what seemed like forever, her eyes held Alix's. A chill that came from another line of existence shivered over Alix, and she murmured, 'Mrs Reed, please.' Caroline shook her head, not unkindly. Go away, the shake meant. Don't intrude. Sheridan was gazing at Alix, coldly, with tear-reddened eyes. Alix saw only Roger's mother.

Em's mouth opened. The mouth trembled, the mouth grew hard, ugly. The mouth pouched forward. She was about to spit, something that Em never would do. Never would think of doing. Spitting was a reflex, an atavism born of misery and despairing grief and absolute hatred. It was all the more terrible because Em, in her forty-eight middle-class years, never had made the age-old gesture that was meant to avert the evil eye, to dispel witch's poison, to show utmost scorn. *I spit on you and yours.* Between her open lips, saliva was a thin vein glinting like a soap bubble. She swallowed convulsively.

Sheridan continued staring at Alix. Vliet had half risen. Not one of the four had spoken or taken their eyes from her.

Clutching her neatly folded clothes, she stood there, unable to move.

And then Dan pulled her towards the wide staircase. In her ear, low and hoarse: 'Alix, sweetheart, may God damn them all to hell forever!'

She recovered. She moved from his protective warmth.

And Gene, emerging from the breakfast room, greeted, 'Dan, Alix, Beverly.' (Beverly, having told Philip of the murders, was hanging up the phone.) 'Come on in.'

'Gene,' Dan's voice was hard. 'Why let the press have more of a field day than necessary?'

Gene glanced over his shoulder at the breakfast room. 'They'll have it.'

'So there's buttons to push.' Dan's harsh loudness overrode discussion.

'Alix, honey,' Gene asked. 'Is there anything I can do? Anything?'

'Please, Mr Matheny,' she said. Her voice didn't waver.

'Roger's things're upstairs, all packed. And his microscope and books're in the car.' She looked puzzled. 'Dan, what should I do about the car?'

'Tomorrow I'll send someone.'

'It's the Mustang,' she said to Gene. 'Oh, and he left his *Anatomy* in the yard.'

'The police took it,' Dan said.

'They never told me,' Alix said. 'Why do you think they didn't?'

'Probably regulations.'

'Mr Matheny, will you see that Roger's parents get everything?'

Gene nodded. He was crying. Through the blur, he saw Beverly, a tall, slender shape in pink stripes, moving towards the open door of the library.

'Buzz!' Dan snapped. 'Get the fuck away from there!'

She was at her father's, and the lines of force in his staircase were wrong, the treads moved like a rope ladder. She gripped the banister, and with effort, descended normally. The three of them, drinking, looked up.

She asked, 'How about one for me?'

'Scotch?' Philip asked.

'Please.'

Dan watched her take the drink. His eyes were narrow, and under them small wrinkles pouched. Dan's eyes pitied her.

'Dan.' She swirled three ice cubes in amber liquid. 'Why not take Mother to dinner?'

'Come home,' Beverly said.

'It's fine here.'

'Here, you don't have a room,' Dan said.

'She has mine.' Philip.

'No-no. Father, I'll take the couch. It's the new line, isn't it? The pull-out?'

'You recognized it,' Philip said, pleased.

'You sent the catalogue. Mother, don't.'

'What?' Beverly asked.

'Cry.'

'I'm not.'

'You've got a look.'

'It's the same name,' Dan said to Philip. 'They'll track her down easier, those damn reporters.'

Philip said, 'I'm unlisted.'

Alix held her glass, not drinking, from time to time raising it to her lips. After a while she glanced at her mother, then Dan. 'Let's get the show on the road, kids.'

Dan came towards her as if to kiss her. She rose. 'Take care,' she said to him.

Beverly, too, was moving in on her. Alix, stepping back, made a smile that was the Great Barrier Reef. Beverly sighed. The sigh lasted, holding Jamie, Roger, death – a trinity of desolation – and for a moment, as Dan opened the door, light folded into itself. Then they were gone.

Alix busied herself, pouring her Scotch, good J&B, intact, down the drain, rinsing the glasses.

'Want to eat at Donkins?' Philip asked.

'I'll scramble us some eggs.'

She pushed hers around the plate and didn't drink the coffee she'd brewed in the Melitta. She insisted on doing the dishes. Keeping things in order was good. Otherwise chaos. But all the time, those voices, soaring in the double-decker room. 'Father, let's take a walk.'

He lent her a jacket, too big and very light, navy quilted dacron, his new sailing jacket. Boats slapped, docks creaked, and the night fog blurred reflections on black water. And then a very strange thing happened. In the darkness she saw Roger. Very clearly. It was as if film were projected onto a screen: Roger stood beyond the torn net, his new racket across his T-shirt, sweat darkening a path down white cotton, drops shining on his forehead, his nose burned from yesterday in the sun. Knees flexed, muscles alert, he watched her serve. And the ball, a clean new Spalding, rose into blue sky, the beginning of *2001*, revolving through endless, countless, unknowable millennia to become a round, white reflection in black water. This morning, she thought, I made that serve this morning. Almighty God in everlasting glory, Prince of Pee-eeeeace. She covered her ears. The music grew. She put her hands in the pockets of her father's jacket and walked faster.

'Hon, let's go home.'

They turned back.

'Thank you, Father.'

'What for?'

For somehow understanding how every bit of me has to be devoted to hanging in there.

When they got back, a lantern-jawed man in a mustard jacket waited by the door. He asked quickly, 'Miss Schorer, are you aware that Giles Cooke has stated under oath that the murders were committed by his orders? Lance Putnam carried them out.'

'Who are you?' Philip asked. 'How did you know to come here?'

And Alix said, 'Orion? But he's dead.'

'He killed himself, after.'

'Orion? Genesis?' Her voice was bewildered. 'They killed Roger?'

'Your, er, fiancé tried to protect Miss Henderson, Cooke says, but he, Cooke, had the others hold him. He said Reed was anti-life, and Miss Henderson, too. Putnam managed the girl alone, but he needed help for Reed. What shape was the body in? Bad?'

Philip had the door unlocked. 'You're trespassing.' He sounded sarcastic rather than angry. 'Alix, hon, come in.'

'Miss Schorer! Was this a grudge slaying? Cooke insists they had it coming to –'

Philip slammed the door. One of the pillows on the couch (new line) was flattened. Alix understood she must plump it. Philip dialled the security guard.

Alix was changing her father's bed when the guard arrived. The guard suggested that Philip hire his cousin, recently retired from the Venice Police Department. So that night Alix sat on a chair facing a freshly made-up bed, while on the steps outside, a grey-haired man sat with a .38 under the old jacket that protected him from sea damp.

3

It was her old room, the room she'd had as a girl.

Dr Porter had come to shoot Demerol into her and, because of this, they assumed she could not think or feel or remember. They assumed she slept. But her eyes were open a fraction, and in the single light she could see, blurrily, the old tallboy and therefore she knew she was in her old room, the same Em, but grieving, tired, numbed, and diminished oh so greatly.

How?

She thought through the drug. How could it have happened? I, always so careful, feeding him his Polyvisol and orange juice. I, sterilizing his teething ring and putting Vaseline on his circumcision. I, standing by his father. Even when it wasn't easy. Sheridan, he still bows his head so I can see the bald spot, telling me of the nastiness, and I reply that I'm his wife and we have our sons and they're all that counts. The girls today, they don't understand. With their Pill and living together and going from one to the next, they don't understand what it is to work at marriage. They don't know. Her! Her!

Em felt a hot redness, unhalted by the drug, pass through her mind. Somewhere far away, Em Wynan Reed moaned and turned her face to clean-smelling pillowslip while, tentatively, her hand inched up to her breast. The sudden shocking cold of her fingertips distracted her and she felt herself drift to another time.

A nurse handing me the baby. The wrong one. No. Not the wrong one, the dark one who looks like Sheridan. But I am careful to hold him just as snugly, for I love him – less, to be sure, but I do love him, for he is mine – and oh, the tenderness when he touches at the side of my breast. He, red and squirmy and open-mouthed, wants the bottle. There. Formula draining. Contented little gurgles and grunts. Mine. Mine. I must see he gets everything, like his brother. Oh, nice and milky is his smell.

Em's fingers squeezed, then fell away.

She made an effort to see Roger at two, three, five. She could not. Nothing.

Ahh, yes.

He looks up at me, his fist clutched around a bouquet, the stems are too short. 'For you, Mommy,' he says. I take the flowers, putting them in a water glass, not smiling, for these are the pansies I planted this morning, yellow and purple, that were my birthday gift. He's only three and thinks they're pretty. For you, Mommy. Vliet calls me Ma. Sheridan says Roger must be spanked for the picking, but I say no, that's not fair. I never told him he mustn't. He's not quick to smile like Vliet, but he's a good boy, no trouble, someone to be proud of in the Family. All *A*s. Harvard. Johns Hopkins. Grandma, I wish you could have seen him a man, my Roger. He was a very good, decent man, my Roger.

But she.

She!

Oh God, forgive me, I wish her dead, too. She, standing there, beautiful for all men to lust after, I could smell the cologne from where I sat. Even then, cologne. Ready for the next one. Now the girls don't care about fidelity and such, they take off their skin-tight pants and lie down with as many men as they can. Nasty.

A long, black hair wrote W-H-O-R-E across Em's brain. She slept.

A little after nine they pulled into Mrs Wynan's drive. Gene, Caroline, and Cricket. Sheridan opened the door. Redness rimmed his eyes, and his shirt collar seemed a size too big for his heavy neck.

Caroline pressed her perfumed cheek to his. 'How wise you were, not going home. We've had one thousand hideous calls, and there're tribes of newspeople camping on our doorstep.'

Gene gripped his brother-in-law's shoulder, all enmity for once forgotten. And Cricket said, 'Uncle Sheridan,' kissing him.

'How is she?' Caroline asked.

'Sleeping,' Sheridan replied.

'Thank God for Dr Porter's magic needle.' Caroline held out a pink box. 'Coffee cake, direct from my freezer.'

Sheridan said, 'Mrs Monk' – Mrs Wynan's current nurse-companion – 'gave us breakfast.'

Caroline was not to be daunted. She set minute pastries on a salver and reheated coffee. They sat around the dining table.

'Vliet, take one,' Caroline insisted.

Vliet bit. He glanced across the table at Gene. 'Beats ours,' he said.

'At the price, Bailey's has to do *some*thing.' And Caroline, chattering continuously through cigarette smoke, pressed coffee and tiny, buttery cakes on everyone.

'Luv,' she asked Vliet, 'did you find one?'

'In his closet,' Vliet said. 'Trust Ma. She'd had it cleaned, and there it hung, in its plastic, for three years.'

'Does it still fit?' Caroline asked.

'Does it still matter?' Vliet replied.

'He didn't own a real suit!' Caroline had tears in her eyes. 'My Gawd, can you imagine any twenty-five-year-old man without a suit in our day? Much less a *doctor*?'

Sheridan said, 'Dad, as long as I can remember, wore the same one to church. Brown and too tight.' His voice held pride in his boyhood poverty.

'What sort of life is it now?' Caroline choked and her tears spilled, as if Roger's lack of a suit managed to sum up the entire tragedy.

'Well?' Sheridan asked Gene.

'Yes, we better.'

The two men stood. Sheridan put on his coat, which had been hanging over the back of his chair.

'You have everything?' Caroline asked. 'A tie?'

'My new striped one,' Vliet said.

'And a shirt? Does he have a clean white shirt?'

'An old one,' Sheridan said.

'It won't fit!'

'Forest Lawn has the secret passed down by ancient Egyptians,' Vliet said. 'It'll fit.'

'I can run down to Brand Boulevard in five —'

'Caroline,' Gene said quietly, 'just calm down.'

She followed them to the door, embracing both.

Em's old room was in front. Gene's muffler on sunken paving must have disturbed her. 'Vliet?' Her voice came plaintive, querulous. 'Vliet, is that Aunt Caroline?'

'Me, luv,' Caroline called. She poured coffee, set two dainty twists of cinnamon on the saucer and, cigarette between her lips, navigated through the living-room to the bedroom hall.

Cricket and Vliet sat on opposing couches. From a gilt frame a young woman, wickedly haughty, looked down on a tall, handsome young man and a tiny blonde cuddling a needlepoint pillow: her descendants.

Vliet held part II of the *Times*. 'Dad tossed the front section,' he said, unfolding the paper, scanning. 'This you won't believe, Cricket. In editorials we have replaced the war in Indo-China.'

Cricket's fingers rubbed the ugly needlepoint.

' "Have We Failed Our Children?" ' he read. 'How's that for a headline? "There is a growing trend to consider churches at best outmoded and at worst hypocritical, even tyrannical. But have we failed an entire generation by not offering adequate moral guidelines?" ' He glanced up at her. '*Fantástico?* "Yesterday a murder was committed that will leave its echo on our decade just as the Manson murders left their imprint on the sixties. A young doctor and a talented actress were held by three youths while a fourth fatally stabbed the victims. This youth then killed himself. He had acted in accordance with the beliefs of a bizarre sect. The leader of this group, a man earlier imprisoned for homicide, stated that this was their punishment for acts contrary to their religious beliefs. Young people, he told police and reporters, seek him out because he is willing to show them a way of life." ' Vliet took a breath. 'Paragraph. "These young killers came from so-called advantaged homes. They had been in no previous trouble with police. They simply had not found the faith that they were looking for in their homes." ' Vliet clucked his tongue. 'Paragraph. "There is no question that many of today's youth seek values formerly found in religion. Now, in a time of national cynicism and disbelief, it is no wonder that they have turned elsewhere. Many find solace in Far Eastern faiths. Or in so-called communal living. A few, inevitably, fall into the clutches of a Giles Cooke. That such a man as Cooke can throw his spell over a group of otherwise peaceable youths is ultimately a fault of society." ' Vliet tapped newsprint. 'Paragraph. "In essence, society has failed by no longer providing boundaries and an ethical structure. We have left our children in a moral vacuum." '

Cricket didn't look up.

'Blessed are the simplistic minded,' Vliet said. He refolded the paper on the coffee table, then thought better of it, going out of the kitchen door to crush it into a dustbin.

'There can't be anything for Ma to find in the family section, can there?'

She shook her head.

He rubbed his neck thoughtfully. 'You haven't said a word, Cricket, since you got here.'

She raised her rounded little chin a fraction to indicate possibly that he was incorrect.

'What's that?' he asked.

'I think it's printed ahead of time.'

'Let's not get garrulous.'

Cricket rested a cheek on worn needlepoint.

'Come on, little cousin, you must have a word or two.' He lit a cigarette. He reached for an Indian brass dish.

Finally she said, 'It's my fault.'

'What?'

'The whole thing's my fault.'

'Let's not have any of that, Cricket. You were selecting the prime cuts with us.'

'Roger met them, Genesis and Orion, through me.'

'Well?'

'That started it.'

'Roger's keen medical eye, that's what started it.'

'Remember in Carmel?' She reached across the narrow mahogany table towards him, then dropped the hand as if she'd burned herself on his cigarette. 'You said they were weird.'

'I don't care for this line of reasoning, Cricket.'

'You warned me. I could've listened.'

'Really. You could've. Except at the time they weren't in business.'

'They were getting weirder,' she said, sighing. 'If I hadn't gone there that Sunday, Roger never would've seen Orion's scab.'

'Christ! More third-rate inductive reasoning.'

'And think of RB.'

'I'd rather know how to avoid thinking of her.'

'She had nothing to do with them. She'd never met Genesis, even.'

'But according to this youth-attracting religion, Cricket, she was corrupt. And therefore deserved to die. And then some.'

'All through me.'

'Don't let's have the *mea culpas*,' Vliet said. 'I'm not up to 'em. One thing we don't need here, Cricket, is more self-blame.'

'How can I help it?'

'Make an effort,' he said, leaning into the couch, riffing his fingers on his knees. 'Siegfried's Funeral March,' he announced.

Cricket's face was intent. 'This weekend Orion was talking crazy. I felt sorry for him, but also I had that sort of uncomfortable, itchy thing. You know. Something's wrong, but you refuse to let yourself think it through.'

'Cricket, no more instant replays, huhh?'

'He said Genesis had let him back into REVELATION. It hit me as far out, but I didn't ask how come, or why.'

'For Chrissakes, forget it!'

'You wanted me to talk.'

'Not like this, I didn't.'

'I've been thinking and thinking.'

'And hasn't it occurred to you that others have their own thoughts?'

'You?'

'Me. If I hadn't been drinking coffee and mulling over the meat, I'd've been there with him. And he'd've had a chance, a chance is all. I mean, don't you remember who insisted we go with you on that jaunt to Carmel Valley?'

She sat forward. From the closed door of the bedroom hall came muted female voices. It was impossible, though, to tell who was talking.

'Without me, none of you would've been there, not in a million years.'

'Cricket, I don't give a damn for whom the bell tolls. I don't wanta hear about it, I don't wanta talk about it, I don't wanta think about it. So shut the hell up!'

The door to the hall opened. Mrs Wynan moved ponderously into the room. Her stockings were knotted below the knees of her thick, veined legs. She held onto a table, then a chair.

'Heading outside, Grandma?' Vliet asked, taking her arm.

'Thank you, dear.'

Vliet opened a French window, warm breezes tagged ecru curtains, and the flat, homely old face lit up.

Said the forgetful Mrs Wynan, 'I do so enjoy seeing you, Roger dear.'

She sat on the morning-shaded patio. Vliet remained where he was. Shoulders heaving, he dropped his face in his hands.

Vliet Reed, sobbing, thinks. Into this world they come alone. Not me. I came half of a twinship, which is closer than kinship and, if at times I felt like the back part of a vaudeville horse, the heavy costume suffocating me and forcing me to follow Roger, I also felt like part of a very exclusive society. Us two. This relationship being severed by the Big Break. Or, as Ma puts it, 'her'. And even after

412

it was schizo, how often I would call him or he would call me, just as the opposing twin had an opposing hand – left him, right me – on the phone for the very purpose. This I can't explain. I'm not the fuzzy-minded sort who would classify it as psychic phenomenon. Still, when I found Roger on that kitchen floor, hamburger, I had a, well, an Experience. Horror, yes. And grief, sure, grief. But more than horror or grief. It was as if certain nerves along my spinal column were being cut, certain areas in me were becoming numb. Part of me will be forever numb. And right now, that part – Roger – lies under the scalpel of some coroner, maybe the great Noguchi himself. Christ, how Roger would've appreciated the performance. Unfortunately he's there in body only.

Roger Reed, always having to buck for sainthood. Who would look after and pay surgical bills for a stranger, a freaked-out, mixed-up San Marino weirdo kid? St Roger, that's who. Now on God's right hand, not mine.

I am half a twin.

Is there such a creature?

Half a twin is better than none.

No, half a twin is none.

He even smelled stronger than me and, Christ, whoever dreamed without him so much of me would be missing?

Vliet does not pursue that which has been taken from him. It is mostly in the area of conscience. Roger always had acted as a sort of detainer: Roger never would be doing this shitty thing, Vliet had thought, and possibly had desisted. This concept is dissolving from the electrical impulses of Vliet's brain.

'Vliet,' Cricket said, leading him to the couch. 'Here,' she said, handing him her damp handkerchief. They had run out of handkerchiefs. Mrs Monk was washing a load now.

4

'I don't see why she can't be there,' Vliet said.

'She's not Family,' Em repeated.

'In this particular case, Ma, it's beside the point.'

'Vliet,' said Sheridan, 'we don't need arguments now.'

Vliet lit a cigarette. Carefully. The Reeds had finished
a late lunch. (Cricket had been taken by her parents to
the downtown offices of Sidney Sutherland, cousin and
attorney.) Em, elbow on her raffia place mat, rested her
cheek in her hand. For once she had let down on appearances and was without make-up, wrapped in an old, too
large robe of Mrs Wynan's, a safety pin holding the
neckline together.

Vliet exhaled. 'Roger would want her.'

'Son, I don't think you understand.' Sheridan still wore
the suit, his good navy suit, that he'd worn while making
the last arrangements for his other son. 'We've decided
The matter's closed.'

Em found a handkerchief in her sleeve. She blew her
nose. 'Family,' she said. 'Only the Family.' Even now, her
voice went respectful as she spoke of Van Vliets.

'She would've been family,' Vliet said.

'No,' Em denied.

'Roger was going to –'

'Vliet, watch it,' Sheridan said.

'– marry her.'

'Never!' Em shrilled.

'Thursday. They were coming to tell you.'

'No!' Em.

'For Chrissake, they might as well have been.'

'They weren't.' Sheridan stood. Erect, almost martial.
He often said, proudly, that he could still fit into his old
sergeant's uniform. 'And you won't keep this up.'

I'm out of my skin about her, Roger had said, and set
about proving it, not endearing Alix to their parents.

Roger had left Vliet one hell of a job.

'Dad, think what Roger would've wanted.'

'I'm not about to tell you again!'

'But –' And then Vliet shut up.

Em had taken off her glasses and was crying. Who can argue with a weeping, grieving mother? Especially if she happens to be yours?

'Hey, Ma, none of that. Doctor's orders.' As he spoke he realized *doctor* was an unfortunate word. She shifted into fierce, gasping sobs. He hugged her. What's here to fight, anyway? A small, frail woman with flesh gone slack who smells of stale tears and liquor, a woman close to fifty, mourning her son.

In truth, Vliet shaped up equally poorly. Even though he was not crying, he had no resources left. He was incapable of further combat. They habeas corpus, he thought, they have the corpse and possession's nine-tenths of the law and is it so crucifyingly important that Alix Schorer be graveside? No, he decided, not if your mother's sobbing hysterically. He blew his nose and went to the cabinet, turning the key on the left side, taking the first bottle that came to hand, pouring Em a quadruple. '*Salud*,' he said. 'Dad?'

'Don't mind if I do.'

By the time they had finished their sherry, Em was snuffling quietly.

Vliet got up. 'See you at dinner, then,' he said.

'Where are you going?' Em asked.

'There's this little thing I gotta do.'

'What?' she wanted to know.

But he was out of the door. For maybe two minutes neither Em nor Sheridan moved.

She wiped her eyes. 'He's going to her.'

'He's worried she'll find out and come, that's all.'

'If it weren't for her, Roger would've been home. Safe and sound.'

'Please, Em. Don't.'

'She came between the boys.'

'There's no point, not now.'

415

'Nothing else ever did. They were so close. It's how we raised them.'

'We did a good job.'

Em's wan face suddenly went anxious. 'Vliet's not angry is he?'

'No. Not Vliet.'

'I am being fair, aren't I? It *is* Family only.'

'And she's not.' The tension around Sheridan's mouth had been loosened by time and grief. 'She's just a little Jew tramp.'

Alix was not at her mother's place. She was, Dan said coldly, not elaborating or inviting him inside, at her father's. Vliet requested the address. Dan scribbled in a black-leather memo book, tearing the scrap of paper. He closed the door. Vliet deciphered directions before starting. Another hot day – he thought of putting down the top, but somehow an open car seemed frivolous.

Boats, thousands of them, enmeshed between docks. Sun rippling on tideless, turgid water. Vliet rechecked the address.

'What is it?' asked a grey man rising from a step.

'Is this Philip Schorer's apartment?'

'Why?'

'Are you Mr Schorer?'

'No.' The man's eyes were frisking him.

'Does he live here?'

'Yes. And you're trespassing.'

'Is Miss Schorer around?'

'She's not seeing anyone.'

'I think she'll see me. I'm Van Vliet Reed.' He gave it the full treatment.

And got the expected results. 'Let me ask Mr Schorer,' said the grey man politely. 'Wait here, please.' He used a key.

Vliet didn't have a chance to light his cigarette. Alix's father was at the door, a fabulous-looking guy, his deep tan set off by white sailing clothes, good ones. Well, Vliet thought, it figures, it figures.

And Alix was saying, 'Vliet', as she came down the stairs. Under her eyes were faint smudges, like a girl who's slept in lavender eye shadow. Otherwise she was perfect. A little too perfect. She might have been posing for a fashion layout, one leg behind her on the bottom step. Except she was better-looking than the models he'd dated. She gave him a smile, the economy-size smile used for mournful occasions. 'Father,' she said, 'this is Vliet. Vliet Reed, my father, Philip Schorer.'

Vliet held out his hand and it was taken. 'Mr Schorer, sir.'

'Philip,' Mr Schorer corrected. And went through the platitudes du jour, how sorry he was, a great loss, and so on and etcetera. He excused himself, tactfully sliding open glass, closing it after himself.

'It's his only place,' Alix said, removing an invisible fleck from a modern couch. *Order, once everything's in order, I'll be in better shape. This damn music won't keep repeating like raw onion.* 'I've got his room. And there's just this.' She gestured, taking in more square footage than is in most houses. Above the kitchen the ceiling was lowered.

'The bedrooms are up there?' he asked.

'Just one. I've got it. The view's terrific.'

A terrific view, he agreed. And in his estimation it was. A billion dollars' worth of boats. Mr Schorer settled into a webbed patio chair, moving a felt-tip pen across a proof sheet.

'He's doing the new catalogue,' Alix said.

'For what?'

'Schorer Furniture.' She moved to the kitchen area. 'Let me fix you lunch?'

'Thanks anyway, but I ate.'

'Oh, that's right. It's almost four. A Coke, then? A drink? Or coffee's ready?'

'Thanks, nothing.' He tapped his cigarette. 'Why aren't you home?'

'You mean Mother's?'

'Yes, Mrs Grossblatt's.'

'She keeps wanting to mother. A lot of body contact and stuff.'

'It gets to you.'

Did I sound a mite off? Vliet's got a very good ear – but if it's so damn good, how come he can't hear this hideous Handel? 'I just don't need any,' Alix said.

And perching on that sterile couch, she crossed her ankles to one side. Toned down, yet crisp. Exactly right. It baffled Vliet. She baffled him. Come to think of it, she always had. There was a mystery about Alix, something mysterious. Untouchable, a perfect, uncrazed Grecian urn in a museum niche, her very impervious hinting at unrevealed pasts, depths, twilit secrets. As he'd been hot to hear her breath coming jagged from beneath him, so he now needed Alix to display grief. He needed to see her lose her cool. He needed proof that his brother, his late other, had meant something to her. On the way over, he'd rehearsed speeches to let her down easy. Forget it, he told himself.

'The funeral,' he said, 'is Wednesday.'

She leaned back, clasping her knees, momentarily withdrawing to some private speculation. *Funeral. Roger wanted cremation – after parts were donated to those in need. But his parts weren't in donatable condition, were they? Oh God, please don't let me break down. I'll never get it together if I do.* 'Where?' she asked.

'Forest Lawn.'

'The main one?'

'Glendale, yes. It won't be in the papers.'

'Understandable,' she said.

'Family,' he said. 'Strictly family.'

For a blink of time he saw, or maybe he hoped he saw, that she swallowed with difficulty. *I never said goodbye, never. My chest is pulling like a cramp, keep moving, that's what they tell you when you cramp up, don't they? Roger, tell them if I'm not there, you won't be, either. What am I going to do, alone? Not go to the funeral. Never say goodbye, ever.*

'You're telling me I'm *persona non grata*?'

418

'I'm sorry, Alix.' Really, he thought, I could have phoned it in kinder. She's smiling, though, so what the hell. His eyes grew moist and he thanked God for giving us Coolray Polaroid sunglasses.

'Flowers, then,' she said. 'I'll send flowers. Where?'

'Forest Lawn.'

'Oh, that's right. You said. The Glendale one. What time?'

'Alix –'

'Not to worry. Flowers. No me. But the florist'll need the time.'

Forever and ever, he thought.

She smoothed an invisible wrinkle in her shorts. 'The time, Vliet?'

'Noon.'

'Noon,' she repeated.

'Uh-huh.'

'I appreciate it, Vliet, you coming to tell me.'

'They feel strongly.'

If only I could shut off the sound track, and that's an idiot's thought, still, it's also a kind of litany against grief, and I'll never say goodbye, never, and my chest does hurt so, and shut off the damn sound.

'I'm sorry,' Vliet said. He wasn't. He couldn't care less. She fried him. He was consumed with anger, rare for him. One trace of emotion was all he asked of her. One trace.

'By now I can handle their attitude.'

'If that's the case, Alix, you're exceptional.'

'No-no. Just used to it.'

They stared at one another, Vliet Reed and Alix Schorer. His face, although he didn't realize it, had the same faint detachment. Her expression, however, cost far more, an unknowable amount that she would never be able to recoup. Yesterday, Vliet thought, yesterday she had knelt, Roger's blood covering her, her slender arms straining at the heavy, inert weight, her voice hoarsely, obsessively repeating Roger Roger Roger. Vliet gazed into shadowed eyes, and the throbbing of a boat's engine came like a heartbeat into the high, sunlit room.

Don't take off the glasses, that'll be worse than anything. She turned abruptly, going to the door. 'Mr O'Hara, there's coffee.'

The grey man smiled. 'Thanks, Alix.'

On the steps, Vliet said, 'You're friends with the watchdog?'

'He's retired. This is his way of hanging in.'

Vliet had gone maybe ten yards when she called to him. He turned, inhaling dock smells of hot tar, gasoline, salt.

She raised a hand to visor the sun. 'Will you give your parents my sympathy?'

'I will,' he lied.

Sun bounced from outsize windows of connecting beige condominiums, and not a sound came from any of them. At the car park, Vliet glanced back. Alix remained on the steps alone, a breeze lifting her glossy dark hair. He was too far to see her expression. He was near enough to see a girl of myth, fair enough to launch these thousand ships. Cold bitch, he thought, raising dark glasses to wipe his eyes. Cunt, he thought. These opinions in no way lessened his devotion.

Chapter Fourteen

I

Hallelujah for the Lord God omnipotent reigneth.

... The kingdom of this world is become the kingdom of our Lord and of his Christ; and he shall reign forever and ever.

King of Kings, and Lord of Lords.

'Where to?'

The man had a maroon birthmark on his left cheek, it was raised and velvety and shaped like a pine cone. His uniform was navy, a slick and cheap dacron.

'Where to?' he repeated.

She looked up at the clock and saw hands pointing to 8:07. On a grey television screen were greyish letters:

> 8:40, FLIGHT 210 WASHINGTON
> 9:10, FLIGHT 88 VANCOUVER
> 9:25, FLIGHT 910 NEW YORK

Washington you can land for Baltimore, Washington is out. Far away, she heard shrill tinkling notes, the *Hallelujah Chorus* being played like Beethoven's Ninth in *Clockwork Orange*. Vancouver? New York? Trying to decide, she gripped her handbag, and behind her ear a man coughed, impatient and, Alix thought, The earlier the better, the sooner the best.

'Vancouver,' she said.

'Round trip?'

'One way, please.'

He took her BankAmericard, punching and writing behind the counter. Wednesday, she thought, today's Wednesday.

'Check your baggage?'

'*Voilà*,' she replied, holding up her big summer bag.

'That's what I call travelling light.'

'The only way to fly.'

'Gate Thirteen, Miss Schorer.' As he smiled the birth-mark stretched, turning a shade paler, to raspberry.

At the moving sidewalk she hesitated, her sandals poised over segments. Her toenails were pretty, polished. Now. Now. The bump ascended sharply, and she grabbed the rubber handrail. So, she thought, and began walking. 'Excuse me,' she said, passing a fat corporal, his belt curved below his stomach. Today, she thought, today is Wednesday. *Mr and Mrs Sheridan Reed request/the absence of your company/at the funeral of their son/Dr Roger Stuart Reed/at twelve o'clock noon on Wednesday the twenty-fifth of June.* Vengeance is Mine, saith the Lord, but others can pull it off, too, don't let anyone kid you. The walk dipped, spilling her onto hard marble. She ran up the escalator, passing two nuns wearing short habits and shiny innocence, a little boy wrapping his tongue around a green sucker, a pair of businessmen lugging overnight cases. So many people I must not bump into, she thought, worried. Then, beyond the window walls, she saw them, taxiing, waiting, landing, taking off. The number soothed her. With so many, one could keep on the move forever and ever. At Gate 13 a woman with wide, feral nostrils told her that the flight to Vancouver was on time. Alix moved into the gift shop to pick a novel. She spelled titles letter by letter, but they made no sense.

'What's good?' asked a tall young man. As he talked, his inadequate yellow Fu Manchu goatee wiggled.

'It's a decision,' she replied.

'I'm going to New York. Where're you headed?'

'Maybe this,' she said, taking out the fattest book.

'*Tolstoy* by Troyat,' he read. 'Sounds heavy.'

'No-no, it's terrific.'

'What's the plot?'

'Oh, murders happen.'

'Sex?'

'Loaded,' she said.

'Tell you what. We'll have coffee and you'll give me a rundown.'

She glanced at the clock. 'Fine.'

Steam fogged her dark glasses and the smell of coffee tightened her throat and the tinny music had a strange menace. Miss Henderson's funeral was attended by many Hollywood notables, the *Times* had said. I told Father I should go, but he had that funny beating in his forehead and he said, 'Alix, better, not', with each word in isolation.

Ketchup made a spot on the counter and she dipped a finger, reddening the tracery of veins at her wrist.

'Hey. Whatcha doing?'

'It's what we use for blood on the set.'

'Know something. I had you spotted as an actress.'

'Sharp.'

'What's the name? Maybe I heard of you.'

'Only bits,' she said.

'Aren't you going to wipe it off?'

As she did, dust motes filled the barnlike enclosure with that terrifying sound.

'I was in *Clockwork Orange*,' she said.

'Hey, far out. Wasn't it made in England?' She could smell the spoiled, charred meat of his hot dog and see white of bread mushed on his palate.

'On location,' she said.

'Who were you?'

'The nameless dead.'

'I don't remember . . .' He swallowed, staring at her. His eyes had flecks of brown swimming in muddy green, like dead leaves on poisoned wells. 'What nameless dead?'

She laughed, a tinkly, rising laugh. 'I'm a waitress.'

'Sure. That's just what you look like. A waitress.'

'At the Silver Fork in Baltimore.'

'Hey, what're you on?'

'Thanks for the coffee.' She deposited the full cup in a lined waste bin, careful to keep it upright.

'Grass?'

'I only work part time, I'm pregnant. I'm going to have twins.'

'Yeah. Acid?'

'Please don't look at me like that.'

'How?'

'Like you hate me.'

'No kidding, you better crash someplace till you come down.'

And then the music cleared and a voice of rustling metal announced: 'Flight Eighty-eight for Vancouver is departing from Gate Thirteen.'

She was in a middle seat over the wing before she realized she'd dropped *Tolstoy* by Troyat in her bag. She'd ripped off a book she'd read twice. The plane was almost empty, but anyway, she put her bag on the seat near the aisle and the swiped paperback on the window seat. Nobody could sit near her. She couldn't bear it if anyone sat near her. What if they touched her? I kissed each inch of his body, she thought, and he mine, and he said you smell of flowers everywhere.

'Care for a drink?' asked a silver-lipped stew, bending over a trolley crowded with miniature liquors and ice and pitchers and a bowl of green olives pregnant with red.

'No-no.' Alix made a smile. 'But thank you.'

'How about a little wake-up coffee?' The stew had a nasal voice as if from a botched nose job.

'I had some in the airport.'

'That was quite a while ago. You look like you could use a pick-me-up. Orange juice?'

Watch it, don't hurt her in her feelings. 'Well, a little Seven-Up,' Alix said.

The girl poured, and Alix, careful their fingers didn't touch, reached. Cautiously she wedged the pliable glass in green serge next to her and moved *Tolstoy* by Troyat so she could sit by the window. Below, a sun-topped cloud cast its shadow across empty hills. And He shall reign forever and ever, she thought, looking down, forever and ever.

Silver Lips was leaning towards her.

Then there were two stews, their mouths moving, but she couldn't hear them until she realized this was because she was singing.

'Oh, I am sorry,' she said.

'S'all right,' said Silver Lips. 'All right.'

'I'm with the Roger Wagner Chorale,' Alix said. 'We're doing the *Messiah* in Vancouver.'

'Honey,' said the other, reaching.

'DON'T TOUCH ME!'

'We won't hurt you.'

'I didn't mean to yell. It's just I have this thing about being touched.'

'Why not come up front with us? There's less chance of touching there.'

'We don't get much rehearsal time,' Alix said. And smiling ahead of them, she balanced herself on empty aisle seats, managing equilibrium.

'Here we are,' said Silver Lips. A uniformed man with a nose like a squashed spoon, maybe the co-pilot, said, 'Join us.' The seats were narrower. The man cleared papers. 'I'm Jack Gruening,' he said. 'What's your name?'

'Alix,' she said. 'Alix Schorer.'

And she heard, or thought she heard, the nasal voice of Silver Lips whisper, 'It is her, I tell you. I saw a picture of her on the news, and I remember thinking how gorgeous. Poor kid, after that, no wonder.' Jack Gruening said, 'Here we go, Alix,' dropping a yellow in her palm, extending a Dixie cup. Why she needed the flight crew's friendship she wasn't sure, but she knew, absolutely, with no ifs-ands-or-buts, that she needed to be buddies with all present, so she held a hand to her oesophagus, forcing down the yellow. Bitterness stayed on her tongue.

'Good girl,' said Jack Gruening.

'Ever been to an Episcopal funeral?' she asked.

Wiry hairs grew above the squash-spoon nose. He said, cautiously, 'Yes.'

'Do they last long?'

'Not too. But Catholic's shorter.'

'Do they say psalms?'

'Resurrection and certain life, that's all I can remember.'

Alix nodded.

They were leaving for lunch at PimPam, the new restaurant in the mall, when Philip called. 'I've arranged for the plane,' he said. Dan drove Beverly to the airport, his hands white on the wheel, the speedometer hovering at seventy-five as he wove in and out of freeway lanes. Beverly sat forward in her seat. Her face was pale, her soft mouth set.

'Buzz, an experience like that, she's distraught. It's normal. Why build it into a crack-up?'

Beverly said nothing. She kept wondering why this drive seemed inevitable. It wasn't until they came to the cemetery, a white mausoleum spilling a fountain down green, tree-dotted hill, that she understood.

'Jamie,' she murmured.

'What?'

'Jamie's there.'

Dan glanced at her. 'This is not your fault.'

'In a way, yes.'

'You are in no way guilty of this one.'

'I feel like it's inevitable, like a Greek tragedy, like I've been on this road since I met you.'

He made a growling noise. Exasperation. He did not, however, put it into words.

She said, 'There's a kind of pattern. If I hadn't left Philip, Jamie wouldn't have been killed. And Alix would have been more – more stable.'

'What makes you so sure?'

'There's no way of untangling one from another.'

'Not if you like stringing coincidences, no.'

Beverly watched through the windshield. 'There're families that're healthy, content. Nothing bad seems to happen to them.'

'So?'

'Then there're others. Tragedy keeps coming at them. One thing after another. Like the Kennedys.'

'The Kennedys're in the limelight.'

'Maybe other families get into God's limelight.'

Dan swerved impatiently around a slow Ford. 'You go on like this, crazy, how can you help her?'

'Sunday she was too normal, you know that. I knew it. But since Philip, since us, she won't let me near her. I couldn't help her. Dan, it's all the same thing.'

'Then how does this Cooke nut fit in? He's a stranger.'

God moves in His wondrous way to torment those on His list, Beverly thought. The cords on her neck stood out. She didn't try further explanation. She couldn't. Her explanations went onto canvas. (Two years later, when she had the show at the Museum of Modern Art, a critic wrote: *Schorer's Scenes of Madness have relevance for all of us. Her eerie cityscapes crackle with a terror where sanity is not possible. Her figures intrude in tentative, sinuous lines, as if aware of their eventual fate. No existentialist – and perhaps here lies Schorer's greatest current appeal – she shows madness as a God-linked chain of cause and effect. As if to remind us, in the left-hand corner of the exhibit's largest, most vigorous work, she has paraphrased Aeschylus: pain falls drop by drop upon the human heart, and against our will comes madness to us by the awful grace of God.* Her reviews for the most part were excellent. Whenever the critic included a reference to her personal tragedies, Beverly would send off a hurt note of protest. She was only too aware that she had, as artists must, used her own suffering. And, far worse, Alix's.)

They swerved off the freeway. Dan, forced to slow by traffic lights on Century Boulevard, reached for her hand. 'Buzz, in the war I saw guys go into shock. They snapped out of it. She'll be fine.' Nonetheless, as he drove between huge airport hotels and non-commercial airstrips, he prayed. Beverly knew better than to plea-bargain with God. A United jet roared so low that one could see passengers looking down, and Dan turned into a wide alley between hangars. And there was Philip, waving.

Dan jerked to a halt. 'Call me,' he said.

Not answering or saying goodbye, Beverly left her door open, running to her ex-husband.

'Phil, where is she?'

'Still in the Vancouver airport.' Philip's voice was under tight control. 'We're ready, come on.'

3

And He shall reign forever and ever/and He shall reign...

Music came, disembodied, from nowhere that she could discover in this closetless motel room suspended above duty-free china and perfumes and toys and sweaters and liquor. People clustered, and she saw her father and mother, foreshortened, hurrying, disappearing beneath her. Father entered first. Mother hesitated at the door. She wore a nice-fitting silk dress, cream and pink stripes, with her pearls coming under the collar.

'You look terrific, Mother.'

'Thank you.'

'Truly. Except for one thing. The pearls should be out.'

Mother bent her neck, adjusting the double strand.

'Perfect,' Alix said. 'Why'd they ask me to stay up here?'

'The terminal is crowded,' Father replied.

'Hey, here you are, the two of you alone. Risqué.'

They talked quietly at her and she turned, staring down into the airport. An old lady dragged a cheap-looking suitcase with a strap around it. Why doesn't someone help her, Alix thought. The woman put down her case, pushing it, agonizingly, with her laced oxford. To draw someone's attention – to get the old woman help – Alix rapped on glass.

Click.

The small treble reached, pulling at the cramp in her chest, and she almost cried the pain aloud. The ring. Of course, the ring. She yanked. Her knuckle halted gold briefly, then it lay in her palm.

'Roger,' she explained, 'lent me this.'

Mother said, 'Gave.'

'For God's sake, Mother, don't touch me! DO NOT! I've got to get it back to them.'

Father said, 'I'm sure he meant you to keep it.'

'It wasn't his. It belonged to his grandmother, no-no, his great-grandmother, and her will states for family only. Like the funeral.'

Mother's eyes, huge questioning ambers.

'It was today,' Alix said.

'I didn't know.' Father.

'It wasn't in the paper,' Alix said. 'One of those cosy family affairs.'

Her parents looked at one another, and for a moment something hovered between them that Alix could understand. Pain.

'I'll return it to the Reeds,' Father said.

'Uhh, I think Vliet,' Alix said. 'It's possible, though, he's booked up today. The funeral.'

'He'll find time,' Mother said in a hard tone that was alien to her.

'Beverly,' Father said. 'Alix, hon, come along.'

He didn't push or pull or touch, he guided by putting out a hand to point the direction. 'This way,' he would say, or, 'Through here,' or, 'Out of that door.' They came to a trim white plane.

'A private jet?' she asked.

'It belongs to a friend of mine,' Father said.

'Wow. Class. Who?'

'Kenny Broders. I wrote you about him, we did the Ensenada race together.'

As the Lear Jet took off, she decided that the music tinkled on a less painful note. 'I'm getting a freebie back to Los Angeles,' she said. 'Oh, and I took a paperback from the airport, LAX, I must've left it on the other plane. Father, could you please pay for it?'

'Sure.'

'Think we could radio Vliet to meet us?'

'That's a fine idea,' her father said, disappearing into the cockpit.

Alix was sitting on the floor and her mother was on the couch. 'I think it was easier for you,' Alix said.

'What, darling?'

'Oh, you know. There was none of this free choice. You didn't have all these decisions. You never would've gone off to Baltimore with Father, would you? Openly and un-wed? Grandma Frances would've set the dogs on you both.' Alix heard herself laugh. 'And look at Dan. He never slept over until after he married you, veddy proper. Veddy committed. Oh, maybe a few beatniks, or what-ever you called them then, they wouldn't get married, but ordinary girls like me – I would've married Roger and had babies, he wanted babies. That's all you did. You didn't think or question. You just went ahead and had husbands and babies.'

'Roger loved you very much,' Mother said quietly. 'He told us.'

'He wanted to get married. But now it's called a trap. No-no. I wasn't afraid of being trapped. The truth is, I was afraid of losing him, and that I couldn't bear. He wanted us to be, though, so we were going to. This Thurs-day.'

'You were?'

Alix nodded. 'And today's Wednesday, and he's being buried. That makes me right, huhh?'

Mother moved to a seat nearer her. Alix shifted to the other side of the plane. So as not to offend, she said, 'It's me. I've got this thing.'

'All set.' Her father was back. 'They're phoning him from the airport.'

'What if they can't get in touch?'

'They will.'

'If?'

'I explained this was urgent.'

'Maybe they have bigger urgencies.'

'Hon, they're doing it.'

'I've got this compulsion thing.'

So he went forward again.

As the plane shuddered, braking in descent, she decided to fix herself. Yet. What if she lost the ring?

'Wear it, why not?' Mother suggested.

'Hey, clever,' Alix said, slipping on the ring. The toilet was tiny and mirrored all the way around and she used eye make-up and struggled with her hair. Airport wind had tangled it beyond comprehension. She was still pulling her wide-tooth Kent comb when Father rapped. 'Alix, you need a seat belt.'

'Am I passable?' she inquired, anxious.

'Beautiful,' Father said.

'Beautiful,' Mother echoed, faintly surprised.

And Alix peered through a dust-laced window. 'It's not the regular landing strip. Vliet won't be here.'

Father said, 'He knows.'

'In that case I've been stood up.'

'Alix,' Mother soothed, 'he's here.'

'In hiding,' Alix said, but as the plane taxied, she saw him, the jacket of his black suit flapping to show oyster-pale lining, his hand at pale hair that blew. She fidgeted by the door as steps were wheeled over, then – although the rungs were out of kilter – she hurried down, stopping a yard short of him. His dark glasses were mafioso eyes, impenetrable, sinister.

'Alix,' he said.

'So they tracked you down.' Keep it light.

'The control guy called,' he said. 'Then Dan.'

'Dan?'

'Your father asked him to.'

'Philip Schorer asked something of Dan Grossblatt? I must be in a bad way.'

'I think not. He sounded sore as hell.'

A 707 shook and roared its landing path, unloading that awesome music like poison gas over them.

'I'm sorry,' she said. Loud.

'No sweat.'

'Hold out your hand.'

His palm came up, the fingers forming a cradle. She

peered at dark crimson with old diamond chips that formed a star, and quickly pulled it off. She extended her arm, dropping the small, warm weight into Vliet's hand.

He was holding it between thumb and forefinger. His nails shone. 'Yours,' he said.

'No way.'

'Every way.'

'You were the one who explained the rules. Female descendants.'

'In this case –'

'Please, Vliet. Don't make this only impossible. That's why we got you here.'

He dropped the ring in his pocket.

'Hey. Forever and ever,' she sang. 'On the plane I did that, and they figured I was losing control. But you hear it, too, don't you?'

'Constantly is all.'

'Then why do they act like I'm a squirrel? It bugged me, keeping the ring. It's weird, in Chalet Gourmet we were talking about ... I forgot what I was going to say. I didn't get to go to Jamie's, either.'

'What?'

'I never said goodbye to my brother, either.'

Vliet's face tensed, reddening as if he were lifting a great weight. 'Alix,' he said slowly, 'what was in the coffin, it wasn't Roger.'

'Pumped up with silicone and all rouged and awful. Grandpa was like that. But I needed to.'

'Alix, I am sorry.'

'I shouldn't be putting this on you. Why did you want to hurt me, you know, about the funeral?'

His teeth showed in a funny little grimace of humiliation, and a United DC-7 tore apart the sky. He raised his arms for her.

'DON'T!' she yelled, then formed a quick smile. 'Sorry. But I seem to have developed this morbid dread.'

'The body contact?'

'Yes. Vliet, why'd they have to cut him there?'

He shook his head.

'You still have it in your pocket, don't you?'

He fished in his pants, showing her the garnet.

She nodded, clasping her hands around her goose-bumpy arms. 'You put it back?'

He showed her again.

'Know something, Vliet? You did want to hurt me.'

He took off his dark glasses, folding them slowly. 'Alix, there's one thing you should know. I love you. I always have loved you. I never stopped. And mostly, you'll admit, it's been pretty damned awkward. So anything I did, or any way I acted, that's the reason. I love you.'

'Thank you,' she said.

'Come on, let's head for the car. We'll go anyplace you want. What's your pleasure?'

'To die,' she said simply. And looked into his eyes, which were wet and Prussian blue, exactly like Roger's, maybe she said the name, maybe she didn't, but she was pretty sure she said, 'Roger, the thing of it is, I can't make it alone. I've tried, but I cannot.'

It began then.

First she stiffened. Her muscles turned rocklike, as if a gland were secreting a coagulant to harden blood in every vein, each artery and capillary. Her breath, trapped, crowded her lungs, suffocating her. Her nails dug into her palms. Her eyes felt as if they would pop from her skull. She knew she was dying and was grateful. The spasm ended. Everything went loose and she was still alive.

'Oh God,' she whispered, 'please let me off Your hook.'

Vliet's face had crumpled. And she understood what had happened.

'I am so ashamed.' She held both hands over her eyes. 'Ashamed.'

Beverly stepped forward. 'Vliet,' she said quietly, urgently. 'She'll let you help her. Here, put this around her.'

Vliet, with awkward, numb fingers, took the ends of a green blanket. Philip, on the plane steps, watched his remaining child.

(After they got Alix to Neuropsychiatric, Vliet said to Beverly, 'I screwed it up, Mrs Grossblatt. I can't handle this kind of situation.'

'It's been a terrible day for you.'

'Roger could, but I can't.'

'You were fine. It's difficult.'

'For me, impossible.'

And Beverly said, gently, 'You told her you love her.'

'But I do. Always, Mrs Grossblatt. And always I've been unequal to the task.' He turned his back to her. 'She picked the right one of us.'

Beverly patted his shaking shoulders. 'It's all right, Vliet, all right.')

The airport ambulance pulled up. Alix, the blanket knotted over her shoulder, stood erect, singing quietly.

Hallelujah.

Chapter Fifteen

I

'They're English.'

'At this distance, Cricket, you must be able to see it,' Vliet said. 'Old Glory's tattooed across their forehead.'

London, an October morning, raw with high clouds that threatened rain. Sixteen months of trial, testimony, and reporters had passed. Cricket had been in England five months, Vliet less than five hours, and they were passing through Rutland Gate, a Regency square (one of Cricket's favourites) from her basement flat to Hyde Park. The couple whose nationality was under fire had just emerged from a creamy, pillared house. A woman, thin, fortyish, dark-haired, and a man, thin, twentyish, with a dark Francis Drake beard. As Cricket and Vliet watched, the couple clasped hands and swung their arms.

'That's the Union Jack,' Cricket whispered.

'US of A,' Vliet whispered back. 'And my money's on it.'

'Five pence?'

'You're on.'

As the couple sidestepped onto cobbled streets to avoid them, Vliet asked, 'Excuse me, but do you have the time?'

'Around eleven, I think.' The woman smiled, showing too much gum as she delivered up her four words in the flat California accent that Cricket acknowledged as pure, non-regional American.

'Maybe five past,' added the bearded young man. The same accent, but anyway his smile, the smile was a dead give-away. Mother and son.

After a couple of houses, Cricket whispered, 'Oedipal.'

'You mean Oedipal City in Orange County? Those grotty jeans on both of them, the expensive jackets – Cricket, I put them in the artier outskirts of Beverly Hills.'

Cricket gave a delighted giggle and fished in her pea coat. Vliet tossed the silver coin on the back of his hand.

'Heads. Here. Yours.' He gave it back to her.

The sixteen months since the murders had altered Cricket in no visible manner. She never thought to let her bright hair curl in any way other than its wont, she bought her clothes used, her expression remained as guileless. She aimed her Nikon when the mood hit. She still would be accepted in a junior high corridor.

Yet changed she was. To the marrow. How could she not be?

That hot June day had marked her indelibly. And the Henderson trial, as it had become known, had left scar tissue.

The Henderson case lay in time (and notoriety) between the Manson murders and the Patty Hearst mystery. All three touched the same raw nerve. They epitomized terrifying aspects of the young. Unorthodox sexual behaviour, long hair, beards, vegetarianism, heavy drugs, the philosophy of revolution, California, dusty bare feet, love-ins, communal living, and – worse of all – baffling violence for no seeming purpose, material or otherwise. Fear was not the sole province of elders. While the Henderson trial raged, students were refusing rides to long-haired hitchers, so what if they were girls?

A case célèbre. Internationally watched. All over the world, newspapers, magazines, and prime time were jammed with details. No cameras were permitted in the courtroom, so there were a million sketches of Genesis and the three Select involved in the murders. REVELATION's lifestyle translated conveniently into headlines: Occult Rites, Drug-Crazed Killers, Bloodletting, New Sex in Carmel Valley. And into book titles: *Vengeance Is Mine* and *Revelation* so far.

And oh, the victims! A lovely, talented movie actress. RB had been presented with a special category posthumous Oscar for *One Step, Two Step*. Loomis Henderson, weeping, accepted for his star and ex-wife, bringing the Academy, always sentimental, to their feet in silent, tearful tribute. The other two victims were almost as juicy. A young doctor with the unique qualities of being a twin and belonging to Los Angeles society, who had lived with his beautiful fiancée. (Alix was described variously as daughter of wealth, tragedy-prone, heiress, child of a well-known woman artist, and currently institutionalized.) It was Lance Putnam, however, in his dual role as murderer and victim, who received the most serious attention. Hannah Arendt's article on him in *The New Yorker* was widely quoted. Sociologists and psychiatrists used Putnam as an example when writing of the phenomenon of those who willingly turn over their minds to a charismatic madman.

During the trial Genesis retained immense dignity. Under oath he testified that he had committed no crime. He was, he stated, the instrument of Higher Justice. And after that he remained silent. An Old Testament prophet in a courtroom chair. His followers and co-defendants sat equally silent. The Select, in white, waited on the steps of the courthouse. After the long trial ended and Genesis was sentenced to the maximum penalty, they stood a twenty-four-hour watch, taking turns reciting REVELATION's commandments. This was just after the California State Supreme Court had abolished the death penalty. Therefore Giles Cooke was remanded to the maximum-security adjustment centre in Folsom Prison. The three Select co-defendants went to San Quentin. The Select returned to REVELATION.

Oddly, the media rarely mentioned Cricket, and even then with no detail. Maybe it had to do with those innocent grey eyes, maybe (as she'd always guessed) she was too small-scale to be of interest. Maybe she'd left REVELATION too early. Whatever the reason, she was covered in depth only on her one day of testimony.

Yet escape she could not.

And there was the major change in Cricket. She no longer lived in the present. The past was with her. They came to her, the quick and the dead. Orion would claw his beard, smiling worriedly at her, or RB would yawn and raise thin white arms. Roger spoke from years of boyhood and sweet young manhood. Genesis, too, came. (About once a week Cricket mailed a blue-tissue aerogram to Folsom: Genesis never replied.) She would receive Vliet, shaken and white, his clothes stained with his brother's blood. The most dread visitor, though, was Alix. How could this be beautiful Alix? This inert creature bloated in fat, the face red-spotted and dead under layers and layers of fat. The only alive part of Alix, fingers like fat moles burrowing incessantly into a loose shift. 'It's the drugs, luv,' Caroline had said, hurrying Cricket away.

Thank God, though, London protected her. Memories didn't come here that often.

They had reached Hyde Park.

'Incredible,' Vliet said.

'Soccer, you mean?' On their left was a field with men in shorts running and kicking with red, strong legs.

'No. Me. My first day in Europe and what am I doing? Racing through sub-Arctic weather to feed – for Chrissake – ducks.'

'Here people walk and talk in parks. It's civilized. But I guess I should've arranged for two seats on that overheated American Express tour.'

'One thing we don't need, Cricket, is the family high horse.' Vliet paused, cupping his hands to light a filter tip. 'Honest, feeding ducks is beautiful.'

At the Serpentine she opened a crumpled brown sack, breaking stale ends of Hovis. Waterfowl wedged through gun-metal water. Vliet, with his fluid grace, squatted, reaching bread to a pair of swans. His hair was longer now, coming over the collar of his black leather jacket. Wind shivered the silky blond strands, then each settled in its preordained place. That hair, that hair was too much. Cricket wanted to kiss it.

He stood, brushing at crumbs. 'The glacial age never ended here.'

'It's not that cold.'

'It's freezing is all. Cricket, think that place is open?'

'Sure.'

And they walked around the lake to a modern pavilion. The place was almost empty. A bespectacled woman sloshed hot milk from a tin pitcher into their coffees, which they carried to curved plastic seats. Vliet drained his, grimacing.

'I can afford,' he said, 'to waste a few days of my well-earned vacation. But Cricket, to live here?'

'What other place has what London does?'

'Bad food is available anywhere, and anywhere you find girls fed on cheap sweets they're as lumpish. Moscow has an equally lousy climate, East Berlin as many ruins, Tokyo is as overcrowded, and Harlem –'

'You've been here before. Why come again?'

'Drink up, Cricket. Or is the idea for me to get brucellosis alone?'

The counterwoman wiped mugs and, it seemed to Cricket, watched them.

'Actually, coffee's better with hot milk than with cream.'

'Ackshly,' he mimicked. 'What's the matter? Forgotten the president's English?'

'You could've gone direct to the Georges Cinq.'

'London has a certain amenity.'

'You just said –'

'Imported from California.'

Blushing, smiling, she felt herself move on the seat. And she thought of a puppy wagging its tail with frantic joy. Vliet was grinning openly at her. She looked at the pale skin on her cup and drank. Normally London's white coffee resembled a hot malted to her. This morning it was gritty and tasted of scalded milk.

Lacing the fingers of both hands, stretching his long arms, he said, 'Better haul ass back to the Hilton. My friend, doubtless, is awake and dying to ride that over-heated American Express bus.'

'Friend?'

'A stewardess. On the plane we realized deep mutual interest. She's never seen London. I'm not up to the moral victory of freezing alone. We're having dinner. You, me, her. At Mirabelle's.'

'I can't.'

'A date? Cancel.'

She shook her head.

Five minutes later he asked, 'Big deal?' They were walking beneath autumnal branches towards Park Lane.

Not replying, she kicked through dead leaves. He let the matter drop. Even if she hadn't been going to a party in South Kensington with Herbert Kuznik, she would have declined. Not jealousy. She never had been able to work up spirit against Vliet's girls, lovely, amiable, and ephemeral as mayflies. So why, she wondered, kicking her way through sodden leaves, was the thought of facing an ephemeral lovely too depressing to bear?

After she left Vliet the thought of the thing in South Kensington depressed her, too. She went into a red phone booth, dialling Herbert Kuznik's bed-and-breakfast, asking a Liverpudlian accent of indeterminate sex to inform Mr Kuznik that Miss Matheny couldn't make the party tonight. She wouldn't see Vliet and she couldn't see Herbert. What sort of sense did it make? And what was the difference? This was like it was.

The following morning she was examining some proofs. Rain spat at the high windows that showed only the lower half of people. Her bell gave its harsh grate.

'Come on, Cricket,' Vliet said. 'Buy you elevensies.'

Rain slanted in icy lines. They bent their heads, hurrying past terraced red-brick houses, ducking into an Old Brompton Road snack bar that smelled of wet clothes and coffee. At the counter a pair of girls talked soberly of David Cassidy.

Vliet shook his hair and took off his coat, ordering, 'Two teas, two toasts.'

'Just tea, please,' Cricket said.

'This is my breakfast,' Vliet said. 'My friend's catching up on her jet lag. And while we're on the subject, what's with your sex life?'

Cricket played with her spoon. In London she was wandering through her usual existence with her usual type of men. Herbert Kuznik was a good example. She had

440

met him two weeks ago at the Wimpy bar on Oxford Street. He was alone, eating a Wimpyburger, hunched over *London from A to Z*. Squarish of mind and body, a sophomore from the University of Arizona, Herbert was sweating out his year's sentence of obligatory drop-out.

'Caroline's panting to hear.'

'Nothing permanent,' she said.

Vliet burst into laughter. The David Cassidy fans turned, approving him with green-rimmed eyes.

'Cricket, oh Cricket. That is a one-night stand. One-night stands aren't the message to take the boss's wife.'

Tea and toast arrived. He took a bite, gazing thoughtfully at her.

He said, 'About Thanksgiving.'

'They don't have it here.'

'They have Guy Fawkes Day. Now will you listen?' He held out a toast triangle. She shook her head. 'Go on,' he said. 'It's safe. Those buns I wouldn't trust, but in my *Fodor* I read English bread is absolutely safe.'

'Vliet,' she whispered, 'they can't tell you're kidding. Stop the Ugly American, please?'

'We're talking about Thanksgiving,' he said. 'Cricket, think of the food. There'll be sweet potatoes, and Ma will tell us she put in orange juice, butter, and sherry and can anyone tell they're canned? And string beans with blanched almonds. Oh, and let's not forget the creamed onions. And the acres of pickled watermelon rind. Ever notice nobody eats watermelon pickles? They take them to leave on their plate. And the noble bird itself, from Van Vliet's, a hen, golden, bursting with oyster stuffing.'

'You're nostalgic.'

'If there's one thing I never am, it's nostalgic. And to prove it, we'll have a minute's silence for the vodka going down Ma's throat in the kitchen. For Chrissake, Cricket, you tell me how anyone can be nostalgic for the looks on reactionary Dad's and liberal Gene's faces as they talk Watergate? And Caroline talking to keep them from talking, and saying she won't eat this and this and this.' With a graceful movement he gathered sugar and cruet in his arms as if hoarding a feast. 'Think of Grandma calling me Roger and you Em.'

Cricket sighed.

'Better,' he said. 'Much better. Far from home, one should mourn one's native festivals.'

Don't do this to me, Cricket thought. She poured milk into her tea. It turned putty-grey, and when she drank, it was cold. She had caught on to what Vliet was doing. She knew him as well as she loved him. Don't do this, she thought. Please. I can't go home.

Chewing on his last triangle, he glanced at his flat gold watch. 'At the Royal Festival Hall tonight they're doing Haydn's *Nelson Mass* with, they say, a two-hundred-and-fifty-voice chorus. You come along and count.'

'I'm busy.'

'Again?'

'It's a two-night stand.'

Laughing, he reconsulted his watch. 'Even she must be up by now.'

'Don't you like her?'

'Should I?'

'For me it's sort of imperative.'

'That, you'll outgrow.' Tossing silver on the counter, he paused behind the two girls, dropping a hand on a shoulder of each. 'I couldn't help overhearing. I happen to be a very close personal friend of David Cassidy, and you're right. He does have integrity, charisma, and smashing honesty. He's the musical genius of our time. There's one problem, one tiny problem is all. Ackshly, he's a thirty-five-year-old female impersonator.'

The girls goggled, then giggled, and one cried, 'You Americans!'

Cricket watched him stride past Harrods, tall above Britishers. The rain had stopped. Shifting clouds bared a crescent of blue, but it would rain again. She should go right home. Instead, she walked among the hatted, gloved, heavy-coated crowds. Winter, she thought, balling her hands in her pockets. The memories were coming at her, fast, in double exposures.

I can't go back to California.

I can't. Her nose was red at its Van Vliet tip, and she walked faster, into a side street. At Rutland Gate she saw the American couple. Today, though, they were a threesome. An older man, bald, managed to open a *Paris Herald* against the wind. She heard him say something about the A's. Passing, she said, 'Hi.' The woman smiled. The bearded young man said, 'Hey there, again,' reddening as he lurched on an uneven cobble. The A's? Sure, she thought, it's World Series time. The A's. Oakland. But who was Oakland playing? Her eyes filled with tears, so much did she yearn to know. She turned to ask. The threesome was disappearing into No. 16.

She felt utterly alone, cut adrift. An exile. Which, of course, was precisely how Vliet intended her to feel.

2

By three o'clock her nose felt tight, her throat raw. 'I haven't had a cold since I got here, so I'm due,' she said to Herbert Kuznik when she cancelled a second time. Around four, rain started again. At five-thirty, there was a knock at her door. Barefoot, tightening her robe, she answered. Vliet. Rain dripped into the hollowed stone at the threshold, and silently across the puddle he handed her a bag of Rosarita tortillas.

'Where'd you get them?' she cried. 'There's none, even at Harrods.'

He came in, taking off his raincoat. The kitchen, which was the entry, once had been used for coal storage and was paved, low. He had to bend.

'It's like this, Cricket. I made a pilgrimage to Westminster, praying long at the tomb of St Esteban de Enchilada, and –'

'Fortnum's?'

'Caroline put 'em on a plane. I took 'em off.'

'You called her? Went to the airport?'

'No need to sob.' He crossed her narrow room to sit on a lumpy couch which opened into a lumpier bed – a PutYouUp, the landlady called it.

'Who's in the Series?' Cricket asked.

'What does that have to do with the price of tortillas?'

'Mind?'

'Oakland and the Mets,' he said. 'We forgot the pies, Cricket. French apple, pumpkin, and mince with lattice pastry on top. And this should please you. Ma's given up on Dream Whip and we're back to the real thing.' He rubbed his palms together. 'Christ, this place is cold. We'll find you something plusher.'

'Like the Hilton?'

'You're not dense, Cricket. How come I'm not getting through?'

'You are,' she said clearly. 'Vliet, I can't go back.'

'Why?'

'I'm happy here.'

'Really.'

She sat on the floor, extracting a Kleenex, blowing her nose.

'Let's hear it again for happiness,' he said.

'I'm ...'

'Come on. Say it again.'

'Until you came I was. No. Not really. I mean ...'

'What do you mean, Cricket?'

She massaged her ankle. 'Home, I kept thinking, all the time thinking. It wasn't guilt.' She sighed. (Guilt affected only matters concerning their son.) 'I couldn't escape. The trial dragged on and on.'

'We have television and papers in Seattle, Cricket. I testified longer than you did, Cricket.'

'But I knew those people. Magnificat, Bethesda, Celestial. It got very bad. I'd be driving someplace and forget where I was going, and there I'd be, on the Pasadena Freeway, heading for Mrs Putnam's. Or on Pacific Coast Highway. Mr Henderson lives in Malibu. He was very broken

up, more than Mrs Putnam. Of course he's old and sensitive, a director and all. Mostly, though, I'd be at Beverly's.
She put up with me. Sometimes she'd get to painting and
forget I was there. Her face is like an El Greco madonna,
all grief and beauty. Steel and sorrow. I mean, how could
anyone live through two murders? Two!' Cricket pulled
out a tissue, not using it. 'Before I left, they let me visit
Alix.'

'They did? How come you never said anything? How
was she?'

Closing her eyes, Cricket saw frantic mole fingers.

'That bad?'

'She's very fat. And quiet. Mother says it's the drugs.'
Cricket paused. 'Poor Beverly. Think how terrible it must
be for her. She's so gentle. And a fantastic painter. Did
you know she's having a big exhibit at the Museum of
Modern Art next spring?'

'And so much for Beverly Picasso's career.'

'Anyway, in Los Angeles, I couldn't escape. And when
I got here, I felt better.' Cricket had a couple of old Brace
Ridge friends who lived in Chelsea, and with them had
figured that on her trust income she could manage.

'And in London you're doing fabulous?'

'At least it's not being pushed on me the whole time.'

'A question, then. Why did you hang around when the
shit was flying? And now it's over, take off? Want to
know what I think? When the trial was on, Cricket, you
could run around and beat your chest remorsefully or play
ministering angel to the bereaved. But now things've
quietened down, there's nothing left for you to do except
atone. And that's what you're doing. Paying your nego-
tiable penance. That's the way I see it, Cricket. You've
pulled on a hair shirt. And you refuse to take it off, even
though it's become quite smelly.'

She said nothing.

He struck a match. 'Ever thought,' he asked over the
flame, 'what your being here does to Caroline and Gene?'

'They said it was fine.'

'They say everything you do is fine, and you know it.

You're hurting them, Cricket, and in a goddamn stupid way.'

Cricket blew her nose more violently than was called for. After a minute Vliet went into the kitchen, running himself a glass of water. The tap was slow.

'That was below the belt,' he said. 'I'm sorry.'

'Are they really hurt? Am I being cruel?'

'You don't have it in you.'

'No, tell me.'

'Cricket, you flunk cruelty.' He turned off the water. 'Listen, I can take the way SOBs stare like I'm a freak. I can take Grandma calling me Roger. I can take the way Ma hovers over me, so proud I'm a Van Vliet like the big kids. Christ, though, she's on the sauce. Really. And Dad – he's pathetic. Whoever figured losing Roger would hit him so hard? I honestly believe he's quit screwing around. But you wanna know what it is really gets to me?'

'Vliet, don't do this,' she said. 'Not to me.'

He went on. 'I can stand everything, Cricket. Except holidays and birthdays and anniversaries. With her wedding-present silver, bowls and platters and little jars, her good cutwork cloth covered. That food. So damn much food. That much food is obscene. And they expect me to eat and eat and eat and make up for Roger. And since I already said it, there's Gene and Caroline. They have sad eyes, too. So I eat your share. Nothing goes down right. I'm a full-fledged ulcer candidate before my time.' He came back into the room. 'Forget any of that crap about you going into self-imposed exile. You always did live in your own peculiar, honest little world.' He leaned on the sink. 'It's me. Me. Me. Cricket, I cannot eat all that damn stuffing and gravy.'

'Please, Vliet.'

He held up his glass, squinting at her through water. 'God is my witness, I cannot face that Van Vliet's butter-ball turkey alone.'

'Here I'm all right. Pretty much.' Her voice faded.

'Cricket, Cricket. Six thousand miles to say this. I need you to be with me.'

A long silence.

'Look, I fly down for every possible holiday and occasion, and some impossible ones. I'll keep doing it. I'll be with you.'

Down the narrow room he was staring at her, so intently that she could feel her heart, and she thought of their son and the events preceding him. Upstairs, a phone rang. Her lips trembled.

Vliet didn't move, but the expression in his blue eyes changed. A warm look. And something more. Pleasure. As if he'd found the key to an Alfa-Romeo on his chain.

'Okay, I won't push it,' he said.

Why should he? He'd won, and he knew it.

She sneezed three times.

'My limey cousin better take her vitamin C.' He pronounced *vitamin* English-style, the first *i* short, the second long. 'And I better move my tail.'

He phoned for a minicab. And was gone.

She found a George V shilling and pushed it in the meter. Electric coals glowed orange. She sat on the thin rug, warm on her front, her back cold, munching a stale tortilla. From time to time she sniffled. The upper lip protruded wistfully.

She listened to the rain fall on a city that, until two days ago, had been her haven.

3

Vliet kept his promise. He flew home so often that by April Gene was saying, 'Joe McAllister's retiring next year. We better break you in while he's still around.' Joe was one of the old-time market men, he ran the seven Southern California warehouses. This was a big promotion, a challenge, a hell of a lot of work.

Alix had been sprung. It took Vliet three months to find

time (get up the nerve?) to call her.

Vliet kept to the middle of the shabby carpet. The apartment corridor was thick with the non-committal hush that underscores muted television laughtracks. The window at the end of the hall was dirty, uncurtained. All the lonely people, he thought, this is where they all come to, and as his finger pressed down on the yellowing buzzer of 117, he saw, very clearly, a fat Down's syndrome face with crazy lipstick. Make her look okay, he thought, I don't ask for the old spectacular, okay is all.

The door opened.

Slender body in magnificent cut white pants, hair shining and curled at the tips as if blown dry by some hip faggot operator, make-up invisible but present. It was as if tragedy had made Alix aware of her unique gift, as if she now understood her luminous perfection demanded trusteeship. She was, without hyperbole, the most beautiful woman Vliet ever had seen – and he'd searched plenty. Relief exploded in him, she held out both hands, and he took them, kissing her forehead.

'You smell good, too,' he said.

The living-room was ferns, wicker, charm, and a ringing phone. Glancing him an apology, she answered.

'Sure ... No-no, not tonight ... Mmm, sad. Sounds fun. ... Six tomorrow? Fine, Vic ... Yes, here ...'

Vliet noted a desk with books. Alix, still on the phone, pressed the rolltop. The desk rumbled shut.

After she hung up, he asked, 'What's that you're hiding?'

'A mess. I'm working on a paper. Didn't Cricket mention UCLA?'

Cricket, who saw Alix, had. 'Full time?' he asked.

'Pretty much.' And the phone rang. As far as Vliet could tell, she made three dates in five minutes. So much for all the lonely people.

Leaving down the drab hall, he asked, 'Not to get personal, but have you considered someplace newer?'

448

'First, it's near Beverly Hills and UCLA. Mother feels more secure if I'm nearby. Second of all, it's cheap. And third, the rooms are good-size, and if there's one thing I cannot stand after being in hatches, it's small rooms.'

'Real finesse,' he acknowledged. 'I haven't heard a crack-up handled so beautifully since my first Sutherland *Lucia*.'

They ate in the Rathskeller in Westwood, surrounded by others in the uniform of casual chic. They drove along Pacific Coast Highway. By the time they neared Malibu, they had talked, briefly, about her stay in Mount Sinai. 'I was stuffed with Thorazine and soggy coffee cake. I weighed in at one ninety-eight when I left.' And Pleasant Elms. 'I went on a diet.' He told her of his job, riding assistant herd on Van Vliet's warehouses, playing down his hard work. He pulled into the Malibu pier parking.

'Buy you a drink,' he said.

'Let's walk.'

So they moved along the dark pier, listening to the hollow crash of waves beneath them. She put her arms on the rail.

'It's been easy,' she said.

'Why the surprise? Isn't it always with us?'

'I was terrified. Vliet, I did crack in front of you.'

He didn't care to open that can of worms. He lit a cigarette.

'It bothers you, my saying that?'

'You never were one for confessionals, Alix.'

She stared down. Breakers roared, ghostly white.

'Dr Emanual says I must be more open with my feelings.'

'You've still got a shrink?'

'One that looks like a lizard.'

'Ahhh. You haven't reached the transference stage.'

'Not yet.' She laughed.

'Openly then, Alix. How do you feel about the date you made with the first joker?'

'Sincere.'

449

'Too sincere to cancel?'

'It's Vic. One of Dan's sons. They're in for a month – they live with his first wife in Rome. Vic's eighteen. No-no. Nineteen.'

'Do you confine yourself to foreign adolescent stepbrothers?'

'Absolutely.'

At her khaki-drab front door, he put his arms around her. She pushed at his chest with her palms, breaking free. 'That's the trouble with the world today. Everything's rush-rush.'

'It's called instant gratification.'

'Never touch the stuff.'

'Then, Alix, you're out of step.'

'Sure I am. You're with a certifiable corkscrew.' And rising on her espadrilles, she kissed his cheek.

In the cool, rarefied atmosphere of rejection, she had managed – with well-known Schorer charm – to shift the onus from rejected to rejectee. From any other girl he would have accepted it, figuring next time, babe, next time. But walking down the long, dingy hall, he muttered, 'Frigid bitch,' aloud, remembering how often he had left her with these words on his lips. The front door was inset with a stained-glass mermaid. You can't step into the same river twice, you can't relive the past. Roger was dead. Alix the same all-American tease. His policy of forget-what-can't-be-helped applied here. Vliet was not given to dramatic gestures, yet pausing in the streetlight, he flipped through his little black book (gold-cornered Gucci) to S. He crossed and recrossed through her name and number.

Alix sat on the edge of her tub, her back straight, her muscles stiff. She heard his Mercedes start and fade into the night. For five minutes she was motionless. Then she stood in front of the mirrored door, looking at herself. At the worst times she had seen nothing in mirrors. Now a girl stared at her with dark, frightened eyes. Was this what other people saw? She lifted her hand, examining the reflected wrist. The hand in the mirror shook.

Turning away, she unbuttoned her jacket, giving it a little shake, examining collar and cuffs for any line however faint to indicate a trip to the cleaners. None. Meticulously she placed shoulder seams to padded hanger. She arranged her pants, cuff to cuff. She hung jacket and pants on the hook above the mirror. Tying back her hair, she washed her face then peered, examining her eyebrows. Continents might shift if one unplucked stub remained.

In bed, propped up on her pillows, she opened her bedside drawer. Always a list maker, Alix had incorporated into her night routine, no matter how late it was, a noting of items to discuss the following morning. She saw Dr Emanual each weekday at eight. Along with the pad, she inadvertently fished out an earlier note (she saved them compulsively) written in a large, unfamiliar hand: *why always blood? isn't death the ultimate desertion?* The big letters wobbled crazily.

She pushed the scrap far into the drawer, writing in her usual neat hand:

> *it was a mistake to tell him i was terrified. i almost left the apartment a half hour before he was due, but forced myself to wait. lizard, does that earn me a gold star?*
>
> *why couldn't i let him kiss me?*

She sat among the pretty flowered pillows questioning the evening. Alix, vigilant. She might walk and talk like others, but she knew she was not like them. Once you lose your footing, once you've slipped into the crevasse, you never can escape the black ice.

Eventually she folded her list. She waited for sleep.

4

Under taut hospital linen, her body had dragged her into the safety of sleep. Food and sleep, that was what she needed.

Always she was empty. When her trays arrived, she would lift the covers: she, who always had been delicate, grabbed with fingers, dribbling down her hospital smock. Finishing, she would reach for a snack. She would find bear claws sticky with sugar, or a box of stale vanilla wafers, or Twinkies, or a pair of bran muffins bridged by a neat square of butter, or See's chocolate softened by warm hospital air. It didn't matter. Food was not for taste. Food was for the emptiness.

She got to know her ceiling. The chaotic soundproofing squares sagged like wet patchwork.

Once – fluorescent tubes held back the ceiling and therefore it was night – her mother wept. Warnings floated around Alix. Terrified, she didn't dare move on her barred bed. She watched amber eyes and twin trickles. Then the lights cracked and the ceiling gave way, oozing red. Alix screamed and screamed and screamed, frantic to make someone understand that the holes were leaking blood.

And after that the ceiling tormented her.

And after that, she didn't know whether it was the same week or month or year or century, Dr Emanual came. A voice lacking condescension and a saurian mouth. Dr E-lizard-ual. Lizard. He had understood her. He had protected her.

I can't sleep with him, I cannot.
Did he suggest it?
No-no.
Then why is it a problem?
I like him. That's brilliant, isn't it? I like him and am

terrified of sleeping with him. Or anyone. Don't you think we're wasting Father's money?

You're my star patient.

Sure.

Why must you demand so much of yourself? We've made progress, so much progress. It's taken tremendous courage on your part to get this far.

(Long silence.)

In high school, sometimes before I went to sleep I'd have this fantasy. I was living in another time.

What other time?

Oh, not real long ago.

Your mother's time?

When she was in school, yes.

Why then?

You want me to say I was jealous and unresolved about her? But isn't that a mite obvious?

Or too difficult to deal with?

No-no. But in the forties sex was taboo.

(Dr Emanual chuckled.)

Shrinks aren't meant to laugh, Lizard. It was more programmed then. You know, there were codes.

Does it reassure you to believe people lived by the Hayes Office?

That's not the point.

What is the point?

She didn't have to. When she didn't, nobody hated her.

Are you saying Vliet hates you, Alix?

Yes. Now he hates me. Maybe he always did.

From what we've discussed, I'd say the reverse was true.

You didn't see the way he bolted down the hall, leaving me. Oh God!

Is how he feels so important?

You know how everybody feels about me is important. This especially.

Why?

I told you. I like him. For God's sake, he's Roger's brother.

Alix, I want you to think about this. You've character-

453

ized last night as threatening. Very. Do you think it's wise to see him again?

Don't worry. He won't call.

He went about his routine. Behind the turreted Assyrian corporate offices built by his great-grandfather were two huge warehouses. Distribution Centres Nos. 1 and 2. They were filled with nine thousand different items to be distributed to seventy-three stores. Currently they were changing over to computer, with the inevitable screwups. Joe McAllister was out with back trouble. Vliet was swamped. He didn't call Alix. Whenever he thought of her, he told himself, Don't call.

Sunday nights he reserved for his parents. The last Sunday in August they went to an Omega Delta alumnae barbeque. Vliet said to himself, what the hell, and got out his little black book. He couldn't make out the crossed-over number. He surprised himself by remembering it.

Alix sounded pleased. She invited him for dinner, that is, if he didn't mind Sam.

'Sam? I think I do mind. Isn't he the one in wholesale blouses?'

'Idiot!' she laughed. 'Sam. My brother.'

Sam opened the door. Skinny, with Chinese eyes, ears that stuck out, and a lot of curly brown hair. Harpo, Vliet thought. What is he? Nine?

Vliet sniffed. 'Pizza?'

'Alix is no peasant. Veal parmigiana.'

And Alix called from the kitchen, 'Fix yourself a drink.'

Bottles sat on the coffee table. 'What's yours?' he called back.

'Scotch for me,' Sam said. 'Alix doesn't drink. She's waiting for NoCal vodka.'

'If you're so funny,' Vliet demanded, 'why don't you have your own talk show?'

The phone rang four times, Sam answered, 'She's in La Jolla.'

The veal was white (unattainable at your local Van Vliet's) and excellently seasoned, accompanied by romaine

454

salad and gnocchi she'd made herself. She sipped the Vouvray he'd brought, absently picking at her food.

Vliet poured her another glass. 'To the pride of Weight Watchers,' he said.

'Food lost its charm after my former debauches.'

'Alix was formerly Godzilla,' Sam said, puffing out his cheeks.

'Why don't you shut up and clear off the dishes?' Vliet asked.

'Alix is the one with waitress experience.'

Vliet laughed, pouring a few drops of wine in the boy's Pepsi. 'I even hate your kid brother.'

Across dirty dishes, Alix smiled. He could compose a million songs about that smile, mysterious, yet the mystery lay in how any smile that perfect of tooth and lip could be mysterious.

Not that they were together every night.

Sundays belonged to his parents. At least three nights a week he remained in his bare office, dining on hamburgers. Family affection among Van Vliets did not reach above a certain managerial level, but what was wrong with that? Here was his Grail. (As Roger had loved medicine, so Vliet pursued a buck.) In the daytime the 275,000 square feet were busy. Conveyor belts carried red plastic baskets and girls packed health-and-beauty items, lift trucks retrieved cartons – canned goods, paper goods, and so on – from thirty feet up. Pallets were stacked according to order sheets from individual stores. Freight trains pulled up to the rear docks. Bananas were hauled from ripening room to ripening room. But at night Vliet would sit alone in his office. He would figure whether it was cheaper to buy Brand X in quantity to inventory (as Joe McAllister preferred doing) or not to get such a good deal but also not to tie up capital. Interest rates were high this autumn. Vliet was aware, very, if this went well, he was one step nearer being chief among the Dutchmen.

Once – he had forgotten an inventory he was going over – he drove back with Alix to the warehouse. She was intrigued by the Spartan offices. No receptionist. A red phone on the wall, and underneath, on plain white paper:

PLEASE DIAL THE EXTENSION
LISTED BELOW FOR THE PERSON
YOU WISH TO SEE.

'Vliet Reed, oh-four-nine,' she said. 'Shall I dial?'

'We're the only ones in the office.'

'Hey.'

'Yeah,' he said, leering.

But he never attempted more than a forehead kiss goodnight. Turandot, Puccini's glacial princess, has asked riddles of her suitors, insoluble conundrums, afterwards impaling their idiot heads on the city walls. Rejection hurts.

Why do you keep on?

We have fun. I like him.

You haven't seen anyone else for two months.

It's called easing back into normal life.

I'll be frank with you, Alix. You should stop.

Why?

He can hurt you.

I don't see how.

You don't choose to see. In your opinion, have you resolved Roger's death?

That, I'll never resolve. No shrink on earth can help me resolve that. You know I still love him.

Let me ask this, then. Have you considered why, of all the men you know, you've selected Roger's twin?

I like him, mind?

He's not Roger. He's much weaker than Roger.

Are you saying I'm acting out?

I'm saying he was never able to accept you for more than your unique surface qualities.

So now he's – God knows – not ready for a freaked-out case?

Does he discuss that aspect?

I told you. Not yet. Is that so bad?

Yes.

Maybe it's my fault. I haven't brought it up. Besides, Lizard, you forgot one detail. Vliet came first.

I'm not forgetting at all.

(A long silence.)

Oh God. How can I be so chicken?

You're brave. Under the circumstances, a little too brave.

I have to reach out. Please, you're meant to help me.

I'm trying to.

Then don't you see how much I need him?

I see two very troubled people who were involved in a trauma they're unable to handle. Justifiably. That doesn't alter the problem. He's not my patient. You are. He and Roger are connected in your mind.

That's obvious.

And you and Roger are connected in his.

I suppose so, yes.

And you don't see the danger?

He resents me and Roger? I doubt if he still could. And if he does, well, I have to risk it. I like him a lot.

That's why I'm asking you to stop. At this point another rejection, or what you inevitably would consider a rejection, could destroy all we've worked for.

5

A white car chased a black car, and Vliet, nursing a brandy snifter, watched. He took his socked feet from the coffee table when Alix returned from stacking her dishwasher. She sat on the couch next to him.

'Which're the good guys?' she wanted to know.

'In the white car.'

'I should've known.'

'What was TV before the car chase?'

She laughed, the white car swerved around a corner, and there was a woman smirking at her brand of margarine.

Alix shifted closer. Vliet could smell her light perfume. French, he decided. She fingered his hand. Christ, he thought, is this a pass? Her touch drifted towards his arm. She looked at him, her lashes gradually closing. He heard a lyrical *My mother never told me about Ultrabrite*, and thought, definitely a pass. Leaning forward, not putting his arms around her, he kissed her. He was aware of phrenetic music of the chase, then paid no attention because her lips were opening and in his ears was a roar as if he were being tumbled in surf, and now he did put his arms about her, easing her back into cushions, nothing planned, mind you, yet how long, oh, how long had he anticipated this moment? The skin, as remembered, a finer texture than silk, more like chiffon, and – he sought under the well-fitted shirt – breasts amazingly delicate yet full. She didn't tense. A distinct improvement. Before, she always had. And he was unbuttoning, unzipping, pulling back clothes. He gave himself over to admiration, half naked, a few strands of shining black hair clinging to her neck, Alix seemed to have arrived from the sea, the foam-born. Venus, for him.

He saw wetness making a path from her eyes to the sides of her hair.

He pulled her clothes together, fastening one button of her shirt. He sat up. Flames rose from the black car. He touched the remote.

'One thing, Alix,' he said. Hurt stuck in his throat like irretrievable celery string, and he gave a small cough. 'I can't be charged with attempted rape.'

She heaved a tremendous sigh and undid the button.

'Believe this or not. Weeping isn't my turn-on.'

She rose, averting her head, hurrying from the room. He heard water. He smoked. She returned, hair combed, clothes in order, sitting on the far end of the couch.

'I'm sorry,' she said. Her hands rested on sharkskin

458

pants. 'I wanted to make contact.'

'Haven't we? The last couple of months?'

'We don't know one another.'

'Biblically speaking, no.'

'We've never talked about Roger.'

'That's bullshit.'

She closed her eyes. She had applied fresh shadow, brown, in a perfect curve. 'We've skidded by his name.'

She loves him, Vliet thought, she did from that first day, she still does. Probably she always will. He could feel it in his gut, that weakness, that grappling of love and hate, that sense of being the inferior, lighter half of a twinship.

'What shall we talk about?' he asked lightly. 'How strong he was? How decent? His interest in medicine?'

'I just want us to be honest, Vliet.'

'Yeah, Roger was high on honesty.' He kept his tone light, and if his words inflicted wounds, well, who had started this? 'Let me guess. Your shrink wants you to define our relationship?'

She nodded.

She's got me in the old psychoanalytic filing system, he thought. Pigeonholing me. With difficulty he went through the mechanics of lighting up.

'Your behaviour passes for honesty,' he said. 'It passes with me, Alix. Maybe not your fabulous medical-research honesty, but adequate for your routine supermarket clot.'

'Do your parents know you're seeing me?'

'As one nears the twenty-eight mark, Alix, one doesn't check in.'

'They don't know.'

'Why should they?'

'And we've never talked about my being crazy.'

'Right off, you dragged in your nervous breakdown.'

'A few sentences. Does that cover eighteen months of insanity?'

Her eyes seemed more intense. The eyes caught him short. Mascara smudged the left. He remembered that nightmare afternoon when he'd failed her under whining jets. The eyes touched him where he hurt. Licking his

459

finger, he leaned towards her, wiping the smudge.

'If talking's what the shrink ordered,' he said, 'fire away, Alix.'

She leaned into the leather couch, staring up. The ceiling was high. Lamps cast fuzzy circles.

'I'm with you,' she said. 'I prefer the surface. Smile and keep safe – does that make sense?' She looked at him. 'No-no. Of course not. Let's see if I can explain.'

She frowned, then nodded. 'In the hospital I ate all the time. The more I ate, the less I was me. That gross body couldn't be me, understand? The fat insulated me from myself. And that's how my personality works. The more smiles and easy talk, the less me.'

'Alix, we all cover up. Let a sleeping neurosis lie.'

'Neurosis?' she said. 'I believed they stored blood, whole blood, in the room over mine. I truly believed. The weight made my ceiling droop. I'd hear a noise and think, Now they're getting some to take downstairs to Surgery, or, Now they're doing a dialysis. I mean, I heard them dragging around the aluminium cans. Imagine? After living with Roger, me visualizing blood stored in old-fashioned milk cans! At times the hospital was over-supplied, and then the ceiling would really sag. One night, Mother was there, it started leaking, and nobody would understand. I tried to explain blood was coming down on me. I went berserk. After that they really laid on the stuff. God! Those drugs! They slime your brain, crushing and strangling you, and you're trapped for eternity. I'd hate Roger for getting killed and leaving me. Of course I tried to kill myself, all nuts do, but I miss him so terribly I would've tried, anyway.'

Her tone stayed in pitch. Vliet had an excellent ear. Her tone remained absolutely normal, and it was this contradiction that got him.

'Lizard – that's what I call Dr Emanual – he understood about blood leaking through the soundproofing holes. You know what he did? The sweet ugly man, he borrowed a ladder and taped up sheets of paper, the heavy brown kind they use for packing.'

Her fingers dug into her thighs. Vliet wanted to hold her poor, anxious hands, wanted to soothe them. Instead, he lit up. Some smoker. One puff and he ground out his cigarette.

'He got the connection, you know, the blood. He was where I was at.' And on and on she intertwined *The Terror on Kings Road* (as the latest book on the Henderson case was entitled) with her lunatic phase. Vliet thought of a Bach fugue played on a theramin, background for a horror movie. He shut her out.

'Vliet?'

He blinked to, realizing she was tilting her head inquiringly at him.

'Alix.'

'Have I blown it?'

'What?'

'Us?' she asked.

A blue spiral of smoke drifted from his volcano of bent, discarded cigarettes. 'If that's your mental-health spiel, Alix, you should know I gave at the office.' Very funny. But how long can you keep up this sort of thing without comedy relief?

Her fingers rubbed into her knees. After a pause, she said, 'I, well, I haven't.'

He understood. Sex. He went to pour more Hennessey's.

She said to his back, 'I was remembering the time we last ... Vliet, I couldn't help ... It's only been you and Roger, ever.'

He brought his drink back to the couch.

'You still here?' she asked.

'Does it look like it?'

'I see you, therefore you are.'

'That's the problem in the world today. Everybody's got a simple answer.'

She laughed.

Her laughter reassured him, and he put down the snifter, finally able to take her hands, caressing the fingers, which were rigid, kissing her, gentle, and she

461

pulled his hands, cupping them over her breasts.

'Nice,' he whispered.

She put her arms around him, and he was able to block – neat and complete – all she'd told him. Alix, flawless of mind and body. 'The bedroom,' he said in her ear.

A line from the bathroom flailed her back as she bent, gracefully skinnying out of pants. 'Mind if we have the lamp?' he asked. She switched one on.

And they lay on eyelet-edged sheets. For a nameless time (or so she'd said) this body had been ugly, but he didn't believe it. This incredibly smooth field of light and dark, this passive field he'd been first to conquer never could have been a swollen horror. He wouldn't have it so. Her breasts were nippled with pearly apricot, and there was the gentle rise and fall of a stomach whose flatness was proof positive: if she'd been bloat, wouldn't this torso have stretch marks? The diffused light shone on them, and he entered into the rite of spring – *sacre du printemps* – forgetting he'd had other girls, none of them counted, only this one, and now he shut his eyes, racing into that dark and mysterious cave where he had sojourned before, yet this time was different, for now through her body he was again linked with his brother, his other, he was again part of his brother, Roger and Alix and Vliet, a trinity that denied death, defied death, contradicting past terrors, and he wanted to help her and console her and tell her he loved her, he loved her and Roger, both. Instead, breathing stridently, he pressed her into tangled custom sheets.

After, he smoked, one arm under her neck. He whistled contentedly, and when the cigarette was finished, rolled over to get up. She held his arm.

'You aren't leaving?' she asked.

'I must.'

'Why?'

'It's after twelve.'

'Vliet, stay tonight.'

He moved her hand. The nails were long, the polish perfect. 'I can't, Alix,' he said.

'Please!' Little muscles under her cheeks worked. And it popped into his mind again, that fat, pasty, Down's syndrome face with the lunatic lipstick.

'Some other night,' he said, quickly heading for the bathroom.

He stood in her tub with the shower curtain closed, letting the hot water race on him, rubbing himself dry with a terry sheet that smelled of her. Dressed, he went into the bedroom. Alix, in sheer, loose white, bent over a pillow.

'Then you are leaving?'

'Alix, we just did this number.'

She stared at him, bewildered, as if she'd just woken.

'Tomorrow's a workday,' he muttered, not caring – even now – to discuss how important his job was to him.

She turned down an immaculate triangle in the space he'd recently occupied.

'My clothes are in the apartment,' he said. 'Want me to show up like a regular warehouseman in my Levi's?'

'You could get up early,' she said. But this time she smiled. The lovely smile rescued him. Other girls in other bedrooms had smiled, inviting him to stay over. A courtesy. Please, thank you, stay.

She went to the door with him. Two palsied old folk were attempting to unlock the next apartment, and their frustrated mumbles filled the dim corridor. He traced the line of Alix's lips, feeling her warm, moist breath, running his finger along the ridge that delineated her mouth. He was amazed by the intensity of his urge to hold her. Tomorrow was Wednesday, a workday. He had to leave now. If he held and kissed her, he would stay. Vliet glanced at the ancients. Having triumphed over lock and key, they were watching.

He took a step back, reaching into his pocket, palming nothing into her hand. 'Not that it wasn't fantastic, chick, but we agreed fifty. A hundred's sheer rip-off.'

Alix gave him that luminous smile. 'For Mother it was easier,' she said.

Terrific, he thought. Now that's something for them to

cackle over. He left on the double. Outside, he stood on the steps. The night was damp, cold, and he could see puffs of his breath. A narrow Westwood street with bumper-to-bumper cars, old apartments, and Vliet Reed, motionless. A car swerved into the garage, headlights momentarily drowning him.

He opened the door with the blue-tailed mermaid, moving on silent feet. He stopped at her door.

Hold it, he said to himself.

First, I gotta get things straight in my mind. She's been there and back, and can I cope with a crazy lady? She's in love with Roger. And then, oddly, because he'd never considered this before: do I want her partially because she is in love with him? She's been in the bin, he thought.

A faint rustle. He wasn't certain where it came from, and the sound could be natural to an old building filled with old people, or – just possibly – the sound could be mindless grieving.

Oh Christ. It's too complicated for me. She's always been too complicated for me. Roger could handle it, not me. I'll phone her first thing tomorrow.

He sprinted down the hall, throwing open the door, not bothering to close it, taking the four steps at once, pounding the half block to the Mercedes. He hunched over the wheel. It was several minutes before he was able to negotiate his key into the ignition, and when he turned it, the radio burst forth with Diana Ross and 'Touch Me in the Morning'.

After he left her, she climbed the stairs, no reason except they were there. She felt bruised everyplace, and very heavy, heavier than she'd been in the hospital. Her legs took effort to move. On the fourth, the top floor, she stopped, exhausted, holding onto the window ledge.

This hall smells mousy, like old people, like madhouses, she thought. He left me. Everyone leaves me. For a moment she saw Vliet with unusual vividness, as he'd looked the moment they went into the bedroom, the sharp tip of his nose, the mouth moving forward, then melting

464

into his lopsided smile, one long, graceful hand extending to help her up from the couch. He smiled at me with Roger's eyes. I don't love him, she thought. I need him. How grasping I am, needing but not loving him. Her thighs felt rubbery, and she sat, uncomfortable, on the narrow window ledge. It's dusty, she thought. Why can't they keep this place decent?

She tried to remember again how it had been when she and Roger had made love. Instead, she remembered how he had been cut. Oh God, she thought, and leaned her forehead on cold, smeared glass. Why don't they get curtains, she thought. Outside, a long-winged insect, trapped in a spider's web, had desiccated. With effort, she raised the window, freeing the corpse.

Alix never had asked quarter either for her madness or her grief. She loathed sympathy. (Pity?) Tonight, among the haunting terrors, she had betrayed herself by pleading on both counts. I asked him to stay, she thought, and he cut out.

I'm not crazy, I am not, she thought, and the weight inside her body pulled her to sit again on the window ledge. I'm alone. So is Vliet. We're utterly bereft, yet how is it we're incapable of holding one another, comforting one another? In the path far below, a bare lightbulb exposed a clump of dented dustbins. She looked up at city stars. Small and pale, she thought. Everything's cold and ugly. Suddenly she remembered that Anna Karenina had seen the world's true ugliness before she threw herself under her appointed freight train. *And the candle by which she had been reading a book full of terrible deceit, misfortune, and evil flamed up brighter than ever.* Alix, at the fourth-floor open window, shivering in her thin white robe, staring into the drab night, thinking of terrible deceit, misfortune, and evil, thinking of Anna's suicide.

Chapter Sixteen

I

Dark had fallen on that New Year's Day, 1975.

The country had a new president and vice-president, unelected Republicans, Ford and Rockefeller, the dollar was falling steadily, gold was almost two hundred dollars an ounce, sugar prices soared, and American tourists were no longer the Romans of the earth. Matters critical to Van Vliets. Yet they continued to go securely about their lives.

The clan had watched USC win the Rose Bowl game on four colour TVs spread through the home of Evelyn (Van Vliet) and Sidney Sutherland, the-ones-with-a-Japanese-son-in-law. They had regathered, and candles made a festive glow for sixty loosely related people, some holding plates of cold cuts, others clinking ice in glasses. Children in bright sweaters cut peppermints from a candy pyramid.

At one end of the huge, curving couch sat Em and Sheridan. At these greater Family get-togethers they clung together, Sheridan almost, but not quite, keeping up with Em drink for drink, both of them intent on drawing Vliet close, their rod and their shield. He sat cross-legged at their feet. Four cousins chattered about a recent Family divorce. Cricket, laughing, chucked the fat infant in the lap of Leigh Sutherland Igawa. Ken Igawa, the Sutherlands' Japanese son-in-law, was American-born, an artist, and the Van Vliets were tolerant of his origins and occupation. Comfortable with themselves, they were able to absorb exotica. Ken was trying to get his elder daughter, a pretty child with the Sutherland red hair and carefully set Oriental eyes, to write *Happy New Year*. 'See, Nan, first you make a line.'

Nan drew an uneven circle, dropped the red Marksalot, shouting, 'Grandpa!' trotting off, leaving a trail of peppermint.

'Yeah yeah yeah.' Ken grinned at Vliet. 'All looks, no brains. Your side of the family.'

'Wasps're no less intelligent than any other ethnic group. It's those unfair IQ tests.'

Ken laughed. 'Where's the girl?' he asked.

'Quick. Give me the comeback.'

'It's like this. Without the fantastic stuff, man, you're naked.'

Vliet pretended laughter. The morning after he'd made it with Alix, a foggy October dawn, she had been re-admitted to Mount Sinai's locked floor, voluntarily and briefly, true, but readmitted. It goes without saying he couldn't face her. What surprised him was the extent of his avoidance. He was a case of shell shock. He had no urge for any female companionship. Zilch. *Nada*. Zero.

He saw his mother's pony ankles move together. Primly. Ken's wasn't her type of remark and, besides, she dis-approved of exogamy. Ointment was needed here.

'I'm with my little cousin.'

Ken laughed. So did Bette Van Vliet.

'Hi, little cousin!' Bette waved, rattling half a dozen gold bangles. 'Get over here with your date. You're not his type, but . . .'

'You'd be surprised,' Vliet said. 'She's my small snail.'

Everyone nearby laughed. Everyone, that is, except Cricket. She tilted her head, peering around legs and long skirts at him. In candlelight he couldn't make out her expression.

She blinked and rose, heading – Vliet assumed – for the recently done-over living-room where a few people sang 'Auld Lang Syne', off-key, to a thumping Steinway. In-stead, she echoed across the hall to the dining-room. Vliet was following her, but Sidney Sutherland, at the piano, called, 'Vliet! Exactly who we need.' So Vliet played the Trojan fight song, and alums, Em and Sheridan joining, sang, 'Fi-yut on for o-old Esss Seeee, fi-yut on to vic-toreeeeeee!' Vliet spread his long fingers in a final major chord, saying, 'No applause, no applause until the final curtain.' He moved to the dining-room. On the table remained two half-eaten turkeys, a ham, bowls of relish, salads, fruit. Cricket wasn't in here. He had kept an eye out. She hadn't come back into the hall. Either she was in the kitchen or the breakfast room. He tried the door to the latter.

'Am I disturbing you?' he inquired.

Cricket, not answering, continued to pile round cookies in front of her. Poker chips. On her right hand she wore a child's gold ring with three seed pearls, and on her left forefinger, pale metal soldered to a green stone. Newberry's, Vliet thought.

'Mmmm, let's see. Not talking is on my little cousin's New Year's list.'

'Don't call me that.'

'You're four-ten. Our mothers are sisters.'

'Next time shout family joke number twenty-eight. You'll get the same laugh.'

'Ouch.' He grinned, sitting in the chair opposite. He tapped his left canine. 'Chocolate here.'

Running her tongue over her teeth, she continued stacking cookies.

Vliet played a tune on the table. 'Know it?' he asked.

She shrugged absently.

'What's eating you?'

She looked at him with those serene grey eyes. 'Small snail,' she said.

He'd used the stupid, impromptu nickname in the family room. 'So?'

She kept gazing at him.

He'd said it to her before, a long time ago. But when? Where? Oh shit, he thought. Arrowhead.

'Not funny.' He couldn't look her in the face. He examined her crap green ring. Her hands were child-size, with round nails, unpolished and unevenly filed.

'Come on, Cricket. There've been others, lots of 'em. Whoever.'

'When you're around, we always break up, me and Whoever.'

'You're a big girl now, or so you tell me. Really. Isn't it

468

about time we put this game to rest?'

'You play, too.'

'Each morning I set aside a full hour. Today I must find a new gambit to keep Cricket on a string.'

'Because of you, I'm in Los Angeles.'

'And it's shattering?' he asked. She was currently living at home. She appeared content as ever. 'Is it?'

'Not so bad as it was.'

'Good. However.' He raised his right hand. 'I hereby vow never again to use my powers of persuasion on my cousin, Amelie Deane Matheny, also known as Cricket Matheny.' He gave his amused smile. The lines around his mouth were permanently etched. 'Come on. Let's get back to the party.'

She had a look of despair. She took a deep breath as if she were diving into a tremendous wave and might never come out. She said, very clearly, four words.

'We had a baby,' she said.

A car backfired. Through an open window the sharp sound burst. Vliet, clutching his chest, gasped, 'They got me.' He looked at her. 'Come again?'

'We had a baby.'

'We who?'

'You and me.'

He dropped his cigarette, retrieving it, rubbing ash from polished parquet with his thumb. 'No,' he denied.

'Yes.'

'Where's it at, then?'

'He.'

'Where?'

'Dead.' Her voice shook. 'He's dead.'

'Listen, being shook makes for a certain lack of empathy. Cricket, I'm sorry.'

The splotches of colour that had risen to her cheeks faded.

'Give me a minute, okay?' he said. And stared at the tip of his cigarette. The fall had doused it. At first her words refused to register. Dead. Who? Dead? A baby. A boy. They had made it once – no, two times – he out of pain,

469

she out of love, and nothing new for either, so how could this be true? Empty soft drink crates were stacked along one wall. Reaching out, he dropped his dead cigarette in one. 'How long did it – he – live?'

'About six hours.'

The unhappiness in her whisper cut through him.

'Not even the night,' she said, hunching over stacked cookies, a hand to her forehead.

Any other circumstance and he would have teased her, consoled her, cajoled her, touched her. In the living-room they sang 'Old MacDonald', a ragged children's chorus drifting through closed doors. *With a blurb-blurb here, a blurb-blurb there.* Cricket took her hand from her eyes.

'Dr Porter decided I was too young to stay on The Pill,' she said. 'I hadn't had the coil put in.'

'What would you've done if he'd been okay?'

'I never really thought it through. I was all happy and excited. And you know me. I was worse then. No plans at all. Having him, that's as far as I thought.'

'Keep him, though?'

The soft upper lip curved in surprise.

'No, you wouldn't give any babies away, would you? How did you keep it quiet? And where was he born – That was when you were at REVELATION, right?'

'Yes,' she said.

Vliet's turn to close his eyes. He saw a bearded figure, bloodied sword in hand. Christ, he thought. 'But this didn't come out with the rest of the garbage at the trial.'

'Only Orion and Genesis knew.'

'Orion dead, Genesis never speaking.' Vliet nodded.

'Genesis was different then. He helped me.'

'Other people there must've seen. Known.'

'The baby was seven months. I never got huge or anything. And Genesis asked me not to tell. He has this thing about collecting secrets. Orion guessed, but he was the only one. Vliet, I feel guilty, so guilty.'

'About what?'

'The baby.'

'Why?'

She stared at him, surprised. 'He's dead.'

'But it's not your fault, Cricket.' He paused. 'Why didn't you tell Caroline and Gene? They never would've thrown you out. They would've helped.'

'With a D&C,' she said.

After a moment he said, 'I suppose so. Cricket, you should've let me in on it.'

'You would've helped the same?' She gazed questioningly at him. His eyebrows raised in helpless, hopeless affirmation. 'Vliet, you just had finished telling me if I ever mentioned, well, the incident, you wouldn't be able to look at me. Ever again. And that was one thing I couldn't stand. Not seeing you. How could I tell you? There was everything to lose.'

She'd been barely sixteen. He took the top cookie from her stack, and centring it carefully on waxed table, inquired, 'Why tell me now?'

Her small face was defeated. 'I just split with David.' (A beefy, silent type, according to Caroline, and no loss at all.) 'I keep going from one to the other. It's connected with you. When I see you, that finishes everything. With everyone.'

'So this,' he managed a painful smile, 'is cold turkey?'

She didn't answer.

She was giving him a strange, impersonal look, as if she were about to photograph him. *With an oink-oink here.* She rose, walking round the table. The back of her long yellow skirt was rumpled.

'Cricket, hey, wait. Please.'

She didn't turn. The door clicked shut.

He sat in a cane-bottomed chair in the Sutherlands' pretty breakfast room, tapping a filter tip on the table. He didn't light it. He had crept into a neutral area of self-hypnosis where time means nothing and cold pads the interior of the skull, protecting the mind. He didn't dare move. If he moved, there was no way of knowing which direction his brain would jump. A black cateress in uniform opened the door, clinking empties into segmented crates. She glanced curiously at him. He didn't move.

When, finally, he rejoined the living, the party was over. Mothers zipped children's jackets. People clustered in the hall, thanking the Sutherlands. Cold air streamed with each opening of the front door. Cricket was pulling on a brownish fur of possible rodent origin.

Cricket, a tiny girl who looked far younger than she was. A freckly girl with a bump-ended nose and yellow hair. In this house were several ladies, his own mother included, who must have looked somewhat similar at the same age. But this one had been involved in a brutal mass murder, had had an illegitimate baby for a day (fantastic telly title, he thought), and slept around. Once she had comforted him. His mother never would have considered sanctioning her body for such purpose. The family called her Cricket-the-hippie-one. Vliet thought of her as Cricket-my-little-cousin-who-loves-me. Now, for the first time, he was recognizing that she existed apart from him and his needs, in her own landscape of barren craters and dangerous, burned-out places. This separate identity made his throat ache with sadness. His fuzzy little mascot gone. Gone forever.

Caroline offered her perfumed cheek for a kiss, Gene gripped his hand. Cricket, lugging an incongruously businesslike camera bag, did not look at him as she slipped into the cold new year.

2

Two nights later, Friday at ten, Vliet stood at the Mathenys' front door. Gene squinted through the peep. 'Oh, it's you.'

'I find myself in the neighbourhood.'

'Where've you been the last two days?'

'I called in sick. Didn't the trucks roll?'

'You never miss. I was worried.'

'But I wasn't sick. Am I fired?'

Gene laughed. 'It's cold, Vliet. Come on in.'

Yellow forms were spread on the den table. In this house, Vliet was surrogate son, not a guest. Gene went back to work. Caroline, snug in a crimson-velvet caftan, watched a black-and-white movie. 'They don't make 'em like this anymore,' she said, smiling up. 'Isn't Claudette the *most*?' She pronounced it French-style. 'Get yourself something to eat, luv, or drink.'

'Cricket home?'

'In her room. Go cheer her. It must be breaking up with what's-his-name. But she's never been like this. A blue funk.'

He hauled himself, arm over arm, up the curving metal, pausing at the dark door. He listened to her even breathing. The room was unheated. Cold penetrated his Norwegian sweater. His pupils adjusted. She was stirring.

'Hi,' he said.

'Mmmm? Vliet?'

'Yes.'

She sat up. She wore a bathrobe. 'Thank you,' she said.

'For being here?' he asked.

'I didn't think you would.'

'Not in character, is it?' he asked, sitting on the end of her single bed. 'Got an ashtray?'

'Use that mug.'

It was on the floor, and he put it between his thighs, lighting a cigarette. 'Why're you in bed?'

'I was up at five-thirty.'

'Early to bed, early to rise, makes a girl smaller than natural size,' he said. 'Cricket, there's a lot I need to know.'

'About the baby?'

'My son.' He gave a curious, atonal laugh. 'I've got a few things to tell you.'

She nodded.

'We're cousins,' he said. 'But there's nothing wrong with the family.'

'I fell. It was raining. Orion wanted me to go to the hospital. With the rain we probably wouldn't've got

473

there. Anyway, Genesis didn't believe in hospitals. Vliet, I knew he didn't.'

'You're not in the neighbourhood of guilty, Cricket. It was a simple premature birth.'

'Whose fault was that?'

'Mine.' Vliet glanced around the dim room. Neat it wasn't. Cold it was. 'Always sleep with the heat off?'

'In winter I wear my robe.'

'So I see. Cricket, know something? You're the only girl I ever talk to. More than opening my mouth, that is.'

'I'm sorry,' she said.

'Why?'

'It sounds so lonely.'

'It is.' He set the mug ashtray back on the carpet. 'I've been doing a lot of thinking these two days.'

'Daddy said you weren't at work. I figured, well, I figured . . .'

'That I'd split?'

'Maybe.'

'What? And give up my red-hot career?'

'Where were you?'

'Going crazy,' he said. 'Listen, that's what I wanta explain.'

Instead of explaining, however, he began to weep.

He leaned onto her bed, shaking and gasping. He wept the tears that hadn't come since Roger's private funeral. He wept for his twin, for poor, brave Alix, and for his unknown son. Rubbing his fists into his eye sockets, Vliet wept for Alix whom he loved and had been unable to help, he wept for an infant who had arrived on the scene too early. He wept for Cricket who was a sweet slob and lived in a room that smelled of photographic supplies. He wept for his parents who sublimated their miseries through him and therefore never could be let in on what a failure he was. He wept for his brother, his conscience, now rotting in a hardwood casket with bronze fittings.

He wept, in truth, as we all weep. He wept for himself. Until this hour it had seemed to Vliet that Genesis had him trapped forever in that hot June day with Handel blaring. Now, though, he accepted the unvarnished verity. It wasn't Genesis who had him trapped.

It was himself.

He wept because, at last, he had accepted his complicity. He had shoved Alix back in the cage. Given a chance, he would have done away with his only begotten son. There were times when he hated his brother, and always he'd envied him. He used people. He used Cricket and used her and used her.

Racked with guilt, Vliet wept into blankets. He could feel her crouching over him, her body warm and soft. He could hear her murmurings in his ear, not words, just comforting sounds.

I don't need to explain, he thought. She takes on faith. She accepts. I can't accept me, but she can.

She'll prevent me from being a hollow man, a straw man, a swindle, a mock turtle. With her I won't be a tin woodsman without heart or conscience, Vliet thought.

He let Cricket take over where Roger had left off.

3

When Vliet told Cricket the baby's death had nothing to do with their being cousins, he had been quoting Dr Bjork, Roger's old mentor. Bjork should know. The man specialized in genetics, sickle cell and otherwise.

That New Year's night, after Vliet had left the Sutherlands', he had driven around the quiet western part of the city. The next two days and two nights, he had branched out, weaving and reweaving through Baldwin Hills, Thousand Oaks, Malibu, Fullerton (where Van Vliet's Distribution Centre No. 3 was), North Hollywood, West Covina, Simi Valley. The megalop loop. He had put well over a thousand miles on the Mercedes. Unable to stay still long enough to eat a meal, he would pause at Van

Vliet's – only Van Vliet's – tearing open Frito bags with his straight white teeth, munching as he drove one-handed. He had shaved with the Remington Electric that he kept in the glove compartment. He was always on the move. He couldn't stop. What amazed him was that Cricket's revelation had been the final straw. He would've figured the murder, the trial, Alix's trips to the country of the mad. But not this. Why this?

He'd had a son.

Thursday afternoon had found him parking on the hilly street between County General Hospital and the USC School of Medicine. Here, in a good-size office that smelled of new paint, sat that elderly genetics miracle man. Bjork. Vliet, pacing between white bookshelves and a window that overlooked a modern court, spewed out the bare story without embellishment or explanation. He spoke as plainly as he could. If he went into emotional responses, there was no knowing how he would react. Bjork's shining skull nodded from time to time. He requested a medical history of the family. Vliet gave him a reasonably complete one. Bjork said, 'We don't know much about human genetics, you understand. But from what you've told me, I'd say you've got as good a background as is possible. In my opinion the child was premature, no more.' Wrinkled hands laced. 'I can't tell you how saddened I was about your brother. A great loss. Such a fine young man.'

'Roger, yes,' Vliet said.

Darkness had fallen. Vliet had found his way around the huge, gaudily lit hospital complex, across a bridge, and onto the nearest freeway, the San Bernardino. He had been in Upland, in a self-service station (*Ladies, We Serve U*), when urgency had overtaken him. Cricket, he had thought, Cricket.

Cricket was inevitable.

Others, of course, do not always see the inevitable as inevitable. Vliet knew it. His gift was oiling difficulties. He set about doing so.

The family – or most of them – were no problem. Vliet, in their minds, was too tall, too elegant for Cricket. That was all. Being first cousins seemed a rather witty quirk. Hadn't they absorbed a Japanese artist, a handsome and rather sadistically inclined Jewish surgeon, a Communist (Gene)? They were worldly people. And thought so well of themselves that they didn't consider themselves at all. They took for granted their large, overtaxed houses, their Revillon furs, their handmade sterling, their inherited *bijouterie* and gems, their Van Vliet noses and stock certificates. If two of them decided to get married, why not? As a matter of fact, there was a delicious fairy-tale aspect here. Look who had snagged their handsome, bewitchingly droll Vliet. Their very own little Cricket-the-hippie-one.

Caroline – Van Vliet to the marrow of her handsome bones – was in seventh heaven. Her child married, and no in-laws to bother anyone!

Em never had been secure like Caroline. She did not take well to the idea.

Early in March, before one of their routine Sunday dinners, Vliet said casually, 'Cricket's coming for dessert. Did I mention we're getting married?'

The parents laughed, imagining this one of their son's inexplicable Family-type jokes. Vliet met their eyes candidly. And silence fell in the small, overly neat living-room. Em paled. Sheridan reddened, his mouth dropping open. The refrigerator kicked on, noisily.

Em spoke first. 'But she's your cousin!'

'Give us good wishes, Ma, not facts.' Vliet sounded amused at her outcry. And this added to Em's confusion.

'Cousins don't marry.' Sheridan had gained weight. Ponderous anger shook his double chin.

'From what I hear, Dad, cousins marry all the time. It's legal in California. Royalty, I hear, don't marry anyone else. Or du Ponts.'

'If,' Em hesitated. 'If there are children.'

'Ma, what's this "if"?'

'Vliet, we're serious.' Sheridan straightened. His wife's Family always had terrified and filled him with baleful envy. Vliet's off-hand explanation, royalty and du Ponts, seemed to Sheridan the ultimate decadence. Now They're marrying only Themselves, he thought. And coming from the Midwest, he was bitterly disturbed. 'The word is incest.'

'Among Catholics,' Vliet agreed. 'Maybe we better get a papal dispensation.'

Sheridan's emotions churned. A staunch anti-Catholic, he was led (as Vliet well knew) into certain interestingly progressive ideologies.

'I have it on the best authority there won't be a single grandchild with more than one head.'

'Vliet,' Sheridan warned.

'Come on, Ma, Dad. You know you're crazy about her.'

'Of c-course we are, Vliet.' Em, embarrassed, was positive that Vliet understood the fine points she and Sheridan were trying to get across. Yet she continued in her sober way. 'We want what's best for Cricket, as well as you. What if something does h-happen? Could you ever f-forgive yourself if anything went wrong with one of the children?'

Vliet's expression changed. He looked older, harder. He rose, pouring himself a drink. Sheridan and Em glanced at one another, the sad, knowing look that can only pass between two people bound together more by defeat than anything else. Their lives had been measured out by her bottles and his petty adulteries, their other son's desertion and death. We better lay off, the look said. After tragedy, parents tend to become lenient. (And, too, Em for a while had suspected Vliet was seeing 'her'.) She went into the kitchen and held tight to the sink. When Sheridan came in and put his fleshy arm around her, she did not shake him off.

Gene's objections were on a profound level. The matter of consanguinity bothered him very little. His wife's family was in good health, mental and physical as well as

478

financial. He, however, had been the fool bestrewing Van Vliet ledgers with large black figures. He had, in his own mind, betrayed his life. He didn't care to see Cricket embark on a similar venture. A vacant alliance. He loved Vliet, but that did not prevent him from seeing the younger man for what he was, a charming egotist, a driving and unscrupulous businessman who was lacking in a way that Gene never could quite put a finger on. Gene would, he told himself, far rather have any of Cricket's quiet, stumbling young men of various races, colours, and religions for a son-in-law.

The wet March Monday after the engagement had been thrown casually at him, Gene waited for the rain to stop. He crossed the puddled loading area to the warehouses. He went directly to Vliet's office. Vliet, on the phone, said, 'I'll get back to you, Dave,' and hung up. 'Gene?' he said.

'Why Cricket?' Gene asked.

Vliet sat down, looking at the man in front of his desk. Gene could have called him, could have forced him into the large, awe-invoking presidential office, but that would have been against Gene's principles. Gene, the boss with ulcers and a liberal's Achilles' heel.

'You must've noticed, Gene. We've always been fond of one another,' Vliet said.

'Not to marry,' Gene replied, and sat on the cheap Naugahyde. 'She's nothing you look for in a girl. She's not pretty, my Cricket.'

'That's not paternal, Gene.'

'I'm her father, I love her. I'm not blind. And you haven't answered my question.'

'After all these years, you're not about to play the heavy father, are you, Gene?'

Gene pressed his thumbnail to his lower lip. He was severe with himself. And in his book, interfering with a child's marriage was despicable. Yet he kept his probing grey eyes on Vliet.

Vliet turned away. 'For Christ's sake, Gene, let it be, let it be.' He spoke harshly. No part of any plan. The words had spilled out.

479

Gene had known Vliet since he was born, and had seen him in every kind of situation. This was a voice he'd never heard. Whose? A stranger's, lost, despairing.

Then Vliet was turning, extending his hand with a smile. 'Come on, think. You're getting Dad for a relation.'

Gene gripped his nephew's extended hand.

Rain had started, harder now. Gene ran around lorries. He was back at his desk, his feet wet, thinking how little he knew of the human heart. That implausible misery in Vliet had been brief. And unforgettable. Gene wished he'd been more tolerant, kinder. Some writer I'd've been, he thought, forever reworking material to make myself sound noble and just. He kept a pair of socks here, and he was pulling them on when he realized he was praying. An agnostic's prayer to his dubious God: If You exist, let her help him, let her be able to help him.

Epilogue

On 20 April, a warm, slightly hazed Sunday, the Eugene Mathenys held Open House for their daughter, Amelie Deane, and Mr Van Vliet Reed, who, six weeks earlier, had driven to Las Vegas to get married.

The bridal couple sat on a patio wall. Em and Sheridan stood nearby. Em would have preferred a receiving line, but Caroline had nixed the idea. A receiving line, Caroline had pronounced, was too *stiff* for words. Still, this being a wedding of sorts, the guests did stop to kiss and congratulate before spreading around the patio and down the terraced hill.

There were sharply delineated groups.

On the narrow grass of the first terrace sat Cricket's friends. ('Is it law, luv, that the fingernails be dirty?' said Caroline *sotto voce* to Gene.) They drank their champagne, earnestly discussing lenses and how to get inside the frame. Vliet's crowd lounged on the pool deck: they seemed to glitter, such was the indecent number of lovely girls. Van Vliets mingled with the Mathenys' friends, greeting one another with champagne-scented kisses and cries of 'Isn't it a delicious day?' and 'I adore that dress!' and 'They just don't get married anymore. This is my first wedding in ages!' and 'Worth missing the old tennis game for, huhh, boy?' Under a yellow-striped awning that had been put up for the occasion, the Reeds' Glendale contingent clung together for safety. Everywhere bloomed tubs of yellow and white daisies.

The musicians, young people in jeans, were wandering back to their station, retrieving viola d'amore, lute, flute, and recorder, drifting into a pleasantly archaic 'Bridge over Troubled Water'. Vliet, with graceful conducting gestures, left his bride, descending to the pool deck to introduce an old Harvard buddy around.

Cricket swung one sandalled foot, oblivious to the social magnets drawing people together. She saw the simple truth. They were enjoying themselves. They were happy. She was happy. Sun had raised a faint shine on her forehead. She wore a yellow lace she'd discovered at a jumble sale. Naturally her mother had tried to coax her into a new dress, indeed, into a trousseau (or, as the enthusiastic Caroline had purposefully mispronounced, a 'torso'), but in the multiple reflections of the fitting-room mirrors, Cricket had seen the incorruptible in her small body denying these elegantly tagged clothes. 'No,' she had said.

Most people think of a wedding as a mountain that, once crossed, presents one with a pleasant or exciting new vista. Cricket had no such concept. Her ability was to give. She lacked the sense of ownership. She did not think of possessing Vliet. Or being herself possessed by matrimony. She was just happy they were together, and this happiness had the evocative power of the classical music Vliet played whenever he was home – she'd moved into his West Hollywood apartment. Those taped chords left in her a sense of surprise, wonder, and inevitability.

Vliet, returning to her, paused to clown a small dance in front of their grandmother's chair. As the smile gathered wrinkles on the bovine face, Cricket felt her own lips echo the smile. Vliet thought he didn't love her, and Cricket knew it. He did. And she knew this. Since his love was uncoloured by romanticism, he missed seeing it.

'You forgot your wedding ring,' Vliet said.

She looked down. She had. He hadn't.

Suddenly they both laughed.

The party, Caroline decided, had the fine, casual ambience she had striven after.

'It's coming off,' she said to Gene.

He put his arm around her waist. 'You worked hard enough.'

'We *should* celebrate a son-in-law who'll support our *dee*-clining years.'

She had thrown herself into the planning, conferring

interminably with Em, overriding her sister's cautious opinion on each issue. Formal invitations versus informal, receiving line or none, refreshments, cut flowers, guest lists. The decision that had thrown Em was that Gene and Vliet would not wear suits at the garden afternoon. 'Well, Sheridan will!' she had cried.

Yet in the midst of the fiercest sibling argument, they would catch themselves. 'It's for the children,' Em would cry. And the tall sister and the short would embrace. Em had almost overcome her reservations. (And besides, Vliet's beautiful girls always had made her uncomfortable.) Caroline was, as she repeatedly told her friends, delirious. She *ad*ored Vliet. (Besides, she had feared Cricket would keep flopping from one bed to the next and never marry.) Neither sister mentioned the close relationship to one another. In Caroline's mind it was just too bourgeois. Em was anxious not to anger her urbane sister. Anyway, the children had eloped, and the matter was out of their hands. Em, hating herself for it, couldn't help wondering if they'd had to.

She turned, peering through her glasses at Cricket. Was that lace a trifle snug? The way the child dressed, fit was impossible to gauge. It actually made Em's head ache when she considered that Cricket might have, before. Yet she couldn't help saying to Sheridan, 'Cricket looks pretty, don't you think?'

Sheridan wiggled his neck, trying to escape his shirt collar. Since Roger's death he'd put on thirty pounds, and his new navy suit was hot, uncomfortable. 'If she'd fix herself up a bit,' he muttered. He never would surmount that thought, *incest*, yet at the same time, he liked his new daughter-in-law far more than anyone else in his wife's Family.

'Hasn't she gained a little weight?'

'Married life agrees with her.'

Just then, Beverly, with Dan, stepped through open sliding glass. Em hadn't seen Beverly for ages. It came as a shock that Beverly's brown hair, which flowed around shoulders slender and straight as a girl's, was threaded with white. She doesn't keep it coloured, Em thought, and pity welled. As an archaeologist cautiously unearths stones of a dead civilization, so Em delved her emotions, discovering to her pleasure that she still felt affection for Beverly Linde. Beverly is a family friend, Em thought. Then she thought, Alix!

Em held up her empty glass. 'I'll be back in a moment,' she said to Sheridan.

'Why not lay off today?'

'I've only had champagne,' she lied, heading for the long portable bar, hoping fervently that Alix, most disputed on the guest list, wouldn't show.

Beverly kissed Cricket. 'I'm so happy for you,' she murmured in her gentle, low voice, and then, when Cricket hugged her, 'Vliet's so very lucky.'

'*Mazeltov*,' Dan said to Vliet.

'Thank you, sir,' Vliet replied.

'How long've you been married?' Beverly asked.

'Four weeks,' Cricket said.

'Six,' Vliet corrected. 'My wife's not much on detail.'

'Mine either,' Dan said. 'There're advantages and disadvantages.' He spoke pleasantly. He did not like Vliet: he had seen in that charnel-house the way Vliet had stared at Alix, he suspected Vliet had had more than a hand in her relapse. But Dan was Gene Matheny's friend. So he was pleasant.

Caroline draped an arm over her tall nephew's shoulder. 'This is a son-in-law. The prime of the species.' She laughed, and they all had to laugh with her. 'Ahh, Beverly, we're aged crones.'

And Gene was there, kissing Beverly, shaking Dan's hand. 'Weren't you bringing Sam?'

'Listen,' Dan chuckled, 'would you give up pitching for this?'

Em, returning with vodka in her champagne glass, caught Beverly's eye.

'Em,' Beverly murmured.

The two women smiled hesitantly, then moved forward with small, Chinese-concubine steps. A long pause. Em's

rouged, wrinkled cheek met Beverly's firm flesh. With the
half kiss came a flood of nostalgia ... Frank Sinatra 78s ...
Apple Blossom cologne ... rationed meat, and meat loaf
centred with a hard egg ... hubba-hubba ... USO parties
... folded rush invitations ... ironed rayon slips and
white cotton gloves and ten o'clock Omega Delta check-
ins, girlhoods lost in a time that had sunk as irretrievably
as Atlantis. In the brief hug, bitterness dissolved.

As they pulled apart, Beverly's eyes were moist. 'Em,
I'm so happy for you,' she said.

'We're very pleased,' Em replied.

'On the way, I thought of your wedding. I guess because
it was in a garden, too.'

'The reception,' Em corrected.

'The ceremony was in St Mark's,' Beverly remembered.

'That's right. You told us to be happy forever and
ever.'

'I did?'

'As we drove away. There were cans tied to the car, and
I heard you calling, "Be happy forever and ever."' Em
spoke in her pedantic way. 'Nobody else used those exact
words.' She paused. 'Beverly, I'm sorry about – I'm sorry.'
And she was silent.

Above them, at the patio entry, stood Mrs Linde and a
greying man with a peculiar wide mouth. Between, in a
tangerine dress of some very soft fabric, Alix. Em had
battled to prevent one of the engraved invitations from
being mailed to Alix. Cricket had wanted her, and so did
Caroline – 'After all, luv, she's the daughter of my oldest,
my *famous* friend.' But Em, in the grip of a sudden
migraine, would have carried the day if it hadn't been
for Gene. He had been disturbed, deeply, when the girl
was excluded from Roger's funeral: a righteous man, he
had felt group-action guilt for her crack-up. 'There won't
be a reception in my house,' Gene had stated firmly,
'unless Alix is invited.' Her! Her! Em had had taut,
menopausal dreams of strangling Alix, smothering her
with a pillow, locking her in a dungeon filled with poison-
ous adders, taking a bread knife and matching the beauti-

ful body with Roger's wounds.

The memory of these dreams hot in her, she couldn't look at Beverly.

'There's Alix,' Beverly said. 'And that's Dr Emanual. He's been looking after her since, well, since.' She swallowed hard.

'Yes,' said Em, avoiding Beverly's eyes. 'And if you'll excuse me, there're two friends I must introduce.'

Caroline said to Beverly, 'Don't look now, but every male at this entire gathering has his tongue hanging out. Who's that with her?'

'Dr Emanual.'

'Oh *yes*. She did call to ask if she could bring a friend. Beauty and the beast. I'll bet he's cuh-razy over her.'

Beverly's old, mischievous smile flickered. 'He's older than God, Caroline, six years older than us.'

'She must have 'em all ages,' Caroline said, glancing over Beverly's shoulder. 'Oh Lawd! The cateress wants me. What can it be *now*?'

And Beverly went towards her mother and daughter, moving slowly around kaleidoscoping groups. Ridiculous, she told herself. Nobody gets rattled saying hello to her own mother or her own child. Except me. I do. With Mother since I left Philip. And with Alix? Oh my God, my poor Alix. Since then, too. Beverly's lips were stiff, and she thought, as she always must, Jamie. She was relieved to find Dan at her side. 'Here,' he said, handing her a glass of champagne. In the warm April sun, very close to her husband, Beverly greeted her mother, her daughter, and Dr Emanual.

Em circulated among her friends. The dichondra was brilliant green, and Em whirled back and forth over it to the bar. One journey found her alone with Caroline.

Suddenly Caroline gripped Em's wrist, muttering, 'Oh shit!'

At the obscenity, Em froze.

'Look,' Caroline ordered. 'Down there.'

Alone, islanded on the grass to the left of the pool, stood Vliet and Alix. Em was at the point where her perceptions came and went, so maybe it was a trick of alcohol. Her glasses seemed to magnify. On her son's face she saw something she'd never seen before. Raw, naked pain. Even from here she could see Vliet's pain.

'They must be talking about poor Roger.'

'That hot and heavy?' Caroline demanded.

Alix was gazing up at Vliet, her eyes seemed tranced, her lips parted slightly. She seemed to have emerged at his bidding from another element, from a world with an atmosphere of heavy dew. The dewiness lay on her skin. A breeze fluttered her chiffon skirt, and the small, hexagonal pattern in Vliet's shirt picked up the tangerine. What a fabulous couple, what style! Caroline thought, then fury overtook her. He's married to *my* Cricket.

And Em was saying, '. . . to Cricket, so there's nothing to worry about.'

'Of course not!' Caroline's whisper was cruel. 'After all, they're married. And that means *happily* ever after!'

'Don't say it like that. He loves her.'

'Did you love Sheridan?'

'Of course. And you, Gene.'

'Oh God! For once, stop mouthing platitudes. We were programmed to get married, that's all.' Her voice transmitted her hurt. 'We didn't dare miss out on the white wedding, the cottage small by the waterfall, the dozen handmade cutwork place mats!'

'You've forgotten.'

'Maybe I was *hot* for his bod. You're right. I've forgotten. Now all I can remember is that he seemed so very clean, and I was expected to be married. But love! Don't give me love!'

Vliet was touching Alix's slender, bare arm, handing her his champagne glass, saying something near her cheek. Sunlight glinted a blinding path in her dark hair, and Vliet's eyes closed in what to Em seemed a paroxysm of misery.

'Then why did he marry Cricket?' she asked, stopping abruptly, flushing. *He had to.*

'How should I know?' Caroline snapped. Suddenly she

began to weep. Annoyed with herself, she sniffed violently, blowing her nose in a cocktail napkin. Em put her glass on a waiter's silver tray, taking a full one, gulping. Someone spoke to her. The voice was an insect whine. Em excused herself. She advanced on the crowded bar and found her sister already there.

Vliet asked, 'What's this bizarre couple, Emanual and your grandmother?'

'They came together.'

'Is he her date or what?'

'Ask Grandma. Of course she's very straight, so possibly she'll refuse to answer on the grounds you're a married man.'

'She's right, I'll grant her that. Really. From here on, I'll have to be more circumspect.' Vliet paused. 'How do I act with you?'

'I was wondering the same.'

'Shall we both punt?'

'It's a crowded field.'

'The thing is, Alix, we must decide. To ignore the last time we were together, or to drag it into the open?'

Musicians floated into 'I'll Remember April', learned for old sentimentalists at wedding gigs.

'I never should've thrown the gory details at you. I was all wrong.'

'You're being generous.'

'It was my mistake, and I'm sorry, Vliet.'

'No, it's me who's sorry,' he said, and his face melted with remembrance of fear and love and triumph that had surrounded her brass bed. He swayed towards her, his mind filling with endearments both lewd and tender. On another level he was aware of pleasantly archaic notes, a clutch of voices, a burst of semi-stoned laughter. My wedding party, he thought. Yet Vliet felt no guilt. Cricket aided and succoured him, she understood him, she nursed his now delicate lusts, she was (and always had been) as much a part of him as his thymus, and what did Cricket or

a thymus have to do with how he felt about Alix Schorer?
Her eyes were on his.

'That night,' he said, hearing his voice, toneless, strange.
'Know how much I wanted to stay?'

'Vliet, what happened, it wasn't your fault. I was at a
bad point.'

'Stop being so goddamn generous. I was chicken of
getting in too deep. Crazy? I've always been in too deep
with you.'

'Vliet, don't.'

'Emanual?'

'I'm going out with him.'

'He's old, ugly, short.'

'And kind. He knows everything. He understands about
me and Roger.'

Vliet touched her arm. 'You're trembling,' he said. And
drugged with love, aching to protect her from small,
lizardlike old shrinks, Vliet felt tears form in his (just
like Roger's) eyes. If I had the Lazarus touch, he thought,
if it were possible, for you, Alix, I would bring him back.
Or resurrect myself into him. He handed her his champagne. 'This'll help.'

She raised the glass.

He said, 'I love you.'

A few drops scattered. *Please.*

'Cricket knows.'

'It's still not to talk about.'

'I have to. Something's changed in me, Alix. It might be
for the worse, but I'm different. And you are, too. You
seem – resigned.'

'Matured is a better word. Let's not go into this.'

'But you do feel for me?'

'I . . . a lot. But Vliet, it's all mixed up with Roger.'

'Yes, Roger.' He blinked the moisture in his eyes.

'Vliet,' she said gently, 'you married the right girl.'

'Really. But in no way, darling, does that alter how I
feel about you.'

And Mrs Linde was saying, 'Have you congratulated

491

Mr and Mrs Matheny, Alix dear?' Vliet wondered how long she'd been there, listening with pearl-hung, transparent old ears. 'Or Mr and Mrs Reed? It's the correct thing.'

'No-no. Not yet.'

Vliet saw a barely perceptible flicker trap Alix's eye. 'I'll have a go at them, too,' he said.

A little ahead of him, Alix moved with a flamenco dancer's provocative grace up the steps towards one woman who had hated her for years and the other woman whose hatred had started only a few minutes ago.

To the left of the house was a slope. Beverly climbed, her heels sinking in the grass. Birds sang in three silver birches that guarded the crest. Near the delicate trees, she stopped, noting shapes and colours with trained eyes. She saw Alix as drifting tangerine, masculine heads turning after her, she saw Mrs Linde, with the segmented movements of age, lower her erect body into a rented white chair. They're my mother and my daughter, she thought. The silver cord might tarnish, but never can it be cut. I love them and am forever bound to them.

Alone, from this distance, she could look at Mrs Linde and Alix without an excess of repentance. She had failed her parents and, in a far more disastrous manner, her children, yet here, under rustling birches, she was able to accept the blame. She had copped out, yes, terribly and tragically, but not from want of love. She was a flawed creature like all else in this imperfect world. Inevitably, in some way, each of us fails, first as a child, then as a parent. Nothing new or profound. The report cards already are printed: we get *F*s as children, *Incompletes* as parents.

Since morning, Em's wedding had been on her mind, and now she was picturing the too-pink stucco of the Wynans' house, she was seeing Caroline, rosy and handsome with graduated pearls knotted. There was Em, dwarfed by a cathedral train. And at a little distance, herself. Beverly alone. In that powder blue with pads widening her shoulders. Three girls. She tried to think of them as daughters. As children of the Lindes and the Wynans. Impossible. Rather, it was as if the three of them had sprung to life in a stylized Rousseau-innocent meadow, breathing less smoggy, more hopeful air. Their goals and dreams they had believed peculiar to that newly peace-blessed Truman era. They had recognized no legacy of the past. They had felt they owed nothing to the past. They had refused to crib from the past. They were the first of a new race.

To wish anyone happiness forever and ever! Could there be any remark more oblivious to lives that had come before? All her observations must have told her that her parents and the Wynans were not happy in the corny Warner Brothers style she had wished for Em and Sheridan. Yet she had meant the words. More, she had expected them to come true, and – oddly enough – had considered babies an essential element. Babies who, it should have been equally apparent, would have their own brave new world.

The shadow of a bird flickered on grass. A breeze jostled a napkin to her feet. Picking up the small square, absently smoothing it, her head tilted towards wisps of party laughter. She saw Dan looking around. Looking for me, she thought. Once she had been shamed by her need for solitude. Now she understood that solitude was the balloon that carried her to the real meaning of her life. Yet she couldn't rid herself of that old guilt. Why do I have to be by my lonesome? Pushing back soft, greying hair, she went quickly down the small incline.

She passed her mother, who leaned towards Mrs Wynan. 'Cricket and Vliet make a lovely couple,' said Mrs Linde, her firm voice betraying none of the indulgence with which most people address the senile. 'I always think there's something so hopeful about a wedding, don't you?'

OUTSTANDING WOMEN'S FICTION IN GRANADA PAPERBACKS

C L Skelton

Hardacre	£1.50	☐
The Maclarens	£1.25	☐
Sweethearts and Wives	£1.25	☐

Christina Savage

Love's Wildest Fires	£1.25	☐

Nicola Thorne

The Girls	85p	☐
Birdie Climbing	85p	☐
In Love	95p	☐
A Woman Like Us	95p	☐

BESTSELLERS AVAILABLE IN GRANADA PAPERBACKS

Leslie Waller

Trocadero	£1.25	☐
The Swiss Account	£1.25	☐
The 'K' Assignment	50p	☐
Number One	85p	☐
A Change in the Wind	40p	☐
The American	75p	☐
The Family	£1.25	☐
The Banker	£1.25	☐
Hide in Plain Sight	£1.25	☐

Patrick Mann

Dog Day Afternoon	60p	☐
Steal Big	85p	☐

Calder Willingham

Natural Child	95p	☐
The Big Nickel	£1.25	☐
End as a Man	£1.25	☐
Eternal Fire	£1.50	☐
Providence Island	£1.50	☐
Reach to the Stars	95p	☐

All these books are available to your local bookshop or newsagent, or can be ordered direct from the publisher. Just tick the titles you want and fill in the form below.

Name ....

Address ....

....

Write to Granada Cash Sales, PO Box 11, Falmouth, Cornwall TR10 9EN

Please enclose remittance to the value of the cover price plus:

UK: 40p for the first book, 18p for the second book plus 13p per copy for each additional book ordered to a maximum charge of £1.49.

BFPO and EIRE: 40p for the first book, 18p for the second book plus 13p per copy for the next 7 books, thereafter 7p per book.

OVERSEAS: 60p for the first book and 18p for each additional book.

Granada Publishing reserve the right to show new retail prices on covers, which may differ from those previously advertised in the text or elsewhere.